CRUCIBLE OF WAR

'BROTHER-CAPTAIN, THEY'RE coming!'

'Who, Covius? I need better information than that!' yelled Uriel.

But before Covius could reply, the signal was suddenly cut off as a fiery explosion blossomed at the far edge of the chamber.

Then through the flames came a wave of screaming foes, their bestial faces twisted in alien hate and their powerful bodies rippling with bulging muscle.

Orks. Hundreds of them. – *from* **Leviathan** *by Graham McNeill*

MACKS HOWLED, AND fired her riot-gun into the ceiling, pumping the grip and blasting the rotten floorboards in a blizzard of wood splinters with each successive shot. Every muzzle-flash lit the mill room for a millisecond

Exploding wood away before it, the Beast smashed through the deck and came down at them.

It was a blur. Just a blur, moving faster than anything had a right to. Macks's riot-gun boomed again. Drusher had a fleeting glimpse of deep purple body plates, a snapping tail of gristly bone, forearm claws like harvest scythes. – *from* **The Curiosity** *by Dan Abnett*

IN THE NIGHTMARE world of the 41st millennium, humanity is locked in a desperate struggle for survival against a relentless tide of aliens. Read tales of heroism and valour in this action-packed selection of savage science fiction stories ripped from the pages of *Inferno!* magazine.

More Warhammer 40,000 from the Black Library

• WARHAMMER 40,000 SHORT STORIES •

STATUS: DEADZONE
eds. Marc Gascoigne & Andy Jones

DARK IMPERIUM
eds. Marc Gascoigne & Andy Jones

DEATHWING
eds. Neil Jones & David Pringle

WORDS OF BLOOD
eds. Marc Gascoigne & Christian Dunn

• GAUNT'S GHOSTS •

FIRST & ONLY by Dan Abnett
GHOSTMAKER by Dan Abnett
NECROPOLIS by Dan Abnett
HONOUR GUARD by Dan Abnett
THE GUNS OF TANITH by Dan Abnett
STRAIGHT SILVER by Dan Abnett

• SPACE WOLF •

SPACE WOLF by William King
RAGNAR'S CLAW by William King
GREY HUNTER by William King

• THE EISENHORN TRILOGY •

XENOS by Dan Abnett
MALLEUS by Dan Abnett
HERETICUS by Dan Abnett

• WARHAMMER 40,000 TITLES •

NIGHTBRINGER by Graham McNeill
WARRIORS OF ULTRAMAR by Graham McNeill
EXECUTION HOUR by Gordon Rennie
SHADOW POINT by Gordon Rennie
ANGELS OF DARKNESS by Gav Thorpe
SOUL DRINKER by Ben Counter
DAEMON WORLD by Ben Counter

CRUCIBLE OF WAR

Edited by
Marc Gascoigne
& Christian Dunn

A BLACK LIBRARY PUBLICATION

First published in Great Britain in 2003
by BL Publishing,
Games Workshop Ltd.,
Willow Road, Nottingham,
NG7 2WS, UK

10 9 8 7 6 5 4 3 2 1

Cover illustration by Adrian Smith

A CIP record for this book
is available from the British Library

ISBN 1 84416 005 X

Set in ITC Giovanni

Printed and bound in Great Britain by
Cox & Wyman Ltd, Cardiff Rd, Reading, Berkshire RG1 8EX, UK

See the Black Library on the Internet at
www.blacklibrary.com

Find out more about Games Workshop
and the world of Warhammer 40.000 at
www.games-workshop.com

IT IS THE 41st millennium. For more than a hundred centuries the Emperor has sat immobile on the Golden Throne of Earth. He is the master of mankind by the will of the gods, and master of a million worlds by the might of his inexhaustible armies. He is a rotting carcass writhing invisibly with power from the Dark Age of Technology. He is the Carrion Lord of the Imperium for whom a thousand souls are sacrificed every day, so that he may never truly die.

YET EVEN IN his deathless state, the Emperor continues his eternal vigilance. Mighty battlefleets cross the daemon-infested miasma of the warp, the only route between distant stars, their way lit by the Astronomican, the psychic manifestation of the Emperor's will. Vast armies give battle in his name on uncounted worlds. Greatest amongst his soldiers are the Adeptus Astartes, the Space Marines, bio-engineered super-warriors. Their comrades in arms are legion: the Imperial Guard and countless planetary defence forces, the ever-vigilant Inquisition and the tech-priests of the Adeptus Mechanicus to name only a few. But for all their multitudes, they are barely enough to hold off the ever-present threat from aliens, heretics, mutants – and worse.

TO BE A man in such times is to be one amongst untold billions. It is to live in the cruellest and most bloody regime imaginable. These are the tales of those times. Forget the power of technology and science, for so much has been forgotten, never to be re-learned. Forget the promise of progress and understanding, for in the grim dark future there is only war. There is no peace amongst the stars, only an eternity of carnage and slaughter, and the laughter of thirsting gods.

CONTENTS

Liberation Day *by Matthew Farrer*
   & Edward Rusk   **9**

The Curiosity *by Dan Abnett*   **35**

Payback *by Graham McNeill*   **65**

The Emperor's Will *by David Charters*   **89**

Fight or Flight *by Sandy Mitchell*   **109**

On Mournful Wings *by Si Spurrier*   **131**

Backcloth for a
   Crown Additional *by Dan Abnett*   **155**

Firestarter *by Jonathon Green*   **181**

Warp Spawn *by Matt Ralphs*   **213**

Leviathan *by Graham McNeill*   **241**

LIBERATION DAY

Matthew Farrer & Edward Rusk

One hundred and fifteen days to liberation

Do not breathe.
Do not move.
The Emperor is my strength.
Faith is my shield.
By the Emperor's Grace I will be saved.
Here it comes...

HE COULD SEE them through the cracked and rusted floor of the pipe. Flickering glow-globes and the lights of the camp threw an erratic yellow cast over green hide and rusted armour, and then over tusks and stiff bristles as the sentry's pet beast began snorting and huffing the air for something it could not see.

The Emperor is my salvation. Challis made his hands still, fought to calm himself.

The yelping changed note and Challis realised it had worked. The rancid meat he had dropped behind the girder had confused the hound and buried his scent. He could hear footfalls again, but the greenskin and its bouncing, yapping hound had moved out of sight. Challis listened carefully, swiped sweat off his forehead. Twenty seconds went by with no returning steps, so he risked a quick crawl to where the pipe swung away from the wall and out over the hangar bay.

Or what had once been a hangar bay. Now it was a slave stockade, bathed in crude arc lights and full of the crack of whips, brutish bellows of command and the cries of the hopeless. Challis allowed himself a moment of rage. Abominations of nature. No mercy. Then he shook his head and focused.

With the sentry out on patrol, the small greenskins left guarding the gate were screeching and squabbling and kicking one another's shins. Clinging to the top of the pipe, Challis inched forward in the dimness, every movement agonisingly loud to his tension-sharpened ears. He was almost above the stockade wall now, close to the limit of the protective shadows. Now or never. With another glance at the brawling creatures, he dropped from the pipe, rolled and ducked behind the smashed chassis of a wrecked vehicle he had seen the greenskins careening around the corridors in. Heart pounding, he wormed his way under the wreck and lay still as advancing footsteps and the yells of the returning sentry put paid to the fight by the gate.

They had not spotted him. He allowed himself a grin. Unnoticed and in one piece, he was inside the slave camp.

Now, the trick of getting out again would be far more difficult.

CHALLIS HAD NEVER been this far into the bay before, but he had studied the place from every perch he could find in the hangar ceiling and now he unrolled a mental map with practised ease. The beasts had ignored the maze of corridors and compartments in the decks and simply built a sprawl of shacks and hovels on the hangar floor as they would have on an open plain. Challis could even see a new one going up: in the middle distance a greenskin had bolted a frame together and was fixing rough metal plates to it, driving the rivets home with well-aimed blows of its forehead.

The layout was crude, but it had made the camp easy to scout. I'm... he glanced around... on the south side, so the slave pens should be... he squinted, there.

Slave pits would have been a better term. Huge holes had been blasted out of the deck, roofed over with tangles of wire and metal and the slaves thrown in with whatever clothes they had on their backs. Many were nearly naked from months of squalor and floggings, emaciated and broken-spirited.

There were greenskins on guard here, and Challis had to stay flat to the deck as he worked around the perimeter. There! A burning device the greenskins used to make the holes was still set up. That meant a new pit, dug for fresh slaves.

He snaked forward to see in. The slaves looked new indeed and were numerous – at least forty or fifty of them – barely wounded and most of their clothing intact. Those would be the ones. The others were as good as dead already. Back in the shadows, he slipped back towards the only shed that the greenskins kept locked.

A gap low in one wall let him crawl in, and his guess had been right – it was the ammunition store. Enough light came in through the rickety roof to make out piles of crude ammo clips, boxes of bombs, battered jerry cans of what smelled like flamer fuel. Challis tugged on a cord about his neck, pulling out the little handheld igniter he had stolen two days before. Looped at his belt was a length of tough, ropy creeper he had found could work as a wick. One end went into the valve on one of the fuel-cans, and after a couple of tries he got a puff of yellow flame out of the igniter and set the dried creeper to smouldering. Adrenaline made his stomach lurch as he wriggled back out of the shed and scuttled for cover. You're going soft, he told himself, too used to fancy charges with amulet-clocks to time them and–

The wick burned faster than he'd expected – there must have been vapour from the fuel-cans in the air. The blast thundered all across the hangar, and Challis fled for cover to a string of booms and cracks as the other munitions blew apart. All around greenskins bellowed to each other and charged towards the flames.

Except one by the slave pen, looking distractedly at the fire engulfing the centre of the camp. Its back was to the mound of solidified slag left from the pit's digging.

Challis ran up the slagpile, pulling two heavy black-bladed knives from his belt. A leap took him onto the beast's broad shoulders, sending it staggering. A second later both blades sank into its neck, cutting its bellows of protest to strangled gurgles. Challis vaulted clear as it staggered away, trying to hold its head on, and ran to the rim of the pit. Staring up at him in the brightening firelight, the slaves looked aghast.

'Who are you?' one haggard face demanded.

'No time! Let's go!' Challis began pulling the spiked roof-bars aside. 'You, the big one. Grab its weapon. You two grab those spanners. The rest of you, here.' A moment more and they began to scramble out.

Getting the slaves out by the route he had come in was out of the question, but he had scouted a path back from the main south entrance too. Its arch came into view between the shacks as they ran, gates hanging open but four more huge greenskins were on guard.

Challis made a quick count. About eight slaves per guard, about half of them with stakes, spanners or whatever they had grabbed on their way out of the pit. Not the best odds, but it would have to do. No time to go looking for more tools or bodies to strip.

'Right, Challis hissed, 'we go through that gate. Anyone here fight before?'

The hulking slave who'd taken the pit guard's cleaver raised his hand, another half-dozen behind him. Challis sheathed one of his knives and pulled a battered laspistol from his knapsack.

'The rest of you follow the armed people in. When I say go, you go! Any of you that can run past, do it! Don't play hero. Once we're past the gate keep heading along the corridor south. After a couple hundred paces you'll reach a fork. Take the left. When you reach the old torpedo gantry, jump down into the large ventilation pipe. It will drop you a few decks down near a waste reclamation plant. Go into the storage cells at the back and wait. Save any questions for after we're out.' He primed his laspistol.

'Emperor bless us,' whispered one of the slaves.

'We pray that He will,' Challis joined the rest of them in the reply. Then: 'GO!'

Running, Challis dropped the first guard with a frantic point-blank headshot. A burst of yellow gunfire in the gloom and two slaves convulsed and flew backward. The big man swung his cleaver down, forcing his target to parry as the other two were mobbed by slaves. Challis ducked low to avoid the sweep of an axe that took the head off the slave to his left.

One guard went down, but there were humans dead underfoot too. Challis shouted at them to go through and bodies raced past him.

The big slave and the guard were still locked together as another guard fell to a wild shovel swing. The last howled with rage as the slaves slipped past them. Challis thrust his knife but was knocked backwards – winded, he looked around and saw more charging towards the gate, while in the distance came the cough and roar of engines. And the last damned guard would not die.

Then the big slave lunged, turning his weapon at the last moment to bypass the guard's counter swing and sink the blade deep into its shoulder, severing its arm and splitting its body. It fell to the deck, bisected and swearing.

'We've got to go NOW!' Challis shouted. A shell whined over their heads.

The big man looked past him and saw what was coming. He gave Challis a sombre grin and hefted the cleaver.

'You go. I'll hold 'em.'

Challis bit his lip. The slave's bravery was humbling. He gave a nod.

'The Emperor will welcome your soul.'

'I gladly give it. Go on.'

Challis turned and ran.

Behind him there was a cry of 'For the Emperor!' against the roars of the enemy, then he was into the south corridor. The left fork. The torpedo gantry. He paused at the lip of the pipe, hoping against hope to hear another human shout from behind him, but there was nothing but the inhuman babble of the greenskins and the revving of engines. Challis turned and dived into the dark.

'YOU'RE GOING TO have to talk to them before long.' It was one of the women, whippet-lean and green-eyed. 'One or two of them are about ready to drop, and another couple are about ready to fight each other.' Challis shook his head.

'We keep moving. They were stirred up already, prowling all over the hulk from half a dozen camps, and this will make it worse.'

They had come to a joist, torn from the ceiling and blocking most of the passage. The slaves crawled under it one by one, stiff and gasping. Challis swung deftly under it by one hand. When he stood up on the far side the woman was watching him still.

'You've been this way before. You know this passage. Do you know where we're going?' He shooed them into motion again before he answered.

'I came this way when I started scouting the slave pens. I've been along here a few times. And it's a lot like home.'

'Home?' Brighter light was filtering in from somewhere through rents in the walls, enough for her to see him more clearly. His hair and beard were iron-grey, his features grizzled, but Challis's skin was pearl-white, almost transparent.

'You're a hive-worlder. A down-hiver, at that.' She found the spirit to grin. 'I don't wonder you've learned your way around. You're in your element here.' He snorted and called ahead.

'Wait. See that spot where the metal's ripped? There's some lichen leaves dropped next to it as a marker. That's the one. Through there.' He turned at a tap on his shoulder; the woman had her hand out.

'I'm Hyl. Thank you for coming in for us.' His expression softened a little and he took her forearm in his old gangers' greeting.

'Challis. Pleased to have you along.'

The crawlspace was an old corridor, crushed to a narrow metal slot and tough to negotiate. It was twenty minutes before they had all passed through to stand on a mesh platform over a giant shaft that blew chilly air up at them. The going was easier here and Hyl soon had breath to talk again.

'I was taken from a ship that this hulk almost hit while we were in the Immaterium. The *Cezarro's Dreaming*. Bonded trader. My father was the chief steward to the guild household. We both dropped into real space and they sent boats out to board us. What world are you from? I didn't realise this thing was big enough to take a planet.'

'Vanaheim. Noatun Hive.'

Her expression changed. 'So Vanaheim's fallen? Throne of Earth, how many of those creatures are there on this thing?'

'Fallen I don't know about. This piece of trash somehow made it practically into orbit before any of the misbegotten bastards up-hive thought to check their scopes.'

'You're a ganger?'

'Not for a few years.' Challis tapped a tarnished silver stud on his tunic. 'Section Commander, Fourth Division, House Skadi Integrated Militia. They dropped onto the hive and broke in at the shoreline. When we started putting up a good fight at the breaches, they dropped a chunk of rock into the sea just outside and sent a wave in that flooded the lower levels. Then they came back in and scooped us up. That's when they got my team. I don't know what happened after that.'

They fell silent as the group scrambled through a gully where the deck was wrenched up at a right angle. At the top of the slope Challis took them into a sloping tunnel full of metal flanges that Hyl realised after a moment were stairs – they were walking down one wall of a stairwell that was on its side. Several slaves were crying with exhaustion now; pulling, cajoling, and carrying one another, they scrambled to the end, crowded into the bottom of the well where a corridor soared straight up over their heads. Challis lit a torch from his igniter and the others flinched away from the sudden glow.

'Listen, now. Not far. Beyond this we'll be safe from any greenskins, even if the breakout stirred them up more than

I think it did. But you're going to need to be careful. All of you get a torch from that pile. Good. There are some spares, get one in each hand if you can. Get them all lit. I made them to be used, I don't want to have wasted my time.'

He stood in a circle of torchlight.

'Listen well. Be quiet and careful. Watch one another's backs. Any movement, keep a flame between you and it and make sure people around you know you saw it.' He stepped back and reached into the tangle of metal wedged across a door that was tilted into a sideways slot. Hyl realised it was a barricade, lashed and riveted across the door and covered with a brutish alien scrawl, but Challis gripped a couple of struts that looked like all the others, slid them aside and vanished through the hole. Warm, musty air came out of the opening.

Hyl looked around as the others shuffled and looked fearfully at the opening. No one moved.

'The hell with you all, then,' she told them, and clambered through the opening with her torch out in front of her. On the other side, Challis watched her stand up, then watched the first of the slaves follow her through and grinned.

One hundred and twelve days to liberation

'WHAT DID YOU mean when we first broke out, when you talked about them all getting stirred up?' Hyl asked.

They were sitting in a dim oubliette behind a hatch that still closed. Their first torches had long since burned down, but Challis had pointed them to a stockpile of replacements and to a fire pit he had made in the hollow of two vent-pipes. The slaves were slurping water from a channel low in the floor and chewing on a bitter lichen that Challis had told them was edible.

'The greenskins? It's how they get when there's a fight in the air. There hasn't been as much squabbling between them as usual, but they still seem to get wind of a fight or a hunt a lot faster when they're bored. I wish I knew how they know when things like this are happening.'

'We think it might be mind-to-mind, sir.'

Challis and Hyl looked around at a slim boy, not more then twenty, the grubby remains of an Adeptus apprentice's braid hanging at the side of his head. He spoke nervously, as if he was unaccustomed to speaking to groups.

'We think they can talk to each others' minds like astropaths can. Ideas, feelings, they can... sort of ripple through large groups of them. It's how they can make armies so fast. And how they can get excited and wanting to hunt even before they actually hear the news that a group of slaves have escaped.'

'An astra-what?' said Challis. 'Talk sense, boy.'

'Sounds like witchcraft to me,' Hyl said, and made an uneasy face. Challis shot her a look, equal parts annoyance and confusion, until she noticed it and explained. 'My father's ship had its contingent of witch-workers – they let starships steer, see where they're going, talk to other ships and planets. But I never knew greenskins had their own.'

Challis scowled at his own ignorance for a moment more then shrugged. Hyl was just realising that Challis had likely never even seen a space ship when he snapped his fingers and made her jump.

'That would explain it.' Both the boy and Hyl looked at him quizzically.

'I found a chamber near the outer hulk when I was first finding my way around,' he explained. 'Dozens of greenskins, scores, all chained together and filling the air with lightning. I saw one or two wyrds in the hive sumps back home, and they made my guts crawl in exactly the same way.'

The boy nodded in sudden excitement at Challis's description. 'Yes, the mutant offshoot! Psychics! We knew they must exist, but we never learned much about what kind of work they do. But what you are saying, sir and madam, it fits well.'

For the first time Challis took a moment to look the boy properly up and down. Had he had choices he wouldn't have saved this one – too thin, too frail-looking, scholar's stoop. But on the other hand...

'Fits, does it? Your name? And you know all this how?' The boy straightened a little.

'Korland, sir. I was apprenticed to the household of Magos Biologis Emmanael Cort on Othera. I was compiling my journeyman's thesis on orkoid behaviour, sir.'

'Orkoid?' Challis asked. He looked at Hyl but she just shook her head and shrugged.

'Orks, sir. That is the proper name for the greenskins. "Ork."'

Challis spat onto the deck. 'The bastard greenskins don't deserve a proper name!' The other slaves looked over then cringed away from the sudden boom in Challis's voice and Korland seemed to shrink visibly. Hyl broke the tension and clapped the boy on the shoulder.

'Oh, the irony, eh, Korland?' she said drily. 'Bet you didn't expect to be studying them from this close to hand.'

Korland hazarded a short laugh, and when Challis simply snorted he started to talk again.

'We were planning to pick up some of the creatures left behind on worlds they attacked. We got too far ahead and arrived at Vanaheim while the hulk was in orbit. One of their ships crippled our engines as we tried to get clear and their boats took some of us before the ship fell into the atmosphere.'

'You sure? The captains of the smaller ships co-operating with the ones on the hulk?' Hyl's tone was sceptical and Challis nodded agreement.

'They can't stop fighting among themselves, from what I've seen since I've been trapped here,' he said. 'They've even divided this craft into territories, as far as I can tell. Some of the greenskins wear different paints, like gang colours, though that doesn't seem to matter much. I've seen ones from the same bunch bash each other around a good amount.' Challis shook his head. 'No, the damn beasts are too dumb to co-operate.'

Hyl added her agreement in turn. 'You must have been boarded straight from the hulk.'

'I intend no insolence, sir, ma'am, but I am sure it was the smaller ship. That was part of our study, to find out how orks co-operate. Normally they don't, as you've seen, but you do find rivals co-existing when...'

The rest were gathering around now to listen, but Korland had frozen under Challis's gaze.

'When what, Korland? What are you saying has got them all working together?'

'I think there's a war on the way, sir. A crusade of some sort, catching up orks from all across the sector. The orks have a word for it, or we think... thought it might be a word, just a kind of bellow...'

Challis swallowed, took a deep breath. Hyl closed her eyes and bowed her head.

'I've heard of them, these great greenskin wars. Great Terra, what have we been caught up in?'

'That's why my master was trying to capture specimens, sir! We thought we might be able to divine the target of the war from them! It fits, sir – the migrations of orks from all around, we've been able to track them, the lack of infighting, the capturing of slaves to build war engines. We just needed to discern the trigger...' Challis's gaze zeroed in on him again. Korland's voice faltered for a moment before he went on.

'A crusade like this usually has a trigger, a focal point, something to turn the orks' aggression outward. I think I know what it is.'

All of the slaves were looking at Korland now.

'The Adeptus Astartes, sir. Master Cort knew something of the ork language, and he told us what he had been able to discern. This hulk, other greenskin ships, they're all being drawn to a system where the orks are at war with the Astartes.'

Challis squinted at him, waiting for an explanation; beside him Hyl's eyes widened.

'The Astartes,' she breathed. 'We're going to be sent to war against the Space Marines.'

'Space Marines?' Challis said incredulously. 'The, what do they call them, the Angels of Death? From the stories and hymns? Lord Dante and all the rest? I've heard some of these names, there was a pageant every year at Noatun. All the tales paint them as gods-in-flesh. You're telling me that's what we're going to be meeting? In a song or a tale, maybe, but...' He looked to Hyl for support but she was shaking her head.

'They are real, Challis, trust me. They came aboard our ship once, long ago when I was a girl. They had come to save our convoy from...' Hyl stopped speaking and bit her lip. She raised her head up to look at the darkness above them and simply said, 'Yes, they are real.'

Korland had folded his arms, as if watching a slow student help an even slower one do their numbers. And as he watched, a fire began to come into Challis's face, the grimness turning to a savage joy.

'Do you realise what you're saying? Either of you? Did you hear that, the rest of you? Don't look so miserable, Korland: you've just given us something to fight for!'

Challis stood and walked around, facing each slave with blazing eyes.

'Don't you understand? This hulk's days must be numbered now! Listen to what Korland is telling us! The Astartes! The Emperor's own! No cowering in tunnels for us, not now! Think of what you have to hold out for! The day when the Astartes break this ship's back and come to free us! Liberation Day!'

Challis threw back his head and laughed.

Fifty-eight days to liberation

THERE WAS A human skull lying in a silt-drift where the corridor crumpled through an angle; despite herself, Hyl had been watching it for several minutes. She was getting used enough now to the fungus-light of these levels to be able to pick out shapes, although it had taken her eyes days to adapt. She had been terrified at first that Challis or one of the others would order that she be left behind as they moved through the Wilds.

Wilds. It had been Korland's term. A great wedge of old ship – Hyl thought it must have been a transport – driven edgewise into the giant wreck that made up the hulk's backbone. The ship was canted over at an angle, sealed off from the surrounding decks as it wrecked them in that long-ago crash, cut off from most of the power supplies, some parts airless and locked in lethal cold, much of it choked with rot and silt that had come from who knew where. When the greenskins had come they had filled the Wilds with their own fungi and feral beasts, closed up whatever openings remained and left them.

'These decks were their larder and their livestock-pen,' Challis had told them. 'Whenever they needed to hunt food or catch beasts to fight for them they would come in hunting parties and seal up behind them when they left again. Shadowing the hunting-packs was how I got to know the ways in and out.'

The Wilds had also been a jail. Hyl shifted in her spot and looked at the skull again. No camps in the outer hull for Challis and the thousands from his hive: in the charge of a different slave-master than her own band, they had been herded into the Wilds and sealed there, perchance to be rounded up again at the end of the voyage but as likely to serve as beast-food before then. Challis had not spoken of how the other captives had died, and the darkness that took his expression at those times meant that no one had pressed him.

She shifted round and looked at the shaft behind her as voices drifted up it.

'It's working, sir. Damn, but it's working! Three more of 'em dead since yesterday and still not one of 'em looks like coming out on top. There'll be more to follow, I don't doubt.'

She could hear the wolfish satisfaction in Cantle's voice, muffled as it was. He had been a maintenance rating aboard his old ship, and knew how to slip through the hulk's crawl-spaces like an oiled shadow. He had been spying on the orks that they had tried Korland's latest theory on: assassinate any large ork and its warband would neutralise itself for days, dissolving in petty brawls as the others fought for dominance. Impending ork-crusade or no, it seemed to be working so far.

Hyl leaned into the shaft and peered down, leaving Luder to guard the corridor with a captured ork pistol that it took the other woman both hands to lift, hefting it by the crude shoulder-stock they had had to make for it before any of the slaves could use it. Below her, the shaft ended in a flattened, malformed plug of metal and ceramite, three dead rocket-ports gaping up at her in the dimness.

It had been Cantle who first recognised it for what it was when they had discovered this shaft: a boarding torpedo, remnant of a long-ago Imperial attack. The shaft – Hyl looked up at the odd, lumpy walls where layers of decking had been half-melted and smashed aside – had been the tunnel it had bored deep into the hulk before it ground to a halt in this wreck's guts. Old as it was, it had cheered the ex-slaves, bone-weary after days of hit-and-run raids and ambushes against the greenskins in the mazes of decking. It was a reminder that somewhere out there were humans, an Imperium, the wait for liberation day.

There were sounds below her. Cantle had squeezed out through a rent in the torpedo's side and was clambering out of the pit it lay in.

Hyl caught his hand and pulled him up to the floor she stood on, and he grinned at her.

'Go on, hop down, have a look. Challis is in pretty good spirits.'

Hyl swung herself over the edge and felt her way downward. The air in the shaft still had a faint tang of oilsmoke: two weeks ago Luder had had the idea of burning stolen motor fuel in the airways, the smoke too thin to affect them but enough to blunt the fine noses of the beast-hounds. They hadn't bothered keeping the fires up since she and Challis had led a sabotage team to blow out an air-seal, opening the orks' kennels into space.

She hoped Cantle was right about their leader's mood. Lucky as the find was, she thought Challis still hadn't forgiven Korland for sneaking off – alone of all things! – to investigate the shaft during his assigned sentry shift. She could remember hearing their argument echoing through the little amphitheatre they used as a base.

'And you wonder why I was angry? This is not a game, child, or some scholarly investigation. Lives are at stake. We need everyone! That includes you and that bucket of learnin' you have. How dare you run off like that, without a word to Hyl, or me, or–'

But Korland had been unrepentant, not letting up until Challis had followed him back out to see the torpedo for himself. Hyl leaned close and fitted her head and shoulders through the gap. Challis was the suggestion of an outline around the little glow of his igniter and, peering about, she could start to make out the dim shapes of corpses, dried and shrivelled, still locked into their pews and sunken into heavy environment suits and carapace armour. Challis was braced against a column that ran down the middle of the torpedo, a column studded with what had to be weapon racks.

'I've got the lockers open, managed to get a look inside. Lasers and stubbers, a grenade launcher I think we can fix, hand weapons. Enough for about half of us. Weapons made for humans, not salvaged ork guns we can barely use.' Hyl clambered through the hole to join him, standing awkwardly on the tilted floor as he pointed to the compartments around them.

'There's damage to this thing. I don't know what caused it, but it looks like that's what killed the crew.' Hyl looked around. The torpedo casing was full of gouges and dents from its passage through the hull, and below her toward the point there was a great circular wound there the skin of the torpedo had been punched inward.

'But look up here,' said Challis. 'The ammo lockers on these things look like they're made to last, and I mean last. Lasgun cells will keep for just about ever, and I think there are even flamer tanks back there that survived the impact.'

Challis grunted with satisfaction as he forced a stiff clamp open and turned around with a matt-grey assault shotgun in his hands.

'We're going to be an army now, Hyl. Not a rag-arsed collection of escapees. Korland's words about the Astartes were an omen, right enough. The Emperor's grace brought us news of our freedom, now He's given us the tools to meet our liberators proudly. Weapons in our hands and the blood of greenskins on our fists.' But Challis's tone was still thoughtful, his eyes hooded.

'Something's still on your mind, though, Challis. What is it?'

'Cantle told me that starships have other kinds of these...' he gestured around them.

'Torpedoes.'

'Torpedoes. But they don't carry warriors, they carry bombs. That's what's preying on me now, Hyl. We can fend off these creatures until this hulk goes into its battle, but the Astartes won't know we are here. We have to find a way to make sure they come to free us instead of just firing on this thing and blowing it to pieces. We need to find a way to tell them we're here.'

Hyl took a breath.

'That's why I came to find you, Challis. I think I know where that chamber of witch-orks you told us about is, and I've been talking to Korland about it. I think we have a way to call the Space Marines to free us.'

Thirty days to liberation

WITCHCRAFT. CHALLIS LOATHED the idea, loathed alien witch-craft even more, but there was nothing else for it now. Challis still couldn't fully accept that space ships needed sorcery to talk to one another, even after Hyl and Korlland had explained it to him as best they could.

Ever since the gut-wrenching half-day when the hulk had fought its way back into real space they had been on edge. And when the scouts had reported a rush of agitated orks to the hangars and gun decks, and distant flares of light beyond the viewports, they knew a battle had begun.

Now he was back at the witch-place, crouched in a breach in the wall of what Hyl said had once been the Navigator cathedral. His eyes wanted to lose focus and the air tasted of metal and felt hot and cold at once, and there was a constant pressured feeling as though they were in a fast-dropping lift. Witchcraft.

Spread out below them was the scene he remembered, no less strange for seeing it a second time. Filling the tiered pews were scores of greenskins, chained together with heavy copper shackles. Some seemed to be concentrating and muttering; others were thrashing and yelling, green sparks flying from their eyes and ears.

The great holograph globe hanging above the chamber was cracked and long broken, but occasionally when a sparking greenskin looked at it it would brighten with green mist and faint images, though the greenskins paid little attention to it. Pictures: outlines of giant craft against the stars or bellowing greenskins in what Challis realised with a jolt were other ships in the fleet.

Oh yes, this was the place alright. The place where these spark-spitting orks talked to others on other ships and helped the hulk's commanders see their enemies. The witch-powered aliens who, Korland had told them confidently, would die of their own excitement as soon as any fighting started, leaving the hulk blinded and the greenskins unable to communicate.

Fine. As long as they made some kind of contact first. The place had taken him a week to find again; the raid had taken three times that long to prepare. There would be one chance only.

The force of the orks' brains beat at his eardrums like surf in a storm, and Challis almost didn't hear the muffled explosion at the far end of the chamber as their bombs went off. Then smoke began to roil from several places along the walls and suddenly the air was filled with screams as the chained orks began to convulse and catch fire. Green smoke spurted from mouths, arcs of power crackled between ears, eyes lit up like emerald searchlights.

Challis kicked open the air vent and rappelled down the wall, the rest of his team behind him. Hyl's shoulder jerked as her grenade launcher recoiled, and flechettes stippled the skins of a dozen howling orks. Challis's shotgun boomed twice and felled a surprised attendant as Kelf's flamer lit the air behind them.

Challis felt his head being crushed in an invisible vice. Next to him, blood was running from Luder's nose and mouth.

In front of them, two orks' heads exploded in showers of green light.

He ran to stand in front of the biggest witch-ork, forced himself to look the creature in the eye. Slowly, so that its brain would blast the image out into the minds of every astropath in the system, he raised his shotgun and spoke.

'My name is Challis. There are humans on this hulk. We beg you, help us in liberation!'

There were shots and cries from behind him, and he forced himself not to flinch.

'Please! If anyone hears this!'

And then, suddenly, the creature straightened from its orkish slouch and stood over him. Its expression changed, its eyes fixed on him. As it spoke in a deep, oddly accented human voice the green steam around it seemed to curl into the suggestion of a helmet and faceplate, curved shoulder-guards and a great cloak.

'Human Challis. I speak from the battle-barge *Ragnarok*. You will undermine the turrets and defeat the shields for the wing of the hulk from which you speak. You will open it for attacks by my company and–'

Challis stammered to speak, 'W-we are poorly armed. I am unsure of where this wing is you speak of. I–'

The ork leaned over Challis, voice booming. 'Pay heed! The place you speak from juts from the side of your misshapen craft like a wing. It is decked with cannon and turrets, guns the orks will use to fire at us as we close the distance to storm it, walls of energy that mean we cannot teleport in to find you.'

Challis fought to think through the psychic yammer around him. He remembered the crater in the front of their boarding torpedo. How could he have been so stupid? They would fly at the hulk and their torpedoes would be shot at, breached, the great Astartes might even perish...

Above him the image faded for a moment as the witch-ork began to convulse, then sharpened and spoke again.

'We shall watch you, Challis, and mount our sortie when your destruction of the defences is done. Even as I speak we are in battle, and the defences must be open in thirty days or our attack may fail. Know that we will fight to liberate you, but know that you must fight too before we can reach you. Do you understand?'

'Yes, yes sir.' The gaze looking at him through the creature's eyes seemed to hold him like an iron clamp.

'We will meet thirty days hence, then. Farewell, human Challis.'

The ork's head slowly crumpled into fragments. Challis felt blood erupt from his own nose. There was a fizzing sensation under his skin. His vision swam as he looked around. With an exultant shout Cantle completed his adjustments to a half-wrecked console and blast shutters slammed over every door from the chambers. In the flames and bedlam they sprinted for their tunnel as, behind them, the last of the orks overloaded in a deafening blast of green light.

Liberation day

UP AHEAD THE barricades had gone up as he instructed. Behind them the ork mob rounded the corner, their fury seeming to intensify with every step, and all around came the distant boom of explosions as the slaves' sabotage did its work.

Kelf was dead, gone in the first of the great detonations they had triggered in the base of the bridge-tower. There had been more orks than anyone had been ready for, and just as Challis was realising that they would never be able to fight their way down the stairs to the power regulators, Kelf had kicked the drum of promethium off the edge of the catwalk they had been fighting on and leapt after it, turning his flamer on himself to become a dying, blazing detonator. They could only hope that the explosion had done enough damage to destroy the shields that the Astartes had spoken of.

The mob filled the width of the large corridor, shouldering one another aside to be at the fore. At the rear, blue smoke jetted from the hulking, armoured greenskin pushing the mass forward. In front of him Hyl and the last of the others were already in place, and with a last burst of energy Challis vaulted the metal beams that formed the front line of the defences as hands reached to haul him up the last stretch of barricade.

Cantle and his scouts were gone as well. Their plan had worked perfectly, using baits and fires to drive a stampede of gnashing beasts into the shafts where the orks fed ammo up to their turrets. The guns had soon fallen silent but Cantle and the others had been cut off and lost, unable to get to the rendezvous point they had fortified. Challis had bid them a silent farewell – he had no illusions that their liberators would have time to comb the tunnels for the missing. The message had left no doubt that the blessed Space Marines were going to have to fight their way in and out of even this one weak spot.

Challis dropped down the far side of the barricade and shots erupted around him: the deep chug of Hyl's grenade launcher, the roar of the high-speed ork cannon that Luder and Korland had learned to work, las and stub bursts. Challis scrambled to his feet and added the last of his shotgun rounds to the fusillade.

Last stand, he thought, glancing over his shoulder at the hull-wall behind them. If the blessed Astartes can't find us soon, it ends here. His shotgun was empty and the orks were a mere dozen steps away.

They'll not find us in time, not now.

The armoured giant was in the lead, shots bouncing off the metal plates riveted to its skin. Challis pulled his knives from his belt and readied himself, tears of rage in his eyes.

To have come so far to have it end like this!

In the last few moments of frantic gunfire the flash of light behind the orks went unnoticed.

The Emperor is my…

Until the shooting started.

A whoosh of flame incinerated the rearmost orks, the humans ducking down to avoid the wash of heat. The chieftain turned, roaring in rage, the motors on its armour rattling and smoking.

Challis lifted his head. Through the smoke and orks he counted ten great silver figures, stepping into firing poses and felling one greenskin after another with sweeping, methodical bursts. In a few moments of deafening gunfire the armoured chieftain was alone, green corpses piled to its knees, and the shooting ceased.

The ork revved its armour into a run and one silver figure stepped forward to meet it, racks of golden blades on each arm crackling with blue energy. The ork's swing never connected; the blue-gold claws turned the creature into a cascade of blood, viscera and metal plates, until after another moment the silver being hoisted the carcass up and flung it aside. The remains flopped to the floor and lay oozing.

And in the silence that took the battlefield now, Challis could hear the explosions change note – no longer muffled and deep but nearby clangs and crunches that he guessed must be Astartes boarding torpedoes hitting home.

FROM BEHIND THEIR last barricade, the slave fighters came out, silent with awe, to meet their liberators over the gore-splattered deck. In the clearing smoke Challis took his first good look at the great Marines.

Their dull silver power armour had golden trim, the eye-pieces of the helms lit with a green glow. Challis looked for a name or badge to identify his liberators, but saw none that he recognised. Korland, frowning, had hurried to catch up with him and opened his mouth to speak. Challis waved him to respectful silence. He was grateful for the boy's brain, but a time like this needed no prattling, no matter how well-educated.

One armoured figure after another regarded his procession. None barred their way, but neither did they offer greetings.

It was the golden-clawed Space Marine, his armour glistening with ork blood, who stepped into Challis's way. The captain's helm was the same golden colour as his claws and the shoulders of his hulking suit were maned by long golden spines, decorated with skulls both old and new. Flanking him were massive figures in duller, baroque armour of a different design, the metal flowing from one plate to another in fluid, organic lines. Looking at them in delighted awe, Challis fell to one knee until the being gestured for him to rise.

Challis spoke first, using the formal High Gothic for addressing a superior.

'Hail Astartes! Hail to our liberators! I am Challis, leader of the slave revolt. We hoped you would come to free us. The Emperor, praise to his name, has answered our prayers!'

Several of the figures around them began to laugh. The sound chilled Challis for a moment before he realised what it must be. The Astartes were showing the joy of victory too. Despite their frightening armour there was humanity in them still. Challis grinned back at them.

The voice was a deep, flat baritone, in an antiquated accent Challis had to pay close attention to.

'And our greetings to you in return, Challis. I am Lord Sliganian, leader of this humble company you see before you. My praise to you, sir – you have led your warriors bravely and well. I have not seen the like for many a year.'

'Thank you, Lord Sliganian. We are honoured by your presence and your words.'

'Indeed you should be. Not many of your kind have gazed upon us this close in many ages.' There was a boom behind them, and the faint sound of gunfire. Sliganian cocked his head for a moment, listening to something.

'I would talk with you more, Master Challis, but now is not the time. Our position here is embattled, not a place to make conversation. The task at hand is your liberation.'

Challis bowed.

'Of course, lord.' He waved his soldiers forward. 'Step forward, all of you. Give praise and thanks! How are we to board your craft, Lord Sliganian?'

'Board? Why?' The giant Marine sounded vaguely puzzled. 'You, Challis, I may bring away with us – you, I have hopes for. But you must know that the liberation you have fought for has been brought to you – you need travel no further in search of it.'

'Lord Sliganian,' Challis began, hearing the puzzlement creeping into his own voice, 'are you saying that you will board and keep this hulk? We must leave it otherwise. I mean, true freedom is in faith and spirit, sir, but...' Korland was tugging at his sleeve, mouthing something. Challis shook him off.

'We may take this creation, Challis, you are right,' rumbled Sliganian, gesturing at the walls. 'Ungainly as it is, perhaps it will be home for a little while. Perhaps it will yield up secrets to us, or perhaps we shall destroy it yet. Do not doubt that we can, now that your own actions allowed us our landing. A hulk is simply another fortress, Challis, and the fortress has not yet been raised that our skills cannot bring down. Our progenitors are ancient and noble. Our citadels are impregnable and our engineers unmatched.'

'Challis!'

'What, Korland? Show respect before the Astartes!' But the boy was corpse-pale with fear, and Challis's alarm deepened.

'Ah, Astartes. We were Astartes once, young one, but no longer. We forswore the title the day the Iron Cage broke Rogal Dorn's conceited puppies and we showed ourselves the masters of those who still clung to their old loyalties.'

Challis's alarm dropped into outright terror. Fragments of forbidden legends, false histories whispered of around barrack-tables deep in the night. The Traitor Legions. Astartes who had – unimaginable thought! – turned from the light and brought blasphemous war against the Emperor. He could feel Korland's hand on his arm, quaking uncontrollably.

'But... you promised... you said you brought liberation...'

Sliganian came to attention and clashed his claws together in a handclap. There was more animation in his voice now, a hideous good humour.

'You are right, young Challis, we must not delay. You have earned your liberation ten times over, you and these brave warriors of yours. Why, your resourcefulness almost reminds me of myself in my younger days, before my time as an Iron Warrior.'

Iron Warrior. The words hit Challis like a hammer. Beside him, Korland wrenched Hyl's grenade launcher from her hands with a shriek.

'Run! We are deceived! We are deceived!'

He never had time to fire. The machine-man forms beside Sliganian began to emit a crackling hum, and raised arms that changed before Challis's eyes. Fingers stretched to become gunbarrels, metal gloves flowed backwards into shapes that hinted at weapon stocks, magazines. Each mutant gun-arm spat once.

Challis looked around. The head full of knowledge that Korland had spent his young life accumulating was burst open, the boy's chest caved in. Blood pooled around the corpse.

Delirious with shock, all Challis could do was stare and whisper: 'Liberation. You promised.'

'And am I not a man of my word, Challis, whatever ingratitude your young companion insisted on showing? Theomandus, quickly, please.'

There was a cry from behind him and Challis spun about. Hyl was struggling in the grip of another armoured giant, this one wrapped in a cloak of spun silver, with eyes that gave off pale, twisting lights and a voice that was a soft, creeping whisper: 'For is it not written that "the common man is like a worm in the gut of a corpse, trapped inside a prison of cold flesh, helpless and uncaring, unaware even of the inevitability of its own doom"? Such a fate do we free you from as we bring your mortal flesh to glorious union with the stuff of Chaos.'

'Yes, indeed it is most well written and right,' Sliganian responded.

'And hath not great Perturabo proclaimed: "The spirit is a machine that is unlocked by Chaos. The flesh is a fortress that we shall overcome"?'

Sliganian bowed slightly: 'Thus sayeth the Warsmith above all.'

Hyl had time for one more cry before a hazy wave of energy tore through her and she began to change.

Her mouth dropped open and a threefold tongue tipped in bone barbs uncoiled from it. Her body ballooned into an obese mass that writhed with parodies of her own face as her arms and legs withered to fleshless sticks and dropped away. And her clear green eyes stayed fixed on Challis's until, mercifully, the sanity left them and the sorcerer dropped the squalling lump of flesh onto the deck.

'And so these proud warriors embrace their freedom,' said Sliganian as the slaves were seized by the Traitor Marines around them. His voice was soft, his tone not unkind. 'Your liberation from your mortality, the liberation you so crave from the rusted chains of your Imperium. A gift that so few understand, a gift that the ignorant fear and flee from. There have been worlds, Challis, where the people have risen as one and fought us when we have tried to give the gift that you asked us for. But when I heard of your call for help I knew we had to make haste to aid you. Truly, this is the gift you have all earned, Challis, and it is my honour to be the instrument by which you will have your sweet, brief taste of freedom.'

The sorcerer moved among them, taking each slave by the arm. Luder became a writhing slug-thing with a crest of dripping quills; the man behind her sprouted lashing tendrils from his mouth and nose and choked on them as his muscles swelled and their convulsions broke his bones. By the time the last of them had had their humanity wrenched away, Challis was weeping freely with rage and despair. Sliganian's hand took his shoulder.

'I know, my young friend, it is a moving thing to witness. The corpse-Emperor has no sway over them now. But for you, my warrior, their leader and inspiration, a greater gift still. My flagship has need of slaves, Challis, the fighting with the greenskins has taken its toll. Be of good cheer, brave human – you have won the right to live out your days in the service of your liberator. Hold your head high, Challis. You need wait no longer.'

The servo-claws of the smiths closed about Challis's limbs and the screaming, weeping human was carried away. As his warriors moved to their pickup points Lord Sliganian looked back at the clump of struggling, yammering Chaos spawn. Nearly half were dead already as their deformed bodies gave out; the rest thrashed and howled on the grimy metal floor.

'It is good and generous work that we do, Theomandus,' Sliganian declared, and his sorcerer bowed. 'I am never so fulfilled as upon a Liberation Day.'

THE CURIOSITY

Dan Abnett

HE WAS, IT is fair to say, already weary of Gershom when the curiosity came to light. Seven years is a long time in any man's career, seven years living and working in grubby tenements, backwater hostels and frontier habs all over the planet. Long enough to feel like a native, and certainly to look like one, although he had been born forty-two years and many million AU distant. The patched worsted suit with shiny, calloused elbows, the slate grey weathercoat, fingerless leather gloves, wire-framed spectacles, the skin of his face etiolated from too many short, wintry days, his thin hair unnaturally black from a biweekly chemical treatment that he purchased and applied himself.

This insipid and forlorn figure stared at his own reflection from the smoked glass screen of the demograph booth.

'Present papers. State name and occupation,' the indistinct form behind the screen said. As he spoke, the words appeared in glowing, block-capital holos on the glass.

He put his crumpled documents into the bare metal drawer below the screen and it gobbled them away with an un-oiled clatter. Hunching low, he aimed his mouth helpfully at the vox grille, and said, 'Valentin Drusher, magos biologis.'

'Purpose of travel?' the voice said, subtitled as before.

'I am a magos biologis, as I said. You'll see I have a permit for travel to Outer Udar stamped by the office of the Lord Governor. He is my patron.'

The shape behind the tinted glass panel paused and then the legend 'please wait' appeared on the screen. Doing as he was told, Drusher stood back, rubbing his hands together briskly to chafe warmth into them. It was a miserably early morning in the last few days of autumn and the terminal was vacant. Outside, it was not yet light; the sky was a patchy blue, the colour of a Tarkoni tarkonil's winter plumage, and the orange glare of sodium lamps reflected in the puddles on the rain-slicked concourse. Drusher studied the reflections and they reminded him of the fluorescent banding on the abdomen of the southern latitude glowmoth, Lumenis gershomi.

The air held the bitter foretaste of another hard Gershom winter closing in. He consoled himself with the thought that he would be long gone before winter came. Just a few more days to tidy up this annoying loose end and then he would be done at last.

The drawer slot clacked open again, his refolded papers laid inside.

'Proceed,' said the voice.

Drusher retrieved his papers, gathered up his bags and equipment cases, and walked down into the boarding yard to find himself a seat on the interprovince coach.

It wasn't hard. The vehicle, a converted military gref-carrier from the Peninsula, was all but empty. An old woman in a purple shawl sat alone, fingering rosary beads as she read from a dog-eared devotional chapbook. A young mother, hard-faced and tired, occupied another bench seat, her two small children gathered up in her skirts. A rough-faced agri-worker in leather overalls nodded, half-asleep, one arm protectively around the baskets of live, clucking poultry he shared his seat with. His hound, lean and grinning, prowled the aisle. Two young men, identical twins, sat side by side, motionlessly intent. Drusher set himself down near the front of the cabin, far away from anyone else. He shooed the dog away when it came sniffing at his bags.

A hooter sounded, waking the agri-worker briefly. The coach's big, caged props began to turn and beat, and the patched rubber skirts of the bulky ground-effect vehicle began to swell out. Drusher felt them drunkenly rise up. One of the little children laughed out in glee at the bobbing motion as the vehicle picked up speed.

Then they were out of the city terminal and roaring up to the state highway, fuming spray into the gloomy dawn.

Outer Udar, the most western and – many said – the most heathen of Gershom's provinces, lay far beyond the Tartred Mountains, forty hours away.

For the first hour or two, he worked on his notes, refining technical descriptions on his data-slate. Such polish was simply cosmetic. He'd been over it a hundred times and the taxonomy would have been published as complete by now. Complete but for the curiosity.

He put his slate aside and took the crumpled voxgram from his pocket, hoping yet again that it was a mistake.

Seven years! Seven damn years of rigorous work. To miss a sub-form of tick-fly, a variant weevil, even a divergent rodentae, well that would just be the way of things. Even, he considered, some class of grazer, if it was localised and sufficiently shy in its habits.

But an apex predator? Surely, surely not. Any systematic taxonomy identified all apex predators in the initial phase of preparation by dint of the fact they were the most obvious of any world's creatures.

No, it was a mistake. The curiosity in Outer Udar was an error. He'd stake his reputation on that.

The rolling motion of the gref-coach began to lull him. He fell asleep, dreaming of the characterising mouthparts of filter snakes, the distinguishing feather-palps of lowland locustae, and the bold, striated beaks of peninsula huskpeckers.

* * *

HE WOKE TO the sound of infant laughter. The coach was stationary, and sleet was dashing against the grey windows.
Blinking, he sat up, and repositioned his dislodged spectacles on his nose. At his feet, the two children had his
sketchbooks laid open and were giggling as they surveyed
the hand-painted images of beasts and fowls.

'Please,' he said, 'please be careful with those.'

The children looked up at him.

'Zoo books,' said one.

'Yes,' he replied, taking the sketchbooks away from their
grubby hands and closing them.

'Why have you got zoo books?'

'I make zoo books,' he said.

They thought about this. Their simple grasp of profes-
sional careers did not reach so far. One nudged the other.
'Are you going to put the beast in your zoo books?' the
nudged one asked.

'The beast?' he asked. 'Which beast?'

'The hill beast. It has teeth.'

'Great large teeth.'

'It eats men up.'

'And swine.'

'And swine. With its great large teeth. It has no eyes.'

'Come away!' their mother called, and the two children
scurried back to her down the aisle.

Drusher looked around the cabin. It was just as he had
last seen it. The agri-worker continued to snooze; the old
woman was still reading. The only change was the twins,
who now sat facing one another, like a mirror.

The cabin door thumped open and flakes of sleet billowed in around several newcomers. A black-robed
demograph servitor, its face a cluster of slack tubes beneath
augmetic compound eyes. A short-haired woman in a
leather body-glove and fur coat, carrying a brown paper
parcel. Another agri-worker, his face chilblained, fighting to
keep his long-haired terrier from snapping at the roaming
hound. A matronly progenium school teacher in a long
grey dress. The short-haired woman helped the matron
with her luggage.

'Leofrik! This is Leofrik!' the servitor called as he walked the cabin. 'Present your papers!'

Each voyager offered up his or her documents for the servitor to scan. Gershom was very particular about its indigents, the side effect of being so close to a war zone. The Departmento demographicae maintained a vigilant watch on the planet's human traffic.

The servitor, waste spittle drooling from its mouth tubes, took a long time studying Drusher's papers.

'Magos biologis?'

'Yes.'

'Reason for travel?'

'I went through all this at the terminal this morning.'

'Reason for travel?'

Drusher sighed. 'Seven years ago, I was commissioned by the Lord Governor of Gershom to draw up a comprehensive taxonomy of the planet's fauna. It is all but complete. However, a curiosity has appeared in Outer Udar and I am travelling there to examine it.'

Drusher wanted to go on. To talk about the extended deadlines he had been forced to request, the increasingly reluctant project funding that had obliged him to take the overland coach instead of a chartered flier, the preposterous idea that he might have missed an apex predator.

But the demograph servitor wasn't interested. It handed the papers back to Drusher and stalked away.

In the meantime, the short-haired woman had taken the seat opposite him. She smiled at Drusher. Her face was lean and sturdy, with a tiny scar zagging up from the left hand corner of her lip. Her eyes were dazzling amber, like photoluminescent cells.

Drusher looked away.

'Magos biologis?' she said.

'Yes.'

'I couldn't help overhearing.'

'Apparently.'

The servitor had dismounted. With a lurch like sea-swell, the gref-carrier rose and got underway again.

'I was told you were coming,' she said.

'What?'

The woman reached into her fur coat – highland fox, if he wasn't mistaken – and produced a wallet which she flipped open to reveal the golden badge inside.

'Germaine Macks, province arbites.'

'You were expecting me, officer?'

'A squirt from the governor's office. An expert on his way. I'm thrilled, of course. It's about time. So, what's the plan?'

'Plan?'

'Your m.o.?'

Drusher shrugged. 'I suppose I'll examine habitat, look for spores, collate cases and get a decent pict or two if I can.' His voice trailed off. In seven years, no official had ever taken such interest in his work.

'And how do you plan to kill it?' she asked.

'Kill it?' he echoed.

'Yes,' she said, chuckling, as if party to some joke. 'That being the point.'

'I don't intend to kill it. I don't take samples. Just descriptive records, for the taxonomy.' He patted his sketchbooks.

'But you have to kill it,' she said, earnestly. 'I mean, if you don't, who the hell will?'

BY THE FIRELIGHT of the great hearth, Baron Karne went on expansively for several minutes.

'The Lord Governor is a personal friend, a childhood friend, and when he makes it known that a scholar such as yourself is coming to my part of the world, I take pains to make that scholar welcome. Ask, and it will be given, magos. Any service, any requirement. I am happy to provide.'

'Th–thank you, baron,' Drusher said uneasily. He looked about the room. Trophy heads, crested with vast antlers and grimacing their fangs, haunted the shadowy walls. A winter storm battered at the leaded windows. Outer Udar was colder than he had dared imagine.

'I wonder if there might have been a mistake,' Drusher ventured.

'How is that?'

'Sir, I am a taxonomist. A scholar. My expertise is in the cataloguing of fauna-forms. The Lord Governor – your childhood friend, as you say – commissioned me to compile a concordance of Gershom's animal life. I've come here because... well, there seems to be a curiosity out here I may have missed. A predator. I'm here to identify it for the taxonomy. Not kill it. I'm no hunter.'

'You're not?'

'Not at all, sir. I sketch and examine and catalogue.'

The baron bowed his head. 'Dear me... really?'

'I'm truly sorry, sir.'

He looked over at the door into the dining room. It was ajar and light slanted through.

'What will I tell them?' the baron said.

Drusher felt desperately out of his depth. 'If you have guests – I mean, to save face – I could play along, I suppose.'

AROUND THE LONG candlelit table were nineteen local lairds and their ladies, the rotund Bishop of Udar and his secretary, and a square-jawed man with sandy-white hair and piercing eyes. His name was Skoh. Drusher wasn't entirely sure who Skoh was. In fact, he wasn't entirely sure of anything any more. The baron introduced him as 'that expert from the city I've been promising'.

'You are a famous hunter, then?' the bishop asked Drusher.

'Not famous, your holiness. I have some expertise in the line of animals.'

'Good, good. So claims Skoh here, but in three months, what?'

'It is a difficult beast, your honour,' Skoh said softly. 'I'd welcome some expert advice. What weapon do you favour, magos? Hollowpoint or shot? Do you bait? Do you use blinds?'

'I... um... favour multiple means, sir. Whatever suits.'

'Aren't you terribly afraid?' asked one of the ladies.

'One must never underestimate the quarry, lady,' Drusher said, hoping it conveyed an appropriate sense of duty and caution.

'They say it has no eyes. How does it find its prey?' asked the bishop.

'By scent,' Drusher replied emphatically.

'Not so,' snapped Skoh. 'My hunters have been using sealed body sleeves. Not one sniff of pheromone escapes those suits. And still it finds them.'

'It is,' said Drusher, 'a difficult beast. When was it last seen?'

'The thirteenth,' said the baron, 'Up in the ridgeway, having taken a parlour maid from the yard at Laird Connok's manse. My men scoured the woods for it, to no avail. Before that, the swineherd killed at Karla. The waterman at Sont's Crossroads. The two boys out late by Laer's Mere.'

'You forget,' said one of the lairds, 'my potman, just before the killings at the Mere.'

The baron nodded. 'My apologies.'

'The beast is a blight on our land,' said the bishop. 'I say to you all, a speck of Chaos. We must rally round the holy aquila and renounce the dark. This thing has come to test our faith.'

Assenting murmurs grumbled around the table.

'Are you a religious man, magos?' the bishop asked.

'Most certainly, your holiness.'

'You must come to worship at my temple tomorrow. I would like to bless you before you begin your bloody work.'

'Thank you, your holiness,' Drusher said.

The outer door burst open, scudding all the candle flames, and a servant hurried in to whisper in the baron's ear. Baron Karne nodded, and the servant hurried out again. A moment later, Arbites Officer Macks was standing in the doorway, dripping wet, a riot-gun over one arm. Her badge was now pinned to the lapel of her leather body suit.

She looked around the room, pausing as she met Drusher's eyes.

'Deputy,' said the baron, rising from his seat. 'To what do we owe this interruption?'

'Another death, lord,' she said. 'Out by the stoops.'

* * *

THE ACREAGE TO the north of Baron Karne's draughty keep was a low swathe of marshy ground given over to poultry farming. Through the sleeting rain, thanks to the light of the bobbing lamps, Drusher could make out row upon row of stoop-sheds constructed from maritime ply and wire. There was a strong smell of mud and bird lime.

Drusher followed the baron and Officer Macks down boarded paths fringed by gorse hedges. With them came three of the baron's huscarls, lanterns swinging from the tines of their billhooks. The weather was dreadful. Icy rain stung Drusher's cheeks numb and, as he pulled his old weathercoat tighter around him, he longed for a hat and a warm fox-fur jacket like the one Macks wore.

There was an odd wobbling noise just audible over the drumming of the rain. Drusher realised it was the agitated clucking of thousands of poultry birds.

They reached the stoops, and trudged up a metal-mesh walkway between the first two shed rows. The bird-dung stink was stronger now, musty and stale despite the rain. Teased clumps of white feathers clogged the cage wire. Macks said something to the baron and pointed. A flashlight beam moved around up ahead. It was one of Macks's junior arbites, a young man by the name of Lussin, according to his quilted jacket's nametag. He looked agitated, and extremely glad to see company at last.

The frame door to one of the stoop sheds was open; Macks shone her light inside. Drusher caught a glimpse of feathers and some kind of metal cylinder lying on the floor.

He followed Macks and the baron into the stoop.

Drusher had never seen a dead body before, except for that of his Uncle Rudiger, who had died when Drusher was a boy. The family had visited his body in the chapel of rest to pay their respects and Uncle Rudiger had looked normal. Asleep. Drusher, with a child's naiveté, had quite expected his uncle to jump up and laugh in their faces. Uncle Rudiger had been a great one for practical jokes.

The body in the poultry stoop wasn't about to jump up or do anything. It was face down, thankfully, its limbs draped in a contorted, awkward way that wasn't a practical joke.

This was one of the baron's farm staff, apparently, a yeoman called Kalken. He'd been doing the night feed, and the metal cylinder Drusher had seen was Kalken's grain-hopper, lying where he'd dropped it in a pile of spilt maize.

Macks knelt down by the body. She looked up at Drusher and made a little jerk with her head that indicated he might want to go outside again. Drusher stuck his hands in his coat pockets resolutely and stayed put. With a shrug, Macks turned the body over.

'ARE YOU ALL right?' Macks said.

'What?'

'Are you all right?'

Drusher opened his eyes. He couldn't remember leaving the stoop, but he was outside in the rain again, leaning against the barn opposite, his hands clenched in the wire mesh so tight he'd drawn blood.

'Magos?'

'Y-yes,' he stammered. 'I'm fine.' He thought it likely that he'd never forget what he'd just seen. The awful flop of the rolling body. The way a good deal of it had remained behind on the muddy floor.

'Take a few deep breaths,' she said.

'I really am fine.'

'You look pale.'

'I'm always pale.'

She shrugged. 'You might as well stay here,' she added, though Drusher felt she'd said it less out of concern for his nerves and more because she knew he wasn't particularly useful. 'I'm going to make some notes in situ.'

'There were bites,' he said.

'Yes,' Macks replied. 'At least, I think so.'

'Measure them. And examine the bite radius for foreign matter. Tooth fragments that might have lodged in the bone. That sort of thing.'

'Right,' she said and turned away.

'Where did it get in?' he called after her.

'What?'

'Where did it get in? Was the cage door open?'

'No. He'd fastened it behind him when we found him.'

'Can I borrow a flashlight?'

Macks got a lamp-pack from Lussin and gave it to Drusher. Then she went back into the stoop with the baron to begin her grisly inspection properly.

Drusher began to walk away down the length of the stoop run, shining his torch in through the cages on either side.

'Don't roam too far, sir!' one of the huscarls called out after him.

Drusher didn't answer. He wanted to roam as far as he could. The thought of being anywhere near that bloody, dismembered mess made him shiver. He was sweating despite the winter gale.

Ten metres down, near the end of the row, he found the wire cage roof of one of the stoops had been torn wide open. Drusher played the torch around. He was near the end fence of the poultry compound, a three-metre timber pale topped with a barbed and electrified string of wires. He could see no hole in the fence or damage to the deterrent wires. Had the beast cleared the wall itself? Quite a leap. There was no sign of spore in the thick mud at his feet. The rain was washing it into soup.

He let himself into the ruptured stoop and examined the torn wire roof. With the rain splashing off his face, he reached up and yanked part of it down, studying the broken ends with his lamp closely.

It wasn't torn. It was cut, cleanly, the tough wire strands simply severed. What could do that? Certainly not teeth, not even teeth that could take the front off a man's face and body. A power blade, perhaps, but that would leave signs of oxidation and heat-fatigue.

As far as he knew – and there was no man on Gershom better qualified – there wasn't an animal on the planet that could leap a three-metre security fence and slice open reinforced agricultural mesh.

Drusher took out the compact digital picter he always carried and took a few snaps of the wire for reference. It came through this cage roof, he thought. Probably landed on it, in point of fact, coming over the fence, cut its way in... and then what?

He looked around. The covered timber coop-end of the shed was dark and unforthcoming.

It suddenly occurred to him that whatever it was might still be there.

He felt terror and stupidity in roughly equal measures. He'd been so anxious to get away from that terrible corpse and prove he was good for something, the blindingly obvious had passed him by.

It was still here. It was still right here in the shadows of the coop-box. Once the idea had entered his brain it became unshakable fact. It really was there, just out of sight in the gloom, breathing low, gazing at him without eyes, coiling to pounce.

He backed towards the cage door, fumbling for the latch. He could hear it moving now, the rustle of straw, the crunch of dried lime on the box's wooden floor.

Dear God-Emperor, he was going to–

'Drusher? Golden Throne! I nearly blasted you!' Macks emerged from the coop-box, straw sticking to her wet hair. She lowered her riot-gun.

'What are you doing here?' she asked

'I was... looking for... traces...' he said, trying to slow his thrashing pulse. He gestured up at the torn cage roof.

'You'll love this then,' she said, and led him into the stinking darkness of the coop-box. The floor was littered with dead poultry, feathers glued to the wallboards with blood. The smell of offal was overpowering and made him gag.

Macks shone her flashlight at the end wall, and showed him the splintered hole in the timbers.

'It came in and went right down through the row of stoops, smashing through each dividing wall until it found Kalken,' she said. She'd come back along that route to find Drusher. The holes were easily big enough for her to get through.

'Killed everything in its path,' she said. 'Hundreds of roosting birds.'

'But it didn't eat anything,' he observed, struggling to overcome his nausea. 'It slashed or bit its way through, but there's no sign of feeding.'

'That's important why?' she asked.

He shrugged. He took shots of the splintered holes with his picter, and then got her to hold the light steady while he measured the dimensions of each hole with his las-surveyor.

'Have you told anyone?' he asked her.

'Told anyone what?'

'The truth about me? About what I am?'

She shook her head. 'I didn't see any point.'

'The baron knows,' he told her.

'Right.'

There was movement outside, and he followed her out of the stoop. Skoh was coming down the walkway through the rain. He'd changed into a foul-weather suit, and was hefting what looked like an autolaser, though Drusher was no expert on weapons. It had a big, chrome drum-barrel, and was so heavy it was supported by a gyro harness strapped around his torso. An auspex target-lens covered his right eye like a patch.

'You've seen the body?' she asked him.

'Yes. My men are sweeping the wood behind the fence.'

'It came right through here,' she said, indicating the run of stoops.

Skoh nodded and looked at Drusher, as if expecting some expert insight from him. When none came, Skoh left them without a word and continued on down the path.

'Who is he?' Drusher asked.

'Fernal Skoh? He's a freelance hunter. Game specialist. The community hired him and his men when it became clear I wasn't up to the job.' There was rich contempt in her voice.

'The bishop doesn't think much of him,' Drusher said.

Macks grinned. 'The bishop doesn't think much of anyone. Skoh's not had much success so far, despite his flashy rep. Besides, the bishop has his own man on the job.'

'His own man?'

'Gundax. You'll meet him before long. He's the bishop's bodyguard. Tough piece of work.'

'Doesn't the bishop think Skoh can get the job done?'

'I don't think anybody does any more. The baron's threat-ening to withhold Skoh's fee. Anyway, Skoh's not the bishop's sort.'

'What?'

'Skoh's ungodly, according to his holiness. His back-ground is in bloodsports. The Imperial Pits on Thustathrax.'

DRUSHER'S REPOSE WAS fractured by lurid dreams of bodies that left steaming parts behind when they rolled over. In the small hours, he gave up on rest, and got out of bed.

He'd been given a room on an upper floor of the keep. It was terribly cold, and the wind and rain rattled the poorly-fitted shutters. Drusher got dressed, activated a glow-globe, and stoked some life into the portable heater. By the light of the globe, he spread out his equipment and note books on the table and distracted himself with study.

There wasn't a land predator in Gershom that even approximately fitted the evidence. Prairie wolves from the western continent, Lupus cygnadae gershomi, were rapa-cious enough, but their pack mentality meant they were unlikely to be lone killers. The great mottled felid of the peninsula taiga, sadly almost extinct, had the bulk and power, and could well have cleared the fence, but neither it nor a prairie wolf would could have cut wire like that. And either would have fed.

Besides, Macks had given him her scribbled findings. There was no foreign matter in the poor yeoman's wounds, but she'd made an estimation of the bite radius. Fifty-three centimetres. Fifty-three!

No wolf came close. The biggest radius Drusher had mea-sured for a felid was thirty-seven, and that had been from a skull in the Peninsula Museum. All the biggest cats were long dead now.

The only thing that came close was Gnathocorda max-imus, the vast, deep ocean fish. But this was Outer Udar. There were no wolves here, no forest cats, and certainly no sharks on the loose.

He looked at the picts he'd made of the holes in the stoop walls. It was hard to define from the splinter damage, but it looked like each gap had been ripped open by a double blow, each point descending diagonally from the upper corners. Like a man slicing an X with two swords.

And what was all this talk about it having no eyes?

LYAM GUNDAX'S EYES were dark and close together. He was a tall, massively muscled man with a forked beard and braided black hair. Drusher could smell his body-sweat, a scent like that of an animal.

'Who are you and what do you want?'

It was early in the day. The rains had slowed to a drizzle, and the land was dark under a grey sky. Outer Udar was a wide skirt of rocky uplands and black forests around the dismal horizon.

Drusher had come to the cathedral only to find his way into the nave blocked by the big, fur-clad Gundax. The bishop's man was decorated with bead necklaces and wrist-straps, heavy with polished stones, charms, Imperial symbols and animal teeth.

'Gundax! Come away!' the bishop called out, as if calling off a dog. He wobbled into view as Gundax stepped back.

'Drusher, my dear child,' the bishop greeted him. 'Pay no attention to my rogue here. This is the magos biologis I told you about,' he told Gundax.

Gundax nodded curtly, his leather smock creaking. His charm beads clattered against each other.

'Walk with me,' the bishop told Drusher.

They plodded side by side down the nave. Drusher made a few admiring remarks about the temple's towering architecture and glorious stained glass work.

'This is a hard parish,' said the bishop. 'Hard and hardy on the edge of beyond. Of course, I'm not complaining. I serve the God-Emperor in whatever capacity he calls on me to perform. And here is as good as any.'

'The Emperor protects,' Drusher said.

'He doesn't seem to be doing that so much here these days,' said the bishop. 'It weakens the faith. I have a tough enough time instilling virtue and belief into the weather-beaten folk of this blasted land, and this beast... it saps every ounce of fibre.'

'It must be difficult, your holiness.'

'Life is difficult. We rise to our tests. But, my dear magos, I fear for the spiritual life of this community almost as much as I fear for its flesh and blood. This thing... this beast... it is not an animal. It is a test of faith. An emissary of Chaos. For it to roam here, unchecked also shows that disbelief may roam here likewise. In every sermon I preach, I declaim as much. The beast is a sign that we have fallen away and allowed taint into our souls. To kill it, to cast it out, we must first reaffirm our faith in the Golden Throne.'

'You make it sound simple, your holiness.'

'It is not, of course! But this beast may be a blessing in disguise. Ultimately, I mean. If it makes us renew our belief and our trust in the absolute sanctity of the aquila, then I will offer thanks for it in time. Only in true adversity may a congregation find its focus.'

'I commend your zeal, bishop.'

'So... do you have any leads? Any expert insight?'

'Not yet, your holiness.'

'Ah well, early days. Come, let me bless you and your work.'

'Your holiness? One thing?'

'Yes, magos?' said the bishop brightly, halting in his tracks.

'You said the beast has no eyes. In fact, that seems to be the popular conviction.' Drusher paused, remembering the words of the child on the coach.

'No eyes, indeed! No eyes, that's what they say.'

'Who, your holiness?'

The bishop paused. 'Why, the folk of Outer Udar. It is what they know of it.'

'I was of the understanding that no one had actually seen this thing. Seen it and survived, I mean.'

The bishop shrugged. 'Really?'

'I know of no eye-witness. No one can offer any sort of description. No one knows the form or size of this thing. Of course, we can make guesses. We know it has teeth from the wounds it delivers, and from that I can estimate the size of the mouth. We know it is small enough to pass through a man-sized hole. And, I fancy, it has shearing claws or talons of some considerable size. But other than that, there is no certainty of its form or nature. And yet... everyone seems certain it has no eyes. Why is that, do you think?'

'Tattle,' smiled the bishop. 'Tavern talk, fireside yap. You know how people invent things, especially if they know nothing and they're afraid. I'm sure it has eyes.'

'I see,' said Drusher.

'Now, come and receive my blessing.'

Drusher endured the short blessing ritual. He didn't feel any better for it.

'I WOULD APPRECIATE your collaboration, magos,' said Fernal Skoh. Drusher raised his eyebrows and hesitated, then let the hunter into his chambers. It was late afternoon, and an ice-wind was rising in the north.

Skoh, dressed in a leather body-glove reinforced with mail links and segments of plasteel armour plate, entered Drusher's quarters in the keep and looked around.

Drusher closed the door after him.

'A drink?' he offered.

'Thank you, yes.'

Drusher poured two glasses of amasec from the flask in his luggage. Skoh was wandering the room. He paused at the table, and looked down at Drusher's spread-out mass of notebooks, data-slates and jottings. Skoh carefully leafed through one of the sketch books, studying each water colour illustration.

Drusher brought him his drink.

'This is fine work,' said Skoh, making an admiring gesture towards the sketches. 'Truly you have a good hand and a great eye. That grazer there. Just so.'

'Thank you.'

'You're no hunter though, are you, Drusher?'

The question took Drusher aback.

'No,' he admitted.

'That's fine,' said Skoh, sipping his drink. 'I didn't think so. You're just one more fool caught up in this mess.'

'I hear you worked the Imperial Pits.'

Skoh looked at Drusher cautiously. 'Who's been talking?'

'Deputy Macks.'

Skoh nodded. 'Well, it's true. Twenty-five years I worked for the arena on Thustathrax as a procurer.'

'What's that?'

'I was paid to travel the wilder worlds of the Imperium trapping and collecting animal specimens to fight in the arena. The odder, the more savage, the better. It brought the crowds in if we had something... unusual.'

'Something like this beast?'

Skoh didn't reply.

'It must have been interesting work. Dangerous work. That's why the bishop doesn't like you, isn't it?'

Skoh managed a small smile. 'The arenas of the Imperial Pits are ungodly, according to his holiness. I was employed by a secular entertainment industry that revelled in blood-letting and carnage. I am, to him, the lowest of the low. And an outsider to boot.'

'What did you want, Skoh?' Drusher asked.

'The baron tells me my fee will be forfeit if I fail to make a kill soon. I have wages to pay, overheads to consider. This job has dragged on. I can kill this beast, Drusher, but I can't find it. I think you can. Help me, and I'll pay you a dividend of my earnings.'

'I'm not interested in money,' said Drusher, sipping his amasec.

'You're not?'

'I'm interested in two things. An end to this slaughter and a personal closure. I was hired to produce a complete tax-onomy of this planet's fauna. Now, at the eleventh hour, I seem to have a new apex predator on my hands. If that's so, it will throw my entire work into disarray. Seven years' work, you understand?'

'You think this is an apex predator that you've missed?'

'No,' said Drusher. 'Not even slightly. There'd be records, previous incidents. This is either a known predator gone rogue and acting abnormally or... '

'Or?'

'It's an exotic.'

Skoh nodded. 'You've been here a day and you're that certain?'

'Yes, sir.'

'Do you have supporting evidence?'

'It doesn't match anything I've turned up in seven years. And it doesn't feed. There is no sign of appetite or predation. It simply kills and kills and kills again. That's the behaviour of a rogue animal, a carnivore that's no longer killing due to hunger. And it's the behaviour of a creature alien to this world. May I ask you a couple of questions?'

Skoh set his empty glass down on the table. 'By all means.'

'Why do they say it has no eyes? Where did that rumour come from?'

'All I know about that is that the lack of eyes is a regular feature of the bishop's hellfire sermons. I presumed it was hyperbolic invention on his part, which has fallen into common rumour.'

'My other question is this: you know what it is, don't you?'

Skoh looked at him. His eyes pierced right through Drusher.

'No,' he said.

BY DAWN THE next day, there had been another death. A swine herder out beyond the crossroads had been killed in the night, and twenty of his saddlebacks along with him. Drusher went out into the sparse woodland with Skoh, Macks, Lussin and two of Skoh's huntsmen.

The air was cold and ice-fog wrapped the hillside. It was ten below. At the swine farm, the bodies of hogs and hogherd alike had frozen into the mud of the pens, their copious blood making ruby-like crystals.

In the steep thorn scrub above the swine farm, Drusher stopped the group and handed out the cartridges he'd prepared the night before.

'Load them into your shotguns,' he said. 'They won't have much range, I'm afraid.'

Macks and Lussin had arbites-issue riot-guns. Skoh had made sure his men had brought short action pump-shots along with their heavy ordnance. Both huntsmen, like Skoh, were weighed down with torso rigs supporting massive autolasers.

'What are these?' Lussin asked.

Drusher broke a cartridge open to show them. Little chrome pellets were packed inside in a sticky fluid suspension.

'Trackers,' he said. 'Miniature tracker units. They have a two thousand kilometre range. I usually use them for ringing birds. In fact I plotted the migration patterns of the lesser beakspot and the frigate gull *Tachybaptus maritimus* over a three-year period using just these very–'

'I'm sure you did a great job,' snapped Macks. 'But can we get on?'

Drusher nodded. 'I've packed them in contact adhesive. If you see anything – anything – then you mark it.'

They made their way up the thorny scarp and entered a stretch of black-birch woodland. Thanks to the fog, the world had become a shrunken, myopic place. Unaided visibility was twenty metres. Stark and twisted black trees hemmed them in, gradually receding into the white vapour. The earth was hard, and groundcover leaves were brittle with frost. The obscured sun backlit the fog, turning the sky into a glowing white haze. Skoh spread the group into a wide line, but still close enough for every person to be visible at least to his immediate neighbour. Drusher stayed with Macks. There was an uncanny stillness, broken only by the sounds of their breathing and movement.

Drusher was bone-cold. Macks, wearing a quilted arbites jacket, had lent him her fox-fur jacket, which he wore over his own weathercoat. His breath clouded the air.

'Do you have a weapon?' she asked.

He shook his head.

She slid a short-pattern autopistol out of an underarm rig, checked the load, and handed it to him grip first.

He looked at it uncertainly, as if it was some new specimen for collation. It had a brushed-matt finish and a black, rubberised grip.

'The safety's here, beside the trigger guard. If you have to fire it, hold it with both hands and aim low because the kick lifts it.'

'I don't think so,' he said. 'I've never been a great one for guns.'

'I'd feel better if you had something.'

'You wouldn't feel better if I shot you by accident, which is likely if you let me loose with something like that.'

She shrugged and put it away again.

'Your funeral,' she said.

'I do hope not.'

They walked on another kilometre or two. Skoh and his hired hands had auspex units taped to their forearms, scanning for movement.

'What was the time of death, do you reckon?' Drusher asked.

Macks pursed her lips. 'Four, four-thirty? The bodies had a residual core temperature.'

'So three or four hours ago?'

The chance of anything still being around seemed very slim to Drusher. Given the Beast's hit-and-run habits, it would be long gone by now. But the cold offered possibilities. It had set the soil hard and solid. Tracks might remain. Drusher kept his eyes on the ground.

They went across open fields, thick with rime, and along the basin of a wooded dell where the fallen leaves had frozen into a slippery mat. The fog was actually beginning to disperse, but down in the hollow it was as thick as smoke. Butcher birds, jet black and armed with shiny hook-beaks, cawed, clacked and circled in the treetops.

Drusher suddenly heard an extraordinary noise. It sounded like an industrial riveter or a steam-powered loom. A puffing, pneumatic sputter interlaced with high pitch squeals.

Macks started to run. Her vox-link crackled into life.

'What is it?' Drusher called, hurrying after her.

He heard the noise again and made more sense of it. One of Skoh's men had opened fire with his autolaser.

He scrambled through the frosty ground-brush, trying to keep up with Macks's jogging back as it slipped in and out of sight between the tree trunks. Twice he went over on the frozen rug of leaves, scraping his palms.

'Macks! What's going on?'

More shooting now. A second weapon joining the first. Stacatto *puff-zwip-puff-zwip*.

Then the dreadful, plangent boom of a shotgun.

Drusher almost ran into Macks. She had stopped in her tracks.

Ahead of them, in a narrow clearing between leafless tindletrees, Skoh lay on his back. It looked like his chest and groin was on fire, but Drusher realised it wasn't smoke. It was steam, wafting up from wretched wounds that had all but eviscerated him. His heavy weapon and part of its gimbal-rig had been torn off and were lying on the other side of the clearing. Huge clouts of fused earth had been torn out of the ground and two small trees severed completely from the fury of his shooting.

'Throne of Terra...' Macks stammered.

Drusher felt oddly dislocated, as if it wasn't actually happening. They walked together, slowly, towards the body of the hunter. He still had his pump-shot clamped in his hand. The end of the barrel was missing.

Macks suddenly swung left, her riot-gun aimed. One of Skoh's men stood on the other side of the clearing, half-hidden by a tree and only now visible to them. He wasn't actually standing. His body was lodged upright by the tree itself. His head was bowed onto his chest, the angle of the tilt far, far greater than any spine should allow. Macks approached him tentatively, and reached out a hand. When she touched him, he sagged sideways and his head flopped further. Drusher saw that only the merest shred of skin kept it attached to the rest of the body.

Drusher was overcome with heaving retches and he wobbled over to the thickets to throw up. Lussin and the other huntsman stumbled into the clearing while he was emptying his stomach.

'Did you see anything?' Macks barked at the other men.

'I just heard the shooting,' Lussin moaned. He couldn't take his eyes from Skoh's awfully exposed entrails.

'That's it, then,' said the hunter. He leaned back against a tree trunk, and clutched his head in his hands. 'Damn, that's it then.'

'It's got to be close! Come on!' Macks snapped.

'And do what?' the hunter asked. 'Two of them, with turbo-lasers, and they didn't kill it.' He nodded to Skoh's body. 'That's my paycheck gone. All my dividends.'

'Is that all you care about?' Lussin asked.

'No,' said the hunter, 'I care about living too.' He took out a lho-stick, lit it and sucked hard. 'I told Skoh we'd wasted our time here. Stayed too long. He wouldn't admit it. He said he couldn't afford to cut our losses and leave. Screw it. Screw him.'

The hunter straightened up and dragged on his smoke-stick again. 'Good luck,' he said and began to walk away.

'Where the hell are you going?' Macks demanded.

'Where we should have gone weeks ago. As far away as possible.'

'Come back!' cried Lussin.

The hunter shook his head and wandered away into the fog. Drusher never saw him again.

'WHAT DO WE do?' Lussin asked Macks. She was prowling up and down, fists clenched. She growled something.

'One of them got a round off, with a shotgun,' Drusher said. His voice was hoarse from vomiting and his mouth tasted foul.

'You sure?' Macks snapped.

'I heard a shotgun,' Drusher said.

'I didn't,' said Macks.

'I think I did... maybe...' Lussin murmured softly, rubbing his eyes.

'Get an auspex!' Macks ordered. Drusher wasn't sure who she was speaking to, but Lussin didn't move. Reluctantly, Drusher approached Skoh's body, trying not to look directly at it. He crouched down and started to peel away the tape that secured the compact scanner to Skoh's left gauntlet.

Skoh opened his eyes and exhaled steam. Drusher screamed, and would have leapt back if the hunter's left hand hadn't grabbed his wrist.

'Drusher...'

'Oh no... oh no... '

The hand pulled him closer. He could smell the hot, metallic stink of blood.

'Saw it...'

'What?'

'I... saw... it...' Thin, watery blood leaked from Skoh's mouth and his breathing was ragged. His eyes were dull and filmy.

'What did you see?' asked Drusher.

'You... were... right, Drusher... I... I did... know what... it was... suspected... didn't want... didn't want to say... cause a panic... and anyway... couldn't be true... not here... couldn't be here...'

'What did you see?' Drusher repeated.

'All the things... I've tracked... tracked and caught in... in my life... for the Pits... you know I worked for the Pits...?'

'Yes.'

'Never seen one... before... but been told... about them... you don't mess with... don't mess with them... don't care what the... the Pits would pay for one.'

'What was it, Skoh?'

'The Great... Great Devourer...'

'Skoh?'

The hunter tried to turn his head to look at Drusher. A torrent of black blood gushed from his mouth and nostrils, and his eyes went blank.

Drusher tore the auspex from the dead man's forearm and got to his feet.

'What did he say?' Macks asked.

'He was raving,' said Drusher. 'The pain had taken his senses away.'

He swept the auspex around and tried to adjust its depth of field. He was getting a lot of nearby bounce from the trackers that had gone wide and pelted the ferns and tree boles.

Two contacts showed at a greater range. Two of the glue-dipped teleplugs anchored to the hide of something moving north-west, just a kilometre and a half away.

'Got anything?'

'Yes. Come on.'

Macks was clearly considering taking one of the heavy turbo-las weapons from the corpses, but that would mean touching them.

'Right,' she said. 'Lead on.'

'Macks?'

'Yes?'

'Maybe I should borrow that handgun after all,' Drusher said.

THEY HURRIED THROUGH the frozen woodland, following the steady returns of the auspex. The fog was burning off now, and the heavy red sun was glowering down, casting a rosy tint across the iced wilderness.

When they paused for a moment to catch their breaths, Macks looked at the magos.

'What?' she asked.

'I was just thinking...'

'Thinking what?'

'Skoh was looking for this thing for months. State of the art track-ware, qualified help. Not a sign. And then, today...'

'He got unlucky. Damn, we all got unlucky.'

'No,' said Drusher. 'If you were the beast... wouldn't today be a good day to turn and take him out? It was his last serious try. He's coming out with a magos biologis at his side, changing tactics. Using taggers.'

'What are you saying, Drusher?'

Drusher shrugged. 'I don't know. It's... convenient, I suppose. This thing is quick and sly enough to do its evil work and stay right out of harm's way. By the time a killing is discovered, it's long gone. Today, we had the best chance yet of catching it. And what does it do? It changes its habits entirely and turns on us.'

'So?' asked Lussin.

'Almost like it knew. Almost like it was concerned that a magos biologis and an experienced tracker might have enough skill between them to pose a realistic threat.'

'It's just an animal. What did you call it? An apex predator.'

'Maybe. But it's what a man would do. A fugitive who's evaded capture this long, but hears that the search for him has stepped up. He might decide the time was right to turn and fight.'

'You talk like you know what this thing is, Drusher,' said Macks.

'I don't. It doesn't fit into any taxonomy I've studied. It doesn't fit into any Imperial taxonomy either. Except maybe classified ones.'

'What?'

'Come on. ' Drusher stood up and hurried on through the copse.

THE AIR-MILL had been derelict for fifty years. Its weather boards had fallen away and the sails of its wind-rotor were flaking. The district had processed its flour here, before the cheaper mass-production plant had opened in Udar Town half a century ago.

Drusher, Macks and Lussin edged down through the chokes of weed brush towards the rear of the ruin. The tracker tags had been stationary for half an hour.

Macks pushed the lap-frame door open with the snout of her riot-gun. They slid inside. The interior space was a dingy cone of timber and beamed floors. The mill-gear ran down through the tower's spine like the gears of a gigantic clock.

It smelled of mildew and rotting flour-dust. Drusher took out the pistol. He pointed upwards. Lussin, riot-gun gripped tightly, edged up the open-framed steps to the second level.

Drusher heard something. A slither. A scurry.

He hung back against the wall. There was something up with the auspex. An interference pattern that was making the screen jump. As if an outside signal was chopping the scanner's returns.

Macks circled wide, gun raised to aim at the roof. Lussin reached the head of the stairs and switched around, sweeping with his gun. Drusher tried to get the auspex to clear.

Lussin screamed, and his gun went off. There was a heavy, splintering sound as he fell backwards down the steps, his weapon discharging a second time.

He was dead. The front of his skull was peeled off and blood squirted into the air.

Macks howled, and fired her riot-gun into the ceiling, pumping the grip and blasting the rotten floorboards in a blizzard of wood splinters with each successive shot. Every muzzle-flash lit the mill room for a millisecond

Exploding wood away before it, the Beast smashed through the deck and came down at them.

It was a blur. Just a blur, moving faster than anything had a right to. Macks's riot-gun boomed again. The creature moved like smoke in a draft. Drusher had a fleeting glimpse of deep purple body plates, a snapping tail of gristly bone, forearm claws like harvest scythes. Macks screamed.

Drusher dropped the auspex and fired his pistol.

The recoil almost broke his wrist. He yelped in pain and frustration, stung hard by the kick. Use both hands, she'd told him.

It turned from Macks, chittering, and bounded across the floor right at him.

It was beautiful. Perfect. An organic engine designed for one sole task: murder. The muscular power of the body, the counter-weight tail; the scythe limbs, like a pair of swords. The inhuman hate.

It had no eyes, at least none that he could see.

Hold the gun with both hands and aim low. That's what she'd said. Because of the kick.

Drusher fired. The recoil slammed up his arms. If he'd hit anything, it wasn't obvious. He fired again.

The Beast opened its mouth. Fifty-three centimetres of bite radius, teeth like thorns. The blade-limbs jerking back to kill him.

He fired again. And again. He saw at least one round flick away, deflected by the Beast's bio-armour.

It was right on him.

And then it was thrown sideways against the wall.

It dropped, writhed, and rose again.

Drusher shot it in the head.

It lunged at him. A riot-gun roared and blew it back. Bleeding from the forehead, Macks stepped up and fired blast after blast. She fired until the gun was empty, then took the pistol out of Drusher's hands and emptied that into it too.

Ichor covered the walls. Frothy goo dribbled out of the Beast's fractured bone armour.

'What is it?' Macks asked.

'I believe,' Drusher replied, 'it's called a hormagaunt.'

But Macks had passed out.

IT TOOK THE better part of an hour for the relief team of arbites to reach them from Udar Town. Drusher had made Macks comfortable by them, and dressed her wounds.

Pistol in hand, he'd carefully examined the beast. The goad-control was easy to find, implanted into the back of the eyeless head.

When Macks came round again, he showed her.

'You need to deal with this.'

'What does it mean?'

'It means this abomination was brought here deliberately. It means that someone was controlling it, directing it in a rudimentary fashion.'

'Really? Like who?'

'I'd start by asking the bishop some questions, and his pet heavy, Gundax. I could be wrong, of course, because it's not my field, but I think the bishop has a lot to gain from something that puts the fear of the God-Emperor into his flock. It steels the faith of a congregation to have something real to rally against.'

'He did this on purpose?'

'It's just a theory. Someone did.'

Macks was quiet for a while. He could guess what she was thinking. There would be an investigation and an inquest. The Inquisition may have to be involved. Every aspect of life in the province would be scrutinised and pulled apart. It could take months. Drusher knew it meant he wouldn't be leaving Outer Udar any time soon. As a chief witness, he'd be required to stay.

Outside, it had begun to sleet again.

'You must be happy at least,' murmured Macks. 'That work of yours, your great taxonomy. It's all done. You've finished.'

'It was done before I even got here,' said Drusher dryly. He nodded at the body of the beast. He'd covered it with a piece of sacking so he didn't have to look at it any more. 'That wasn't part of my job. Just a curiosity.'

'Oh well,' she replied with a sigh.

He went to the mill door, and gazed out into the sleeting wilds. Ice pricked at his face. Gershom would be keeping him in its chilly grip a while longer yet.

'Could I keep this jacket a little longer?' he asked Macks, indicating the fur coat she'd lent him. 'It's going to be a cold winter.'

PAYBACK

Graham McNeill

GUNSMOKE AND BRICK dust filled the stinking bedroom, blasted clear by the gunfire from outside. Cornelius sat below the window with his back to the wall, holding his stubber between his knees as he thumbed more cartridges into the breech. Shouted commands and the sound of running feet told him he didn't have much time before Constantine's men came for him. As he loaded the weapon he kept his laspistol trained through the broken mirror door. Low moans and anguished cries drifted from the landing outside, and the mutant whore's shrill screaming from the bed grated on his already taut nerves.

He snapped the stubber's breech shut and aimed the gun at the shrieking mutant.

'You'd better shut up unless you want to be next,' he growled, nodding towards the bullet-riddled body of Trask, his naked body lying on top of the bloody bed-sheets.

Trask's heavy boots hung over the end of the bed, the laces dangling to the floor. Cornelius shook his head at his former partner's lack of class. Only a low-life like Trask would pay

for one of Mama Pollyanna's girls and take her to bed with
his boots on.

The girl in question clutched a spattered blanket around
her, her black eyes wide and her whipping tongue stretched
fully a foot from her mouth as she screamed the place down.
A thick mane of fiery orange hair spilled around her feline
face, running in a mohawked trail down her spine. Her skin
was bronzed and smooth, like honey, and he could well
understand why Trask had picked her. What other talents
her mutations had granted her in her profession he could
only guess at.

He heard heavy footfalls and whispered conversation
from outside the room as a spray of bullets and las-bolts
ripped through the window, splintering the frame and raining broken glass to the floor. The girl screamed again and
pounced from the bed, clawing at him with her nails as two
of Constantine's thugs burst into the room, shotguns at the
ready.

Cornelius fired twice, both shots going wild as the naked
girl kicked and punched, dragging her long, painted nails
down his face while shrieking like a banshee. He rolled and
hammered his elbow into her face, snapping her head back.
The first thug opened up with his shotgun, blasting a plate-
sized chunk of brickwork from the wall.

Cornelius swung the unconscious girl around in front of
him, using her body as a shield, and blew the back of the
shooter's head clear with a single las-bolt. The second gun-
man hesitated, trying to draw a bead on Cornelius without
hitting Mama's most requested girl. Cornelius didn't give
him a chance to regret his mistake and shot him in the belly
with his stubber. The man screamed and crumpled, clutching his bloody midriff.

Cornelius threw the mutant girl onto the bed as an explosion above him rained timber and plaster from a hole
blasted in the ceiling. He saw shapes through the pall of
smoke and dived forwards, scooping up a fallen shotgun
and rolling onto his back below the hole.

Pain tore at him as the synth-flesh bandage Monque had
applied ripped free and blood ran down his side. He racked

the shotgun's slide and fired upwards three times, hearing the screams of wounded men and the thump of bodies on the floor above him.

Keeping the shotgun aimed through the hole in the ceiling, Cornelius scrambled to his knees, turning and putting a las-bolt through the skull of the second man who'd come through the door as he weakly reached for his fallen weapon.

He crawled back to his position beneath the window, sweat pouring from his face as he heard the wailing sirens of approaching Special Security Agent Rhinos.

Cornelius swore silently to himself.

How had he allowed things to get so messed up?

'CORNELIUS BARDEN?' SAID the girl. 'I've not heard of you before.' 'No reason you should have,' replied Cornelius. 'I'm new on Karis Cephalon.'

The girl nodded, cocking her head to one side. 'Trask says you killed six men at the spaceport when you jacked these weapons.'

'Trask talks too much,' said Cornelius.

The girl smiled in agreement and he was again struck by how young she was. Trask's contacts had set this meeting up, but he'd had trouble believing that this girl, Lathesia, could actually be the leader of the mutant resistance here in Cephalon. But she knew her stuff and he was impressed by her easy confidence.

'Hey, easy, Con! I'm standin' right here,' whined Cornelius's partner, Milos Trask.

Both Cornelius and Lathesia ignored him.

'Is it true though? Did you kill them?' she pressed.

'Yes, I killed them. So what?' shrugged Cornelius.

'So what indeed,' agreed Lathesia. Her black eyes glittered in the dim light cast by the hooded glowlamps as she knelt and lifted a blue-steel plasma gun from one of the packing crates sitting on the ground between them.

'Who did these belong to?' she asked, tapping her fingers against the scorched side of the crate where a shipping marking had once been stamped.

'What do you care?' replied Cornelius.

'I don't.'

'Then why ask?'

'I just wanted to see if you'd tell me,' shrugged Lathesia, handing the plasma gun to one of the two heavily-built men flanking her. Both were mutants, their skin a mottled purple and their limbs grossly swollen. Cornelius could tell they were just itching for an excuse to use the battered rifles – antique PDF surplus – they carried. Though if this deal went through, the mutant resistance would suddenly become a whole lot better armed and he'd be a whole lot richer.

There was just one catch.

'Red' Ivan Constantine.

Selling weapons to mutants was treading on Constantine's toes and if the arms dealer knew about this deal, he'd be lethally opposed to it.

Cornelius knew this deal was dangerous and his senses were electric. Everyone was nervous. Everyone but him and Lathesia.

The deal vibed strange. The deal vibed wrong.

Trask was tight as a drum. Sweat stink and nervous energy poured from him in waves. Cornelius didn't like it. It smelled of set-up. But of who?

He shook his head with a smile. 'You want to go direct to source next time. Cut out the middle man.'

'Something like that,' nodded the teenage girl, running a hand through her dark hair, and even in the dim light, Cornelius could make out the scabbing flesh on her arms. Aside from her eyes, it was one of the few visible signs of her mutant heritage.

Anyplace else, she'd be ostracised, but here in the mutant ghetto, he was the outsider.

She caught his gaze and smiled humourlessly.

'Do you have a problem that I'm a mutant?'

'Not so long as you pay us, little girl,' said Trask, unashamedly ogling her curves.

The largest of Lathesia's mutant guards stepped forward, lips pursed together.

'Call her that again and I'll put bullets in you, Trask,' he snapped.

Trask raised his hands in mock terror and laughed, 'Ooooh, the mutants are mad at me! I'm so scared.'

The mutant raised his rifle, but Lathesia stopped him with a curt gesture.

Cornelius masked his annoyance at Trask, again regretting his decision to hook up with the man on this venture. It had seemed like an easy score; selling arms at inflated prices to the mutant population of Karis Cephalon, who were too dumb to realise they were being ripped off. Ever since they had heisted the guns from the spaceport, Trask had been nothing but a liability, his loose mouth and lack of personal hygiene at odds with Cornelius's stoicism and careful grooming. But for his contacts within the mutant underground, Cornelius would have killed him the moment they'd made their escape from the heist.

'I don't give a damn if you're a mutant, xeno or pureblood,' said Cornelius. 'Your cash is as good as anyone else's.'

Lathesia locked eyes with him, holding his gaze for long seconds until, at last, she nodded, apparently satisfied with his answer. She waved her hand to the less aggressive of her companions, who stepped forwards with a burlap sack, secured at the neck with a rope drawstring. He tossed it at Cornelius's feet, where Trask seized upon it with a whooping laugh. Cornelius kept his eyes on Lathesia as Trask lifted out bundles of tied bills and fed them into an auto-counter. The machine flickered quickly through the money, its tiny machine spirit checking denominations and for counterfeit bills.

At a shade over two metres, Cornelius Barden was of above average height, and his build was that of a pit-fighter. His shoulders were wide and powerful, his waist narrow and his chest slabbed with thick muscle. He wore a long greatcoat, hiked over the butt of his stubber and his silver hair and beard reflected the torchlight. Every movement spoke of control.

Over the mumbled counting of Trask, Cornelius heard a scrape of metal. He made sure not to move, but his senses cranked up a notch. Someone was out there. Not SSA. Not this deep in the mutant ghetto; the alarm would have been sounded long ago and they'd be roaring in with bullhorns and searchlights. No, this was something else. Constantine? Log that as a possible.

Trask finished counting the money and pulled the bag's drawstring tight.

'We happy?' asked Cornelius.

'Damn straight we happy, Con,' said Trask, dropping the auto-counter into the sack, slinging it over his shoulder and backing away from the mutants. Cornelius lost sight of Trask as he moved beyond his peripheral vision. He heard another scrape. Boots on gravel. Upgrade the Constantine possibility to a probability.

Closer now, more steps. Lathesia noticed it now, eyes narrowing, unable to see much beyond the torchlight. She shot a hurried glance at Cornelius. He shook his head and reached for his stubber. She whipped out a heavy revolver and sprinted for cover.

Gunshots split the night, pistols and lasguns. Cornelius felt a whipcrack sting of bullet fragments against his cheek. Something snatched at the hem of his greatcoat as he dived towards a built-up pile of debris.

One of the mutants was down, his guts burned open by twin las-blasts. The other returned fire into the darkness, screaming in defiance.

Very dumb, thought Cornelius as a flurry of bullet impacts cratered his chest. A final shot took off the top of his head. Cornelius heard the boom of Lathesia's gun and low crawled back the way he'd come, trying to spot the attackers and, more importantly, Trask and the money. Lathesia was on her own. He owed her nothing.

He heard scrabbling feet, ten metres west, and made his way through the rubble towards it as a voice echoed through the night.

'Barden! I know you can hear me, so you listen good eh? I only want my money. This turf, it mine, and you know it. Just hand over the money and I call it even! What you say to that, huh?'

Cornelius had seen Ivan Constantine, though had never spoken to him. But he knew instinctively that the thickly accented voice was his. He silently backed away from the source of the shout. If Constantine thought he was dumb enough to answer, then they had a lot to learn about Cornelius Barden.

He ghosted through the detritus of the mutant ghetto, putting as much distance between him and Constantine. The deal was done and he wanted to get out of here before the arms dealer's men realised he was gone. He had to find Trask. Quickly. Give the man ten minutes and he'd blow the score in dice games or on a girl. His partner would have no compunction about ditching Cornelius the moment it looked like he was in trouble, but Cornelius didn't blame him. He'd do the same.

The noise he'd been circling towards resolved itself as a man, crouched low with a long-barrelled lasrifle. Cornelius drew a power knife and thumbed the activation rune, the blade glowing faintly with lethal energy.

Two steps and he closed the gap, wrapping his thick arms around the man's neck. His victim's arms came up, clawing. Cornelius hammered the full length of the power knife through the man's armpit and into his heart. The man's struggles ceased instantly. Cornelius eased the corpse to the ground, too late catching the click of a hammer easing back behind him.

He spun. He caught a muzzle flash and a silhouette. Fiery red pain flared in his side. He fell, blood pumped, hot and fast. He snapped off a couple of shots – wide. His vision blurred as he hit the ground hard. Fireflies spun before his eyes. More shouts sounded behind him. Constantine's men coming for him.

The one who'd shot him turned and ran from the shouts. His direction and his sweat stink told Cornelius who it was.

Trask.

HE RAN. HE stumbled. He fell. But he kept going. Gritting his teeth and pressing his hand hard into the wound, he kept going. Several times his pursuers came close, but each time he hunkered down, fighting to keep his breathing quiet and even. He almost blacked out twice, biting his lip till it bled to keep from slipping into unconsciousness. His body was running on pure adrenaline, but he could feel his strength fading fast. He had to keep moving, to stop was to die.

He pulled a stimm inhaler from his coat and took a huge breath. Fresh vigour poured through his limbs as the Spur took effect. It was risky taking a stimm when he'd lost so much blood, but what choice did he have?

Blood soaked his fatigues and filled his boot, leaving bloody prints in his wake. He needed help badly and there was only one place in Cephalon where he could get it.

It was nearly a kilometre away in the old royal quarter, but he had no choice.

CHIRURGEON MONQUE PULLED back the bolt on his door, unlocking the six padlocks that secured the steel door to his ad-hoc surgery. He was no stranger to midnight callers and was therefore not surprised to see the slumped form of a man gripping the metal frame of his door. There had been gunshots earlier, but with increased SSA crackdowns and riots breaking out almost daily, that wasn't unusual.

He knelt beside the man, pressing his fingers against his neck. There was a pulse: erratic, but strong.

Monque checked the street in both directions to see if this man had brought trouble to his door, but there was nothing to be seen other than the usual collection of vicious night-owls that prowled the streets of Cephalon in this unsavoury district.

He lifted the man's blood-soaked coat, grimacing as he saw the bullet wound in his side. He rolled the man over onto his side, shaking his head as he saw there was no exit wound. Which meant the bullet was probably lodged deep in a vital organ or had fragmented on a bone, shredding his intestines.

Monque sighed and replaced the man's coat over his wound.

He said, 'I think you might be out of luck, my friend.'

As he made to stand, the man's hand reached up, gripping him tightly, and Monque was amazed at his strength.

'I have money,' he hissed, thrusting a handful of bills towards Monque.

Monque snatched them from the man's hand and smiled.

'Well, why didn't you say so?' said Monque and dragged Cornelius inside.

CORNELIUS TOOK ANOTHER swig from the bottle, feeling the cheap rotgut sear its way down his gullet. As filthy a concoction as it surely was, it dulled his senses to the agony in his side. He drank again and laid his head back on the table.

'I'll add that to your bill,' said Monque, wheeling over a rusted gurney laden with surgical instruments.

'Whatever. Just get on with it, damn you,' said Cornelius as Monque snapped on a pair of surgical gloves.

The chirurgeon took the bottle from Cornelius's fingers, placing it on a nearby cabinet filled with vials of coloured solutions. A gurgling medicae transfuser pumped fresh blood into his body, and he experienced a moment of panic as he suddenly wondered where it came from. Was it mutant blood? Might it be infected with the plague that had swept through the mutant population in the last few weeks? Would it make him like the twisted wretches he'd seen eking out a slave's existence in the mutant ghetto?

Monque saw his concern and chuckled.

'Don't worry; it's clean. And anyway, despite what the priests will tell you, mutant blood is just like yours and mine. Their corruption is of the soul, not the blood.'

The chirurgeon selected a plastic hypo-syringe from the tray before him and stabbed the needle into a bottle filled with murky liquid. He half-filled the injector and tapped it before squirting a few droplets from the needle to release any remaining air bubbles.

'Is that sterile?'

'Probably not,' admitted Monque, 'But it will help the pain. It's a little concoction of my own actually. I call it Ease…you know, because it helps–'

'Ease the pain, yeah, I get it,' groaned Cornelius.

Monque sniffed, piqued at having his witticism ruined, and jabbed the needle into Cornelius's arm with rather more force than was necessary. Cornelius winced, but smiled dreamily as the pain suppressant went to work almost instantaneously. Whatever other flaws Monque had, he brewed some damn fine chemicals.

Cornelius watched as Monque replaced the hypo on the tray and lifted a set of thin-legged forceps. The pain from his wound was still there, burning like a hot coal in his belly, but he felt strangely removed from it, as though it belonged to another person.

His thoughts, normally so quick and sharp, flowed like syrup, meandering their way towards a conclusion whose point was forgotten by the time his numbed brain even remembered that there was one. It wasn't a sensation he particularly liked.

Monque lifted clear the bloody leather of his coat and shook his head again.

'The bullet has pushed dirt and burnt leather into the wound. You'll be lucky if you don't get an infection from this.'

Cornelius tried to answer, but his tongue felt too heavy to form the words. Monque smiled.

'Don't try and speak, the Ease will make that next to impossible.'

'Right,' slurred Cornelius and Monque's eyebrow rose a fraction.

Monque returned his attention to the wound and wiped it clear with a sodden rag. Blood pulsed weakly from the hole.

He extended his little finger and forced it into the bullet hole, twisting and prodding inside Cornelius's belly. He shook his head and pushed deeper, past the knuckle, rooting around for the hard touch of the bullet.

'Well at least it didn't strike any bone and fragment,' murmured Monque to himself.

Cornelius watched as more blood spilled across his belly, pooling beneath him on the table and dripping to the cracked tile floor. He groaned in pain, the none-too-tender ministrations of Monque penetrating even the fog of his

Ease. He felt the forceps push into his flesh, Monque rummaging around in his belly for the bullet.

Monque grimaced. 'I can feel the Emperor-damned thing, but I can't quite reach it yet.'

He swapped the forceps for a surgical scalpel, pressing the sharp blade against the ragged edge of the bullet hole, cutting it wider and spreading the wound. He picked up the forceps once again and dug into Cornelius, tugging at the reluctant bullet.

Cornelius gripped the metal rails at the side of the table, knuckles white.

Three more times, Monque widened the wound with the scalpel before eventually the bullet came free in a wash of blood.

Cornelius roared in agony, ripping the metal rails free from the table.

He flopped back into a sticky red pool, the table awash with his blood.

Monque lifted the forceps and held them before Cornelius's eyes.

The bullet was less than a centimetre long, a flattened oval of silver steel spattered red.

He felt his strength fading again as Monque said, 'There, that wasn't so bad, was it?'

Cornelius blacked out.

SUNLIGHT BREAKING THROUGH a clear polythene window woke him. Cornelius blinked his gummed eyes open and licked his cracked lips. Then the pain hit him and he groaned. He lay on a stinking pallet bed, the thin sheet stained and malodorous. He pulled it back and looked at his bruised and raw flesh. A synth-flesh bandage had been applied to his wound.

He tried to push himself upright, but gave in as pain zipped up his side and set off supernovas in his head. He contented himself with propping himself up on his elbows and checking out his surroundings.

Through the window he could see the spire of the Amethyst Palace the locals called the Needle of Sennamis, which meant he was still in the old royal quarter. Probably still at Monque's then. How long had he been out? He rubbed a hand across his face, judging the stubble there to be a night's worth of growth.

The room was dirty, the tiles that remained on the walls cracked and stained a mouldy green. A bare wooden floor lay deep in dust, and footprints led from the door to the bed. An upturned packing crate with a faded medicae stencil served as a makeshift table beside the bed. His guns lay on the crate. He checked both, unsurprised to find both empty.

The door opened. Instantly Cornelius swung his laspistol round.

'I do hope you're not planning on using that in here,' said Monque, setting a vial and syringe next to Cornelius's stubber.

'That depends.'

'Oh, on what?'

'On who comes through that door.'

Monque nodded, preparing another hypo-syringe from the bottle. 'I knew the moment I saw you, that you were trouble.'

'So why help me?' asked Cornelius, setting down his pistol.

'I have many weaknesses, my friend, and money is first among them. You gave me quite a sum last night. Don't you remember?'

'No.'

'Well, it was enough to run roughshod over my otherwise highly-tuned sense of self-preservation, I can tell you. However, having said that, I want you out of here. I can smell trouble on you and when it finds you: be somewhere else. I have enough of my own without your type bringing me more.'

'I'll be gone within the hour,' promised Cornelius, 'I have to find someone.'

'I just bet you do. I wouldn't want to be him, whoever he is,' said Monque.

'No, you wouldn't,' agreed Cornelius, grabbing Monque's hand as he pressed the needle of the syringe against his forearm.

'What's in that?'

'It's a dose of Ease, but don't worry, it's much weaker than the shot I gave you last night. It'll help the pain, but won't turn your head inside out.'

Cornelius released the chirurgeon's arm and allowed him to spike his vein.

The plunger was halfway when Cornelius heard the creak of a door opening downstairs. He whipped his arm away from Monque and wrapped his hand around the chirurgeon's neck.

'Did you tell anyone I was here?' hissed Cornelius.

Monque gasped, dropping the hypo and shaking his head furiously.

'No! I swear! Why would I?'

'So how did Constantine's men know to find me here?'

'Constantine? Ivan Constantine?' spluttered Monque. 'Emperor's holy blood! I knew you were trouble.'

He heard heavy footfalls on the stairs. The snap of a weapon being cocked.

'How did they know I was here?' demanded Cornelius again.

'There were a dozen or more people on the street last night!' wheezed Monque, his face purpling. 'Any one of them could have told Red Ivan you were here if his men wanted to find you.'

Cornelius swore, knowing Monque was right. 'Where's the energy pack? Quickly, before I break your damn neck.'

Monque nodded hurriedly. The footsteps neared the door. Floorboards creaked.

Monque reached into a pouch at his belt and pulled out a silver-steel laspistol power pack.

Cornelius grabbed it and slammed it home.

The door burst open. Cornelius aimed the laspistol.

Monque hit the floor. Bullets ripped through, cratering the wall above him. Cornelius rolled from the bed, crying out as pain engulfed his side. He put his first lasbolts through the door, but couldn't see if they hit anything.

The barrel of an autogun poked around the door, the barrel flaring as wild shots tore up the bed. Dust, smoke and roaring noise filled the room. A shadowy figure lurched inside, spraying the room with bullets.

Lying on his back, Cornelius gripped his pistol two-handed and squeezed the trigger three times.

The figure grunted and staggered backwards. For good measure, Cornelius fired three more times, pitching his victim through the window.

Monque poked his head above the level of the bed, looking through the torn, flapping polythene.

'Did you kill him?' he asked.

'I damn well hope so,' said Cornelius, 'because I don't have any more power.'

Monque threw Cornelius the pouch of ammunition.

'You need to go now,' he said emphatically.

CORNELIUS WAS AS good as his word, leaving Monque's surgery within minutes, dropping another handful of crushed bills onto the bloody operating table on his way out. With his guns loaded, Cornelius left Monque's through the back, taking great pains to ensure he was unobserved.

His wound pulled tight. It bled a little. It hurt a lot.

But he'd been lucky. Had Trask's bullet been a few centimetres to the right, he'd be in the ground by now. He made his way through the streets of Cephalon, the city sweltering and stinking in the heat. Hover carriages passed him and shuttles screamed overhead, heading towards the spaceport as he limped from the royal quarter. He kept clear of the main arterial routes through the city, heading north towards the mutant ghetto.

He passed posters of Space Marines, promising him that His warriors were protecting him, devotional slogans painted on building sides and PDF recruitment posters.

He couldn't go back to the place he'd stowed his gear; Trask would surely have betrayed its location to Constantine.

It didn't matter. There was nothing there he'd miss. He carried all his money with him and anything else he needed he could buy or steal.

But first he needed a place to rest up for a few days. He wasn't strong enough to take on Constantine yet.

Finding lodgings was easy enough. Cornelius paid for three nights in a run down flophouse, run by a fat man with an eye-patch and a shotgun. Cornelius greased him with some bills. He found his room, a filthy, bug-infested firetrap. He slept for sixteen hours.

He spent the time building his strength, working out his strategy.

Find Trask. Kill Trask. Take whatever was left of the score. Pretty simple really.

The days blurred. Cornelius stripped his weapons, preparing special hand-loads for the stubber. Dumdums and man-stoppers. One-shot killers.

He ate in his room, he drank in the flophouse's excuse for a bar. He listened to the talk.

Riots had erupted in the mutant ghetto again. SSA snatch squads hit suspected mutant resistance safe houses, killing anyone they found. The mutants reciprocated, ambushing two SSA patrols and bombing several mercantile trading houses.

Rumour was that the ambushes had been carried out with some brand new weaponry. Weaponry the mutants weren't supposed to have. Questions were bound to be asked by senior members of the SSA and Cornelius knew it wouldn't take them long to come up with his name. Even if Constantine didn't give him up, SSA snitches would hear it from Trask's flapping mouth.

Simmering tension filled the streets. Gunshots became endemic.

People talked of revolution. Cornelius saw opportunities.

Cephalon's movers and shakers tried to put a soothing spin on events. Holocasts of Cardinal Kodazcka showed the holy man appealing for calm from his pulpit. The powerful mercantile families called for the Governor to maintain order and protect their holdings. Nothing was forthcoming from the Amethyst Palace but stony silence. Rumours flew that the Governor was missing. Said rumours were denied vehemently.

As night drew in on the third day, Cornelius holstered his pistols, filled his belt loops with speed-loaders and pulled on his greatcoat. He'd rested long enough and though he was nowhere near fully fit, he was strong enough to take out Trask.

Time to get going. Where would Trask go?

The answer came easy: gambling dens and whorehouses.

THE NORTH-EAST QUARTER of Cephalon was a haven for mutants, desperadoes, killers, thieves and deviants. If Trask was going to be anyplace, it would be here. Cephalon by night was loud, brash and unashamed. The wild scions of the wealthy families slummed it here, trolling the whorehouses and dope dens for thrills they couldn't get elsewhere.

The streets heaved with bodies. Dealers sold their wares from street corners. Women sold themselves from shadowed doorways. Voices were raised and flashing neon bathed everything in rainbows of sickly light.

Cornelius moved through the crowds, his eyes constantly in motion as he scanned faces. He changed direction often, checking for anyone following him. He saw no one, but in this place there could be a dozen people tailing him and he wouldn't know it.

Trask was here somewhere; he could smell him.

He pictured Trask's narrow, pale face, trying to think like him. Brothels, drug dens and dice halls lined the roads. Where to start? He picked one at random, easing through the doors and circulating.

Smoke from bac-sticks and cheap cigars hugged the ceiling. Gamblers and hustlers filled the den, but Cornelius knew this place was out of Trask's league. He'd know he'd get fleeced here before he'd finished his first drink.

Cornelius ruled out twelve more places before he found Mama Pollyana's.

The moment he saw the place he knew he'd hit paydirt. Trask would riff on this place.

An ugly, sprawling stucco pile with neon and holo-streamers cavorting above the roof. Flame-wreathed columns spurted fire either side of the ribbed oval doorway

as revellers drank and howled before the building. A hugely
fat woman paraded before the entrance with a bullhorn,
extolling the virtues of Mama's girls.

Mutant tail, the best there is. Come inside and do the
twist.

Cornelius marched up the worn steps and brushed off the
fat woman's hand, noticing the scarred texture of her mutant
flesh.

Trask was here. He was sure of it.

THE BARMAN WAS a mutant. All the workers in Mama
Pollyana's place were; the bar staff, the bruisers, the whores,
the singers and the gunmen loitering in the shadows. He
tagged four mutants with guns. None looked threatening.
Two of them guarded the stairs that led upwards to the private booths. If Trask was here, that's where he'd be.

Cornelius ordered a glass of amasec, sipping the drink
slowly and panning across the room. Three girls gyrated to a
pounding soundtrack on a stage at the far end of the wide
hall, thrusting their altered bodies towards the baying
crowd. Unlike the vast majority of mutants, most of these
girls had escaped the worst horrors of their condition; the
atrophied limbs, the scaled skin or distended, molten faces.

One girl's bikini top had been extensively modified to
accommodate her altered physique while a whipping, pre-
hensile tail swished behind the second. Barely a metre tall,
she nevertheless had her fair share of whooping admirers.
Cornelius couldn't see any visible mutations on the last girl
until she leapt onto a silvered pole and spun around it, her
every joint twisting in unnatural ways. She bent herself backwards, flipping her legs through a loop of her arms and
vaulted over the heads of the other girls. She landed on her
hands, spinning onto her feet to rapturous applause.

Cornelius grinned, imagining how versatile she could be
in her chosen profession. Working girls circulated the bar
and Cornelius caught the eye of a young woman wearing a
scarlet rubber bodyglove, strategically holed to best display
her wares. Her skin was patterned with red blotches and
dozens of multi-coloured electoos writhed beneath her

flesh, rotating and swirling with the discolouration of her skin to form a kaleidoscope of colours and images. The birth of a star, a swelling sunrise and a bleeding heart.

She smiled, coquettishly angling her head to one side and sashaying towards him, unlacing her upper bodice. She leaned on the bar next to him and lifted his amasec, draining it in a single swallow.

'You want to buy me another?' she asked, leaning forward and giving Cornelius a glimpse of her multi-coloured flesh.

Cornelius shook his head. 'No. I want to go upstairs.'

She grinned. 'You don't mess about, do you?'

'Not if I can help it, no,' said Cornelius, sliding a roll of bills across to her.

'Alright then, honey,' purred the girl, slipping the cash into her cleavage and playing with his collar. 'I can be real nice to you, or I can be sure to punish you if you've been bad. If you know what I mean.'

Cornelius nodded and allowed himself to be led towards the stairs. He played meek as the armed mutants checked him out. The girl walked ahead of him, the rubber of her outfit gleaming as it stretched tight across her backside.

The landing at the top of the stairs curled around the hall below, the wood-panelled walls studded with mirrored doors. Opaque from inside, transparent from the outside, the views were designed to titillate.

Electro-candles flickered, held aloft in bobbing suspensor fields. Business must be booming.

The girl turned left, beckoning him with a curling finger. Instead, Cornelius turned right, checking out the rooms on the opposite side of the landing. He heard the girl call after him, but ignored her, pressing his face to the glass of each door in turn.

There. Cornelius smiled humourlessly as he saw Trask's skinny legs poking from under a bedsheet and his lank hair flopping over a girl with a bright orange mane.

He pushed open the door and drew his laspistol. Trask leapt from the bed, his face going from indignant rage to sheer terror in the space of a second.

'Con! You're alive!'

'No thanks to you, you bastard,' replied Cornelius, back-handing his pistol across Trask's jaw. Trask dropped, blood sprayed the wall and teeth flew. Trask's girl screamed.

Behind him, he heard the girl who'd led him upstairs shout for the armed mutants at the bottom of the stairs. He picked up Trask, his jaw drooling blood to the carpet.

'Where's my money?' demanded Cornelius.

Trask shook his head and Cornelius hit him again, hard. Once in the face, once in the gut. Trask folded, but Cornelius held him up.

'I'm going to ask you once more, Trask. And then I'll put my fist through your face.'

Before Trask could answer, Cornelius heard the mutant gunmen outside. He released Trask and dropped to his knees, swinging round and emptying his clip through the mirrored door. He heard screams and the sound of falling bodies.

Trask grabbed for a pistol beside the bed, but Cornelius was ready for him and batted it from his hands, sending it crashing through the window. As the window shattered, he saw upturned faces and a group of armed men making their way through the crowds of people towards the brothel. He recognised Constantine at the centre of the group and cursed as he realised he'd been set up.

They knew he'd go after Trask and just waited for him to put his head in the noose.

He locked eyes with Constantine, hearing him bark orders and seeing his men raise their weapons. He dropped to the floor as bullets and las-bolts blasted through the window and popped chunks of brickwork from the wall.

Trask's torso disintegrated under the fusillade, his body torn to pieces. He flopped onto the bed, the mutant whore's screams reaching new heights.

Cornelius kept his head down as bullets peppered the outside wall, rising to his knees and firing both his guns into Constantine's men. Most of his shots went wide, but four went down. Screams filled the street.

Constantine's men scattered, running for the entrance to Mama Pollyana's. Cornelius emptied the stubber, ducking back to reload.

Things were now officially messed up.

THE WAIL OF sirens told Cornelius that the SSA were now on their way. He risked a glance out the shattered window, seeing three black Rhinos lumber down the street and grind to a halt just in front of the brothel.

Constantine was nowhere to be seen. Was he already inside or had he made good his getaway when he'd heard the sirens? It didn't matter at the moment, Cornelius had to avoid capture first. If the SSA got hold of him, it wouldn't take them long to link him to the stolen guns and the mutant resistance's ambushes.

He leaned over, wincing as fresh blood leaked from the wound in his side and shook his head at Trask's foolishness as he pulled out the sack Lathesia had given them from under the bed. There was bound to be some cash missing, but there was still a satisfying weight to it.

Quickly, he slung the bag and holstered his pistols. He discarded the shotgun he'd fired through the ceiling – the SSA would shoot a man with a shotgun on sight – and slipped from the room.

He stepped over the two mutants he'd shot through the door and into a scene of utter bedlam. At least two dozen SSA agents were trashing the joint; clubbing aside mutants and purebloods as they dragged anyone they could lay their hands on outside. Their shock mauls rose and fell in time to the thumping music. Flashing strobes rendered everything surreal.

The brothel's patrons screamed, desperate to escape.

He saw a lone SSA agent behind the bar. The agent clubbed the barman, splitting his skull open and pounding his brains out. Cornelius vaulted the balcony, landing feet-first on the SSA agent's neck and breaking his back. He rolled, keeping out of sight behind the bar, gritting his teeth in pain. Holding his injured side, he dragged the dead agent towards him.

He shucked off his greatcoat and swiftly began stripping the agent's armour and uniform. A thrown tankard shattered mirrored glass and liquor bottles above him.

Cornelius worked fast, pulling on the agent's grey trousers and jacket. Swiftly he buckled on the heavy breastplate and took the agent's helmet, slipping it on and sliding down the visor. Grabbing the agent's shock maul, he rose to his feet and slammed it down hard on the dead barman, shouting, 'Filthy mutant scum!'

Still gripping the burlap sack, he made his way round the bar and waded into the mass of bodies, clubbing his way towards the main doors.

The SSA agents ignored him, but a young man wearing expensive clothes tried to barge past him. He slammed his fist into his face twice, breaking the man's nose and rendering him insensible. Cornelius dragged him through the door and down the steps of the brothel to the waiting Rhinos.

Flashing lights on the troop transports cast a flickering glow across the brothel. Jeering crowds filled the street behind the black troop vehicles. SSA agents manned pintel-mounted guns as a line of troops bundled the brothel's patrons into the holding cells in the back of the vehicles.

Cornelius walked confidently towards the furthest Rhino, hauling the staggering young man towards the SSA agent standing there. He glanced round. All attention was focussed on Mama Pollyana's.

'One for the cells,' said Cornelius. He pushed his victim into the SSA agent, who grabbed the falling man. Cornelius stepped close and hammered his upturned palm into the agent's windpipe. The man dropped, gagging for breath, and Cornelius pushed both men into the back of the transport.

He ditched the stolen helmet and unclipped the breast-plate. He kept the shock maul and jogged away from the transports, quickly joining the concealing ranks of the crowd. He gripped the money sack tight, his other held tight over the synth-flesh bandage as he pushed his way through.

Even as he made his way from Mama Pollyana's, he grinned wolfishly as he saw Ivan Constantine lurking at the back of the crowd in the shadowed doorway of a derelict

building. Two of his thugs stood either side of him, the
bulge of firearms clearly visible.

Taking an oblique route, he circled towards them, his
thumb hovering above the activation rune of the shock
maul. A small circle of space surrounded the arms dealer, his
bodyguards allowing no one to come too close to their boss.
Cornelius knew stealth was out of the question and pressed
the activation rune of the shock maul, marching straight
towards the group.

The nearest bodyguard saw him coming and moved to
intercept.

Cornelius slammed the maul across his face, breaking his
jaw. The second drew a bead on him with his gun. Cornelius
didn't give him a chance to fire, driving the crackling
weapon into his groin and dropping him to the ground. The
stench of scorched flesh hit his nostrils.

Constantine drew a silver laspistol. Cornelius smashed
the maul across his hand, breaking fingers, then drove it
hard into the arms dealer's gut. Constantine dropped to his
knees.

Cornelius kicked open the sagging door behind Constantine and, gripping him by the hair, dragged him inside.
Cornelius pulled the wheezing Constantine to the furthest
corner of the burnt-out building.

He pulled his stubber, emptied out half the shells and
spun the barrel. He showed Constantine, then jammed it
under his jaw.

'You know who I am?' asked Cornelius.

'You're a dead man,' sneered Constantine.

'Wrong answer,' said Cornelius and pulled the trigger.

The hammer slammed down on an empty chamber. Constantine yelped.

'Now I'll assume that was just a necessary show of
bravado,' continued Cornelius, 'and that you're ready to listen to me now.'

Constantine bit his lip and Cornelius smiled, placing the
cash Lathesia had paid him beside him.

'I could kill you now, Ivan, but I'm not going to. I've killed
a bunch of your men, but I'm not going to kill you.'

Seeing Constantine's puzzled expression, Cornelius said, 'Here's the deal. You're buying your life with this money. I don't kill you, walk away with whatever Trask's left me of it and we call this whole sorry mess even. Live and let live, agreed?'

Constantine said nothing, his eyes blazing hatred.

Cornelius pulled the trigger again.

The hammer clicked down on another empty chamber.

'Alright, alright!' snapped Constantine, but his eyes told another story.

Cornelius nodded and rose to his feet. 'Smart decision, Ivan. I figure there's got to be enough money to be made on this Emperor-forsaken planet to keep us both happy. And I just know you're smart enough to know that we can be useful to each other.'

'Very well,' hissed Constantine. 'I won't have you killed for this, but pull a stunt like this again and you're a dead man, Cornelius Barden.'

Cornelius shrugged. 'I can live with that. It's all just part of the game, Ivan,' he said.

He turned and disappeared into the flickering glow of Cephalon's night.

THE EMPEROR'S WILL

David Charters

A LONG LINE of ships stretched away into the dark reaches of the outer system. More than sixty vessels in all, among them survey ships and recovery vessels, giant transports and tiny scouts, as well as fearsome vessels of war. Their crusade had lasted fifteen years of their time, as they had entered and re-entered the warp. But on Taran III, the homeworld of their Chapter, their battle-brothers had aged nearly a hundred. The men aboard the ships were tired and the ships themselves seemed wearier still. Most had suffered damage and the warships bore the scars of many battles down their armoured sides.

Yet for all their weariness, they were still proud, and joyful at the prospect of homecoming. Aboard the giant transports were the prizes they had sought for the Emperor who commanded them – ancient artefacts from lost civilisations, treasures from a dozen strange worlds, specimens and recordings and survey results to last a thousand scholars' lifetimes.

They carried people, too – the Emperor's loyal subjects, representatives of the survivors from systems isolated in the great warp storms. Their peoples had long since given up hope that the Imperium would reach out to find its lost children – until the day the great ships of the Storm Warriors' fleet had appeared in the skies over their home-worlds.

And lastly they brought with them memories, of lost comrades, of acts of heroism, of the *Battleaxe* and the *Lionheart* and their courageous crews who would never return home, memories that would be recorded in the annals of the Chapter upon their return.

But now they had been diverted. Their homecoming was to be delayed as urgent messages summoned them to undertake one final task for their Emperor before He released them for rest and meditation beneath the silver skies of Taran III.

FROM THE VIEWING port of the *Sirius*, Tesra IV loomed large and forbidding. It was a giant by any standards. Much of its atmosphere was heavily polluted with thick, dark clouds obscuring the surface. Only at its northern pole, where the bitter cold had kept human settlement at bay, was there a clear view of what had once been a stark but beautiful ice planet.

Chapter Master Calan turned from the viewing port to face the assembled officers in the wardroom.

'I understand that some among you are impatient for the assault to begin?'

It was framed as a question, but Calan's stern glare at the Marine officers made it clear that no answer was expected. He turned back to the viewing port. He could just make out the shape of the nearest vessels to the mighty battle-barge.

'Our forces are still assembling. By tonight the *Valiant* and her escorts will have joined us. Tomorrow, battle-brothers from the Black Templars will be here, and I expect a mixed force of cruisers and destroyers to arrive from Elara Prime...' He paused, his voice betraying what might have been uncertainty. 'And there may be other reinforcements as well.'

'Sir?' It was Captain Kortar, commander of the First Company, an officer whose courage verged on recklessness or even insubordination, and who typically failed to maintain the respectful silence of his brother officers in the presence of the chapter master.

Calan's voice was firmer now as he spoke.

'Kortar, when the position is clearer, you will be informed. First I need to reflect further on our situation myself. We are assembling an overwhelming force around Tesra IV, and there can be no doubt as to our ultimate victory, nor to the fate of the rebels who have chosen to take the path of treachery. But first we must be certain that we best serve the Emperor's interests. I do not yet have that certainty. I shall retire to my quarters to meditate. Attend to your duties, gentlemen!'

Calan turned and strode from the room, his scarlet cloak sweeping behind him. The sergeant standing at the wardroom door shouted, 'Attention on deck!' and the officers leapt to their feet as their chapter master left them. The sergeant followed Calan from the room and the officers relaxed. Several of them left to return to duties elsewhere aboard the *Sirius*, but most remained, confounded and intrigued by their leader's uncharacteristic caution in the face of the rebels on Tesra IV.

Kortar was first to speak. 'Why are we waiting? Why sit here in easy detection range of the enemy, doing nothing? We have five hundred Marines aboard the *Sirius*, a hundred more aboard *Ilyan* and *Tigris*, and enough firepower to tear a hole in their defences.'

'Perhaps, now we are so close to home, he is minded to lose as few of our brothers as possible.' The officer speaking was a young lieutenant named Marek, a promising warrior building a reputation for fighting carefully planned actions with few casualties, unlike Kortar, whose victories – impressive though they were – had often been won at great cost to the Chapter. 'Intelligence suggests that the conspirators are few in number, but that the governor is among them and has persuaded the garrison that we are the enemy and that we are serving the Dark Forces. If they carry that off, then we may end up destroying loyal servants of the Emperor while the rebel scum look on and laugh.'

'What of it?' replied Kortar angrily. 'The invasion is inevitable. We are merely wasting time here.'

'You may both be right,' came a calmer, more thoughtful voice. Chaplain Dusal was standing by the viewing port. 'If we must fight, then let us do so when we have truly over-whelming force. We were nine hundred strong when we left Taran III. Three hundred of our battle-brothers will never see those silver skies again. Perhaps that's enough. Perhaps the Emperor honoured us with this task precisely because we have suffered and we are tired and we will not rush thought-lessly in. The rebels aren't going anywhere. And there's always a chance that they'll surrender themselves to the Emperor's mercy when they see we mean business.'

Several others murmured in agreement and the gathering dispersed, with some officers returning to their quarters and others going to brief their men. Kortar cursed and kicked over a chair as he left to begin his daily ritual of close combat training. At least that should allow him to let off steam.

SEVERAL DECKS BELOW, kneeling in darkness in his quarters, Calan prayed to the Emperor for guidance.

JUST BEFORE MIDNIGHT, warning lights went on in the Opera-tions Room. Klaxons blared and Calan was called to the bridge. The officers on duty might have noticed that he looked tired when he arrived, but they were too discreet to remark upon it.

'Status?' he asked as he seated himself in the captain's chair.

'The *Valiant* has been sighted, sir – approaching on vector four-zero-nine.'

Calan looked at the central viewing screen.

'Maximum magnification!'

At first she seemed like a tiny speck in the distance, then around her six other specks appeared and slowly the mighty battleship and her six escorts began to take shape. The *Valiant* had been scheduled to meet the returning Storm Warriors in the Magellan Sector, to take charge of the trans-ports and other Imperial vessels and escort them to the bases where they would be received and their cargoes and survey records examined. Now both found themselves diverted to Tesra IV.

'*Sirius* to *Valiant*. This is Calan, chapter master of the Emperor's Storm Warriors and commander of the battle-barge *Sirius* and its accompanying task force. Welcome. Assume position in the vanguard of the fleet. *Sirius* out.'

He watched as the enormous battleship slowly passed the *Sirius*, great scars disfiguring her armoured sides. Her escorts followed smoothly behind.

The duty officer moved to the communicator to close the comm-link to the *Valiant*, but as he did so he paused and looked closely at a monitor. 'Sir – we have another contact coming from the same bearing as the *Valiant*. A small craft, could be an Imperial shuttle. Scanning now.'

At last, thought Calan, now I shall have clarity.

'Sir – the shuttle is hailing us. He doesn't appear to have visual, but I'm putting him on loudspeaker.'

Calan sat back in his command chair and waited while the hiss of static faded and he could make out the words coming from the loudspeaker.

'This is Imperial shuttle *Aurora*, hailing Imperial task force. We request permission to dock with your flagship. We have one passenger aboard. Code Indigo.'

Code Indigo, thought Calan, ignoring the startled faces on the bridge, an inquisitor. Now things truly will become clearer. He looked towards the duty officer. 'Signal them to come aboard. I will receive our visitor in my quarters.' He stood and had turned to leave the bridge when behind him a voice shouted, 'They've fired something! The shuttle's fired something!' A klaxon sounded and warning lights started flashing.

'Identify that missile!' shouted Calan. 'Who are they firing at?'

The duty officer was leaning over the shoulder of a young crewman at another monitor. 'Sir – it's not a missile at all. It appears to be a drop pod. We detect one life form aboard. It's heading for the planet's surface, moving very fast.' He turned and looked at Calan. 'Sir – they've got fighters down there, and a lot of firepower. Whoever he is, I don't give much for his chances.'

Neither do I, thought Calan, whoever he is, he must be very brave or very stupid.

'Sir – *Ilyan*'s hailing us. Captain Sovak requests permission to talk to you.'

'Put him on.'

This time there was visual, and Calan looked into the steely blue eyes of the officer commanding the strike cruiser, a man who might one day succeed him as chapter master.

'Sir – you will have seen that the shuttle has launched a drop pod towards Tesra IV. I don't know if he's friend or foe – he could be trying to reach the rebels to assist them, or he may be on the Emperor's business. Do you want me to blow him out of the sky, or clear a path for him through the enemy defences?'

Once again Calan understood why he felt such confidence for the future of the Chapter. With such men – clear thinking, bold, decisive – the Emperor's foes had good reason to fear. Calan closed his eyes for a second to think. *Help him, serve the Emperor and let the Emperor's will be done.* Calan started. It was as if someone was talking inside his head. 'Help him! Clear his path! Ensure that he reaches the planet at all costs. Other vessels stand aside. *Ilyan* and *Tigris*, you have weapons free – fire at will. May the Emperor's will be done!'

HUNDREDS OF KILOMETRES below the task force, swarms of fighters were emerging on the edge of the atmosphere, racing to intercept the drop pod. As they approached the tiny pod it seemed to accelerate and started to dodge and weave. The fighters closed in, mirroring its movements and firing lance-like bursts of laser cannon at it. The fate of the tiny craft looked inevitable, until suddenly an enormous laser bolt from the *Ilyan* ripped through the fighter formation, incinerating many of them, and the strike cruiser and her sister vessel surged forward into their midst. Several of the fighters were too slow to dodge the oncoming cruisers and were smashed in fiery explosions by the accurate fire as the ships raced towards the outer atmosphere of the planet, covering the descent of the tiny drop pod.

On the bridge of the *Sirius*, Calan shook his head in wonder as his cruiser captains threw their ships around space like fighter jets. 'They're following the pod right down into the atmosphere!' shouted one of the crewmen on the bridge.

They watched in awe as the cruisers descended behind the tiny drop pod. Every weapon on the cruisers seemed to be firing, blasting at the rebel fighters like giants troubled by gnats. As they entered the atmosphere their hulls glowed and seemed to be ablaze, and the fighters peeled off as their heat shields threatened to overload. The pod itself only accelerated further, glowing like a shooting star and then turning off rapidly towards the frozen north and disappearing to land somewhere in the arctic wastes. *Ilyan* and *Tigris* turned off in the opposite direction, racing through the skies of the polluted planet, leaving multiple sonic booms and hurricane-like tail winds in their wake.

'Unsubtle, I think you'll agree, but effective. If the rebels were in any doubt about our presence here before, they're certainly under no illusions now.'

Calan span at the unfamiliar voice.

'Forgive me, chapter master. My shuttle docked while you were otherwise distracted. I am Inquisitor Andrijssen. I am here by order of the Inquisition to assist and advise you in this grave matter. With your permission, I would welcome the opportunity to talk further with you about the situation on Tesra IV.'

Calan looked at the tall, stooped figure swathed in a dark cloak, his face and head concealed by a hood. 'Of course, my lord inquisitor. It is an honour to welcome you aboard the *Sirius*. Shall we retire to my quarters?'

THE FLEET HAD been in orbit around Tesra IV for eleven days. A company of Black Templars arrived on the second day and further reinforcements continued to assemble. The captain commanding the Templars made clear his frustration at the delay. His men were renowned for their close combat skills and their great physical strength, even by the standards of the Adeptus Astartes, and they wanted to fight. By contrast he found the Storm Warriors' chapter master a strange character, his destiny lying in the far reaches of deep space far from the planet he called home, braving the warp with its dangers and its unpredictability on his Chapter's great crusades. Their commander seemed to have a different perspective on the timing of human affairs, returning home after a century-long crusade, but the Templar longed for the simple, straightforward virtue of a short, sharp fight. The motto of the Black Templars was *No pity! No remorse! No fear!*, and he yearned to swing the thunder-hammer of his forces and bring forth righteous redemption upon the traitors down below.

Aboard the *Sirius* even the normally calm Chaplain Dusal was heard to mutter about time wasting. Kortar was beside himself. He had put three of the Chapter's close combat instructors in the sick bay as he worked out his frustrations in the training chamber. From the *Valiant* came courteous but increasingly impatient enquiries as to Calan's intentions. Lord Admiral Dacius, commanding the *Valiant*, was technically in command of the fleet in space, but was required to defer to Calan in respect of the planetary assault. His own officers had even suggested that the *Valiant* launch its own assault, bombarding the planet and then landing invasion parties selected from their own highly-trained boarding crews. Dacius had quashed the idea, standing firm against the unrest amongst his officers but still he could not hide his own frustration.

Finally on the tenth day the captains of *Ilyan* and *Tigris* had defied convention and joined with several of the escort commanders and the Black Templars' captain in coming aboard for 'consultations' with Calan. Calan listened to their requests for clarification and then sent them away, retiring to his quarters to meditate and pray with the mysterious Inquisitor.

FAR BELOW ON the planet's surface, the winds howled around the Winter Palace of His Most Glorious Excellency Ignatius the Third, governor of Tesra IV by Imperial command. The Winter Palace was Ignatius's favourite retreat, a haven of tranquillity on an over-developed industrial planet, much of which had slowly turned into a single giant city. He had once heard it called a hive-world, and that was increasingly what it was, with its forty billion inhabitants, its vast underground factories and dormitories, and the mining operations that penetrated almost to the planet's core.

It was a world of enormous wealth, yet it was also a desolate place whose atmosphere had been poisoned by industrial pollution. Only in the arctic north could a man walk freely on the planet's surface and breathe the air without the help of apparatus. Few people ventured there, however, because of the ferocious arctic climate with its bitter winds, icy temperatures and sudden storms. It was about as brutal a place as a man could imagine, thought Ignatius as he walked from his well-heated private chambers towards the gate that led outside to the spectacular ice gardens with their centuries-old frozen sculptures. Whenever he stayed at the Winter Palace he spent fifteen or twenty minutes at the start of each day in the ice gardens. He enjoyed the sense of privacy and seclusion in them and liked to look up at the mighty Mount Okram, the tallest mountain on the planet, in whose shadow the Winter Palace had been built a thousand years before.

Mount Okram occupied a special place in the consciousness of all native-born Tesrans. In primitive times young men had attempted to climb it for the honour of their peoples and as a test of manhood. The lucky ones turned back while they could. There was no known account of an unaided climber reaching the summit and returning alive. In more recent times attempts had been made to land on the summit from the air, but even large craft could not manoeuvre safely in the storms that constantly swept the summit. Teleport tests had been tried with volunteers, but the metallic ores at the heart of the mountain upset the delicate positioning apparatus with catastrophic – and fatal – consequences. The result of all this was that Mount Okram remained unconquered, nature's last bastion in a world devastated by mankind. Ignatius found it fitting that the mountain should provide the backdrop to the palace. He was surrounded on three sides by the walls and fortifications of the palace grounds with their heavy weapons emplacements and reinforced bunkers, while to his rear an impregnable force of nature protected him.

Today Ignatius had a concern of a different type. He had received a message from the Imperial task force circling the planet. He was to receive a visit from the chapter master of the Storm Warriors, no less, to 'conduct enquiries on behalf of the Emperor'. He was surprised that the Imperial forces were taking such a delicate approach. By this time he would have expected them to have charged in with a full-scale planetary assault, which would have suited him perfectly. Then they would have discovered – to their cost – that the armouries of Tesra IV that had equipped the Imperial Navy so magnificently over the centuries could also produce land-based weapons. Ignatius had personally overseen the secret installation of concealed batteries of nova cannons, missile silos and other defences. When the Imperium attacked they would be blasted to atoms.

With the Emperor's forces destroyed, he, Ignatius the Third, would control not just Tesra IV, but the entire sector. It was risky, of course, but he had friends that even his closest accomplices knew nothing about. His periods of unexplained absence over the past three years had in fact been well spent securing new allies, allies who understood and appreciated him, who would support him and his rule, powerful, ruthless allies who would make the Imperium think twice before attempting to re-take this sector.

As he thought of his powerful friends, he reached inside his robe and gently rubbed the dark, ornate medallion that hung around his neck. Even to wear such an object was punishable by death, but it amused Ignatius to feel it around his neck at meetings of the planetary council. Soon there would be no planetary council – he looked forward to personally ending the lives of some of its more troublesome members in the most barbaric fashion. But first he needed a victory, a decisive victory over the Imperial fleet circling overhead to show them all that they could not resist his power.

He had been tempted to fire the nova cannons almost two weeks ago when a bizarre incident had occurred. A drop pod was launched from the Imperial fleet, his fighters moved to intercept it, and two strike cruisers intervened, chasing away his fighters and risking their own destruction by entering the planet's atmosphere. His advisors still had not determined if they were pursuing or protecting the drop pod, since the pod had veered off and crashed on the other side of Mount Okram. His forces had found it burnt beyond recognition in the arctic wastes. Whatever its secrets might have been, they had gone to the grave with its unknown pilot.

Ignatius opened the door to the ice garden. A bitter gust of wind blew in a flurry of snow. He shivered. It was an unusually cold day. Or perhaps he was uncharacteristically nervous. Today he would meet a chapter master for the first time. It should be entertaining, he thought to himself, looking up at the mountain towering above him. I've never killed a Marine before.

High up on the mountainside, overlooking the Winter Palace far below, part of the rock face appeared to move and take on human form. Slowly a figure became apparent, gliding smoothly across the rocks in a snake-like movement, and barely visible beneath a camouflage cloak. The icy wind howled across the slope, blowing flurries of snow and ice before it. The slowly moving figure was the only living thing in sight. Everywhere was desolation and bitter, icy cold. The figure stopped at a gentle rise in the slope and moved into position behind it. It had been a long trek from the carefully incinerated drop pod, and an even tougher ascent. Now he would have to wait, possibly for many days, and it would be brutally uncomfortable. But the waiting figure was capable of great patience and had endurance beyond the capacity of normal men. If he had to wait, then wait he would, for he was in the service of the Emperor and he would do his duty.

'ARE YOU SURE you want to do this alone?' Chaplain Dusal looked at Calan as he walked slowly across the main deck of the *Sirius's* dock towards his shuttle, struggling to contain his objections.

Calan paused. 'You know that there is no other way. It is the Emperor's will.'

'It's also very foolhardy. He may kill you out of hand.'

'No. An older, wiser servant of the Emperor than I once said, "Know your enemy". Ignatius is a vain, conceited man. He will want to toy with his prey.'

Dusal nodded towards the inquisitor who had followed them to the dock, but now stood apart from them, shrouded in his dark cloak, his face hidden beneath his hood.

'You're taking a lot on trust. I'd feel happier if you'd at least allow us to teleport some Terminators in behind you. Kortar would kill to lead them.'

Calan laughed. 'I believe he would. But my decision is made.'

Dusal smiled and shrugged. 'I've served you long enough to know that no purpose is served by arguing with you. Very well – good luck!' Calan held out his hand. The chaplain clasped it firmly, wondering if it was the last time.

Calan turned and entered the shuttle, the hydraulics whined as the hatch shut behind him and then the engines roared powerfully as they ignited. Dusal stepped back. 'May the faith of the Emperor and his strong right arm guard you and guide you.' He turned and headed back to the bridge.

THE ROARING SOUND of powerful thrusters interrupted the moaning of the wind around the Winter Palace. Ignatius looked up from his desk and stared out through the thick armoured glass window at the landing pad. An Imperial shuttle was landing in the grounds, painted in the distinctive scarlet and gold livery of the Storm Warriors.

A strange Chapter, thought Ignatius, and one for which my friends have a particular loathing. They will be pleased with me for this. He turned to his aide standing beside the head of his personal bodyguard, an ogryn accustomed to killing on command for his master. 'Our guest has arrived. I trust that all the arrangements are in place to take care of him?' It was the third time that morning that he had asked the question. Both men knew that Ignatius's attempt at grim humour concealed his fraying nerves.

'Yes, master, we are ready to take care of him as soon as you give the signal.'

'Good, then we had better meet him. Is he alone?'

'Just the pilot, master. He won't be a problem.'

'Very well, let us receive him in the ice garden.'

THE TALL, POWERFUL figure of the chapter master walked slowly amongst the giant ice sculptures, his scarlet cloak flapping around his ancient ceremonial armour. Unusually for someone of his calling, he appeared to be unarmed, save for an ornate ceremonial dagger at his waist. He paused from time to time to gaze appreciatively at some particularly fine work.

'Greetings, my honoured guest!' cried Ignatius as he approached, followed by his retinue of servants and bodyguards.

'Greetings, governor. It seems you are a fortunate man, blessed with many fine things.'

Ignatius bowed, 'It is the Emperor's will. All good things flow from Him. To what do we owe the unexpected honour of your visit?'

'To the Emperor's work. Reports have reached us, troubling reports my lord, of treachery planned but not yet executed, of petty gods secretly worshipped by those who feign loyalty to the Imperium. That is what brings me to Tesra IV!'

'By my honour, I swear that I will do my utmost to rid this planet of any who plan treachery against the Emperor!' Ignatius was red in the face, sweating slightly despite the cold. But he took comfort from his surroundings, from the visible trappings of power around him, his bodyguards, the palace's defences, and the towering presence of Mount Okram in the background.

To Ignatius, Calan seemed typical of the brutish force that constituted the Adeptus Astartes. He had cropped grey hair and a granite face with piercing grey eyes. One half of his face was hideously scarred. His very calmness exuded menace and Ignatius's servants stepped back while his guards nervously fingered their weapons.

'Oh, but you will, governor, you most certainly will do your utmost. I have here a list of those who are guilty of these crimes – a list that includes many of your closest friends and associates, your own family, and of course at the head of the list yourself, Ignatius the Third, governor by Imperial command.' Calan held out a small scroll that bore the seal of the Inquisition. 'You will order the arrest of all those on the list, and ensure that they receive the full force and benefit of the Emperor's justice. You will do this immediately. And then, my lord governor, you will continue to rule Tesra IV in the Emperor's name – except that this time you'll mean it. In future you will truly be the most diligent and loyal of the Emperor's servants.'

Ignatius gasped as he took the list and stepped back out of reach to break the seal and scrutinise it. To his astonishment, he saw dozens of names listed, along with the posts held by the plotters. Most astonishingly of all, Ignatius's own name was at the top. This was extraordinary – his entire plot had become known. For a moment he almost panicked. And then he focused once more on the solitary figure before him. This arrogant brute stood before him now, alone and unsupported, challenging him without benefit of weapons or allies.

Ignatius stepped forward. 'How dare you challenge me?' he roared. 'In your arrogance you have come to my world, to my palace, where I rule! You will never leave here alive. Beg me now for mercy and I may grant you a quick death.'

Calan stepped forward and stood close to Ignatius so that their breath mingled in the cold air. He looked mournfully into the governor's eyes, the edge of hardness tempered by what seemed to be a profound sorrow and weariness.

'You disappoint me, governor, but you do not surprise me.' He turned and stared towards the summit of Mount Okram, looking for something that could not be seen with the naked eye.

MANY THOUSANDS OF metres above the men in the ice garden, the assassin crouched unmoving, oblivious to the cold, staring through the sniper-scope at the scene below, awaiting the signal from the chapter master. When it came he spoke aloud for the first time, though only the wind and the snow could hear, 'Divine Emperor, Protector and Benefactor of mankind, guide this thy weapon on its path of righteousness!' When he squeezed the trigger there was an almost inaudible *phuuut* and then he relaxed, no longer conscious of the scene below him, and started thinking about the long climb back down the mountain.

It had been a challenge, but it was not the greatest that he had faced in the Emperor's service, nor would it be the last. Like all members of the Officio Assassinorum he knew that one day he would face a situation for which his skill would be insufficient, where the odds were too great and his luck would finally run out.

But not today, he thought as he started to disassemble the rifle.

IGNATIUS FELT SOMETHING sting his neck, and touched it gingerly as if expecting an insect bite – except that there were no insects at the Winter Palace. His hand came away with a smear of blood on it. He looked up at the mountainside, visibly shocked, his hands and knees starting to tremble.

'What… what have you done to me?'

'The Emperor's will, governor. The Emperor's servants are everywhere. There can be no escape, no hiding from his divine retribution. Your days of treachery are over. Running in your veins is a poison. It was made according to a formula so ancient that its origins are no longer recorded. It is untraceable and incurable. It will kill you, slowly and painfully, in less than twenty-four hours…'

Ignatius gasped and staggered as if about to faint.

'Unless you take this.' Calan held out a small glass phial containing a clear liquid. 'This is not a cure, it merely delays, by twenty-four hours, what would otherwise be an agonising death. You will not be able to replicate it. Its secrets are known only to the Officio Assassinorum. But as a loyal servant of the Emperor you will be sent regular supplies. Because you are His loyal servant, aren't you, Ignatius?'

Calan's eyes were suddenly empty, devoid of feeling or compassion. Ignatius felt as if he was staring at Death itself. 'Treachery!' he screamed. At this, with a screaming whine of overloaded hydraulics and the thumping and crashing of heavy metal feet, a dozen Sentinels rose from behind the furthest line of sculptures and smashed through the ancient artwork to form a circle around the chapter master. Ignatius's retinue scattered, save for his bodyguards, who dropped to their knees with sidearms in the firing position.

Calan looked around calmly, taking in the weapons trained on him from the Sentinels and the nervous, frightened eyes of the rebels manning them. 'It is time, governor, for you to make a decision.' His voice was icy calm, at the same time menacing and yet offering the prospect of reassurance, of salvation. 'It will not be the most difficult decision that you take in the coming weeks, but it is the most important.'

Ignatius could already feel that something was happening inside him. He was starting to sweat profusely, his hands were shaking and he found it hard to gather his thoughts. His mouth was dry and he started to sway. Deep inside he felt only darkness, anguish and utter despair. He looked around at the guards manning the Sentinels. They were waiting for the order to fire. His bodyguards were waiting too, their weapons trained on the unprotected head of the chapter master. He thought of his allies in their hidden chambers deep beneath the planet's surface, waiting for his signal to strike. And he realised that all of it was useless. He was doomed and he had no choice. Tears filled his eyes and he choked back a sob.

'Of course, my lord,' he wailed. 'The Emperor's loyal servant will do his bidding at all times!' His legs shook and tears ran down his face as he fell to his knees.

'Come, come, Ignatius, let us not forget our dignity,' soothed Calan. 'You are governor by Imperial command. You should not show such emotion in public. There is much work to be done – there are arrests to be ordered, there is treachery to be punished, terminations and interrogations to be carried out. Shall we start with one or two members of your own family, perhaps as a way of demonstrating the strength of your devotion to the Emperor?'

'Yes, my lord,' wailed the broken, defeated man. 'By the Emperor's command, His will shall be done!'

ON THE BRIDGE of the *Sirius*, the duty officer called down to Calan's quarters. 'Sir, something extraordinary is happening on Tesra IV.'

When he entered the bridge, Calan stared in wonder at the giant viewing screen. At more than a dozen points on the planet's surface, huge explosions were erupting, sending flames tens of thousands of feet into the atmosphere.

'Sensors indicate nova cannons, sir. They must have been concealed on the planet's surface. They started detonating about ten minutes ago. It looks as if they're destroying their own defences.'

'Sir!' A crewman called over to Calan. 'Sir – planetary defence forces are airborne. I'm detecting nearly a thousand short-range orbital launches. Probably fighters but could include some bombers and assault craft. It looks like they're launching everything they've got, and they're heading this way.'

Calan relaxed into the command chair and allowed himself a gentle smile. 'Advise the fleet to go to action stations, but do not fire except at my command.'

'Sir – they're hailing us. The Tesran pilots are hailing us.'

The bridge crew were staring at Calan, as puzzled by his relaxed demeanour now as at any time since the shuttle had returned him safely to the *Sirius* just eight hours ago.

'Put it on the loudspeaker.'

The words as they came through were crackly at first, but the meaning soon became clear.

'…welcome Imperial forces… invite you to land on Tesra IV… escort you safely to landing zones…'

Word quickly spread through the ship. For a moment Calan was puzzled as he tried to identify a strange roaring sound, like the noise of some great machine – and then he realised it was the sound of thousands of cheering voices echoing around the corridors, as Space Marines and crewmen gathered at monitors and viewing ports to watch the spectacle unfolding around them.

The bridge door opened and Kortar came storming in.

'Don't say they're surrendering! The filthy yellow scum! We should request powers of exterminatus to cleanse this filth.'

'No, Kortar.' Calan looked at the angry younger man. 'They are not surrendering. We are their allies and they are welcoming us as allies should. The evil on this planet has already been cleansed, by subtler, more precise methods than you and I are accustomed to. The Emperor's will has been done, and we shall all live to celebrate our homecoming.'

Kortar stared at Calan, for once lost for words, his face looking fit to burst. And then he too laughed out loud and let out a great whoop of joy. The crusade was finally over, and the Emperor's will had indeed been done. From the decks of the *Sirius* thousands of voices broke into song, as Marines and Chapter-serfs, naval crewmen and Imperial officers sang the Chapter's anthem, 'We Praise Thee, Imperator', and the thoughts of the Marines and their chapter-serfs turned again to homecoming and the silver skies of Taran III.

'Sir – we have messages of congratulations coming in from *Ilyan* and *Tigris* and from the Black Templars. And Lord Admiral Dacius wishes to speak to you.'

'Put him on,' ordered Calan, feeling suddenly weary with the exertions of the past few days.

The images of the planet's surface disappeared from the main viewing screen and were replaced by the impeccable admiral, seated in his finest Imperial Navy drill uniform on the bridge of the *Valiant*.

'My Lord Calan, for five hundred years the *Valiant* has fought the foes of the Imperium, and twenty-seven admirals raised their flags aboard her before I was granted that great honour. But I would happily wager that none has seen a finer day than this. I have fought alongside many fine comrades from the Astartes, and together we have conquered and crushed the foes of the Imperium, often at great cost.

But never have I found myself saying that it was a privilege not to fight alongside a brave comrade. Please accept my congratulations, my compliments and my gratitude. With your permission, my lord, the Imperial Navy will take control of the situation on Tesra IV, leaving you free to resume your journey.'

Calan sighed. 'The privilege was mine, lord admiral, and I happily release Tesra IV to your command.'

The image on the screen faded and Calan turned to Kortar. 'Kortar!' he snapped, making the burly captain leap to attention. 'Sir!' he bellowed, standing rigidly at his formidable best.

'Kortar,' said Calan more softly, 'We're going home. Signal farewell and Emperor's speed to the Imperial vessels that accompanied us and order all Chapter vessels to form line astern, *Ilyan* and *Tigris* to bring up the rear.'

'Yes, sir!' shouted Kortar, eagerly rushing to the comm-set. He looked up happily as the signals went out, and was puzzled to see Calan slumped exhausted in his chair. In his mind's eye Kortar was already home beneath the silver skies and was rushing headlong into the warm, golden waters that lapped against the shore of the Great Ocean.

But Calan was elsewhere, somewhere out in the warp, remembering lost comrades, recalling the glorious sacrifice of the *Lionheart* and the *Battleaxe*, and reflecting on the tasks yet to come, as the Chapter healed its wounds and prepared itself once again to journey out into the warp on its next crusade.

But we'll be wiser now, thought Kortar, you've taught us wisdom and patience, and that we must not let our strength blind us to the needs of true victory. Next time we shall be more formidable than ever before. This will be your gift to the Chapter, my Lord Calan. *May the Emperor's will be done!*

FIGHT OR FLIGHT

A Ciaphas Cain story

Sandy Mitchell

*Like any newly-commissioned young commissar I faced my first
assignment with an eagerness mixed with trepidation. I was, after
all, the visible embodiment of the will of the Emperor Himself;
and I could scarce suppress the tiny voice which bade me wonder
if, when tested, I would truly prove worthy of the trust bestowed
upon me. When the test came at last, in the blood and glory of
the battlefield, I had my answer; and my life changed forever.*

— Ciaphas Cain, 'To Serve the Emperor:
A Commissar's Life,' 104. M42

IF THERE'S A single piece of truth among all the pious hum-
bug and retrospective arse-covering that passes for my
autobiography, it's the last four words of that paragraph.
When I look back over the past hundred years of cowardice,
truth-bending, bowel-loosening terror, and sheer dumb luck
that somehow propelled me to the dizzy heights of Hero of
the Imperium, I can truthfully point to that grubby little
skirmish on a forgotten mining world as the incident which
made me what I am.

I'd been a fully-fledged commissar for almost eight weeks when I arrived on Desolatia IV, seven of them spent travelling in the warp, and I could tell right away that my new unit wasn't happy to receive me. There was a single Salamander waiting at the edge of the landing field as I stepped off the shuttle, its sand-scoured desert camo bearing the markings of the Valhallan 12th Field Artillery. But there was no sign of the senior officers that protocol demanded should meet a newly-arrived commissar. Just a single, bored-looking trooper, stripped down to the bare minimum of what might pass for a uniform, making the best of what little shade the parked vehicle offered. He glanced up from his slate of 'artistic engravings' as I appeared, and shambled in my general direction, his boots kicking up little puffs of the baking yellow dust.

'Carry your bag, sir?' He didn't even attempt a salute.

'That's fine,' I said hastily. 'It's not heavy.' His body odour preceded him like a personal force bubble. The briefing slate I'd glanced at before making the joyous discovery that the transport ship was stuffed with crewmen still under the fond illusion that games of chance had something to do with luck had mentioned that the Valhallans were from an ice world, so it was no surprise to me that the baking heat of Desolatia was making him sweat heavily, but I'd hardly expected to be met by a walking bioweapon.

I overrode the gag reflex and adopted an expression of amiable good humour that had got me out of trouble innumerable times during my years at the schola, as well as into it as often as I could contrive.

'Commissar Cain,' I said. 'And you are...?'

'Gunner Jurgen. Colonel sends his apologies, but he's busy.'

'No doubt,' I said. The ground crew were starting to unload the cargo, anonymous crates and pieces of mining machinery larger than I was floated past on lift pallets. The mines were the reason we were here; to ensure the un-interrupted supply of something or other to the forgeworlds of the Imperium despite the presence of an ork raiding party, which had been unpleasantly surprised to find an Imperial Guard troopship in orbit waiting for a minor warpstorm to subside when they arrived. Precisely what we were defending from our rapidly dwindling foes would be somewhere in the briefing slate, I supposed.

The mine habs loomed above us, clinging like lichen to the sides of the mountain their inhabitants had all but hollowed out. To a hive boy such as myself they looked comfortably nostalgic, albeit a little on the cramped side. The total population of the colony was just a few hundred thousand, including elders and kids; just a village really by Imperial standards.

I followed Jurgen back to the Salamander, weaving through the thickening scrum of workers; he walked straight towards it, unimpeded, the miasma from his unwashed socks clearing a path as effectively as a chainsword. As I swung my kitbag aboard I found myself wondering if coming here had been a mistake after all.

THE JOURNEY WAS uneventful; nothing so assertive as a landmark interrupted the monotony of the desert road once the mountains had diminished behind us to a low smudge against the horizon. The only thing even approaching scenery was the occasional burned-out hulk of an ork battlewagon.

'You must be looking forward to getting out of here,' I remarked, enjoying the sensation of the wind through my hair and revelling in the fact that perched up behind the gunner's shield, I was mercifully insulated from Jurgen's odour. He shrugged.

'As the Emperor wills.' He said that a lot. I was beginning to realise that where his intellect should have been was a literally-minded adherence to Imperial doctrine which would have had my old tutors at the schola dancing with glee. If they'd ever deigned to do anything so undignified, of course.

Gradually the outline of the artillery park began to resolve itself through the heat haze. It had been sited in the lee of a low bluff, which rose out of the parching sand like an island in a sea of grit; the Valhallans having adapted their instinctive appreciation of blizzard conditions to the sandstorms prevailing here without too much difficulty. Bulldozed berms extended out from the rockface, extending the defensive perimeter into a rough semi-circle blistered with sandbagged emplacements and subsidiary earthworks.

The first thing I made out with any clarity were the Earth-shakers; even at this distance they were impressive, dwarfing the inflatable habdomes that clustered around the compound like camouflaged mushrooms. As we got closer I made out batteries of Hydras too, carefully emplaced along the perimeter to maximise cover against air attack.

Despite myself, I was favourably impressed; Colonel Mostrue obviously knew his business, and wasn't about to let the lack of a visible enemy lull him into a false sense of security. I began to look forward to meeting him.

'So you're the new commissar?' He glanced up from his desk, looking at me like something he'd found on the sole of his boot. I nodded, picking an expression of polite neutrality. I'd met his sort before, and my preferred option of breezy charm wouldn't cut it with him. Imperial Guard commanders tended to distrust the political officers assigned to them, often with good reason. Most of the time, about all you could hope for was to develop a tolerable working relationship and try not to tread on one another's toes too much. That worked for me; even back then I realised commissars who threw their weight around tended to end up dying heroically for the Emperor, even if the enemy was a suspiciously long way away at the time.

'Ciaphas Cain.' I introduced myself with a formal nod of the head, and tried not to shiver. The air in the habdome was freezing, despite the furnace heat outside, and I found myself unexpectedly grateful for the greatcoat that went with my uniform. I should have anticipated Valhallan tastes would run to air conditioning which left your breath vapourising when you spoke. Mostrue was still in his shirt-sleeves while I was trying my best not to shiver.

'I know who you are, commissar.' His voice was dry. 'What I want to know is what you're doing here?'

'I go where I'm sent, colonel.' Which was true enough, so far as it went. What I didn't mention was that I'd gone to considerable trouble finding an Administratum functionary with a weakness for cards and an inability to spot a stacked deck that almost amounted to a gift from the Emperor; who, after a few pleasant social evenings, had left me in a position to pick practically any unit in the entire Guard to attach myself to.

'We've never had a commissar assigned to us before.'

I tried on an expression of bemused puzzlement.

'Probably because you don't seem to need one. Your unit records are exemplary. I can only assume...' I hesitated just long enough to pique his interest.

'Assume what?'

I feigned ill-concealed embarrassment.

'If I could be frank for a moment, colonel?' He nodded. 'I was hardly the most diligent student at the schola. Too much time on the scrumball pitch, and not enough in the library, to be honest.' He nodded again. I thought it best not to mention the other activities which had consumed most of the time I should have spent studying. 'My final assessment was marginal. I suspect this assignment was intended to... ease me into service without too many challenges.'

Worked like a charm, of course. Mostrue was flattered by the implication that his unit was sufficiently well-run to have attracted the favourable notice of the Commissariat, and, if not exactly pleased to have me aboard, was at least no longer radiating ill-concealed suspicion and resentment. It was also almost true; one of the reasons I'd settled on the 12th Field Artillery was that there didn't seem much for me to do there. The main one, though, was that artillery units fought from behind the lines. A long way behind. No skulking through jungles or city blocks waiting for a laser bolt in the back, no standing on the barricades face to face with a screaming ork horde, just the satisfaction of pulverising the enemy at a safe distance and a quick cup of recaff before doing it all over again. Suited me fine.

'We'll do our best to keep you underemployed.' Mostrue smiled thinly, a faint air of tolerant smugness washing across his features. I smiled too. If you let people feel superior to you, they're childishly easy to manipulate.

'GUNNER ERHLSEN. OUT of uniform on sentry duty.' Toren Divas, Mostrue's subaltern, glared at the latest miscreant, who had the grace to blush and glance at me nervously. Divas was the closest thing to a friend I'd made since I arrived; an amiable man, he'd been only too happy to hand over the chore of maintaining discipline among the troops to a proper commissar now one was available.

'Who isn't in this heat?' I made a show of reading the formal report, and glanced up. 'Nevertheless, despite the obvious extenuating circumstances, we have to retain some standards. Five days' kitchen duty. And put some trousers on.'

Erhlsen saluted, visibly relieved to have escaped the flogging normally prescribed for such an infraction, and marched out between his escorts, showing far too much of his inadequately patched undershorts.

'I must say, Cai, you're not quite what I'd expected.' Erhlsen had been the last defaulter of the day, and Divas began to collect his documentation together. 'When they told us we were getting a commissar...'

'Everyone panicked. The card games broke up, the moonshine stills were dismantled, and the stores tallied with inventory for the first time in living memory.' I laughed, slipping easily into the affable persona I use to put people at their ease. 'We're not all Emperor-bothering killjoys, you know.'

The habdome rocked as the Earthshakers outside lived up to their name. After a month here, I barely noticed.

'You know your job better than I do, of course.' Divas hesitated. 'But don't you think you might be a little... well...'

'Too lenient?' I shrugged. 'Possibly. But everyone's finding the heat hard to cope with. They deserve a bit of slack. It's good for morale.'

The truth was, of course, that despite what you've seen in the holos, charismatic commissars loved and respected by the men they lead are about as common as ork ballerinas;

and being thought of as a soft touch who's infinitely prefer-
able to any possible replacement is almost as good when it
comes to making sure someone's watching your back in a
firefight.

We stepped outside, the heat punching the breath from
my lungs as usual, and were halfway to the officer's mess
before a nagging sense of disquiet at the back of my mind
resolved itself into a sudden realisation: the guns had
stopped firing.

'I thought we were supposed to lay down a barrage for the
rest of the day?' I said.

'We were.' Divas turned, looking at the Earthshakers.
Sweat-streaked gun crews, stripped to the waist, were secur-
ing equipment, evidently more than happy to cease fire.
'Something's–'

'Sir! Commissar!' There was no need to look to identify
the messenger; Jurgen's unique body odour heralded his
arrival as surely as a shellscream presaged an explosion. He
was running towards us from the direction of the battery
offices. 'Colonel wants to see you right away!'

'What's wrong?' I asked.

'Nothing, sir.' He sketched a perfunctory salute, more for
Divas's benefit than mine, a huge grin all but bisecting his
face. 'They're pulling us out!'

'YES, IT'S TRUE.' Mostrue seemed as pleased at the news as
everyone else. He pointed at the hololithic display. 'The 6th
Armoured overran the last pocket of resistance this morning. They should have completed cleansing the entire world
by nightfall.'

I studied it with interest, seeing the full dispersion of our
units for the first time. The bulk of our forces in this hemisphere were well to the east, leaving a small, isolated blip
between them and the mines. Us. The orks had fallen back
further and faster than I'd expected, and I began to realise
just how merited the Valhallans' reputation as elite shock
troopers was. Even fighting in conditions about as hostile to
them as they were ever likely to encounter, they had ground
a stubborn and vicious enemy to paste in a matter of weeks.

'So, where next?' I asked, regretting it instantly. Mostrue turned his pale eyes on me in the same way my old tutor domus used to do at the schola, when he was sure I was guilty of something but couldn't prove it. Which was most of the time, incidentally, but I digress.

'Initially, the landing field.' He turned to Divas. 'We'll need to get the Earthshakers limbered up for transport.'

'I'll see to it.' Divas hurried out.

'After that,' the colonel continued, changing the display, 'we're to join the Keffia task force.' A fleet of starships, over a thousand strong, was curving in towards the Desolatia system. I was impressed. News of the uprising on the remote agriworld was only just beginning to filter back to the Commissariat when I'd been dispatched here; the Navy had evidently been busy in the last three months.

'Seems a bit excessive for a handful of rebels,' one of the officers remarked.

'Let's hope so,' I said, seeing the chance of regaining the initiative. Mostrue looked at me again, in evident surprise; he'd obviously thought he'd put me in my place the first time for having the temerity to interrupt.

'Do you know something we don't, commissar?' He still pronounced my title as though it were a species of fungus, but at least he was pretending to acknowledge it. That was a start.

'Nothing concrete,' I said. 'But I have seen indications...'

'Other than the size of the fleet?' Mostrue's sarcasm got a toadying laugh from some of the officers as he turned away, convinced he'd called my bluff.

'It was only gossip really,' I began, letting him savour his phantom triumph for a moment longer, 'but according to a friend on the Warmaster's staff...'

The sudden silence was truly satisfying. That the 'friend' was a minor clerical functionary with a weakness for handsome young men in uniform, when she wasn't sorting files and making recaff, was a detail I kept to myself. I went on as though I hadn't noticed the sudden collective intake of breath.

'Keffia might have been infested by genestealers,' I finished.

The silence lengthened while they digested the implications. Everyone knew what that meant. A long, bloody campaign to cleanse the world metre by metre. Virus bombing from orbit was the option of last resort on an agriworld, which would cease to be of any value to the Imperium if its ecosystem was destroyed.

In other words, years of rear echelon campaigning in a temperate climate, chucking high explosive death at an enemy without any means to retaliate in kind. I could hardly wait.

'If this is true,' Mostrue said, looking more shaken than I'd ever seen him, 'we've no time to lose.' He began to issue orders to his subordinates.

'I agree,' I said. 'How close is the fleet?'

'A day, maybe two.' The colonel shrugged. 'The astropaths at regimental HQ lost contact with them last night.'

'With the entire fleet?' I was getting an uncomfortable tingling sensation in the palms of my hands. I've felt it a great many times over the years since, and it never meant anything good. No reason why an Imperial Guard officer should find the lack of contact ominous, of course. To them the warp and anything to do with it is simply something best not thought about, but commissars are supposed to know a great deal more than we'd like to about the primal stuff of Chaos. There's very little which can cast a shadow in the warp so powerful that it can cut off communication with an entire battle fleet, and none of them are anything I want to be within a dozen sub-sectors of. 'Colonel, I recommend very strongly that you rescind the orders you've just given.' He looked at me as if I'd gone mad.

'This is no time for humour, commissar.'

'I wish I was joking,' I said. Some of my unease must have been showing on my face, because he actually started listening to me. 'Put the whole battery on full alert. Especially the Hydras. Call regimental headquarters and tell them to do the same. Don't take no for an answer. And get every air defence auspex you can on line.'

'Anything else?' he asked, still visibly unsure whether to take me seriously or not.

'Yes,' I said. 'Pray to the Emperor I'm wrong.'

UNFORTUNATELY, I WASN'T. I was in the command post, talking to the captain of an ore barge which had made orbit that morning, when my worst fears were realised. He was a florid man, running slightly to fat, and visibly uncomfortable communicating with an Imperial official, even one as minor as me.

'We're the only thing in orbit, commissar,' he said, clearly unsure why I'd asked. I flipped through the shipping schedules I'd requisitioned from an equally bemused mine manager.

'You weren't due for another week,' I said. The captain shrugged.

'We were lucky. The warp currents were stronger than usual.'

'Or something very big is disturbing them,' I suggested, then cursed myself for saying it. The captain wasn't stupid.

'Commissar?' he queried, clearly considering most of the possibilities I already had, and probably wondering if there was time to make a run for it.

'There's a large Navy task force inbound to pick us up,' I reassured him, half truthfully.

'I see.' He obviously didn't trust me further than he could throw a cargo shuttle, sensible man. He was about to say something else, when his navigator interrupted.

'We're detecting warp portals. Dozens of them!'

'The fleet?' Divas asked hopefully at my elbow. Mostrue shook his head doubtfully.

'The auspex signatures are all wrong. Not like ships at all...'

'Bioships,' I said. 'No metal in the hulls.'

'Tyranids?' Mostrue's face was grey. Mine was too, probably, although I'd had longer to get used to the idea. Like I said, there wasn't much that could cast a shadow in the warp that big, and with genestealers running rampant a couple of systems away it didn't need Inquisitor Kryptmann to join the dots. I turned my attention back to the freighter captain before he could cut the link.

'Captain,' I said hastily, 'your ship is now requisitioned by the Commissariat. You will not break orbit without explicit instructions. Do you understand?'

He nodded, somberly, and turned to shout orders at his crew.

'What do you want an ore scow for?' Mostrue looked at me narrowly. 'Planning to leave us, commissar?' That was precisely what I had in mind, of course, but I smiled thinly, pretending to take his remark for gallows humour.

'Don't think I'm not tempted,' I said. 'But I'm afraid we're stuck here.'

I called up the tactical display. Outside, the staccato drumbeats of the Hydras opened up, seeking the first mycetic spores to breach the atmosphere. Red dots began to blossom on the hololith, marking the first beachheads. To my relief and as I'd expected, the 'nids had homed in on the largest concentration of visible biomass: the main strength of the regiment. That would buy me a little time.

'Where did they come from?' Divas asked, an edge of panic entering his voice. I found myself slipping into my role of calm authority. All my training was beginning to pay off.

'One of the splinter fleets from Ichar IV.' The segmentum was full of them, fallout from the Ultramarines' heroic victory over Hive Fleet Kraken almost a decade before. Scattered remnants, a tiny fraction of the threat they'd once presented, but still enough to overwhelm a lightly defended world. Like this one. 'Small. Weak. Easy pickings.' I slapped him encouragingly on the back, radiating an easy confidence I didn't feel, and indicated the data coming in from the ore barge's navigational auspex. 'Less than a hundred ships.' Each one of which probably held enough bioconstructs to devour everyone on the planet, but I couldn't afford to think about that just now.

Mostrue was studying the display, nodding thoughtfully.

'That's why you wanted the barge. To see what's going on up there.' Most of the regimental sensor net had been directed downwards, towards the planet's surface. 'Good thinking.'

'Partially,' I said. I indicated the surface readouts. Our air defence assets were doing sterling work, but the sheer number of spores was unstoppable. Red contact icons on the surface were beginning to make the hemisphere look like a case of Uhlren's pox. 'But we'll need it for an evacuation too.'

'Evacuate who?' The suspicious look was back on Mostrue's face again. I pointed to the mining colony.

'I'm sure you haven't forgotten we have a quarter of a million civilians sitting right next to the landing field,' I pointed out mildly. 'The 'nids haven't noticed them yet; thank the Emperor for underground hab zones.' Divas dipped his head at the mention of the Holy Name, pulling himself together with a visible effort. 'But when they do they'll think it's an all you can eat smorgasbord.'

'Will one barge be enough?' Divas asked.

'Have to be,' I said. 'It'll be cramped and uncomfortable for sure, but it beats ending up as Hormagaunt munchies. Can you get things started?'

'Right away.' Now he had something to do, Divas's confidence was returning. I clapped him on the back again as he turned to leave.

'Thanks, Toren. I know I can rely on you.' That should do it. The poor sap would take on a carnifex with a broken chair leg now rather than feel he'd let me down. Which just left Mostrue.

'We'll need to buy time,' I said, once the young subaltern was out of the way. The colonel looked at me, surprised by the change in my demeanour. But I knew my man; plain speaking would work better with him.

'The situation's worse than you were letting on, isn't it?' he asked. I nodded.

'I didn't want to discuss it in front of Divas. He's got enough to cope with at the moment. But yes.' I turned to the tactical display again. 'Even with every shuttle they can lay their hands on, it's going to take at least a day to get everyone aboard.' I indicated the main tyranid advance. 'At the moment the 'nids are here, engaging our main force. When they notice the colony...'

'Or overrun the regiment.' Mostrue could read a hololith as well as I could. I nodded.

'They'll head west. And when they do we'll have to hold them for as long as we can.' Until we're all dead, in other words. I didn't need to spell it out. Mostrue nodded, gravely. Small crystals of ice drifted down from the ceiling as the Earthshakers got back to work, abrading the odds against us by the most miniscule of fractions. To my surprise he held out his hand, grasping mine and shaking it firmly.

'You're a good man, commissar,' he said. Which just goes to show what an appalling judge of character he was.

Now I'D SET everything in motion there was nothing to do but wait. I hung around the command post for a while longer, watching the red dots blossom in the desert to the east of us, and marvelled at the tenacity of our main force. I'd expected them to be annihilated within a matter of hours, but they held their positions doggedly, even gaining ground in a few places. Even so, with the steady rain of mycetic spores delivering an endless tide of reinforcements, they were only delaying the inevitable. Mostrue watched tensely, stepping aside to afford me a better view as he noticed my presence. Under other circumstances I'd have gloated quietly over my sudden popularity, but I was too busy trying to suppress the urge to run for the latrines.

'We've you to thank for this,' he said. 'Without your warning they'd have been all over us.'

'I'm sure you'd have coped,' I said, and turned to Divas. 'How's the evacuation coming?'

'Slowly,' he admitted. I made a show of studying the data, and smiled encouragingly.

'Faster than I'd expected,' I lied. But fast enough. If I was going to join them I couldn't wait too much longer. Divas looked pleased.

'Nothing more I can do here,' I said, turning back to Mostrue. 'This is a job for a real soldier.' I gave him a moment to savour the compliment. 'I'll go and spend some time with the men. Try and boost morale.'

'It's what you're here for,' he said, meaning 'frak off and let me get on with it, then.' So I did.

Night had fallen some hours before, the temperature plummeting to levels the Valhallans were almost comfortable with, and the guardsmen seemed happier, despite the prospect of imminent combat. I wandered from group to group, cracking a few jokes, easing tension, instilling them with a confidence I was far from feeling myself. Despite my personal shortcomings, and I'd be the first to admit that they're many, I'm very good at that side of things. Which is why I was selected for the Commissariat in the first place.

Gradually, without seeming to have any specific destination in mind, I was heading for the vehicle park. I'd almost reached it when I ran out of time.

'They're here!' someone shrieked, opening up with a lasgun. I whirled at the distinctive crack of ionising air, in time to see a trooper I didn't recognise going down beneath a dark, nightmare shape which plummeted from the sky like a bird of prey. I didn't recognise him because his face was gone, eaten away by the fleshborer the thing carried.

'Gargoyles!' I shouted, although the warning could barely be heard above the unearthly shrieking which presaged a bioplasma attack. I leapt aside just quickly enough to avoid a seething bolt of primal matter vomited up by a winged horror swooping in my direction. I felt the heat on my face as it went past, detonating a few yards away and setting fire to a tent. Without thinking I drew my chainsword, thumbed the selector to full speed, and waved it over my head as I ducked. Luck was with me, because I was rewarded by a torrent of stinking filth which poured down the neck of my shirt.

'Look out, commissar!'

I whirled, seeing it swooping back towards me in the light from the fire, screaming in rage, ragged entrails streaming behind it like a banner. Erhlsen was kneeling, tracking it with the barrel of his lasgun, leisurely, as if he was at a recreational target shoot. I threw myself flat, just as he squeezed the trigger, and the thing's head exploded.

'Thanks, Erhlsen!' I waved, rolled to my feet, and drew my laspistol left-handed. He grinned, and turned to track another target.

Time to be somewhere else, I thought, and ran as hard as I could towards the vehicle park. On the way I shot frequently, and swung my humming chainsword in every defensive pattern I could recall, but whether I hit anything only the Emperor knows. Apparently I struck a heroic figure, though, shrieking what was taken for a stirring battle cry rather than an incoherent howl of terror, which encouraged the men no end.

The Hydras were firing continuously now, stitching the air over the compound with tracer fire which looked dense enough to walk on, but the gargoyles were small and fast-moving, evading most of it with ease. Craning my neck around for potential threats, I saw most of the guardsmen taking whatever cover they could find; anyone left out in the open was in no condition to move by this time as the flesh-borer fire and bioplasma bolts rained down furiously. My attention thus diverted, I tripped, going down hard on something which swore at me, and tried to brain me with the butt of a lasgun.

'Jurgen! It's me!' I said, blocking frantically with my forearm before he could stave my skull in. Even over the smell of the gargoyle guts I could tell who it was without looking. He'd dug in between the tracks of a Salamander, protected from the blizzard of falling death by the armour plating above him.

'Commissar.' He looked relieved. 'What should we do?'

'Get this thing started,' I said. Anyone else might have argued, but Jurgen's dogged deference to authority sent him out into the open without hesitation. I half expected to hear a scream and the wet slap of a fleshborer impact, but after a moment the engine rumbled to life. I took a deep breath, and then another. Relinquishing the safety of overshadowing armour plate for the exposed deck of the open-topped scout car seemed almost suicidal, but staying here for the main assault would be worse.

With more willpower than I believed I possessed, I holstered the pistol, tightened my grip on the chainsword, and
rolled out into the open.

'Up here, sir.' Jurgen reached down a grubby hand, which
I seized gratefully, and swung myself up behind the autocannon. Something crunched under my bootsoles: tiny
beetle-like things, thousands of them, discharged by the gargoyles' fleshborers. I shuddered reflexively, but they were
dead, not having found living flesh to consume in their brief
spasm of existence.

'Drive!' I shouted, and was almost thrown off my feet as
Jurgen accelerated. I ducked below the gunner's shield,
dropped the melee weapon, and opened fire. It had little
effect, of course, but it would look good, and anyone seeing
us would assume that the extra firepower was the reason I'd
commandeered the vehicle.

Within moments we were beyond the camp perimeter,
and Jurgen began to slow.

'Keep going!' I said. He looked puzzled, but opened the
throttle again.

'Where to, sir?'

'West. The mines. As fast as you can.' Again, I was expecting questions, doubts, and from any other trooper I might
have had them. But Jurgen, Emperor bless his memory, simply complied without demur. Then again, in his position I'd
have done the same, relieved to have been ordered away
from the battle. Gradually the noise and fireglow began to
fade behind us in the night. I was just beginning to relax,
estimating the time remaining until we reached safety, when
the Salamander shook violently.

'Jurgen!' I yelled. 'What's happening?'

'They're firing at us, sir.' He sounded no more concerned
about it than he did about making his regular report as
latrine orderly. It took me a moment to realise that he trusted
me to deal with whatever we were facing. I pulled myself up
to look over the gunner's shield, and my bowels spasmed.

'Turn!' I screamed, as a second venom cannon blast scored
the armour plating centimetres from my face. 'Back to the
compound!'

Even now, after more than a century, I still wake sweating from dreams of that moment. In the pre-dawn glow the plain before us seemed to move like a vast grey ocean, undulating gently; but instead of water it was a sea of chitin, flecked with claw and fang rather than foam, rolling inexorably on towards the fragile defensive island of the artillery park. I would have wept with disappointment if I wasn't already too terrified for any other emotion. The 'nids had outsmarted me, sweeping round to cut us off and block our escape.

I bounced off the hull plating, falling heavily back into the crew compartment, as Jurgen threw one of the tracks into reverse and swung us around, practically on a coin. My head cracked painfully against something hard. I blinked my swimming eyes clear, and recognised it as a voxcaster. Something like hope flared again, and I grabbed the microphone.

'Cain to command! Come in!' I screamed, voice raw with panic. Static hissed for a moment.

'Commissar? Where are you?' Mostrue's voice, calm and confident. 'We've been looking for you since we drove off the attack...'

'It was a diversion!' I yelled. 'The main force is coming from the west! If you don't redeploy the guns we're all dead!'

'Are you sure?' The colonel sounded doubtful.

'I'm out here now! I've got half the hive fleet on my arse! How sure do you want me to be?' I never found out, as the aerial melted under the impact of a bioplasma blast. The Salamander shook again, and the engine howled, as Jurgen pushed it up past speeds it had never been designed to cope with. Despite my trepidation I couldn't resist peering cautiously over the lip of the armour plate.

Merciful Emperor, we were opening the distance! The incoming fire was becoming less accurate as the scuttling swarm receded slowly behind us. Emboldened, I swung the pintel-mounted bolter around and fired into the densely packed mass of seething obscenity; there was no need to aim, as I could hardly miss hitting something, but I pointed it in the general direction of the largest creature I saw. As a rule, the larger the creature the higher it was in the hive hierarchy, and the more vital it was to co-ordinating the swarm. And seeding swarms, I vaguely recalled from some long-forgotten xenobiology lecture, tended to be thinly supplied with them. I missed the tyrant I'd spotted but one of its guard warriors went down, mashed instantly to goo by the weight of the swarm scuttling on and over it.

The compound was in sight now, ant-like troopers lining the fortifications, and, Emperor be praised, the Hydras rumbling into position to defend them, their quad-barrelled autocannon turrets depressing to face the oncoming tide of death. I was just beginning to think we might make it–

When, with a loud crack and a shriek of tortured metal, our howling engine fell silent. Jurgen had pushed it too far and we were about to pay for that with our lives. The Salamander lurched, slipping sideways, and slewed to a halt in a spray of sand.

'What do we do now, sir?' Jurgen asked, hauling himself up out of the driver's compartment. I grabbed my chainsword, suppressing the urge to use it on him; he could still be useful.

'Run like frak!' I said, demonstrating the point. I didn't have to be faster than the 'nids, just faster than Jurgen. I could hear his boots scuffing in the sand behind me, but didn't turn, that would have slowed me momentarily, and I really didn't want to see how close the swarm was getting.

The Hydras opened up, shooting past us, gouging holes in the onrushing wall of chittering death, but barely slowing it. Lasgun bolts began following suit; although the small arms fire would only be marginally effective at this range, every little helped. Return fire from the warriors was sporadic, and directed at the defenders behind the barricades rather than us, the hive mind apparently deciding we weren't worth the bother of singling out. Suited me fine.

I was almost at the berms, encouraging shouts from the men in the emplacements ringing in my ears, when I heard a cry from behind me. Jurgen had fallen.

'Commissar! Help!'

Not a chance, I thought, intent on reaching the safety of the barricades, then my heart froze. Ahead of me, angling in to cut us off, was the huge, unmistakable bulk of the hive tyrant, accompanied by its attendant bodyguards. It hissed, opening its jaws, and I dived to one side expecting the familiar blast of bioplasma, but instead a ravening blast of pure energy detonated where I'd stood seconds before, throwing me to the ground. I rolled upright, moving as far away from it as I could, and found myself running back towards Jurgen. He was on the ground, a hormagaunt about to disembowel him with its scything claws, and its brood mates lining up to dice what was left. Caught between the 'gaunts and the hive tyrant the choice was clear; I had an outside chance of fighting my way through the swarm of smaller creatures, but going back would mean certain death.

'Back off!' I screamed, and swung my chainsword at the 'gaunt attacking Jurgen. It just had time to look up in surprise before its head came off, spraying ichor which smelled nearly as bad as Jurgen did. He rolled to his feet, snapping off a shot from his lasgun that exploded the thorax of another, which I'd barely had time to register was about to eviscerate me. Looked like we were even. I glanced around. The rest of the brood were hemming us in, and the tyrant was getting closer, looming huge against a sky reddened by the rising sun.

Then suddenly the tyrant wasn't there, replaced by shreds of steaming flesh which fell almost leisurely to the sand, its attendant warriors exploding around it. One of the Hydras had rolled around the edge of its emplacement to get a clear shot, the hail of autocannon rounds taking the entire group apart at almost point blank range.

I swung the chainsword to block a sweeping scythe from the closest 'gaunt, and missed as it abruptly pulled away. The whole swarm was hesitating, milling uncertainly, deprived of its guiding intelligence.

'Fire! Keep firing!' Mostrue's voice rang out, clear and confident from the barricades. The gunners complied enthusiastically. I swung the chainsword again, fear and desperation lending me superhuman strength, carving my way through the 'gaunts like so many sides of grox.

Abruptly the swarm broke, scattering, scuttling away like frightened rodents. I dropped the chainsword, trembling with reaction, and felt my knees give way.

'We did it! We did it!' Jurgen let his lasgun fall, his voice tinged with wonder. 'Emperor be praised.' I felt a supporting arm go round my shoulders.

'Well done, Cain. Bravest thing I've ever seen.' Divas was holding me up, his face alight with something approaching hero worship. 'When you went back for Jurgen I thought you were dead for sure.'

'You'd have done the same,' I said, realising the smart way to play it was modest and unassuming. 'Is he–?'

'He's fine.' Colonel Mostrue joined us, and looked at me with the old tutor domus expression. 'I'd like to know what you were doing out there, though.'

'Something didn't feel right about the gargoyle assault,' I improvised hastily. 'And I remembered tyranids tend to use flanking attacks against dug-in defenders. So I thought I'd better go out and take a look.'

'Thank the Emperor you did,' Divas put in, swallowing every word.

'You could have assigned someone,' Mostrue pointed out.

'It was dangerous,' I said, knowing we'd be overheard. 'And, let's be honest, colonel, I'm the most expendable officer in the battery.'

'No one in my battery's expendable, commissar. Not even you.' For a moment I saw a flicker of amusement in those ice-blue eyes and shivered. 'But I'll remember your eagerness to volunteer for dangerous assignments in future.'

I'll just bet you will, I thought. And he was as good as his word, too, once we got to Keffia. But in the meantime he had one more favour to do me.

'I'VE BEEN THINKING, commissar.' Mostrue glanced up from the hololith, where the image of our newly-arrived fleet was enjoying a rare turkey shoot against the vastly out-numbered bioships. 'Perhaps I should assign you an aide?'

'That's hardly necessary, colonel,' I said, flattered in spite of myself. 'My workload's far from excessive.' That wasn't the point, though, and we both knew it. My status as a hero of the regiment demanded some recognition, and assigning a trooper as my personal flunkey would be a public sign that I was fully accepted by the senior officers.

'Nevertheless.' Mostrue smiled thinly. 'There was no shortage of volunteers, as you can imagine.' That went without saying. The official version of my heroism, and my self-sacrificing rescue of Jurgen, was all over the compound.

'I'm sure you'll make the right choice,' I said.

'I already have.' Suspicion flared, and I felt the pit of my stomach drop. He wouldn't, surely...

My nose told me that he had, even before I turned, forcing a smile to my face.

'Gunner Jurgen,' I said. 'What a pleasant surprise.'

ON MOURNFUL WINGS

Si Spurrier

THE SKY BECAME *a mirror, reflecting the ocean's anger. Tangled clouds flexed and boiled, wrestling for supremacy of the horizon.*

A wall of wind and dust and water ripped from the maelstrom like a talon snatching at the land.

Someone screamed.

Everyone died.

ICA LURCHED AWAKE, the memory of screaming voices withdrawing into his mind.

Around him the glider shuddered, inexpertly-fitted fuselage protesting at the pressures beyond. A rusted bolt dropped from the seal above his head and clattered on the floor.

He couldn't bring himself to care.

Dalus slept fitfully beside him. Ica wondered if he shared his twin's dark-rimmed eyes, prematurely lined features and weary, malnourished complexion. Probably. Sleep had become tortuous since… since then.

Dalus mumbled and fidgeted in his uncomfortable seat, disturbed.

The glider's descent became more pronounced and several passengers, all boys of thirteen, whispered urgent prayers of protection. A tortured creak announced the deployment of ancient landing gear.

Let it break, said a voice in Ica's head. Let it hit the runway and splinter into a thousand pieces. Let us spin along that narrow strip of plascrete above Table City, detonating like a messy citrusbloom and sitting there, half buried under granite landslides, flaming and screaming and dying.

There had been a priest in the tiny Ecclesiarchy chapel at Kultoom, a priest with one eye and one flickering ocular implant. He had scars on both cheeks and the bulge of dogtags concealed beneath his sackcloth robes. Sitting there in the shuddering glider, wishing for oblivion, Ica remembered the priest's words with a guilty wince. 'Seek not escape from misery in death,' the voice droned, eye clicking and whirring in the gloom, 'for He That Is Most Mighty gathers not the Selfish Dead to his side.'

The priest was dead now. Everyone in Kultoom was dead now.

THE GLIDER LANDED amid the rain lashed chimneys of Table City with the baby scream of salt-clogged brakes. Its confused passengers disembarked meekly.

The principal city of Gathis II was a desolate metropolis: a scaled-up echo of the tribal communities and lugubrious villages dotting the few areas of planetary dry land. Ramshackle dwellings clustered around one another for protection, smeared with the planet's only resource: chamack oil.

Produced from the pulped remains of chamack weed, the viscous sludge was exported by the Administratum as a cheap but foul-smelling sealant. Day and night the cargo gliders ferried their odoriferous loads from distant island-tribes, a whole year's harvest barely filling a single glider. Competition for access to the aquatic plantations was fierce and regularly bloody.

Ica pushed his face against rain-splattered blast shields as an enormous vessel lifted from the ground, clouds of dust writhing like gaseous tendrils.

'Wonder where they go?' Dalus said, tired-looking eyes tracking the slab of metal into the brooding rain clouds.

Ica nodded. Inside, a voice said: It doesn't matter. Nothing matters.

'Keep moving!' someone called, and both twins returned to the winding line of youths, herded along by men in thick rain-cloaks. They trudged through the skyport, between looming parades of Imperial ships with their massive, mysterious engines.

'Question not your lot in this life,' the priest had said, his his dead voice echoing through Ica's mind. 'Be content to serve Him-Upon-The-Throne – however humble your station.'

Along the line Ica could see inquisitive eyes goggling at the gargantuan treasures looming on either side. Their expressions said, 'How do they work?' 'Where do they go?' 'What's out there?' But they'd never know; never leave the rain-pocked surfaces of Gathis; never see the stars.

And nothing they had ever done would be remembered.

A building loomed ahead, archaic façade crumbling. Its steep sides, surmounted by spines and sneering gargoyles, stood incongruous among the surrounding dockyards. With growing unease Ica realised the youths were headed directly for a gaping set of loading doors on the building's side.

Above, carved from vast stone slabs, stretching in a magnificent halo of angular symmetry, was a set of stylised feathers, angular and black. Not the graceful arcs of Administratum heraldry, with their sweeping curves and adamantium omegas; but rather squared and clipped, arranged in a brutal phalanx. And at the crux of the jagged raptor wings, watching with mute melancholia, an ivory-white death-masque cast its gaze down upon the column of youths.

A winged skull.

THE SKY RUMBLED *distantly. The twins barely bothered to look up. 'Another storm,' Dalus grumbled, tinkering with his stretch-wings. Ica pushed at a ratchet joint and nodded.*

'*Mountain ghosts having a brawl, father?*' he grinned.

The twins' father smiled, features creasing like old leather. He leaned over Ica's shoulder and helped tighten the wing-brace, tousling his son's hair warmly. 'That they are, son.'

Across the room, Dalus watched the movement closely, then returned to improving his glider with renewed vigour.

ICA HAD NEVER seen so many people. The interior of the building seemed endless, ebony horizons pulling away on every side, gazing down upon an infinite ocean of young, bewildered heads.

'Every male of age thirteen to be present at Table City upon the thirteenth day of the thirteenth lunar month of every year. By Imperial command.'

Every year the same: the gliders would come to Kultoom and collect the youths. And sometimes, once in every decade, not all of them would return.

Inducted into the Imperial Navy, the rumour went.

Or sent as cannon fodder to fight the orks.

Or offered as a sacrifice to the Emperor's glory.

Or any one of a thousand different possibilities, all of them rich with uncertainty and legend.

Sent to appease the angry mountain ghosts, one rumour went.

Something far above screeched like a craghawk and a shape parted with the ceiling-shadows, resolving into a metallic platform suspended upon chains. The murmuring of thousands of youths arose throughout the chamber, a choir of fear and uncertainty.

The platform creaked to a pendulous halt far above and silence spread like a net.

The air was greasy and tense, spiderlegs scuttled up the spine and static whispered through the ears and nose.

Spotlights flickered to life, each a miniature thunderclap.

'Look,' Dalus said. Ica followed his gaze and there, threading through the crowd, were the black-robed minders who had ferried the boys from the gliders. Every so often they would stop, lizardlike, and tilt their heads, then scurry off again in another direction. Sometimes they'd look up at the

distant platform as if someone stood there, watching, directing.

And then they began to Choose. A hand would reach out
and tap at a shoulder, blindly feeling for – what? And then
three or four of the ebony figures would close in, dragging
away each victim in a knot of limbs.

Ica had expected shrill pleas for help: oh Emperor,
don't let them take me! But no, those who were taken
seemed placid, cowed somehow. Not one of them cried
out.

Then something stabbed at Ica's mind. Something that
crawled through his brain and knew everything. Something
that said, Yes, you're correct not to care. You're already dead,
and you know it.

And when black-gloved hands closed on his arms and
hauled him away into the shadows, he didn't cry out in
alarm. He didn't even mutter a prayer under his breath
because, after all, what good would it do?

Unconscious and drifting, Ica knew he'd never see Kultoom again. Never net slippery lacefish from his father's
dirigible, never glide in frantic circles above the tribe's submerged chamack-patch, watching for theft-raids from
neighbouring tribes.

There was no Kultoom to go back to. The dirigible had
been pulped and hurled away into the shrieking skies. The
other tribes had come and, unchallenged, plundered his
ancestors' Chamack nurseries.

Someone slapped him, hard, and he vomited.

Next to him, Dalus said 'aack' and dribbled blood. To
each side of Ica unconscious youths were dragged awake
with punches and kicks, courtesy of those same black-
cloaked figures from before. The one looming over him
grunted, satisfied with Ica's alertness, and stepped clear. The
twins traded uncertain looks.

They knelt in a line of some thirty youths – those dragged
from the building in the skyport, Ica supposed – on a rocky
plateau. All around them towered the colossal crags of the
Razorpeak Mountains, casting their ugly shadows far across
the churning seas below.

Somewhere down there, Ica thought, is Table City, where thousands of bewildered youths are climbing back aboard gliders for the journey home, thanking the Emperor and wondering what had happened to those few who had been taken...

Ica tried to remember how he'd arrived at this dizzying place, but his memory faltered. There had been pain, briefly, then the vaguest sensation of machinery and engines – yes, he recognised the sound from the skyport – rising in volume.

To himself, he said, It doesn't matter how you got here. Nobody cares.

'Chapter serfs,' said a voice, thick with authority, 'that will be all.'

The black-robed men bowed mechanically, quickly descending a stairway hewn into the mountainside. Otherwise, the outcrop was empty, dwarfed by its parent mountain, with only a small cave in the vertical cliff-face nearby that could have concealed a person. Ica fixed his eyes on the rocky maw and tried to focus.

Something moved inside.

Something that twisted the light like mercury.

Something huge that somehow shifted with fluid grace.

Something that hulked forwards, polished facets decorated by ivory whorls, smouldering with reflected light. Panelled mirror-gauntlets curled around a blood-red staff and somewhere in the centre of the whole impossible being a pair of melancholy eyes stared out with incalculable wisdom and sadness. A metallic hood, pressed down over the sallow face, seemed to crackle with barely restrained energy.

'I am Thryn,' the behemoth said, mournful voice shivering along Ica's spine, 'Librarian Secundus of the Adeptus Astartes.'

The words meant nothing. Faces twisted by misery and fear, the youths stared as the Librarian took another step, mirror-armour shattering the light. Shoulder guards flexed, and Ica glimpsed again the mournful skull with its stretched wings, engraved upon the metal. The man's pale face drilled its hard gaze into each boy in turn.

'You have been chosen,' the voice said, 'alone among thousands. Chosen not for your strength or your courage, not for your souls or your bodies. You've been chosen because you, each in their way, already understand an immutable truth.

'You understand that you are already dead.'

Somewhere to Ica's left, a boy sobbed quietly.

'Disaster, loss, injury... a lifetime of exclusion and isolation – these are the memories you share. You must understand that whatever you feel, however great your grief, it is a mere nothing: an invisible fraction of the despair shared throughout our Imperium.'

Again something scuttled into Ica's brain, twitching its way through his memories. And when next the Librarian spoke, the voice seemed to enter Ica's very mind. 'You've been brought here to die. You must understand. Cherish your mortality. Cling to it. Today each of you will perish with such certainty that you are, in a sense, already dead – just marking time until the end.

'Behold the despair.'

And the ethereal fingers in Ica's skull sunk deeper and twisted, bringing forth...

...*screaming voices, and his mother's fingernails broke, one after another, until her grip was wrenched clear and she diminished into the maelstrom, screaming his name for help...*

...*and howling creatures with scarlet eyes and green skin like rotten leather clashed their tusks as women screamed and babies cried and cities burnt...*

...*and his father's workshop disintegrated, vindictive lightning obliterating the chaff as it circulated up into the banshee skies...*

...*and multitudes were slaughtered, and monstrosities stalked through bloody streets, chitin clacking, and not one horrified scream was louder than any other, and to every sufferer the world is ended, their life destroyed, and it was happening a million times over...*

...*and Ica screamed and Dalus screamed, although neither was heard, and outside the chapel detonated in a whirligig storm of masonry, and somewhere amongst the debris the old priest*

*thrashed his limbs as the candles he'd so recently lit impaled him
before racing away on the wind...*

*...and the ghostly vessel swept past in a multicoloured broad-
side, unleashing colossal energies in an actinic torpedo volley that
punched gaping mouths into the blast shields, and a hundred
thousand human ants wordlessly shrieked the last of their oxygen
into the void...*

*...and they didn't see their father die, but they heard his voice
as the gather-hall sealant crumbled like dry leaves and haemor-
rhaged into the hurricane, and his howl of terror seemed to go on
for ever and ever and ever and...*

*...and the lightning claws, writhing with evil, moved faster
than the eye could follow, flaring against His force sword's rune
patterned blade, and when finally the ivory power armour splintered and the Warmaster's talons reached inside, on a million
worlds a trillion humans sank to their knees, and nothing would
ever be the same again...*

...and the despair never ended.

ICA OPENED HIS eyes and prayed for death. All that he was
would be nothing. The suffering of the universe eclipsed his
own utterly. Nothing mattered.

'You will enter the cave,' the Librarian ordered, words alive
with psychic energy, impossible to disobey. 'You'll enter the
cave and inside you will die. You will rise through caverns of
fear and violence, and with every footstep you draw closer to
oblivion.'

The grave voice halted, and Ica tried to stand, turning to
see his brother already rising up.

As usual.

Always first.

Others followed, desperate to obey the Librarian's command despite their aching minds. Thryn's silver gauntlet
lifted, unfolded a single digit, and silently directed the
youths into the cave.

One boy, further along the line, didn't stand. His eyes
stared blankly, wide and lifeless. Ica understood. The weight
of sadness had been too much to bear.

* * *

ICA PINWHEELED HIGHER, *stretchwings fully extended. Every arm movement tilted him fractionally, sending him soaring above and across Kultoom Island.*

'Good, Ica! Good!' his father shouted up, cupped hands framing his proud face. 'Don't overbalance – that's it! Perfect!'

Above Ica, Dalus glided in a series of long, lazy spirals. 'How's this, father?' he called, voice almost lost in the chasm of air.

The twins' father glanced away from Ica momentarily, nodding. 'Good.'

Ica peered up at his brother to exchange a smile in celebration of their first flight. But Dalus was frowning, and when he noticed Ica staring, his smile was too brief and too forced, before he manoeuvred his glider away.

TORCHES FLICKERED IN brackets, flames guttering with each movement of the air. Finally all the youths were inside, silent and cowed by the psychic trauma.

Inside Ica's head, a voice said: All dead, dead, dead, dead, dead...

Then the door closed.

One moment the daylight streamed in through the cave entrance, framing the wide figure of the Librarian against the rain-streaked outcrop beyond. The next; iron blast doors slipped from grooves with a thunderclap clang and sealed the youths inside.

The youths exchanged uncertain glances. One boy, voice barely more than a whisper, said 'W-what's happening...?' Nobody replied.

Something hissed, and Ica turned to find water bubbling from a crack in the floor, veils of steam rising from the rapidly enlarging puddle. Nearby, Dalus sniffed at the air. 'Stinks of sulphur...'

Again the voice invaded Ica's brain, the measured tones of Librarian Thryn filling his mind with its patient, mournful inflection. All the youths tilted their heads as if listening intently, and Ica knew that they too heard Thryn's words.

'Millennia ago, an object fell from the sky among the Razorpeak Mountains. Its impact shattered apart the crust of this planet, destabilising it forever.

'It – like us – dies one second at a time. One day its core will solidify, its oceans will freeze and its people will starve. Until then it whiles away its mortality with fiery temper tantrums and indignant earthquakes.

'You are standing at the centre of this world's deepest despair.'

Ica returned his gaze to the growing puddle at his feet, now rising in a small hump of boiling fluid. He could feel its heat, even standing back. Across the floor of the chamber another fissure began to weep.

'Once every year,' the voice droned, 'lava flows beneath the Razorpeaks vent into the tunnels beneath your feet, filling them with scalding water.

'Within an hour this cavern, and all those above it, will be submerged. You will breathe boiling fluid. You will gag silently as the air is burnt from your lungs. This chamber has a single exit. Take it, don't take it. Either way, you have minutes to live.'

The psychic contact ended, leaving Ica dizzy and nauseous.

An orifice in the rock nearby gurgled, hissed, then roared in incandescent fury. Water exploded forth, a mallet striking at the rockface and shattering into a million shards of liquid and steam.

A boy screamed, vapour rising from his blistering face like a shroud.

And Ica thought: So, this is it. Better to die now. Welcome it. Cherish it.

Except...

Except there's nothing left to lose, and dying in the next chamber is as good as dying here...

Frowning, not understanding why, Ica drove himself onwards, stepping towards the tunnel leading up and away. As quick as a wraith, Dalus streaked past him, rushing to be the first through. And behind them came the others, eyes dead, driven on only by the realisation that it made no difference.

The boy who clutched at his face, shrieking unintelligibly in pain, was left behind, cries becoming fainter and fainter, finally falling silent with a single water-choked sob.

ON THE DAY *it happened, the twins had sneaked into the gather-hall through the broken synthiplex panel at its rear.*

Outside it was raining, and the droplets hammered on the building's corrugated roof like a harvest of gallberries, all falling at once. Outside the people of Kultoom tribe, as normal, laboured away their small, blind little lives.

Ica and Dalus were mighty kings, contesting the hand of a fair princess.

They were hero and villain, struggling for dominance.

They were Emperor and Horus (although neither knew which was which).

They were alien and human, or heretic and redeemer, or mutant and puritan.

Throughout the deserted hallway their wooden Jenrak-staves clacked together, whistling in broad sweeps and jabbing viciously. Giggling uncontrollably, feinting and lunging, Ica and Dalus were warriors.

And then their father heard their voices and crawled inside, demanding to know why they'd left their chores. Dalus had said they'd wanted to practise so they could defend the Chamack from neighbour tribes, but their father had seen it was a lie. He grinned slyly, and said, 'Fine. So, fight.'

So, beneath his stern gaze they'd fought. But the fun was gone, and every lunge that found its mark was rewarded with a curt 'Good', and every clumsy back step elicited a burning silence from the gallery where their father stood, shaking his head or muttering.

And it wasn't a game any more, so Ica drove his stave deep into Dalus's stomach.

'A good hit,' their father said.

And it wasn't fun any more, so Dalus battered aside Ica's defence and smashed his brother across the cheek. Ica dropped to the floor, blood ebbing from his nose.

And their father rushed to Ica, checking for broken bones. And he looked up at Dalus, standing over him in a confusion of shame and triumph, and said:

'Stupid boy. Always going too far!'

And outside the thunder rumbled, and Kultoom waited for death.

BONES CLATTERED ON the floor with every footfall. Steam churned behind the youths like the breath of a daemon, hot in pursuit of its prey. They drew closer together, staring into the face of razor-sided agony.

The cavern was bisected by a living cobweb of mossy lichen, clinging to strand upon strand of fibrous stalks and coiling roots. Another tunnel, again leading upwards, yawned on the other side of the mossy partition. But the web, glowing with bacterial luminescence, bore thorns. As long as Ica's finger, they sprouted like butcher-hook talons, curved like scimitars and equally as sharp. Tiny spines beneath the hood of every blade waited to barb any hapless victim, lacerating flesh and splitting sinews. The forest of daggers, five deep, reached from cavern wall to cavern wall, from stalactite-strewn ceiling to uneven floor.

Somewhere, deeply enmeshed, hung a skeleton – its empty eyes watching Ica, saying, you're like me. You're all like me. All dead.

The tunnel from the previous chamber was already submerged, scampering air bubbles cratering the swiftly rising surface. Clouds of steam, reeking of sulphur, coiled insidiously amongst the boys.

Ica pushed himself forwards. Once the impetus to move on had taken root, once the inertia – urging him to give up – had been overcome, driving forwards was not so hard. He turned and, yes, there was Dalus, already approaching the dagger-thorns.

What difference does it make? Ica pondered. Might as well.

The first thorn ripped apart his thin jerkin and prised open his skin, a frosty fire that blossomed warmly.

The next hooked into his shoulder, scraping the dark places inside against bone and nerves. He groaned in pain and gritted his teeth.

Keep going.

The next thorn turned his thigh into a ploughfield of flesh-ribbons.

Something hit his cheek and he glanced around, where a small youth sprayed arterial redness from a gaping wound in his neck. The boy's eyes rolled upwards with something like relief.

Behind Ica, others were pushing through, moaning with each new open wound. To the rear somebody screamed as the boiling water trickled over the lip of the previous tunnel and scorched an unshielded foot.

Ahead, Dalus pushed further into the tangle, incisions covering his arms and legs. He gripped at a branch, hauling himself forwards – only stopping to inspect his lacerated palms. He glanced briefly at Ica, as if checking his brother was still there, still watching, then frowned and barged his way forwards.

A thorn dragged itself along Ica's brow, and he blinked against the red wetness oozing into his eye. He moved forwards, sliced and diced, not caring; feeling the pain with abstract distance – registering its presence but not its effect. An arm broke free, a chequerboard of cuts marking its surface.

A growl of triumph ahead broadcast Dalus's release. Dalus stopped and turned, panting and bleeding, as slowly his brother wrestled free. Something splintered, a mossy crack of parting twigs, and Ica stepped clear.

He turned to look back at the others, some almost liberated, others hopelessly enmeshed, watching with eyes already rheumy and lifeless in death.

Some youths hadn't even tried to get through. They stood or sat on the other side, impassively waiting for their doom as the water bubbled ever higher. Ica nodded, understanding how they felt, and turned away.

Dalus was already climbing towards the next tunnel. Ica blinked bloody tears from his eyes and followed.

THE SKY QUAKED, *electric ribbons chasing across the horizon. Wind plucked at what few trees grew on Kultoom Island, eliciting a creaking and groaning that vocalised the tribe's anxiety.*

Tribesmen looked to the churning clouds and spat, cursing the dismal weather. The priest, dribbling in his zealousness, shouted a prayer to the Emperor, vying with the thunder to be heard. His oratory finished, he entered the chapel and sealed the door.

Windkites were hastily rescued from mid-air gyrations; chamack harvesters were moored securely, and everywhere was the sound of slamming shutters and doors.

The sky went black.

In their hut, Ica and Dalus, footfalls heavy with sulky indignation, descended into the damp darkness of the cellar. Their mother's voice followed after.

'...and stay down there 'til you learn obedience! If you can't be trusted to finish your chores, seems to me you can't be trusted to use a wing-glider either!'

At this the twins both gagged in alarm, turning to the cross-armed silhouette at the top of the stairs with a cry, 'But–!'

'But nothing, night take you! No gliding for a month! And now your father's out in the rain, fixing up that Emperor-damned panel , and who knows where he'll find cover if the storm hits and how we'll survive if he's hurt and why can't you be obedient like Father Lemuel says and...' The whinnying voice faded away as the door slammed and their mother stalked off to bolt the shutters.

In the darkness, Ica sniffed back the blood in his nose. He could feel Dalus glaring across the room.

THROUGH CHAMBERS AND caverns, they ran. Scalding water churned from every crevice, dousing the flickering torches one-by-one.

In one chamber the floor was a gravelpit of smouldering embers, heated by fire-red magma that cooled, sludgelike, in scattered puddles. The youths – those who dared – scampered across in a flurry of yelps and explosions of sparks. Some fell with a howl into the curdling lava, clawing at the air and shrieking until their skin charred and their lungs filled with fire.

In one cavern a firestorm of shrapnel and smoke burst from some hidden alcove among the stalactites, reacting to the unblinking red eye of a motion sensor embedded in one wall. Some of the adolescents lurked at the room's entrance, dividing their terrified glances between the rising water behind and that glaring ruby light, choosing who would live and who would die. Others rushed by, ducking and dodging. Their flesh and bone was dissolved in the resulting whirlwind of metal, screams ripped away in a rush of smoke and dust. A few – those who neither hesitated nor rushed – made it through.

In one chamber the ground gave way to an echoing chasm lined by splintered bones. Only by leaping across then scrabbling amid the jagged handholds of the opposite rock face could the youths pass. The screams of those who fell, punctuated by the splintering cracks of impact, echoed throughout the hollow mountain forever.

And always the water rose, dogging at their heels, curling its tendrils, wrapping everything in a sulphurous haze. The mountain filled from the base upwards, and with every step the remaining air grew hotter and more stifling.

Ica, muscles protesting, passed obstacle after obstacle, forever convinced that each test would be the last. Only by accepting his own death could he march across scorching coal fragments. Only by understanding he was nothing could he amble unhurriedly past an unflickering motion sensor. Only by knowing that he was dying one second at a time, that he was already dead and forgotten, that nothing he had ever done would be remembered, could he hurl himself into the abyss, then clamber, hands and arms lacerated, to his feet.

He was surviving and he didn't care.

And all the time, driven on like some unstoppable dervish, Dalus was one step ahead; turning back to watch Ica but never rushing to his aid when he faltered. Their clothes hung in shreds, their skin was a patchwork of scrapes and cuts. Once Dalus had turned to Ica, eyes burning, and said: 'Try to keep up, brother…'

And then they passed through the final cavern and entered a tunnel that twisted and grew narrower, coiling slowly downwards. Ica, palms and knees shredded, struggled to keep sight of his brother's retreating form.

'Dalus?' he panted. 'T-the water, it'll...'

'I know,' came the curt reply. 'It'll come down after us.'

The tunnel grew steeper, walls closing in until the brothers writhed, wormlike, using only toes and elbows. How many youths remained behind them Ica didn't know. He couldn't turn his head, even if there were light. He was blind, a maggot within a mountain.

The ghost of a scream filtered along the corkscrew tunnel: a million kilometres away. Somewhere far above scalding water lapped at the edge of the descending shaft, waiting...

Ica could see it happening, in his mind. The water – at first only a few droplets – would ebb its way over the lip of the cavern. As it rose the trickle became a stream, then a river, then a tsunami that tumbled down through the passageway, growing faster and faster as the walls grew closer, roaring in sulphurous fury.

And then there was light. Hurting Ica's eyes, making him wince. And there was Dalus, worming his way from the tunnel, shredded legs kicking as he exited.

And the mountain shook as the waterspout filled up, and all around the air began to rush by, driven on by the wall of liquid rage charging at his heels.

And the sun didn't look sweet when he saw it, and he felt no relief at the freshness of the air. He was still dead. Still forgotten.

Only two other youths clambered from the tunnel behind them, faces pale and eyes ringed as if they had been existing underground for years.

They stood on a ledge, jutting from a sheer rockface on the mountainside, and the ground fell away in all directions. The distant ocean was a pond of ripples from this height. And beyond, with sides so sheer that even the craghawks could find no nesting spots, was the Ghostmountain: the tallest of all the Razorpeaks, its very existence a toothy, snarled challenge to the clouds.

Ica stared at it and murmured, 'Emperor preserve...' Its enormity compacted his misery, reminded him of his scale. You are nothing, he told himself. You are nothing and in a moment you will die, punched from this ledge by a fist of water. Maybe your bones will shatter at the impact, driving shards of ivory into your brain. Maybe you'll die quickly. Or maybe you'll be cannoned out into the air, screaming as the water burns your skin and your eyes dissolve. Maybe you'll plummet, arms thrashing, to the fanged rocks at the base of the mountain.

Maybe you'll die in pain. Maybe you won't.

But you'll die. It's so certain that you'll die, you might as well already be dead.

And look, there's nowhere left to go. Nowhere left to run.

And the mountain shook, and the water roared, and Ica remembered.

His mother, screaming as the storm hit and the roof of the hut separated like a jigsaw, trying to wrench open the cellar door to seek sanctuary. She buried her fingernails in the rotten wood of the strut support as behind her the walls of the house went convex and shredded like paper.

'Look,' grunted Dalus curtly, returning Ica to reality. He pointed towards a tangled shape at the farthest corner of the ledge.

A twisted morsel of canvas, stretched to near-tautness by a metal frame, protruded like a shark-fin. Other components – rusted spring mounts and ragged tail rudders, decaying tensile pins and mangled harness struts – lurked within the heap.

'Gliders…' Ica mumbled numbly. Behind him the mountain growled.

And the voice in his head whispered: So you can go on.

Might as well.

Nothing to lose.

Dalus was already beside the pile, snatching at the decaying apparatus, selecting the best glider kit. He hefted the concertina stretch wings onto his back and began buckling the harness around his chest, eyes glowering in determination. Ica, legs ready to collapse beneath the despair filling his mind, simply reached out a hand and dragged at whatever random assemblage it touched. The wings hung shredded and near useless, the harness little more than crossed bandoliers of pleated chamack-twine.

Doesn't matter. Put it on.

The mountain bellowed, a bull-roar of fury. The air rushing from the tunnel mouth became a physical force, pushing the twins backwards towards the edge. One of the other youths lunged for the pile of gliders, eyes wide. The final survivor simply stood and stared, waiting.

Then the world was thrown on its head.

KULTOOM TRIBE DIED. *Kultoom Island shredded like an almost dead body, thrashing itself uselessly, flailing at its tormentor and struggling to hold in its own viscera.*

The storm closed with hungry malevolence; anonymous and implacable.

The universe, with no more regard than a man might have for an insect beneath his boot, reached out and expunged a population.

WITH A COCKROACH snap the wind unfurled the tattered wings of Ica's glider and threw him across the distant ocean. From the corner of his madly oscillating view he registered the mountainside erupting in a gargantuan waterspout, cascading downwards in sheets of rainbow-infested spray – but it was distant, unimportant. A scream dwindled on the howling wind.

Then it was all gone: obliterated in a dizzying split second, and when reality coalesced Ica was gliding erratically, stranded within a gulf of air. The breath, sucked from his lungs, returned in heaving gasps, his head pounding with the angry rhythm of his pulse. Nearby, fighting for stability, Dalus swooped past, stretch wings fully extended. Petulant turbulence buffeted Ica and he over tilted, tumbling briefly in a flurry of mangled wings and tail blades. The descent flattened into an awkward, crippled equilibrium, doomed to fail before long.

The third youth, who had snatched at the pile of gliders moments before the water thundered from the tunnel, cried out nearby. Ica's gaze darted sideways to see the ragged collection of components he'd selected parting like crumbling earth, fragmenting in a cloud of wafting fabrics and spinning shards of metal. The small shape at its epi-centre, arms flailing uselessly, tumbled away towards the ocean. He screamed all the way.

Dalus's trajectory levelled out, once again in front of Ica, and he turned to deliver another infuriating grin, sunken eyes twinkling in – what? Triumph?

Then both twins stared forwards, driven on by the furious gales ripping between the razorpeak summits. To fly into the wind was impossible, retaining balance and altitude was the only recourse. So, bloodied and scarred, exhausted physi-cally and mentally, the twins were silent as before them the Ghostmountain loomed closer.

AFTERWARDS, THE WORLD *was black. Not the dull, dry black-ness of a firestorm or some other act of violence, but rather the polished blackness of sea-slippery rock. The very earth had been torn apart, cleaved up from the rocks below like a scalp from a skull. And yes, there was debris, but not much: no dev-astated huts or mangled vehicles, but rather scattered patches of dust that might once have been homes, or the splattered bloodspray of liquid metal, melted and hurled away by vicious lighting.*

Ica and Dalus crawled from the cellar that had become their burrow, and stared at all that was left of their lives.

On the first day, and even the second, there was no real pain. The despair had yet to descend and instead they wandered the pulverised island in a fugue.

On the third day the reality began to crystallise. They would cry occasionally, though somehow never enough to satisfy the hidden despair. The need to express, to vent, went unresolved. They could not bear to look at one another, nor speak.

On the fourth day, when hunger began to cramp their stom-achs, the numbness began to return. They would find some distraction or task – some beleaguered seabird or semi-successful fishing attempt – and all would seem normal, until the mind allowed itself to wander and the memory of… of events returned. And every time the pain would return: an endless loop of remem-brance and reaction.

On the fifth day the glider came.

'Every male of age thirteen to be present at Table City upon the thirteenth day of the thirteenth lunar month of every year. By Imperial command.'

It almost passed over, sighting from its aerial vantage nothing but the wasted remains of a community: a tribe reduced to a naked rocky crag by the tempest whims of an unstable world.

But Dalus flashed light from a jagged shard of mirror at the distant wraith, and it began the long spiralling descent that would bring it to the last survivors of Kultoom Island.

And they went aboard to die.

TWICE ICA'S STRETCH wings hissed as fabric tore, and twice he found himself lurching impossibly to the left or right, preparing for the terminal descent to the waves below.

Twice the voice in his mind said, Yes – let me die! And twice he righted himself, somehow finding the stability to continue. The Ghostmountain no longer loomed across the horizon of the world. This close, it was the world.

'Where will we land, brother?' Ica called ahead to where Dalus effortlessly hung aloft. His brother didn't reply. Ica called out again, louder this time, 'I said, 'where wi–''

'I heard.' Dalus looked back, piercing his twin with a stare. 'And how should I know?' Then he adjusted his shoulders, dipped forward and streaked ahead.

At times the wind seemed to reach underneath Ica, a seemingly gentle hand to cradle his exposed form, only to hurl him high into the air, or drop away from underneath, leaving him tumbling and helpless. At such moments only fatalistic momentum – the certainty that it made no difference whether one went on or gave in – allowed him to struggle against the pockets and troughs of resistance to stay level.

Every second brought him closer to the Ghostmountain until it seemed to become a planet, tumbling across the horizon of Gathis, to inevitably collide, showering all of existence in chaotic planetary viscera and arterial lava. Ica found himself wishing it would, that he could ride the crest of that fiery cataclysm and burn out in the air, an insignificant spark.

In his abstract state he barely felt the fingers of power that once more delved into his mind. He could barely summon the energy to retch, gagging uselessly at the psychic contact. The voice of Librarian Thryn entered his brain again, stabbing at the back of his eyeballs.

'There…' it hissed, and unbidden his eyes swivelled to a craggy rockface, where – if he winced against the stinging air and focused – he could make out a shadowy recess above a flat ledge. Another cave. Ahead he could see Dalus reacting similarly, face turning to the distant platform.

So the twins tilted their exhausted, ruined bodies towards the ledge, and clumsily, awkwardly, descended.

THE STONE FELT like a bed of feathers, welcoming and cushioning Ica's tumbling form. In some distant part of his brain he was aware of the ruinous landing, vaguely noting the spreading pain but unable to wince or groan.

Dalus was already on his feet, of course. He cast off his stretch wings in a blur, then clenched his fists and punched the air in triumph.

'First!' he called out to the mountain, spinning to stare at his panting brother with eyes full of madness. 'I beat you!'

Ica stammered, uncertain. 'W-what?'

'I beat you. I came first.' Dalus's grin extended further still, an ugly gash in his sallow, pale features. 'Now we'll die, b-but it won't matter because... because when we do you'll know I'm best, and the world will know I came first, and, and–' The grin became something else – a grimace of pain and rage which bubbled up from his eyes and sent tears streaking across his face until his voice cracked and he couldn't continue. Ica stared, astonished and terrified at his twin's tantrum, unable to understand. For the first time since he could remember Dalus looked like a child – shredded and exhausted by a hateful world – but a child nonetheless, with all the petulance and pettiness a child should command.

Then the wind seemed to be rushing directly down upon their heads: a warm gale that grew hotter and hotter. Ica tilted his tired neck and there, descending on a mantle of

smoke and superheated air, was Librarian Thryn. Like a pair
of shimmering wings unfurling from his colossal shoulders,
twin streams of heat diminished slowly until his massive
feet crunched upon the rocks and his metallic form settled.

'Survivors…' he said, sunken eyes drinking in their features. 'Survivors who are dead, and yet live. Hm. Have a care
with feelings of relief, young ones. You'll die yet.'

Ica struggled against the energy filling his brain, twisting
his groans of exhaustion into words. 'W-why? Why do these
things to us?'

Thryn smiled, psychic hood crackling. 'Let us see…' he
hissed.

And the energies reached out and infiltrated the twins'
minds, and they saw–

*Ica's mind was a mountainside. A descending slope of anguish
that neither levelled off nor ended abruptly in a chasm of fatal-
ism. It rushed onwards, descending too far into misery to ever
consider turning about and rescaling, yet too steep and unbroken
to ever reach its suicidal conclusion.*

Ica's own life was worth nothing to him.

To go on, unfeeling and uncaring, was just as easy as giving up.

Librarian Thryn smiled to himself.

Dalus's mind was a minefield of bitterness and pain.

*In every challenge, in every task, there was judgement. There
was his father's attention, grudgingly given and rarely compli-
mentary. There was his mother's love, distant and awkward.*

*And there was Ica. Ica, his father's favourite. Ica, to whom his
mother cried out before her death. Ica who was loved and spoilt.
Ica who could do no wrong. Ica who was an hour older than he.
Ica who would inherit their father's chamack. Ica who, by dint of
sixty Emperor-damned minutes, mattered.*

*Dalus's own life was worth nothing to him. All that mattered
was outdoing his brother, coming first, finally demonstrating to
his parents – far too late – that he the younger brother, he the
runt, he the scorned and unloved and uncared for, that he was the
better!*

*To go on, raging and jealous and desperate for attention, was
far easier than giving up.*

Librarian Thryn frowned.

When reality returned, the wind howled like a child. Ica opened his eyes to a world refracted by tears and Thryn's mournful voice filling his mind.

'All of creation suffers, young ones. Only in accepting our own mortality can we... make a difference. Only in bearing the burden of our failures can we find the strength to go on. Only in detachment from glory, or honour, or jealousy... from life itself can we hope to spare others from grief.

'We are Doom Eagles. And we are already dead.'

A silver gauntlet raised to point at Ica, the extended digit filling his world.

'You may enter, young one. Enter and discover the Eyrie of the Doom Eagles. Enter in humble and thankful service of the Golden Throne. But remember: you have not survived, this day. You are dead now. Never forget.'

And Ica stood, numbly. Nothing was real. Nothing mattered. The wind screamed, almost tearing him away into the abyss, and he staggered, step by step, into the gloom of the cave. Behind him, he knew, Librarian Thryn followed, his hulking frame stalking gracefully into the welcoming shadows beyond.

And he didn't look back, but he could hear the blast door closing, shutting out the rain. He could hear the wind, growing stronger by the second. And he could hear his brother, sobbing gently. Moments before the blast door closed, moments before Ica's life as a peasant of Gathis ended and his non-life as a Doom Eagle began, he heard his twin cry out to the empty, aching universe:

'But I came first! It's not fair!'

And Ica said to himself: No, it's not fair. It's life.

The Ghostmountain sealed with a thump, and the twins, each in their own way, died.

BACKCLOTH FOR A CROWN ADDITIONAL

An Inquisitor Eisenhorn story

Dan Abnett

LORD FROIGRE, MUCH to everyone's dismay including, I'm sure, his own, was dead.

It was a dry, summer morning in 355.M41 and I was taking breakfast with Alizebeth Bequin on the terrace of Spaeton House when I received the news. The sky was a blurry blue, the colour of Sameterware porcelain, and down in the bay the water was a pale lilac, shot through with glittering frills of silver. Sand doves warbled from the drowsy shade of the estate orchards.

Jubal Kircher, my craggy, dependable chief of household security, came out into the day's heat from the garden room, apologised courteously for interrupting our private meal, and handed me a folded square of thin transmission paper.

'Trouble?' asked Bequin, pushing aside her dish of ploin crepes.

'Froigre's dead,' I replied, studying the missive.

'Froigre who?'

'Lord Froigre of House Froigre.'

'You knew him?'

'Very well. I would count him as a friend. Well, how very miserable. Dead at eighty-two. That's no age.'

'Was he ill?' Bequin asked.

'No. Aen Froigre was, if anything, maddeningly robust and healthy. Not a scrap of augmetics about him. You know the sort.' I made this remark pointedly. My career had not been kind to my body. I had been repaired, rebuilt, augmented and generally sewn back together more times than I cared to remember. I was a walking testimonial to Imperial Medicae reconstruction surgery. Alizebeth, on the other hand, still looked like a woman in her prime, a beautiful woman at that, and only the barest minimum of juvenat work had preserved her so.

'According to this, he died following a seizure at his home last night. His family are conducting thorough investigations, of course, but...' I drummed my fingers on the table-top.

'Foul play?'

'He was an influential man.'

'Such men have enemies.'

'And friends,' I said. I handed her the communiqué. 'That's why his widow has requested my assistance.'

But for my friendship with Aen, I'd have turned the matter down. Alizebeth had only just arrived on Gudrun after an absence of almost eighteen months, and would be gone again in a week, so I had resolved to spend as much time with her as possible. The operational demands of the Distaff, based on Messina, kept her away from my side far more than I would have liked.

But this was important, and Lady Froigre's plea too distraught to ignore.

'I'll come with you,' Alizebeth suggested. 'I feel like a jaunt in the country.' She called for a staff car to be brought round from the stable block and we were on our way in under an hour.

FELIPPE GABON, ONE of Kircher's security detail, acted as our driver. He guided the car up from Spaeton on a whisper of thrust and laid in a course for Menizerre. Soon we were cruising south-west over the forest tracts and the verdant cultivated belt outside Dorsay and leaving the Insume headland behind.

In the comfortable, climate-controlled rear cabin of the staff car, I told Alizebeth about Froigre.

'There have been Froigres on Gudrun since the days of the first colonies. Their house is one of the Twenty-Six Venerables, that is to say one of the twenty-six original noble fiefs, and as such has a hereditary seat in the Upper Legislature of the planetary government. Other, newer houses have considerably more power and land these days, but nothing can quite eclipse the prestige of the Venerables. Houses like Froigre, Sangral, Meissian. And Glaw.'

She smiled impishly at my inclusion of that last name.

'So... power, land, prestige... a honeytrap for rivals and enemies. Did your friend have any?'

I shrugged. I'd brought with me several data-slates Psullus had looked out for me from the library. They contained heraldic ledgers, family histories, biographies and memoirs. And very little that seemed pertinent.

'House Froigre vied with House Athensae and House Brudish in the early years of Gudrun, but that's literally ancient history. Besides, House Brudish became extinct after another feud with House Pariti eight hundred years ago. Aen's grandfather famously clashed with Lord Sangral and the then Governor Lord Dougray over the introduction of Founding Levy in the one-nineties, but that was just political, though Dougray never forgave him and later snubbed him by making Richtien chancellor. In recent times, House Froigre has been very much a quiet, solid, traditional seat in the Legislature. No feuds, that I know of. In fact, there hasn't been an inter-house war on Gudrun for seven generations.'

'They all play nicely together, these days, do they?' she asked.

'Pretty much. One of the things I like about Gudrun is that it is so damned civilised.'

'Too damned civilised,' she admonished. 'One day, Gregor, one day this place will lull you into such a deep sense of tranquil seclusion that you'll be caught with your pants down.'

'I hardly think so. It's not complacency, before you jump down my throat. Gudrun – Spaeton House itself – is just a safe place. A sanctuary, given my line of work.'

'Your friend's still dead,' she reminded me.

I sat back. 'He liked to live well. Good food, fine wines. He could drink Nayl under the table.'

'No!'

'I'm not joking. Five years ago, at the wedding of Aen's daughter. I was invited and I took Harlon along as... as I don't know what, actually. You weren't around and I didn't want to go alone. Harlon started bending his lordship's ear with tales of bounty hunting and the last I saw of them they were sprinting their way down their fourth bottle of anise at five in the morning. Aen was up at nine the next day to see his daughter off. Nayl was still asleep at nine the following day.'

She grinned. 'So a life of great appetites may have just caught up with him?'

'Perhaps. Though you'd think that would have shown up on the medicae mortus's report.'

'So you do suspect foul play?'

'I can't shake that idea.'

I was silent for a few minutes, and Alizebeth scrolled her way through several of the slates.

'House Froigre's main income was from mercantile dealings. They hold a twelve point stock in Brade ent Cie and a fifteen per cent share in Helican SubSid Shipping. What about trade rivals?'

'We'd have to expand our scope off-planet. I suppose assassination is possible, but that's a strange way to hit back at a trade rival. I'll have to examine their records. If we can turn up signs of a clandestine trade fight, then maybe assassination is the answer.'

'Your friend spoke out against the Ophidian Campaign.'

'So did his father. Neither believed it was appropriate to divert funds and manpower into a war of reconquest in the sub-sector next door when there was so much to put in order on the home front.'

'I was just wondering...' she said.

'Wonder away, but I think that's a dead end. The Ophidian War's long since over and done with and I don't think anyone cares what Aen thought about it.'

'So have you got a theory?'

'Only the obvious ones. None of them with any substantiating data. An internecine feud, targeting Aen from inside the family. A murder driven by some secret affair of the heart. A darker conspiracy that remains quite invisible for now. Or...'

'Or?'

'Too much good living, in which case we'll be home before nightfall.'

FROIGRE HALL, THE ancestral pile of the noble House Froigre, was a splendid stack of ivy-swathed ouslite and copper tiles overlooking the Vale of Fiegg, ten kilometres south of Menizerre. Water meadows sloped back from the river, becoming wildflower pastures that climbed through spinneys of larch and fintle to hem the magnificent planned gardens of the house; geometric designs of box-hedge, trim lawn, flowering beds and symmetrical ponds. Beyond the sandy drive, darkened woods came right down to skirt the back of the great hall, except for where a near-perfect sulleq lawn had been laid. Aen and I had spent several diverting afternoons there, playing against each other. A kilometre north of the house, the gnarled stone finger of the Folly rose from the ascending woods.

'Where to put down, sir?' Gabon asked over the intercom.

'On the drive in front of the portico, if you'd be so kind.'

'What's been going on here?' Alizebeth asked as we came in lower. She pointed. The lawn areas nearest to the hall were littered with scraps of rubbish – paper waste and glittery bits of foil. Some sections of grass were flat and yellow as if compressed and starved of light.

Tiny stones, whipped up by our downwash, ticked off the car's bodywork as we settled in to land.

'OH, MY DEAR Gregor!' Lady Freyl Froigre almost fell into my arms. I held her in a comforting embrace for a few patient moments as she sobbed against my chest.

'Forgive me!' she said suddenly, pulling away and dabbing her eyes with a black lace handkerchief. 'This is all so very terrible. So very, very terrible.'

'My deepest sympathies for your loss, lady,' I said, feeling awkward.

A houseman, his arm banded in black, had led us into a stateroom off the main hall where Lady Froigre was waiting. The blinds were drawn, and mourning tapers had been lit, filling the air with a feeble light and a sickly perfume. Freyl Froigre was a stunning woman in her late sixties, her lush red hair, almost flame-pink it was so bright, pulled back and pinned down under a veil coiff of jet scamiscoire. Her grief-gown was slate epinchire, the sleeves ending in delicate interwoven gloves so that not one speck of her flesh was uncovered.

I introduced Alizebeth, who murmured her condolences, and Lady Froigre nodded. Then she suddenly looked flustered.

'Oh, my. Where are my manners? I should have the staff bring refreshments for you and–'

'Hush, lady,' I said, taking her arm and walking her down the long room into the soft shade of the shutters. 'You have enough on your mind. Grief is enough. Tell me what you know and I will do the rest.'

'You're a good man, sir. I knew I could trust you.' She paused and waited while her current wracks subsided.

'Aen died just before midnight last night. A seizure. It was quick, the physician said.'

'What else did he say, lady?'

She drew a data-wand from her sleeve and handed it to me. 'It's all here.' I plucked out my slate and plugged it in. The display lit up with the stored files.

Death by tremorous palpitations of the heart and mind. A dysfunction of the spirit. According to the the medicae's report, Aen Froigre had died because of a spasm in his anima.

'This means...' I paused, '...nothing. Who is your physician?'

'Genorus Notil of Menizerre. He has been the family medicae since the time of Aen's grandfather.'

'His report is rather... non-specific, lady. Could I present the body for a further examination?'

'I've already done that,' she said softly. 'The surgeon at Menizerre General who attended said the same. My husband died of terror.'

'Terror?'

'Yes, inquisitor. Now tell me that isn't the work of the infernal powers?'

There had, she told me, been a celebration. A Grand Fete. Aen's eldest son, Rinton, had returned home two weeks before, having mustered out of his service in the Imperial Guard. Rinton Froigre had been a captain in the Fiftieth Gudrunite and seen six years' service in the Ophidean Subsector. Such was his father's delight on his return, a fete was called. A carnival feast. Travelling players from all around the canton had attended, along with troupes of musicians, acrobats, armies of stall holders, entertainers, and hundreds of folk from the town. That explained the litter and faded patches on the lawn. Tent pitches. The scars of marquees.

'Had he any enemies?' I asked, pacing the shuttered room.

'None that I know of.'

'I would like to review his correspondence. Diaries too, if he kept them.'

'I'll see. I don't believe he kept a diary, but our rubricator will have a list of correspondence.'

On the top of the harpsichord was a framed portrait, a hololith of Aen Froigre, smiling.

I picked it up and studied it.

'The last portrait of him,' she said. 'Taken at the fete. My last connection with him.'

'Where did he die?'

'The Folly,' said Lady Froigre. 'He died in the Folly.'

THE WOODS WERE damp and dark. Boughs creaked in the late afternoon wind and odd birdsong trilled from the shadows.

The Folly was a stone drum capped by a slate needle. Inside, it was bare and terribly musty. Sand doves fluttered up in the roof spaces. Cobwebs glazed the bare windows.

'This is where I found him,' said a voice from behind me.

I turned. Rinton Froigre stooped in under the doorframe. He was a well-made boy of twenty-five, with his mother's lush red hair. His eyes had a curious, hooded aspect.

'Rinton.'

'Sir,' he bowed slightly.

'Was he dead when you found him?'

'No, inquisitor. He was laughing and talking. He liked to come up here. He loved the Folly. I came up to thank him for the fete that he had thrown in my honour. We were talking together when suddenly he went into convulsions. Just minutes later, before I could summon help, he was dead.'

I didn't know Rinton Froigre well, though his service record was very respectable, and I knew his father had been proud of him. Aen had never mentioned any animosity from his son, but in any noble house there is always the spectre of succession to consider. Rinton had been alone with his father at the time of death. He was a seasoned soldier, undoubtedly no stranger to the act of killing.

I kept an open mind – literally. Even without any invasive mental probing, it is possible for a psionic of my ability to sense surface thoughts. There was no flavour of deceit about Rinton's person, though I could feel carefully contained loss, and the tingle of trepidation. Small wonder, I considered. Uncommon are the citizens of the Imperium who do not register anxiety at being quizzed by an inquisitor of the Holy Ordos.

There was no point pressing him now. Rinton's story might easily be put to the test with an auto-seance, during which psychometric techniques would simply reveal the truth of his father's last moments to me.

Rinton walked me back to the Hall, and left me to my ponderings in Aen's study. It was as he had left it, I was told.

The room was half-panelled and lined for the most part with glazed shelves of neatly bound books and data-slates. Discreet glow-globes hovered around the edges of the room at head-height, set to a low luminosity, and a selection of scroll-backed couches and over-stuffed chairs were arranged in front of the high-throated ceramic fireplace with its wood-burning fusion stove.

The desk, under the diamond-paned west windows, was a wide crescent of polished duralloy floated a metre off the carpet by passive suspensor pods. The desk was clean and bare.

I sat at it, depressing slightly the hydraulics of the writing chair – I was half a head taller than Aen Froigre. I studied the mirror-smooth, slightly raked surface of the desk. There was no sign of any control panel, but a gentle wave of my hand across it woke up heat-sensitive touch-plates engraved into the duralloy's finish. I touched a few, but they needed Aen's touch – probably a combination of palmprint and genekey – to unlock them.

That, or Inquisition-grade software. I unpinned my Inquisitorial rosette, which I had been wearing on the sternum of a my black leather coat, and slid open the signal port. Holding it low over the desk, I force fed the touch-plates with several magenta-level security override programs. It gave up the fight almost at once, opening systems without even the need for passwords.

Built into the stylish desk – an item of furniture that had clearly cost Aen a lot of money – was a fairly powerful cogitator, a vox-pict uplink, a message archive, two filing archives, and a master control for the simple, limited electronic systems built into the Hall. Separate pages of each file and message could be displayed as a facsimile on the blotter plate and a touch of a finger turned them or put them away. Aen had destroyed all paper records.

I played with it for some time, but the most interesting thing I found was a log of invoices for services provided at the fete, and a list of the invitations. I copied both into my own data-slate.

Alizebeth and Gabon arrived while I was busy with that. Alizebeth had been interviewing the household staff, and Gabon had been out, walking the grounds.

'There were over nine hundred guests here, sir,' he said, 'and maybe another five hundred players, musicians, entertainers and carnival folk.'

'Where from?'

'Menizerre, mostly,' he replied. 'Local entertainers, a few troubadours and some street tumblers from the biweekly textile market. The biggest individual groups were Kalikin's Company, an acclaimed troupe of travelling actors, and Sunsable's Touring Fair, who provided the games and rides and diversions.'

I nodded. Gabon was as thorough as usual. A short, spare man in his one fifties with cropped black hair and a bushy moustache, he had been with the Dorsay Arbites for about seventy years before retiring into private service. He wore a simple, refined dark blue suit that had been ingeniously tailored to hide the fact that he was wearing a handgun in a shoulder rig.

'What about you?' I asked Alizebeth. She sat down on one of the couches.

'Nothing scintillating. The staff seem genuinely shocked and upset at the death. They all react with outrage at the idea your friend might have had any enemies.'

'It seems quite clear to me that he did have some,' I said.

Alizebeth reached into the folds of her gown and fished out a small, hard object. She tossed it across onto the desk top and it landed with a tap. There it extended four, multi-jointed limbs and scurried across onto my palm.

I turned the wriggling poison-snooper over and pressed the recessed stud on its belly. A little ball of hololithic energy coalesced above its head-mounted projector and I read it as it slowly scrolled around on its own axis.

'Traces of lho, obscura and several other class II and III narcotics in the garden area and the staff quarters. Penshel seed traces found in the stable block. More lho, as well as listeria and e. coli in small amounts in the kitchen section... hmmm...'

Alizebeth shrugged. 'The usual mix of recreational drugs one might expect, none in large quantities, and the kitchens's as hygienic as anywhere. You'd probably get the same sort of readings from Spaeton House.'

'Probably. Penshel seeds, they're quite unusual.'

'A very mild stimulant,' said Gabon. 'I didn't know anyone still used that stuff. Time was, it was the drug of choice in the artists' quarter of Dorsay, back when I was on the force. The seeds are dried, rolled and smoked in pipes. A little bohemian, an old man's smoke.'

'Most of the outdoor traces can be put down to the visiting entertainers,' I mused, 'plus a little off-duty pleasure from the staff or loose-living guests. What about the stable block? Are any of Froigre's ostlers penshel smokers?'

Alizebeth shook her head. 'They'd cleared large parts of the stable area to provide spaces for the fair stall-holders.'

I put the snooper down on the desk and it wriggled back and forth for a few moments until it got enough purchase to right itself. 'So nothing untoward, in fact. And certainly no significant toxins.'

'None at all,' said Alizebeth.

Damn. Given the description of Aen's death, I had been quite sure poison was the key, perhaps some assassin's sophisticated toxin that had not shown up on the initial medicae report. But Alizebeth's snooper was high-grade and thorough.

'What do we do now?' she asked.

I passed her my data-slate. 'Send the contents of this to Aemos by direct vox-link. See what he can come up with.'

Uber Aemos was my ancient and trusted savant. If anyone could see a pattern or make a connection, it was him.

EVENING FELL. I went outside, alone. I felt annoyed and frustrated. In fact, I felt thwarted. I'd come there as a favour to my old friend's widow, offering my services, and in most respects I was overqualified. I was an Imperial inquisitor, and this was most likely just a job for the local arbites. I had expected to have the entire matter sewn up in a few hours, to settle things swiftly in a quick, unofficial investigation, and leave with the thanks of the family for sparing them a long, drawn-out inquest.

But the clues just weren't there. There was no motive, no obvious antagonist, no aggressor, but still it seemed likely that Aen Froigre had been killed. I looked at the medicae report again, hoping to find something that would establish natural causes.

Nothing. Something, someone, had taken my friend's life, but I couldn't tell what or who or why.

The evening skies were dark, stained a deep violet and smeared with chasing milky clouds. An early moon shone, passing behind the running trails of cloud every minute or so. A wind was gathering, and the stands of trees beside the lawn were beginning to sway and swish. The leaves made a cold sound, like rain.

I walked over to my flyer, popped the cargo trunk and took out Barbarisater. I slowly freed it from its silk bindings and drew the long, gleaming blade from its machined scabbard. Barbarisater had been an heirloom sword, a psychically attuned weapon from the forges of distant Carthae and slaved to the minds of the generations of warrior women who had wielded it. Enhancing its strength with pentagrammic wards, I had used the long sabre in my battle against the heretic Quixos, during which struggle it had been broken below the tip. Master swordsmiths had remade the blade from the broken main portion, creating a shorter, straighter blade by rounding off and edging the break and reducing the hilt. A good deal smaller than its old self, now more a single-handed rapier than a hand-and-a-half sabre, it was still a potent weapon.

Naked, in my hand, it hummed and whined as my mind ran through it and made it resonate. The incised wards glowed and sobbed out faint wisps of smoke. I walked out over the grass under the seething trees, holding the blade out before me like a dowsing rod, sweeping the scene, letting the blade-tip slide along the invisible angles of space. Twice, on my circuit of the lawns, it twitched as if tugged by sprite hands, but I could discern nothing from the locations.

But there was something there. My first hint of a malign focus. My first hint that not only was foul play involved, but that Lady Froigre might be right.

Though they had left only the slightest traces behind them, infernal powers had been at work here.

* * *

ALIZEBETH CAME INTO my room at eight the next morning. She woke me by sitting down on the side of my bed and handed me a cup of hot, black caffeine as I roused.

She was already dressed and ready for work. The day was bright. I could hear the household coming to life: pans clattering in the kitchen block and the butler calling to his pages in the nearby gallery.

'Bad storm in the night,' she said. 'Brought trees down.'

'Really?' I grumbled, sitting up and sipping the sweet, dark caffeine.

I looked at her. It wasn't like Bequin to be so perky this early.

'Out with it,' I said.

She handed me a data-slate. 'Aemos has been busy. Must've worked all night.'

'Through the storm.'

'There was no storm up his way. It was local.' I didn't really hear that reply. I was caught up in a close reading of the slate.

Failing to cross-match just about every detail I had sent him, Aemos had clearly become bored. The list of guests I had sent him had led to nothing, despite his best efforts to make connections. The caterers and performers had revealed nothing either. No links to the underworld or cult activity, no misdeeds or priors, except for the usual clutch of innocent and minor violations one might expect. One of the travelling actors had been charged with affray twenty years before, and another had done time for grievous wounding, that sort of thing.

The only item that had flagged any sort of connection was the description of Aen Froigre's death. Aemos had only turned to that rather vague clue once he'd exhausted all others.

In the past twenty months, eleven people in the Drunner Region of Gudrun, which is to say the coastal area encompassing Menizerre, Dorsay and Insume all the way to Madua chapeltown, had died of a similar, mystery ailment. Only a tight, deliberate search like the one Aemos had conducted would have shown up such a connection, given the scale of area involved and the size of population. Listed together, the deaths stood out like a sore thumb.

Here, Aemos had come into his own. Another clerk might have sent those findings to me and waited for direction, but Aemos, hungry to answer the questions himself, had pressed on, trying to make a pattern out of them. No simple task. There was nothing to demographically or geographically link the victims. A housewife here, a millkeeper there, a landowner in one small village, a community doctor in another, seventy kilometres away.

The only thing they had in common was the sudden, violent and inexplicable nature of their demises: seizures, abrupt, fatal.

I set down my cup and scrolled on, aware that Alizebeth was grinning at me.

'Get to the last bit,' she advised. 'Aemos strikes again.'

Right at the last, Aemos revealed another connection.

A day or two before each death, the victim's locality had been paid a visit by Sunsable's Touring Fair.

LADY FROIGRE WAS most perturbed to see us about to leave. 'There are questions here still...' she began.

'And I'm going to seek the answers,' I said. 'Trust me. I believe my savant has hit upon something.'

She nodded, unhappy. Rinton stepped forward and put his arm around his mother's shoulders.

'Trust me,' I repeated and walked out across the drive to my waiting flyer.

I could hear the sound of chain blades, and turned from the car to walk around the side of the hall. One of the trees brought down in the night's freak storm had crushed part of the stable block and the housemen were working to saw up the huge trunk and clear it.

'Is that where you detected Penshel seed?' I asked Alizebeth when she came to find out what was keeping me.

'Yes,' she said.

'Fetch my blade.'

I called the housemen away from their work, and walked into the collapsed ruin of the stable, crunching over heaps of coarse sawdust. The ivy-clad tree still sprawled through the burst roof.

Alizebeth brought me Barbarisater and I drew it quickly. By then Lady Froigre and Rinton Froigre had emerged to see what I was doing.

Barbarisater hummed in my hand, louder and more throatily than it had done the previous night. As soon as I entered that part of the stable block, the particular stall the tree had smashed, it jumped. The taste of Chaos was here.

'What was this used for?' I asked. 'During the fete, what was this area used for?'

'Storage,' said Lady Froigre. 'The people from the fair wanted to keep equipment and belongings out of sight. Food too, I think. One man had trays of fresh figs he wanted to keep out of the light.'

'And the hololithographer,' said Rinton. 'He used one of those stalls as a dark room.'

So HOW DO you find a travelling fair in an area the size of the Drunner Region? If you have a copy of their most recent invoice, it's easy. The fair-master, eager to be paid for his services at Froigre Hall, had left as a payment address an inn eighty kilometres away in Seabrud. From the invoice, I saw that Aen had been asked to mail the payment within five days. The fair moved around a great deal, and the travelling folk didn't believe much in the concept of credit accounts.

From Seabrud, we got a fix on the location of Sunsable's Fair.

They had pitched on a meadow outside the village of Brudmarten, a little, rustic community of ket-herds and weavers that was flanked by a lush, deciduous woodland hillside to the east and marshy, cattle-trampled fields below at the river spill to the west.

It was late afternoon on a hot, close day, the air edged with the heavy, fulminous threat of storms. The sky was dark overhead, but the corn was bright and golden down in the meadows, and pollen balls blew in the breeze like thistle-fibres. Grain-crakes whooped in the corn stands, and small warblers of the most intense blue darted across the hedges.

Gabon lowered the limo to rest in a lane behind the village kirk, a pale, Low Gothic temple in need of upkeep. A noble statue of the Emperor Immaculate stood in the overgrown graveyard, a roost for wood doves. I buckled on my sword and covered it with a long leather cloak. Gabon locked the car.

'Stay with me,' I told Alizebeth, and then turned to Gabon. 'Shadow us.'

'Yes, sir.'

We walked down the lane towards the fair.

Even from a distance, we could hear the noise and feel the energy. The arrival of the fair had brought the folk of Brudmarten and the neighbouring hamlets out in force. Pipe organs were trilling and wheezing in the lank air, and there was the pop and whizz of firecrackers. I could hear laughter, the clatter of rides, the ringing of score bells, children screaming, rowdy men carousing, pistons hissing. The smell of warm ale wafted from the tavern tent.

The gate in the meadow's hedge had been turned into an entranceway, arched with a gaudy, handpainted sign that declared Sunsable's Miraculous Fair of Fairs open. A white-eyed twist at the gateway took our coins for admission.

Inside, on the meadow, all manner of bright, vulgar sights greeted us. The carousel, lit up with gas-lamps. The ring-toss. The neat, pink box-tent of the clairvoyant. The churning hoop of the whirligig, spilling out the squeals of children. The colourful shouts of the freak show barker. The burnt-sugar smell of floss makers. The clang of test-your-strength machines.

For a penny, you could ride the shoulders of a Battle Titan – actually an agricultural servitor armoured with painted sections of rusty silage hopper. For another penny, you could shoot greenskins in the las-gallery, or touch the Real and Completely Genuine shin bone of Macharius, or dunk for ploins. For tuppence, you could gaze into the Eye of Terror and have your heroism judged by a hooded man with a stutter who claimed to be an ex-Space Marine. The Eye of Terror in this case was a pit dug in the ground and filled with chemical lamps and coloured glass filters.

Nearby, a small donation allowed you to watch an oiled man struggle free from chains, or a burning sack, or a tin bathtub full of broken glass, or a set of stocks.

'Just a penny, sir, just a penny!' howled a man on stilts with a harlequined face as he capered past me. 'For the young lady!'

I decided not to ask what my penny might buy.

'I want to go look at the freak show,' Alizebeth told me.

'Save your money... it's all around us,' I growled.

We pushed on. Coloured balloons drifted away over the field into the encroaching darkness of the thunderhead. Corn crickets rasped furiously in the trampled stalks all about us. Drunken, painted faces swam at us, some lacking teeth, some with glittering augmetic eyes.

'Over there,' I whispered to Alizebeth.

Past the brazier stand of a woman selling paper cones of sugared nuts, and a large handcart stacked with wire cages full of songbirds, was a small booth tent of heavy red material erected at the side of a brightly painted trailer. A wooden panel raised on bunting-wrapped posts announced 'Hololiths! Most Lifelike! Most Agreeable!' below which a smaller notice said 'A most delightful gift, or a souvenir of the day, captured by the magic art of a master hololithographer.' A frail old man with tufted white hair and small spectacles was seated outside the booth on a folding canvas chair, eating a meat pie that was so hot he had to keep blowing on it.

'Why don't you go and engage his interest?' I suggested.

Alizebeth left my side, pushed through the noisy crowd and stopped by his booth. A sheet of flakboard had been erected beside the booth's entrance, and on it were numerous hololithic pictures mounted for display: some miniatures, some landscapes, some family groups. Alizebeth studied them with feigned interest. The old man immediately leapt up off his chair, stowed the half-eaten pie behind the board and brushed the crumbs off his robes. I moved round to the side, staying in the crowd, watching. I paused to examine the caged birds, though in fact I was looking through their cages at the booth tent.

The old man approached Bequin courteously.

'Madam, good afternoon! I see your attention has been arrested by my display of work. Are they not fairly framed and well-composed?'

'Indeed,' she said.

'You have a good eye, madam,' he said, 'for so often in these country fairs the work of the hololithgrapher is substandard. The composition is frequently poor and the plate quality fades with time. Not so with your humble servant. I have plied this trade of portraiture for thirty years and I fancy I have skill for it. You see this print here? The lakeshore at Entreve?'

'It is a pleasing scene.'

'You are very kind, madam. It is handcoloured, like many of my frames. But this very print was made in the summer of... 329, if my memory serves. And you'll appreciate, there is no fading, no loss of clarity, no discolouration.'

'It has preserved itself well.'

'It has,' he agreed, merrily. 'I have patented my own techniques, and I prepare the chemical compounds for the plates by hand, in my modest studio adjoining.' He gestured to his trailer. 'That is how I can maintain the quality and the perfect grade of the hololiths, and reproduce and print them to order with no marked loss of standard from original to duplicate. My reputation rests upon it. Up and down the byways of the land, the name Bakunin is a watchword for quality portraiture.'

Alizebeth smiled. 'It's most impressive, Master Bakunin. And how much...?'

'Aha!' he grinned. 'I thought you might be tempted, madam, and may I say it would be a crime for your beauty to remain unrecorded! My services are most affordable.'

I moved round further, edging my way to the side of his booth until he and Alizebeth were out of sight behind the awning. I could hear him still making his pitch to her.

On the side of the trailer, further bold statements and enticements were painted in a flourishing script. A large sign read 'Portraits two crowns, group scenes three crowns, gilded miniatures a half-crown only, offering many a striking and famous backcloth for a crown additional.'

I wandered behind the trailer. It was parked at the edge of the fairground, near to a copse of fintle and yew that screened the meadow from pastures beyond the ditch. It was damp and shaded here, small animals rustling in the thickets. I tried to look in at one small window, but it was shuttered. I touched the side of the trailer and felt Barbarisater twitch against my hip. There was a door near the far end of the trailer. I tried it, but it was locked.

'What's your business?' growled a voice.

Three burly fairground wranglers had approached along the copse-side of the booths. They had been smoking lhosticks behind their trailer on a break.

'Not yours,' I assured them.

'You had best be leaving Master Bakunin's trailer alone,' one said. All three were built like wrestlers, their bared arms stained with crude tattoos. I had no time for this.

'Go away now,' I said, pitching my will through my voice. They all blinked, not quite sure what had happened to their minds, and then simply walked away as if I wasn't there.

I returned my attention to the door, and quickly forced the lock with my multi-key. To my surprise, the thin wooden door still refused to open. I wondered if it was bolted from inside, but as I put more weight into it, it did shift a little, enough to prove there there was nothing physical holding it. Then it banged back shut as if drawn by immense suction.

My pulse began to race. I could feel the sour tang of warpcraft in the air and Barbarisater was now vibrating in its scabbard. It was time to dispense with subtleties.

I paced around to the front of the booth, but there was no longer any sign of Bequin or the old man. Stooping, I went in under the entrance flap. An inner drop curtain of black cloth stopped exterior light from entering the tent.

I pushed that aside.

'I will be with you shortly, sir,' Bakunin called, 'if you would give me a moment.'

'I'm not a customer,' I said. I looked around. The tent was quite small, and lit by the greenish glow of gas mantles that

ran, I supposed, off the trailer supply. Alizebeth was sat at
the far side on a ladderback chair with a dropcloth of cream
felt behind her. Bakunin was facing her, carefully adjusting
his hololithic camera, a brass and teak machine mounted
on a wooden tripod. He looked round at me curiously, his
hands still polishing a brass-rimmed lens. Alizebeth rose out
of her seat.

'Gregor?' she asked.

'The good lady is just sitting for a portrait, sir. It's all very
civilised.' Bakunin peered at me, unsure what to make of
me. He smiled and offered his hand. 'I am Bakunin, artist
and hololithographer.'

'I am Eisenhorn, Imperial inquisitor.'

'Oh,' he said and took a step backwards. 'I... I...'

'You're wondering why a servant of the ordos has just
walked into your booth,' I finished for him. Bakunin's mind
was like an open book. There was, I saw at once, no guile
there, except for the natural money-making trickery of a fairground rogue. Whatever else he was, Bakunin was no
heretic.

'You took a portrait of Lord Froigre at the fete held on his
lands just the other day?' I said, thinking of the picture on
the harpsichord back at the hall.

'I did,' he said. 'His lordship was pleased. I made no
charge for the work, sir. It was a gift to thank his lordship
for his hospitality. I thought perhaps some of his worthy
friends might see the work and want the like for themselves,
I...'

He doesn't know, I thought. He has no clue what this is
about. He's trying to work out how he might have drawn
this investigation to himself.

'Lord Froigre is dead,' I told him.

He went pale. 'No, that's... that's...'

'Master Bakunin... do you know if any other of your previous subjects have died? Died soon after your work was
complete?'

'I don't, I'm sure. Sir, what are you implying?'

'I have a list of names,' I said, unclipping my data-slate.
'Do you keep records of your work?'

'I keep them all, all the exposed plates, in case that copies or replacements are needed. I have full catalogues of all pictures.'

I showed him the slate. 'Do you recognise any of these names?'

His hands were shaking. He said, 'I'll have to check them against my catalogue,' but I knew for a fact he'd recognised some of them at once.

'Let's do that together,' I said. Alizebeth followed us as we went through the back of the tent into the trailer. It was a dark, confined space, and Bakunin kept apologising. Every scrap of surface, even the untidy flat of his little cot bed, was piled with spares and partly disassembled cameras. There was a musty, chemical stink, mixed with the scent of Penshel seeds. Bakunin's pipe lay in a small bowl. He reached into a crate under the cot and pulled out several dog-eared record books.

'Let me see now,' he began.

There was a door at the end of the little room. 'What's through there?'

'My dark room, along with the file racks for the exposed plates.'

'It has a door to the outside?'

'Yes,' he said.

'Locked?'

'No...'

'You have an assistant then, someone you ordered to hold the door shut?'

'I have no assistant...' he said, puzzled.

'Open this door,' I told him. He put down the books and went to the communicating door. Just from his body language, I could tell he had been expecting it to open easily.

'I don't understand,' he said. 'It's never jammed before.'

'Stand back,' I said, and drew Barbarisater. The exposed blade filled the little trailer with ozone and Bakunin yelped.

I put the blade through the door with one good swing and ripped it open. There was a loud bang of atmospheric decompression, and fetid air swept over us. A dark, smoky haze drifted out.

'Emperor of Mankind, what is that?'

'Warpcraft,' I said. 'You say you mix your own oxides and solutions?'

'Yes.'

'Where do you get your supplies from?'

'Everywhere, here and there, sometimes from apothecaries, or market traders or...'

Anywhere. Bakunin had experimented with all manner of compounds over the years to create the best, most effective plates for his camera. He'd never been fussy about where the active ingredients came from. Something in his workshop, something in his rack of flasks and bottles, was tainted.

I took a step towards the dark room. In the half-light, things were flickering, half-formed and pale. The baleful energies lurking in Bakunin's workshop could sense I was a threat, and were trying to protect themselves by sealing the doors tight to keep me out.

I crossed the threshold into the dark room. Alizebeth's cry of warning was lost in the shrieking of tormented air that suddenly swirled around me. Glass bottles and flasks of mineral tincture vibrated wildly in metal racks above Bakunin's work bench. Jars of liquid chemicals and unguent oils shattered and sprayed their contents into the air. The little gas-jet burner flared and ignited, its rubber tube thrashing like a snake. Glass plates, each a square the size of a data-slate, and each sleeved in a folder of tan card, were jiggling and working themselves out of the wooden racks on the far side of the blacked out room. There were thousands of them, each one the master exposure of one of Bakunin's hololiths. The first yanked clear of the shelf as if tugged by a sucking force, and I expected it to shatter on the floor, but it floated in the air. Quickly others followed suit. Light from sources I couldn't locate played in the air, casting specks and flashes of colour all around. The air itself became dark brown, like tobacco.

I raised my sword. A negative plate came flying at my head and I struck at it. Shards of glass flew in all directions. Another came at me and I smashed that too. More flew from the shelves like a spray of playing cards, whipping through the air towards me. I made a series of quick *uwe sar* and *ulsar* parries, bursting the glass squares as they struck in. I missed one, and it sliced my cheek with its edge before hitting the wall behind me like a throwing knife.

'Get him out of here!' I yelled to Alizebeth. The trailer was shaking. Outside there was a crash of thunder and rain started to hammer on the low roof. The hurtling plates were driving me back, and Barbarisater had become a blur in my hands as it struck out to intercept them all.

Then the ghosts came. Serious men in formal robes. Gentlewomen in long gowns. Solemn children with pale faces. A laughing innkeeper with blotchy cheeks. Two farmhands, with their arms around each other's shoulders. More, still more, shimmering in the dirty air, made of smoke, their skins white, their clothes sepia, their expressions frozen at the moment they had been caught by the camera.

They clawed and tugged at me with fingers of ice, pummelled me with psychokinetic fists. Some passed through me like wraiths, chilling my marrow. The malevolence hiding in that little trailer was conjuring up all the images Bakunin had immortalised in his career, ripping them off the negative plates and giving them form.

I staggered back, tears appearing in my cloak. Their touch was as sharp as the edge of the glass plates. Their hollow screaming filled my ears. Then, with a sickening lurch, the world itself distorted and changed. The trailer was gone. For a moment I was standing on a sepia shoreline, then I was an uninvited guest at a country wedding. My sword hacking and flashing, I stumbled on into a baptism, then a colourised view of the Atenate Mountains, then a feast in a guild hall.

The ghosts surged at me, frozen hands clawing. The innkeeper with the blotchy cheeks got his icy fists around my throat though his face was still open in laughter. I chopped Barbarisater through him and he billowed like smoke. A sad-faced housemaid pulled at my arm and a fisherman struck at me with his boat hook.

I began to recite the Litany of Salvation, yelling it into the leering faces that beset me. A few crumpled and melted like cellulose exposed to flame.

I heard gunshots. Gabon was to my right, firing his weapon. He was standing on the pier at Dorsay at sunset, in the middle of a inter-village game of knockball, and a harvest festival, all at the same time. The conflicting scenes blurred and merged around him. A bride and her groom, along with five mourners from a funeral and a retiring arbites constable in full medals, were attacking him.

'Get back!' I yelled. Barbarisater was glowing white-hot. Thunder crashed again, shaking the earth. Gabon shrieked as the bride's fingers ripped through his face, and as he stumbled backwards, whizzing glass plates chopped into him like axe heads.

His blood was in the air, like rain. It flooded into the ghosts and stained their sepia tones crimson and their pale flesh pink. I felt fingers like knives draw across the flesh of my arms and back. There were too many of them.

I couldn't trust my eyes. According to them, I was standing on a riverbank, and also the front steps of an Administratum building. The locations overlaid each other impossibly, and neither was real.

I leapt, and lashed out with my blade. I hit something, tore through and immediately found myself rolling on the rain-sodden turf behind the trailer.

Lightning split the darkness overhead and the rain was torrential. The storm and the bizarre activity around Bakunin's booth had sent the commonfolk fleeing from the meadow. The trailer was still vibrating and shaking, and oily brown smoke was gushing from the hole in the side wall I'd cut to break my way out. Inside, lights crackled and flashed and the phantom screaming continued. The warpaint was berserk.

Bakunin appeared, looking desperate, with Alizebeth close behind him. He put his hands to his mouth in shock at the sight of me torn and bloodied.

'Where is it?' I snarled.

'Third shelf up, above the workbench,' he stammered. 'The green bottle. I needed tincture of mercury, years ago, years ago, and an old woman in one of the villages gave it to me and said it would do as well. I use it all the time now.

The emulsions it mixes are perfect. My work has never been better.'

He looked down at the grass, shaking and horrified. 'I should have realised,' he muttered. 'I should have realised. No matter how much I used, the bottle never emptied.'

'Third shelf up?' I confirmed.

'I'll show you,' he said, and sprang to the trailer, clambering in through the hole I had smashed.

'Bakunin! No!'

I followed him inside, tumbling back into the jumble of landscapes and the maelstrom of screaming ghosts. Just for a moment, a brief moment, I saw Aen Froigre amongst them.

Then I was falling through another wedding, a hunting scene, a stockman's meeting, a farrier's smithy, the castle of Elempite by moonlight, a cattle market, a–

I heard Bakunin scream.

I deflected three more deadly hololith plates, and slashed through the thicket of howling ghosts. Spectral, as if it wasn't there, I saw the workbench and the shelves. The green bottle, glowing internally with jade fire.

I raised Barbarisater and smashed the bottle with the edge of the shivering blade.

The explosion shredded the inner partition wall and lurched the trailer onto its side. Dazed, I lay on the splintered wall, sprawled amongst the debris of glass and wood.

The screaming stopped.

SOMEONE HAD CALLED the local arbites. They moved in through the crowds of onlookers as the last of the rain fell and the skies began to clear.

I showed them my credentials and told them to keep the crowd back while I finished my work. The trailer was already burning, and Alizebeth and I threw the last few hololith prints into the flames.

The pictures were fading now. Superimposed on each one, every portrait, every landscape, every miniature, was a ghost exposure. An after-image.

Bakunin, screaming his last scream forever.

FIRESTARTER

Jonathon Green

'WELL, SOMEONE KNOWS who it was!' Antrobus Vetch yelled at the cowering Gravalax Mune, his reedy voice becoming even more high-pitched as he berated his underling. 'Someone informed the Arbites that the cargo had been brought into Hive Primus. We've already established it was those whispering Delaque snakes from the Network who first found out about it, but it wasn't them who told the authorities, was it, hmm?'

'No, my lord,' Mune replied, 'we are certain of that. The Network are information-brokers. They sold the information about the deal on to a third party. Your spies have confirmed that much.'

'Yes, my agents are very thorough,' Vetch said, suddenly quietly conspiratorial. He fixed his servant with his beady, black pinpricks of eyes. 'Well, some of them are,' he added, 'but that doesn't change the fact that someone else informed the Adeptus Arbites, does it, hmm?'

'No, my lord,' Mune responded weakly.

'Well how do you suggest we find out who did, hmm?' Vetch screeched, flecks of spittle flying from his thin lips.

Gravalax Mune averted his gaze from the enraged Guilder, unable to bear his piercing gaze. His heart pounding, Mune desperately tried to think of a solution to Vetch's problem but his mind with fogged with panic. All he could think of was what his master might do to him if he didn't come up with a decent suggestion, or rather what the Guilder would get his servitor slaves to do to him.

Antrobus Vetch wasn't an imposing man physically. He was tiny, well under two metres tall, with spindly limbs and a head that seemed slightly overlarge in proportion to the rest of his body. The overall effect made Vetch seem like an overgrown infant. The long, jade green robe that he wore did nothing to detract from this appearance: when he stood up it covered his feet and dragged along the ground behind him.

But it was the power he wielded that was terrifying. He controlled practically all the trade in the sector, from Tunnel Town and Steel Canyon as far as Toxic Sump and Mercury Falls. Several gangs, including the notorious Orlock Dangar's Dogs, were in his pay. He ran a mining operation at Downer's Deep and effectively owned the populace of Piston Broke. At his word previously prosperous gangs had been declared outlaw, whole mutant settlements had been razed to the ground and half the local Ratskin tribes paid him fealty. It seemed that there wasn't anyone in the sector who didn't either owe Vetch a favour or have good reason to want the Guilder dead, and in a fair number of cases both. But Vetch was rich and riches bought good protection.

But wealth wasn't enough for Antrobus Vetch. What he wanted was acceptance from those he saw as his equals in the Spire. He wanted out of the Underhive and the ork had been his ticket uphive, until person or persons, as yet unknown, had sabotaged the smuggling operation! The ork had been destined for the private zoo of the planetary governor, Lord Helmawr himself. Vetch had wasted thousands on bribing off-world contacts, not a credit of which he would ever see again, thanks to the interference of the Network's client. And now Gravalax Mune was facing the wrath of the thwarted Guilder.

His mind racing, trying to think of a way out of the apparent impasse they had reached in trying to uncover Vetch's betrayers, Mune took in the chamber around him, as if looking for inspiration from anywhere at all.

Vetch's lair was sumptuously decorated as befitted a Guilder of his power and influence. Turquoise velvet drapes jostled with colourful, spider-silk wall hangings for the eye's attention. The glittering, stained glass dome of the chamber – depicting the skull and portcullis badge of the Merchant Guild – was supported at regular intervals by Malvolion jade-marble pillars. To these were chained Vetch's veiled and voluptuous concubines, none of whom wore any item of apparel that might detract from the beauty of their physical form.

The small man leaned forward in his throne, knuckles whitening as his talon-like fingers gripped the arms. 'Well, if we were waiting for you to think of a plan we'd be here 'til the feast of the Emperor's Ascension,' Vetch ranted. 'So it's a good thing that I already have one, isn't it, hmm?'

Mune breathed a sigh of relief. 'Please would you enlighten your humble servant, my lord?'

'We already know of someone who knows the identity of our informer,' Vetch said, a thin smile spreading across his pale lips.

'We do?' Mune said, a glimmer of hope entering his consciousness. Maybe he wasn't bound for Vetch's prison mine after all. Concentrating, he tried to marshal his thoughts. Then it came to him and he was filled with a renewed sense of foreboding: 'You don't mean–'

'The Network! Of course I do!'

Mune looked anxiously from one servitor to the next and found himself wondering how he'd look with a rock drill in place of an arm. 'But the Network have been declared outlaws. You did it yourself for their part in ruining the deal. There's a bounty on all their heads. Every two-bit gang from here to the Effluous will be on their tail, hoping to get even a fraction of the reward you're offering.'

'Which is why you have to find them first,' Vetch snapped, the smile gone from his face, 'or to be more precise, their leader. What's his name? Sisken, isn't it, hmm?'

'I believe so, my lord.'

'Well then, what are you waiting for?' Vetch sank back into his throne. 'Hire someone to capture Sisken if you have to and then do whatever's necessary to extract the information we require.'

'Yes, my lord,' Mune replied without any sense of optimism.

Mune bowed, turned and walked sullenly towards the bulkhead doors at the end of the chamber, two servitors dropping into line behind him.

'Oh, and Mune?'

Mune turned back to his spiteful employer: 'My lord?'

'No mistakes. It can get very cold at the bottom of Deep Three in Stalag Slag Hole, you know, hmm?'

WITH RATTLING THUDS three cylindrical metal objects landed in the centre of the compound of an old water treatment plant. The anxious Delaque gangers stationed around the compound turned to see what had made the noise. In a series of small explosions the photon flash flare grenades detonated. The effect was that of three small suns going supernova in the centre of the compound, bathing the treatment plant and the Delaques in blinding white light.

Photo-visor in place, Nathan Creed – downhive desperado, hired gun and sharp-shooting bounty hunter – grabbed the chain links of the fence in front of him and started to climb. In four heartbeats he was over the razor wire-topped fence. In another three he had crossed the compound. It took only one to drop the screaming, disorientated leader with a tensed, flat-handed chop to the back of the man's neck. Creed caught the unconscious man as he slumped forwards and hefted the Delaque's dead weight over his shoulder. Without even breaking a sweat he covered the twenty metres to the gate.

A wide-muzzled stub gun, held in one hand, barked twice and the stumbling gate sentries fell. A third shot shattered the padlock holding the gates shut. Kicking them open with a booted foot the bounty hunter was through and out into the wastes of the badzones.

From the moment the grenades had detonated the whole operation had all taken less than a minute.

By the time any of the gangers recovered, their blurred vision slowly returning, Sisken, their leader, and the bounty hunter were long gone.

'HERE HE IS, BOSS,' the hairy scummer said, pushing the doctor roughly before Gravalax Mune.

The Guilder agent looked the scientist up and down, taking in the long lab coat buttoned to the neck, smeared with blood and engine oil. A shiny metal plate made up half the dome of the scientist's head, and long, straggly white hair hung down to his shoulders below it.

'Doctor Isaiah Haze, I presume,' the man said with a snide grin.

'That's right,' Haze said, wringing his bony hands nervously, 'but most people call me Doc.'

Haze in turn studied the gangling figure in front of him. He was as thin as a lashworm and, from the grim set of his features, Haze could easily believe he had the temperament to match. The man wore voluminous purple robes that billowed around his scarecrow-like form when he moved, like a face-eater caught in a vent-gale. Hung around his neck on a heavy chain was the skull badge of the Merchant Guild. But what stood out more than any of this was the crest of his employer, an entwined gothic A and V, tattooed onto his forehead, his slicked-back hair making it stand out even more. Two imposing servitors – each bearing powerful-looking robotic limbs with cruelly sharp claws and crushing vices in place of hands – flanked the Guilder agent.

'And you are?' Haze asked, turning his attention back to the scarecrow.

'Mune. Gravalax Mune. Bond-servant of Guilder Antrobus Vetch.'

Doc Haze felt decidedly uncomfortable. He had been removed from his lab by two Underhive scum, who he had taken for gangers in need of his considerable surgical skills and had then dragged him into the badzones to this place – the ruined shell of an Ecclesiarchy chapel – to bring him before an agent of one of the most feared and powerful men in the Underhive.

The doctor looked around him. Fractured pieces of soot-blackened stained glass windows still clung to the leaded rims of gothic window arches. A granite pulpit, the faces of the figures carved around its sides defaced by heretics long ago, stood before the broken plinth of an altar. Ten metres above it hung a dusty black marble Imperial eagle, its wings outstretched over the end of the nave, its two heads survey-ing the scene below with cold stone eyes. The place must have been abandoned centuries ago as the city-mountain of Hive Primus grew ever upwards, taking the righteous with it, leaving only the wretched, the dispossessed and vermin to worship at this shrine to the Emperor of humanity.

'What can I do for you, Mune?'

'I want you to perform an operation for me. A very deli-cate operation.'

'And why couldn't it have been performed in my lab?'

'How shall I put this?' Mune mused. 'It is a sensitive mat-ter. You will be handsomely rewarded, of course.' There was never any suggestion that Haze would refuse and the doctor knew better than to even try.

'Well, where am I supposed to work? Where are the tools I'll need? And where's the patient?' Haze asked irritably, con-tinuing to wring his hands in anxiety.

'This way,' Mune said turning and walking towards an archway in one wall. His hulking cyborg bodyguards fol-lowed. Feeling the muzzle of an autopistol pressed against his back, reluctantly Haze followed, accompanied by his own foul-smelling, unshaven 'bodyguards', their feet crunching on the broken tesserae of the ancient mosaic floor.

Mune led the way down a flight of wide, shallow steps into a vaulted crypt. And then Doc Haze saw something which made his heart leap.

Standing in the centre of the chamber was a reclining chair of gleaming steel sections and brass attachments. Numerous telescoping arms emerged from the upper part of the chair, ending in magnifying lenses, cutting blades and syringes. The gothic piece of antiquated machinery was supported by a brass pedestal, which had yet more pedals and levers sprouting from it. Iron clamps at strategic places completed the ensemble. It looked as if the device had been designed with maximum discomfort in mind.

'I know it's not what you're used to,' Mune said, taking in the crypt with a wave of an arm.

'Amazing,' the Underhive surgeon gasped. 'It's beautiful. A work of art.'

'Sorry?' Mune looked at the doctor, his brow furrowing. 'Oh, I see. The chair. Yes, I suppose it is.'

'What I wouldn't give for one of these.'

'Doctor?'

'Huh?' Haze looked up, Mune's enquiry shaking him from his reverie. 'Um, what procedure was it you wanted me to perform, exactly?'

'A cerebral fluid extraction,' Mune stated. 'I believe that it's colloquially known as a "brain drain".'

Doc Haze looked at the stick-thin man in amazement.

'You have performed one before, haven't you?' Mune asked, a hint of concern creeping into his voice.

'Of course,' Haze lied, excited at the prospect of being able to use the arcane surgical device. He had never performed such an operation in all his long years in the Underhive, but he knew the principles of it.

The procedure had a near legendary status among the medical practitioners of the Underhive. The process was complicated but basically involved extracting, and then purifying, fluid from the brain of a subject. The resulting extract, once mixed with a cocktail of stimms, could then be injected into the brain of another, giving the receiver the original subject's memories. It was rumoured that some uphive nobles utilised the process to relive the thrill of exciting, dangerous or even life-threatening experiences without ever leaving the safety of the Spire. Assuming that the operation was successful, the only side-effect of a brain drain for the subject was that it left them with large gaps in their memory. Those who injected the cerebral fluid of others into their own brains faced the prospect of a crippling addiction, culminating in a total loss of their own identity as the memories of others fractured their minds into a myriad of split personalities.

'I'll need to test the equipment, of course,' Doc Haze said slyly, running a hand over the cold metal of the chair.

'No time for that,' replied Mune. 'Our "patient" will be here any time now.'

As if on cue there was the sound of footsteps on the stairs and Doc Haze looked round. Pushing a bald, manacled ganger before him, a tall man, swathed in a long leather coat and wearing a wide-brimmed hat that hid his face in shadow, entered the crypt. At his hips were holstered two large stub guns and as the man moved Haze caught glimpses of the skull and crossbones bounty seals attached to the long tails of his coat.

'Creed,' he stated coldly.

'Hello again, Doc,' the bounty hunter replied in a down-hive drawl, seeming just as pleased to see the Underhive surgeon as Haze was to see him. Grabbing hold of his manacled prisoner with a strong hand, Creed pushed the ganger to his knees in front of the Guilder agent. 'Here's your man, Mune.'

As the ganger looked up at Mune, Haze felt suddenly sick. He already knew this man and now he knew what Antrobus Vetch was after. Haze wanted to vomit.

'Ah, Sisken,' Mune addressed the ganger. 'How the mighty are fallen, the leader of the Network brought low before Gravalax Mune.'

Although his eyes were hidden by dark-tinted goggles it was obvious the ganger was glaring at Mune. 'I know what you want,' Sisken hissed, 'but I'll never tell you! You'll never get it out of me!'

'Never tell me?' Mune pondered. 'I'm quite sure of that, but never get it out of you?' He turned his gaze towards the gothic contraption and the filthy scientist standing next to it. 'I wouldn't be so sure about that.' Sisken's face fell as he followed Mune's gaze and his already sallow complexion turned almost completely white. 'Strap him in.'

As the Delaque gang leader struggled and protested futilely, the two scummers removed Sisken's manacles and the servitor bodyguards forced him into the operating chair. Doc Haze secured the last restraint around the ganger's head.

'Work quickly, doctor,' Mune instructed Haze. 'But remember – no mistakes!'

Muttering something unintelligible to himself under his breath, the surgeon set to work.

The bounty hunter looked on, his face an emotionless mask. As the doctor positioned the syringe at the base of his prisoner's head Creed took a crumpled packet of smokes from a pocket. Putting a cheroot to his lips he began looking for his lighter.

Haze looked up. 'You know I don't like people smoking when I'm operating.'

The bounty hunter shot him a dark look and, producing a gleaming lighter from another pocket, lit the cheroot.

'Just get on with it!' Mune snapped and the whirring of servos from one of the servitor's prosthetic claws encouraged Haze to put aside all thoughts of hygiene and proceed without further complaint.

But all the while his mind was racing. He knew Sisken, leader of the Delaque gang of information-brokers called the Network. It was they who had sold him the information about Antrobus Vetch's operation to bring an ork into Hive Primus for Lord Helmawr's private zoo. And it had been Haze who had leaked the same information to the authorities, forcing Vetch to dump the illegal alien in the Underhive. Haze had planned to study the ork's regenerative abilities so that he might apply them to his own surgical skills, making his services invaluable to any Underhive gang. And what could Antrobus Vetch want with the leader of the Network other than to find out who sold him out? Once Haze had carried out the brain drain on Sisken, anyone injecting the man's cerebral fluid would discover Doc Haze was the culprit Vetch was after and he would be as good as dead!

But how could he get out of the inevitable? If he botched the brain drain on purpose Mune would have him killed on the spot! And even if he could somehow dispose of Mune and all his bodyguards – not to mention Creed – Vetch would only send others to find out what happened. Whichever way he looked at it he was doomed! If only he had more time maybe he could tamper with the evidence, but time was one thing he didn't have. Then he noticed the small phial of lubricant sitting on the tray next to the reclining chair and a smile spread across his lips as he began to formulate a plan.

There was the sudden roar of gunfire and shattering glass from the chapel above. Haze jumped, almost stabbing his patient with the syringe.

'We're under attack!' Mune squealed.

Unholstering his two wide-calibre stub guns, Creed ran up and out of the crypt, taking the steps two at a time.

'Now you'll be sorry,' Sisken hissed in a voice barely more than a sibilant whisper.

'Go!' Mune yelled at the two scummers who were now looking first at the Guilder agent and then at each other in agitated confusion. 'The operation must be completed!'

At a nod from Mune one of the hulking servitors herded the reluctant scummers out of the crypt.

CREED SPRINTED ACROSS the broken floor of the chapel as bullets and las-rounds impacted in the crumbling wall behind him. Ducking down beneath the glassless arch of one of the ruined chapel's windows he took a deep breath, letting it out in a long, controlled exhalation as he readied himself. 'Let's go, girls,' he muttered under his breath and then rose into a half-crouch, pointing his guns over the sill of the window.

Peering across the rubble-strewn plaza in front of the chapel, at first glance Creed picked out eight pale-skinned, bald-headed figures positioned behind the ruins of concrete walls thirty paces from him, although he suspected there were probably as many more hidden out of sight. Each of them wore a pale-brown leather coat, not unlike his own apart from the emblem of a sump snake on the lapels – the badge of House Delaque – and their eyes were protected by black-tinted goggles or implanted filter screens. They were armed with an assortment of autoguns, bolt pistols and las-weapons.

Another round of fire peppered Creed's position but this time he replied with two shots of his own, fired off in quick succession. A large Delaque wielding an autogun, exposed in a breach in the barricade, fell backwards, blood already oozing from two bullet wounds in his chest. Easy target, Creed thought.

There was the chatter of autogun fire as the ganger's trigger finger spasmed in his death-throes, cries of anger from the Delaques and a yelp of pain. Creed grinned to himself.

'Come on, fellas,' he muttered under his breath, 'it's no fun when you do it to yourselves!'

Then the bounty hunter was aware of the crunching of mosaic tiles under booted feet behind him and the scummers dashed into cover in the chapel, the threatening form of Mune's servitor bodyguard behind them.

Another fusillade of shots smacked into the crumbling chapel. Creed rose onto his haunches, fired off another couple of dum-dum rounds and another Delaque dropped, blood dribbling from a hole in his filter screen. The bounty hunter ducked back into cover as the rest of the besieging gangers replied to his attack with more las-blasts and bolter rounds.

The two scummers looked at him in awed amazement and Creed heard one of them gasp, 'He's good!'

He glowered at them as a searing las-round gouged its way through the sill of the window. 'When you ladies are quite ready,' he drawled, 'maybe you'd like to earn the right to keep your stinking hides?'

In embarrassment the hired scum fumbled the safeties off their autopistols and aimed haphazard fire at the Delaque gang, hitting almost everything but the gangers. Creed made up for their waste of ammunition, making each one of his shots count. One dum-dum round clipped a man's shoulder, sending the Delaque's own raking auto-fire streaking towards the roof of the dome. A second round took out another ganger's kneecap, the screaming man dropping his pistol as he clamped his hands over the ragged wound and his leg gave way under him. A third hit the lasgun gripped by a snarling Delaque, his face a mess of scar tissue, ruining its firing mechanism and sending the weapon flying into the ruins.

The explosive bark of Creed's point-six-six calibre stub guns and the wild rattling chatter of the scummers, autopistols was joined by a chugging roar as the servitor, its metal feet planted squarely on the ground, opened fire with an autocannon attachment mounted on its grotesquely over-large robotic right arm.

Under the watchful eyes of the Imperial eagle, the chapel's defenders did their best to repel the Delaques.

THE CONCUSSIVE FORCE of an explosion rocked the crypt. Doc Haze's sweat-slicked hand slipped on the handle of a control lever. 'No mistakes, remember?' his Guilder overseer screeched as he almost rammed the syringe needle deeper into the Delaque leader's brain, rather than removing it.

'I'm doing my best,' Haze snapped back, 'considering the circumstances!'

Gravalax Mune said nothing else, merely indicating the monstrous slave-machine standing next to him, with a flick of his head. Cursing under his breath, the doctor withdrew the syringe from the silent, semi-lobotomised Sisken and disconnected the phial containing the sample of cerebral fluid. Haze gripped the phial tightly in his hand, lest it slip from his sweaty palms. He wasn't only sweating because he was working in a war-zone – more than anything it was due to his increasing sense of anxiety at how he was going to avoid giving Antrobus Vetch's agent the evidence that it was he who had scuppered his master's plans!

For a moment he actually considered dropping the glass container – he could make out it slipped from his grasp when the next explosion came from the chapel above – but he realised just as quickly that it would be futile. Mune would have him killed there and then, and ask questions later. He would have to think of another way out of this. And then it came to him.

'I just have to purify the sample,' Haze explained to the Guilder agent, 'then we'll be done.'

Placing his own body between Mune and the centrifuge device fixed to the back of the operating chair Haze emptied Sisken's brain drain sample into the purification chamber with one hand while he rummaged in the pocket of his grimy lab coat with the other.

WITH A WHOOSH of super-heated air a second fireball streaked through the chapel window and impacted against the huge Imperial eagle. 'Helmawr's rump!' Creed cursed as he felt the heat-wash on his skin. *Someone's using a flamer*, he thought. *Looks like things could get a little hot!*

For the first time in a long time Creed felt outgunned. His initial assault on the Network had used up the last of his grenades. All he had left now were his two stub guns, with a couple of dozen rounds in total, and as a last resort his bootknife. *Time I paid a long overdue visit to Hackbut's Arms House*, he considered, *if I make it through this.*

There were only three of them left defending the chapel. The taller of the two scum had stupidly stuck his head around the side of a pillar to assess the situation only to have it blown off by a bolter shell. The fat scummer had gone to pieces after that, being possessed by a palsy that made his poor aim even worse.

The Delaques seemed to have called up some reinforcements. Through the smoke Creed caught glimpses of a man with a shock of orange hair moving among the bald gangers. *Hired gun*, the bounty hunter mused. *Probably the one with the flamer.*

At that moment a third ball of fire hurtled through the open archway like a comet and slammed into the servitor. The blast threw the hulking slave-machine backwards into the chapel's altar. The heat of the fireball melted cable-bundles and ignited the ammunition packed into the breach of its autocannon attachment. The resulting explosion shredded the organic parts of the servitor and tore apart its bionic implants.

Creed looked across at the remaining scummer to see the fat man lying in a puddle of his own pooling blood. Several shells from the servitor's exploding arm had hit him from behind. 'Friendly fire,' the bounty hunter muttered grimly to himself.

Two more shots took out two more gangers and emptied both stub guns. Ducking down again and pressing his back against the wall Creed reloaded both weapons with practised ease. He would have to make every round count: after this there weren't enough for another reload.

Taking a deep breath he flung himself sideways, rolling past the open doorway and taking out two Delaque juves who had been advancing while he reloaded. Back in cover he peered around the doorjamb and did a swift headcount.

'Well, girls,' he said, addressing his smoking guns. 'Three down and one to go in here. At least five of them still out there, along with the new hothead. My kind of odds!'

Creed brought down one Delaque after another while – compared to the crackshot gunslinger – all they seemed capable of was peppering the chapel walls with bolter shell impact craters.

And then Creed was suddenly aware of something else. The incessant gunfire had stopped. All he could hear was the crackling of the flames around him, the pinging of his own cooling stub guns and the sound of feet running away over the broken plaza. Cautiously the bounty hunter looked around the doorjamb to see the flapping coat tails of half a dozen Delaque gangers fleeing into the gloom of the waste-zones beyond. But on the other side of the plaza the orange-haired man still moved between the fractured concrete walls, ignoring the fleeing gangers.

'Well, girls,' Creed said. 'One to go.'

With a scream like a discharging plasma cannon three fiery missiles crashed into the chapel. Creed was thrown to the ground by the force of the blasts and covered his head as he was showered with splinters of glass and burning shards of masonry.

'Looks like it's time for a change of plan,' the bounty hunter muttered, as the Imperial eagle burned.

* * *

DOC HAZE POURED the last drop of the scummer's brain drain sample into the centrifuge and, with the practised sleight of hand of a sideshow con artist, slipped both phials into his pocket. At the flick of a switch the device started spinning. Yet another explosion shook the chamber, dust showering from cracks in the vaulted ceiling. 'How long?' Mune snapped.

'A couple of minutes,' Haze hazarded.

'That's about two minutes longer than you've got.'

Both the scientist and Guilder agent spun round on hearing Creed's distinctive drawl behind them.

'What do you mean?' Mune demanded.

'Work it out yourself,' the bounty hunter snarled, pointing at the unconscious Sisken. 'Your guest's friends have come to rescue him back and they've got some help. It's time we were out of here!'

'But how?' Doc Haze panicked, wringing his hands. 'The only way out of here is the way you just came in!'

'Oh, I don't think so,' Creed said, turning his piercing gaze on Mune. 'I doubt Antrobus Vetch's trained lashworm would have set all this up without including more than one escape route. Where is it?' Creed said, spinning round and pointing a stub gun at the tattoo on Mune's forehead.

Mune glanced towards his remaining bodyguard.

'Don't even think about it,' Creed hissed. 'I'll put a bullet between your eyes if you so much as blink.'

Yet another explosion from above rocked the crypt and the roof shook as something heavy crashed down onto the floor of the chapel above.

'First give me the sample,' Mune said, reaching out a hand.

Doc Haze looked to the bounty hunter. 'Do it,' Creed said. The surgeon halted the spinning centrifuge and removed the phial containing the partially 'purified' extract. He tossed it to the Guilder who caught it with a grimace of annoyance.

'Now we go,' Creed stated, pulling back the hammer of the stub gun.

Saying nothing, Mune turned and moved swiftly towards a shadowy archway, previously hidden in the shadows of the far corner of the crypt. In a moment he was through it and gone, followed by the stomping servitor. The bounty hunter and the scientist crossed the crypt quickly towards the exit. When they were only metres away from the archway a ball of white-hot flame streaked over their heads, scorching the hairs on the back of Creed's neck. The fireball smashed into the roof above the archway, sending lumps of smoking rubble crashing down in front of it.

Creed spun round. Standing at the foot of the steps was the orange-haired man he had seen with the besieging gangers. Creed saw that as well as a shock of orange hair, the man had a nasty scar running along the side of his head, from his right temple down to behind his ear under the hairline. He was wearing a pair of black leather boots that covered his legs up to the knees. As well as a grubby pair of rat-hide britches and an unwashed, sleeveless undershirt, the man wore a black sleeveless jacket that looked like it could have been crudely stitched together from spider-skin and that left his muscular arms bare. His features were set in an expression of fury or pain – Creed couldn't tell which – and he advanced with his hands open without a weapon in sight.

Questions crowded Creed's mind. Why was a hired gun, who had previously been wielding a flamer to such devastating effect only moments before, now standing in front of him unarmed? Why was the hired gun still here when those who had hired him had fled?

Creed felt a tug on his arm and looked round to see the crazed scientist quaking behind him, his expression imploring him to move.

'What are you so scared of?' Creed asked Haze angrily. 'He's one man and he's unarmed!'

'Because the good doctor recognises me,' the man said, a cruel smile playing over his grimacing features. 'You do recognise me, don't you, Doc?' the man stated. 'No, don't bother answering. I can tell from the look of ashen-faced panic that you do.'

'I don't believe I've had the pleasure,' Creed snarled, levelling both stubbers at the stranger.

'The name's Ignus Mander,' the man said and then winced. 'My quarrel's not with you, bounty hunter, but if you get in my way I will kill you.'

'And anyone who gets in the way of Nathan Creed has got a whole heap of trouble coming!' Creed retorted, starting to squeeze both triggers.

'Have it your way,' Mander replied coldly.

'Creed!' hissed Doc Haze who was still cowering behind the tall, imposing figure of the bounty hunter. 'Just shoot him and then we can get out of here!' Despite his desperation to leave, the doctor seemed rooted to the spot.

Creed increased the pressure from his trigger fingers. Suddenly he gave a yelp of pain and let go of both guns. Creed looked down at the palms of his hands. Both were covered in large red weals and blistering skin, which stung like a milliasaur bite. Inexplicably, in a matter of seconds the metal of the stubbers had become white-hot, as if they had been heated in a furnace. Creed hugged his hands to his sides in an attempt to dull the pain.

'Now we run!' Haze shouted, pulling sharply on Creed's arm.

The burning pain still overwhelming his senses, forgetting his precious guns the bounty hunter allowed himself to be dragged away by the desperate doctor, who now seemed to have found the motivation to flee. The two of them stumbled through the archway and into the passageway beyond, following Mune's escape route. Vetch's agent and his heavy-duty bodyguard were gone and neither Creed nor the doc knew which ripperjack's nest the tunnel would lead them into next. All they knew was that it would lead them away from Ignus Mander and that was good enough for now.

As the two of them fled Creed heard Mander calling after them, 'You can run, Doc! You can run!' And run they did.

DOC HAZE WAS panting for air like a dying asthmatic as he and Creed came to a halt behind a power relay station. The bounty hunter seemed to have recovered himself after the initial shock of Mander's attack but his hands were a mess of suppurating blisters. After gasping for air, doubled up with his hands gripping his knees for a minute or two, he took a roll of bandage from a pocket and bound Creed's hands. 'How does it feel now?' Doc Haze asked.

'Like I washed my hands in a chem pool,' Creed grumbled, 'but I'll live. Look, we can't hang around here for long before this Mander catches up with us again, so when you're done let's get moving and maybe you can tell me exactly who you've skavved off this time!'

Doc Haze cast his mind back to the last time he had seen Ignus Mander and felt sick to the pit of his stomach.

'If I tell you the whole story, Creed, you must promise to protect me from him. The man's a lunatic! You must kill him! Help me now and I'll see you're well rewarded.'

'Like last time?' the bounty hunter muttered sullenly. 'We came to an agreement.'

'Huh!' Creed grunted. 'It was the same after the Fester Hole incident.'

'I fixed your arm after your run-in with the Kaynn Clan Gang, didn't I?' the doc protested. 'This time I'll make it up to you. Any upgrade you want.' The doc faltered at these words as he considered what he was about to tell the bounty hunter. 'We'll think of something.'

Creed's face remained an inscrutable mask as he cast his eyes back over the area of wasteland they had crossed.

'All right, Doc,' he said at last. 'Although my better judgement tells me I'm a scavvy's uncle for doing so, it looks like we're in this together now so it's in my best interests if I know as much about this scavver as possible if I've got to take him out.'

Quelling the sickening fear that gripped him, Doc Haze began to relate the whole sorry tale to his would-be protector. 'It was a couple of years ago. I tended to Mander after he was shot in a gunfight out at Steel Canyon. I pulled seven pieces of lead out of him but one remained: a bullet lodged in his brain. By rights it should have killed him, only it hadn't. I tried to remove it but something went wrong.'

Haze looked at Creed guiltily and saw at once that the bounty hunter's previously emotionless features were now contorted in a grimace of horror. 'How many times have you fixed me up, Doc?'

'It was a one-off. Honestly! To this day I still don't know what went wrong,' the doc gabbled. 'The more I picked at the bullet the further I ended up pushing it into his cerebellum. You know what some tech-biologis believe about that part of the brain?'

'No, Doc, but something tells me it's got something to do with how Mander made my girls give me the kiss-off.'

'It is popularly held in scientific circles that the cerebellum is the source of psychic powers.'

'Wyrds,' the bounty hunter said with a scowl.

'Exactly,' Haze confirmed. 'Only in some people these powers lie dormant in their subconscious. In most cases these powers never reveal themselves, but then in others some catalyst awakens these latent powers – the onset of adolescence, a sharp blow to the head–'

'Having a bullet pushed into your brain by some lunatic surgeon!'

Haze looked away from Creed rubbing his hands together nervously.

'And how do these powers manifest themselves?' Creed pressed.

'Some psykers can control others by willpower alone, others can move objects physically with their minds and some can manipulate the molecules in objects or even the air around them to heat them to boiling or melting point.'

'So Mander's a pyro.'

'Looks like it.'

'How come Mander's never come after you before? I sure as hell would've done!' Creed said darkly.

'I was based down in Perdition back then. Once I'd patched Mander up as best I could and handed him back to his gang-friends heavily sedated, Veral and I packed up and moved out. I suppose it was only a matter of time before he caught up with me.' Haze looked thoughtful for a moment. 'Thinking about it, once the Network got involved it was inevitable. Those information-junkies and their "Father" don't miss a trick, unfortunately! This way it looks like Mander got the chance to have his revenge and get paid for it at the same time.'

'Whatever,' the bounty hunter drawled. 'Let's face facts. Mander's going to catch up with us sooner or later, I haven't got my guns and that wasn't a flamer he was using during the assault on the chapel at all.'

'Sounds like a pretty concise summary of the situation.' Grimacing, Ignus Mander stepped out from behind the transformer station, fists clenched in front of him.

'How long have you been standing there?' Haze squealed.

'Long enough,' Mander said and winced again. 'I think the only bit you missed out, Doc, was the fact that the bullet you left inside my head means I live in a state of perpetual agony that even drugs can't suppress!'

'I know the perfect cure for a headache,' Creed snarled. 'It's just a shame I haven't got my painkillers with me.'

'I've already told you once, you're not my enemy,' Mander said, addressing the bounty hunter, 'but if you keep on like this you soon will be.'

'We'll see about that,' Doc Haze retorted, displaying a little more bravado now he knew that Creed was fighting for him. 'You'll rue the day you came after Doc H – aargghhh!' the doc screamed, and doubled up in crippling, burning agony.

'Doc?' Creed half-whispered. 'What are you doing to him?' the bounty hunter demanded, turning back to Mander. The pyromaniac was staring intently at the doc and Creed was sure he could see wisps of flickering flame dancing around the psyker's clenched fists. 'Oh no you don't,' Creed hissed and charged at the wyrd.

Mander immediately turned his piercing gaze on the running bounty hunter. Creed was sure he could see distant fires, burning like cold stars within the pyro's unblinking eyes. Creed faltered, feeling his whole body flush with heat, as if he had run five kilometres rather than five metres. He blinked as sweat ran into his eyes.

Putting a hand to the slick-wet skin of his forehead he wiped the sweat from above his eyes. His brow felt like it was burning up as his body temperature soared. It was as if he was suffering from the worst case of sewer-swamp fever ever recorded. He could feel his soaking undershirt clinging to his back. Then he realised that even his bandages were becoming damp as sweat ran down his arms. He began to feel dizzy as the unbearable heat threatened to overcome him.

Without his guns and in danger of becoming totally incapacitated as he was, Creed reacted instinctively. Turning, through sweat-blurred eyes Creed saw Doc Haze's horrified face mere metres away. Forcing his legs to move, overheating muscles protesting bitterly, the bounty hunter staggered forward, bundling the panicking scientist in front of him. His head spinning, Creed saw the black ellipse of an open shaft ahead of them. As they closed the distance between themselves and the hole Creed heard the sound of running water growing ever louder over the pounding of his own heart. At the same moment the smell of scorched leather assaulted his nostrils.

Looking down at his coat as he ran, Creed could see smoke rising from the battered material. With a whoomph the flapping coat tails burst into flame. Without a moment's hesitation the bounty hunter pulled the coat off and flung it aside, losing his hat at the same time. Then the black gulf was before them and, shoving the doc ahead of him, Creed half jumped and half fell in the cold, enveloping darkness.

He hit the fast-flowing stream next to the dazed doc and a cloud of steam rose from the water around him. At once Creed could feel his body temperature dropping to a more healthy level. He sat up and let out a long sigh. Doc Haze was sitting stunned in the middle of the watercourse, the effluent stream, which glowed with faint phosphorescence, swirling past him.

'I never want to feel like that again,' Creed said, running a wet hand through his close-cropped greying hair.

Doc Haze looked at him for a moment, his mouth open in amazement.

'How can you be so calm?' he managed at last. 'Mander just tried to make you spontaneously combust!'

'Come on, doc,' Creed said grimly, ignoring the scientist's question. 'We've got to keep moving. That bastard isn't going to stop now until both of us look like the main course at a scavvy barbeque.'

The pipe was almost large enough to stand upright in. Following the flow of the polluted water downstream, crouching slightly, the bounty hunter and the scientist jogged into the gloom.

GRAVALAX MUNE STOOD in front of the heavy bulkhead door, dusting off his robes and tapping his foot impatiently, waiting for security clearance. The servitor stood statue-still behind him, no concept of 'being kept waiting' or 'impatience' within its programmed brain.

There was a sudden click followed by an electronic whirr and a port opened within an eye-socket of the Guilder skull badge that formed an integral part of the steel door. An optical probe, looking like an iron and glass eyeball, emerged from the hole on a telescopic armature. It stopped centimetres from Mune's face. The Guilder agent glared at the probe. The probe whirred and clicked as its camera eye focused and then jerked back abruptly.

The artificial eye descended on its metal stalk so that it could scan the Guild badge hung around Mune's neck. After a few seconds there was an electronic chirrup and the probe retracted back into the port, which closed behind it. Hinges groaning, with a hiss of compressed air the bulkhead door swung slowly open.

'Access granted,' the tinny voice said in a metallic monotone. Taking a deep breath Mune stepped through the doorway into Antrobus Vetch's lair, the silent servitor clunking after him.

CAUTIOUSLY CREED PEERED over the edge of the pipe while the panting doc hung back. The pipe had twisted and turned, like so many other conduits between the domes of Hive Primus, until it came to an abrupt end in the side of another derelict dome. 'Well?' Haze shouted over the background roar. 'How far down is it?'

The phosphorescent liquid swirling around Creed's booted feet ran out of the end of the sluice pipe and fell several metres before joining the hundreds of gallons of muddy brown water pouring out of a much wider opening below them. The stench of hydrogen sulphide assailed Creed's nostrils as an endless stream of pollutants thundered into the effluent lake twenty metres below.

'Put it this way, doc, the fall won't kill you,' the bounty hunter said with no trace of humour in his voice. *But whatever's in that lake might*, he added to himself.

'Do you know where we are?'

'Yes. The local chem-prospectors call it the Bilgespill Drop, although you won't find many of them out here without gasmasks and protective suits because of the toxins constantly being pumped into the dome. The air-recyclers aren't that reliable down here.'

'So where do we go from here?'

Creed looked back along the shaft: 'Well, back that way is our friendly pyromaniac. So I guess our only real option is down.'

Clinging onto one side of the pipe's mouth, the bounty hunter leaned out over the end and scanned the surrounding area for another way down. A ripperjack's-swing away was a rusted ladder that descended to a grilled walkway that was sprayed by the waterfall. Creed pulled himself back into the pipe and looked the scientist up and down. 'Doesn't look good,' he sighed.

'Could we lower ourselves down?' Haze asked, obviously not relishing the prospect of jumping.

'You got a rope?'

The doc edged closer to the bounty hunter and dared a glance over the edge of the pipe. 'By the Spire!' he gasped.

'Doc!' Creed yelled over the deafening roar of the water. 'Can you swim?'

The bounty hunter was suddenly aware that he was heating up again. Wishing that his worst fears would prove unfounded he turned around slowly. Standing in midstream ten metres away, his grimace of pain and anger illuminated by the phosphorescence in the water, was Ignus Mander. As his body temperature began to rise it seemed to Creed that Mander's orange hair was aflame at the tips.

Mander relaxed his hands, the wisps of flame dissipated and the bounty hunter was freed of the unbearable burning sensation that was gripping his body. 'Caught between a rock and a hard place,' the pyro taunted. 'Or should that be a drop and a hot place?'

Quickly, Creed weighed up the various options. He could try and take Mander now: he was sure he could beat him in a fistfight, despite the pyro's obvious upper body strength. But would he be able to reach Mander before he cooked him from the inside out?

'Do you know what it's like, Doc, living in constant pain?' Mander asked walking slowly towards them. 'A thousand white-hot needles lancing every nerve ending whenever you move?'

'It was an accident!'

'I suppose I should be grateful though,' Mander said, ignoring Haze's plea. 'If it wasn't for you I wouldn't be able to do this!'

The pyro's fists bunched. Creed and Doc Haze doubled up in agony as they were assaulted by a blast of pyro-kinetic energy.

Nothing else for it, the bounty hunter decided as his head began to swim. Gritting his teeth against the building pain Creed threw himself bodily out of the end of the pipe grabbing the doc by the collar of his lab coat as he did so. Then there was nothing but air beneath them. Semi-conscious from Mander's assault the two men dropped like stones, only dimly aware of the rotten egg stink of the torrent of the effluent waterfall buffeting them until with a tremendous splash they hit the roiling surface of the lake below. Oily waters closed over them and they sank into the murky grey depths.

NATHAN CREED OPENED his eyes, which immediately started to sting in the polluted waters. Freed from the agony of his own body overheating by the enveloping waters of the lake Creed's natural survival instinct took over. From the light of glow-globes above permeating the turbid waters he could see the doc only a matter of metres away, dragging himself towards the surface of the lake with unpracticed strokes. Not many inhabitants of the Underhive could swim at all – there weren't many bodies of water this close to Hive Bottom that were safe to swim in, for one reason or another – but from Creed's long years of experience in the badzones he would have drowned long ago if he hadn't been able to swim.

The two men clambered out of the stinking green pool and began the unpleasant task of cleaning themselves off. Doc Haze wiped a mass of sludgy suds from the metal dome of his head and then, grimacing, doubled up as he vomited polluted water from his protesting stomach.

'You don't want to swallow too much of that stuff, Doc,' Creed said, trying to remove glistening jelly-slime from his numbed right arm.

'I didn't intend to,' Haze coughed before retching again.

'We can't hang around here,' the bounty hunter said, matter-of-factly. 'Mander will find a way down sooner or later.'

Creed was suddenly overwhelmed by unfamiliar emotions. Here was an opponent who would not stop, driven by pain and hatred to exact his vengeance no matter what. Creed had never been in such a situation before and he didn't like it. For the first time in his life in the Underhive he felt utterly helpless.

The bounty hunter looked out across the broken landscape of the dome.

Or perhaps I'm not so helpless after all.

In the distance, glowing chlorine-green gas vented into the toxic atmosphere of the dome and amongst the other acrid smells assailing his nose Creed could pick out the distinctive reek of methane. They were standing at the edge of a gas-geyser field: pockets of flammable gas produced by various industrial processes and life-support systems elsewhere in the Hive collected here, issuing forth in blasts at regular intervals when the pressure became too great. Creed smiled. It was time to use this inhospitable terrain to his advantage.

Haze spat the last of the muck from his mouth: 'Where do we go from here?'

'That way,' Creed said, pointing with his left arm towards the cracked plain and the venting gas-geysers.

* * *

'WHERE ARE YOU going to run now, bounty hunter?' Ignus Mander asked, his tone derisive.

The bounty hunter stood only a metre away from the edge of a precipice that ran a hundred metres in either direction. Doc Haze was slumped against a rockrete boulder close by, coughing violently. It looked like the doc hadn't got long to go in this toxic environment. Mander had the two of them cornered at last. There was no more running for them now, not unless they wanted to save Mander the trouble of killing them – but where would be the satisfaction in that?

The bounty hunter looked a mess, his close-cropped greying hair wet with oily water, his undershirt stained brown by slime and effluent, his right arm hanging uselessly at his side, covered in angry red weals, and grubby bandages, oozing pus, wrapped around both hands. The doc had called him Creed, Mander considered.

'So, which one of you shall I kill first?' Despite the white-hot needles lancing his brain, Mander savoured the moment, looking first to Creed, then to the doc, then back to–

The bounty hunter sprang forward, rapidly closing the distance between them. The pyro hit him with a bolt of energy but in his arrogant complacency he had given the man the time he needed.

Creed bowled into Mander, and sent them both sprawling in the carbon-black dust. Instinctively, Mander threw out his hands to break his fall and his psyker power was broken.

'Not so tough now, are you?' the bounty hunter spat, wrestling Mander to the ground by the shoulders.

'We'll see about that,' Mander retorted and brought his knee up into Creed's stomach. The bounty hunter doubled up, winded, and Mander pushed his opponent away. Faster than any ordinary man, the grizzled gunslinger was up and at him again, each punch he landed like the pounding of a sledgehammer. Mander retaliated, his muscles bunched.

The two men traded blows, marking each other hit for hit. Creed was determined to keep Mander occupied with his fists so that he wouldn't have the opportunity to use his pyro-kinetic powers. However, despite the bounty hunter's resilience, it was obvious that Creed had been weakened by the hunt.

Slowly but surely, Mander was winning. Finally, in a skilfully executed move, the pyro kicked Creed's legs out from under him and as his knees buckled, delivered a double-handed blow to his chin. The bounty hunter collapsed into the dirt, his sides heaving as he gasped for air in the polluted atmosphere.

Mander clenched his fists, ready to deliver a killing blast of pyro-kinetic energy. 'Well, do you have anything to say before I roast you like a spitted swine?'

'Yes,' Creed said, spitting a mouthful of ash from his bleeding mouth. 'Can a condemned man have one last smoke? You've won, Mander, so let me die with good, honest tobacco smoke tarring my lungs.'

Flushed with exhilaration, having won the fight, Mander felt the magnanimity of the victorious. He was even almost able to forget about the continual splitting headache he lived with every minute of his life. 'Why not?'

With his left hand Creed pulled a sodden, crumpled packet of cheroots from a pocket in his britches.

'They're a bit wet,' he said, almost apologetically.

'Not a problem,' Mander replied.

The pyro leant over the stricken man, bringing his hand close to the tip of the soaking cheroot Creed placed between his lips. With a flick of Mander's fingers the end of the cheroot sizzled into glowing life, the tightly wrapped tobacco drying in seconds.

'Thanks,' Creed said, 'idiot!'

Complacency had been his enemy again. Mander hadn't seen Creed clasp the piece of broken pipe in his strengthening right hand. The improvised maul connected with the side of Mander's head with a crack. The blow sent him reeling. Suddenly unable to maintain his balance, or to use his legs properly, Mander collapsed heavily over a small rent in the ground.

His head ached but, it slowly dawned on him, not with the lancing needle-pain of the bullet lodged in his brain. This was a dull throbbing ache at the side of his head that blurred his vision. My skull's probably fractured, he thought, almost happily, but the bullet's been dislodged, maybe only slightly, but no more constant agony!

In the same instant Mander realised – without having to test the fact – that his powers were gone along with the agonising pain.

His eyes swimming in and out of focus, the stunned Mander looked towards the figure of Creed advancing towards him. The bounty hunter still gripped the rusted iron pipe in one bandaged hand and the now-lit cheroot was held between the thumb and forefinger of the other. There was a hiss of gas escaping under pressure and Creed was silhouetted against a glowing green jetting cloud. Moving his head slightly Mander could see other cracks in the floor of the dome and, with his ear pressed to the ground, he could hear the rumble of erupting gas pockets.

Released of the pain he had lived with ever since Doc Haze botched the operation to remove the bullet from his brain, Mander was suddenly filled with a moment of clarity: Creed had lured him right into the midst of the gas geysers.

Mander was caught in a sudden blast of gas, with the force of a compressed-air hose, as the geyser he was sprawled across vented. Through the distortion in the air around him and his owned blurred vision he saw Creed flick the cheroot, saw it tumble end over end towards him and then there was nothing but an acetylene white flare and the heat of a smelting furnace swept over him.

ANTROBUS VETCH SAT perched as regally as he could manage on his throne-like chair and fixed Gravalax Mune with a hungry stare. 'So, you have it,' the Guilder acknowledged, looking to his agent's open hand and the prepared syringe resting within it.

'Yes, my lord,' Mune simpered. 'The sample has been purified and is ready for insertion.'

'Excellent, excellent!' Vetch was almost giggling in excited anticipation. 'Well then, what are we waiting for, hmm? Give the syringe to Three-Six-Four.' Mune placed the syringe within the proffered pallid hand of the waiting servitor. 'Then close your eyes.'

Mune felt his erstwhile bodyguard's metallic claw clamp down hard on his shoulder. 'My lord?'

'I'm told it's easier to make sense of the newly-implanted memories if you block other sensory input.'

A cold chill passed down Mune's spine and sweat beaded on his forehead.

'There's also a period of disorientation but that isn't supposed to last for long.'

'But, my lord!' the panicking agent spluttered.

'You didn't think I'd inject the sample into myself, did you, hmm?' Vetch snapped, cutting off Mune's imminent protest. 'There could be anything in that syringe! And anyway, have you not heard the expression, why have a pit slave and dig yourself? Now we'll find out who was responsible for fouling up the biggest operation we've ever set up!'

The excitedly leering Vetch nodded to the slave-machine holding Mune. The man felt a sudden stab of pain in the base of his skull that made him gasp and then the plunger was depressed.

Mune's mind was suddenly filled with a torrent of images as the fluid from Sisken's brain and the lubricant were injected directly into his brain. Mune's retinas burned and he screwed his eyes tight shut in an attempt to stop the stinging sensation. One after another the memories poured through his cerebral cortex.

He was standing before an accident cogitator engine in a red lit chamber listening to the instructions of 'Father'. He was drinking in Snake Eye Sam's gambling den. He was in the centre of a wire-fenced compound when suddenly everything went white. He was standing before himself, Gravalax Mune, and was listening to his own voice telling him to bring Doctor Isaiah Haze to him. He was half-conscious being carried over a man's back – a man who wore a long leather coat.

The images continued. Gradually his scrambled consciousness began to make sense of the rush of memories. He 'remembered' being in Snake Eye Sam's. He 'remembered' assisting in planning the operation that would bring an ork into Hive Primus for Lord Helmawr's zoo. He 'remembered' speaking with Doc Haze... And at last Mune came to a terrible conclusion.

'Well?' he heard Antrobus Vetch's reedy whine as if he were a long way away. 'Who sabotaged the operation, hmm?'

Mune began to speak, neurotransmitters racing at the influx of serotonin, unable to censor what he was saying. 'I-I-It was me,' he spluttered, saliva dribbling from the corner of his mouth. 'I betrayed you!'

'GOING SOMEWHERE, DOC?' Haze spun round, his heart pounding. Standing in the wrecked doorway of the scientist's ransacked lab was Nathan Creed. He looked more like his old self compared to the last time Haze had seen him. He had recovered his hat and coat, although the later was rather singed around the edges, and the bounty hunter's stub guns hung holstered at his waist. His undershirt, however, was still almost black with grime and he had acquired some gloves from somewhere to protect his scolded hands.

'Much as I'd like to make idle chit-chat I have to pack!' Haze growled, scooping the contents of an instrument drawer into a large bag. The doc's servitor, One-Eight-Seven, was already holding two full packs.

'Why?' Creed drawled, taking a long drag on a smouldering cheroot.

'Because, in case you hadn't worked it out yet, Antrobus Vetch now knows that it was me who sabotaged his ork-smuggling operation, and any minute now a whole host of pit slaves and hired scum are going to descend on this place so that that vindictive bastard-son-of-a-ripperjack can extract more than his pound of flesh! That's why!'

'Oh, I don't think that's very likely,' the bounty hunter said, still smiling. 'Not since Vetch thinks that it was actually Mune who betrayed him.'

'What?'

'Our mutual friend Gravalax Mune is at this moment being prepared for "reassignment" to Stalag Slag Hole.'

Doc Haze strode over to the bounty hunter and clasped his shoulders, giving him a friendly shake. 'Then I'm free! I don't need to leave! I owe you one, Creed. You saved my life from than maniac Mander and now I'm free to live it out in peace!'

'Until the next time,' Creed muttered, 'and you actually owe me two.'

'Two?' Haze let go of his saviour and took a step back, eyeing the downhive desperado suspiciously. 'What do you mean, two?'

'I know why Vetch thinks it was Mune who betrayed him. I saw you mix the brain fluid with the lubricant when I entered the crypt the second time. I'm sure Vetch would like you to explain it all to him, as well as who really sabotaged the ork smuggling operation. I always suspected it was you, doc.'

Haze felt the blood drain from his cheeks. 'So, what do you want in return, Creed?' he asked sourly.

The bounty hunter took another long drag on his cheroot and exhaled a great cloud of blue-grey smoke. 'I'll let you know,' he said and, tipping his hat to Haze, Nathan Creed turned and strode out of the lab.

And as the bounty hunter left, Haze was sure he could hear him laughing.

WARP SPAWN

Matt Ralphs

PETTY OFFICER DRANT manoeuvred his wheelchair closer to the edge of the loading ramp and peered out into the gloom. The light from the cargo hold spilled out before him, illuminating a portion of the landing compound; it looked like a vast frozen lake, shining dully in the encroaching dusk. He drummed his fingers nervously on the arm rests and shivered as frigid tendrils of cold penetrated through his tunic. The crisp evening chill steamed his breath and he blew on his fingers, inwardly cursing his captain, who at this very minute was probably tucked up in bed. As far as his aging eyes could tell, the cargo port was empty and still. He cursed and waited, stewing in his own disquiet.

Where were they?

A few small spacecraft, mostly private merchant clippers, sat squat and silent, their hulls softly lit up orange by the sodium lamps that battled valiantly against the deepening dark. These ships, although large, were dwarfed by the vessel Drant looked out from. Guild freighter *Sable Bess*, nearly a kilometre from stubby snout to square cut fins, loomed up massively. Her holds were laden with military supplies destined for the Imperial Guard, and she patiently waited for departure at dawn.

But she was not yet fully laden. There was more cargo still to arrive.

Drant activated a comm-link on the bulkhead and it buzzed into life.

'Private link, captain's quarters,' he whispered.

'Unable to respond. Please speak up,' a mechanical voice replied.

Drant smacked the offending device in exasperation.

'Private link, captain's quarters,' he repeated, louder this time.

He waited, fidgeting nervously – then looked round towards the loading ramp, his pale face panicked.

Voices!

He retreated back into the shadows behind a bulkhead mainstay, terrified by the seemingly deafening noise his chair made in the quiet that surely anyone could hear. In his haste to hide he bumped into a loading cradle, toppling a precariously balanced pot of grease which he managed to grab in the second that two arbites rounded the corner onto the ramp. They stopped and peered up, shining their torches into the hold.

At that moment the comm-link connection to the captain's quarters was made and the line opened with a crackle. Drant's eyes widened and his grip on the greasy pot slipped; it overturned, spilling two litres of stinking axle grease onto his uniform.

The arbites heard the comms unit bleep, and hurried up the ramp. A rough voice, heavy with sleep, crackled over the connection.

'Captain Matteus here. That you, Drant?'

The arbites exchanged perplexed looks, and one touched the 'respond' icon.

'Er, good evening, captain, this is perimeter patrol, Private Hu speaking. Any reason you're paging an empty hold?'

Drant held his breath, waiting for his captain's reply. S'blood, it'd better be good! There was a slight pause, then:

'Dammit, that connection's still faulty. Where're you speaking from, trooper?'

'Says hold one-forty on the floor, sir,' Hu replied, slightly bemused.

'Answer me this, Hu. How can a freighter captain such as myself, charged with supplying the brave men of the Imperial Guard with important equipment, be expected to run a tight ship when his supposed comm-link with engineering patches him through to an empty cargo hold?'

Drant could see Hu grin at his colleague, and relief swept through him. They were going to get away with it!

'I can't answer that, sir,' Hu chuckled. 'But I suggest you get it fixed before departure.'

'Good advice, trooper. Thanks for checking up on us. I'd better close that hold door now.'

'Understood, sir. Safe voyage.'

'Emperor protects.'

The connection clicked off.

Drant let out his breath as the arbites ambled down the ramp, idly swinging their power mauls, and disappeared into the night. He whirred back over to the comms-unit and reconnected back to the captain's quarters.

'That actually you, this time, Drant?' Matteus growled.

'Yes, sir,' Drant replied. He kept the exasperation he felt out of his voice and replaced it with a weary tone of irony. 'Our extra cargo is not here and the compound arbites are, as you've just experienced, somewhat alert tonight.'

'I should hope they are, that's their job. And calm down, our cargo will be here. They paid in advance so I don't much care if they turn up or not, though I suspect they will. They seemed… keen, shall we say, to leave this sector entirely. Told me the local gangers were after them. Behind in protection money. Sad.' Matteus paused as if reflecting on something. 'They had a little girl too…'

'You and your hard luck cases,' Drant muttered. 'We were nearly caught with those Cumanian refugees in the silage ducts last year. I don't need this kind of excitement. It was too much excitement that lost me my legs.'

Then you've nothing to worry about, old friend,' Matteus replied slyly. 'You can't lose your legs twice.'

The connection cut off, leaving Drant alone again in the silent cold. He scanned the perimeter of the compound for any signs of movement, getting more nervous with every passing minute. The next half hour dragged by until two figures carrying a limp bundle appeared from behind some loading frames and dashed over to the cargo ramp. He didn't know whether to feel relieved or frightened.

After a successful launch, with the planet Vrantis III receding into nothing more than a bright light behind her, the *Sable Bess* began preparations for the warp jump. Her decks were alive with activity as the crew busied themselves with maintenance and routine duties. Captain Matteus found Drant outside the infirmary.

'All well?' he asked.

Drant eyed him darkly. 'Well enough. They're in hold one-forty.'

'Good. As planned then,' Matteus replied. 'Was the girl with them?'

Drant regarded his captain shrewdly. 'Is that why you took this contract on, Matteus? Because of the little girl?'

Matteus glanced down. 'They paid. That's all the reason I need.'

Drant snorted, unconvinced. 'She was asleep, looked dead to the world.'

The phrase echoed in Matteus's mind.

Dead to the world. She's dead to me now, or may as well be. Where is she now? While she is gone, I will know no peace. Ten years since… It felt like a prison sentence.

Matteus collected himself, as Drant looked on trying to read his inscrutable face.

'Check on them would you, Drant? Make sure the child's not sick.' He paused, thinking. 'I may move them somewhere more comfortable for the journey.'

Drant grunted and whirred off down the corridor. Matteus closed his eyes for a second, then turned on his heel and strode towards the bridge.

* * *

A SCENE OF organised chaos greeted him when he arrived. He watched the hurried preparations from a darkened alcove in the bulkhead. He could see Lieutenant Eusoph, his rangy second-in-command gesticulating to the pilots as they busily entered data into the ship's main computing engine and conducted last minute safety precautions. Dozens of servitors crouched before banks of machinery, checking and cross-checking numbers that flooded their screens in endless reams. Black-clad crewmen hurried around taking gauge readings; and amongst all this movement and bustle two robed tech-adepts glided, anointing both men and machines with blessed oil from silver tureens. Noticing Matteus in the shadows, Eusoph looked questioningly at him, but his captain waved his hand, allowing him to continue conducting the final preparations himself.

The atmosphere was tense. Matteus had lost count of how many warp jumps he had undertaken, but always he felt a giddy, nervous excitement at this point in the proceedings. Safety checks be damned, he thought; we're in the power of the warp now, anything can happen.

'One minute,' Eusoph snapped over the bridge-vox. 'Be ready.'

The noise and flurry of activity slowly petered out and then ceased altogether. All eyes turned to the huge stained glass window that monopolised the starboard side of the bridge. The coloured glass depicted a stylised outline of the *Bess* surrounded by a halo of protective light, which was itself surrounded by a horde of ravening daemons. This impressive diorama was part of a wall that sealed off the navigator's chamber. The bridge crew stared at the twisted and wizened man behind the window, who himself overlooked them from a cradle that hung on dozens of chains from the high ceiling. He looked like a living sacrifice.

Although the imperfect surface of the window blurred and distorted his form he could clearly be discerned; silent, apart, but omnipresent to a crew that regarded him with a mixture of fear and awe. His body was wrapped in a harness of interlinked straps that swung gently to and fro. A mass of cables and wires extruded from the mummified creature's face, linking him to the ship's navigation equipment and the engine servitors below decks. The only human features visible were sightless milky eyes, flat nostrils and the thin line of his mouth. The third eye that allowed this otherwise blind man insight into the flux of the warp was hidden by a circular metal plate, which fitted snugly around his domed forehead. Upon this was etched the outline of a staring eye.

Eusoph cleared his throat. 'Navigator?' he prompted.

The cocooned man shuddered, as if waking from a deep sleep. His mouth opened and a voice like sandpaper on rust rasped over the vox-com.

'I am ready,' he said. From the floor before him a large screen rose up elegantly on a jointed support pillar. His mind activated the metal plate on his head which opened up like a flower, allowing his third eye access to the warp field as it appeared on the screen. 'The warp is ready,' he said after a few seconds. 'It is time.'

Eusoph nodded. 'Blast shields down,' he said.

Matteus gazed out of the viewing port before him. Staring back was a vista of stars, bright and clear against the blackness. It was starkly and coldly beautiful. Matteus shivered. With a heavy grating sound, a thick shield began to lower over the forward windows and the stars blinked out one by one as it slowly ground down into position. With a solid thump it stopped and locking bolts snapped into place.

Tech-Priest Iotep Kull, garbed in a silver trimmed black cowl, bowed low before the main engine control board, and whispered the final initiation sequence that would ignite the warp engines. A deep booming throb began to seep up from the decks below, as the power unleashed from the warp core in the bowels of the ship was distributed to the engines themselves: the Machine God was awake. Matteus could feel it emanating through the soles of his boots.

'Prepare for warp entry,' Eusoph said, his voice tight with tension. 'On the captain's command.'

Matteus settled down into his giant leather chair, savouring the moment, 'Now, if you please,' he said, indicating to Kull. Kull, flanked on either side by two priests swinging incense pendulums, lifted his face up to the towering bank of instruments that blinked with dozens of glowing runes. Streams of heavy smelling vapour issued forth from fluted pipes to settle in miasmic layers around his feet.

'Ignis, aduro, illustro!' he intoned.

The engines crackled into violent life and the ship lunged forward. The navigator strained to steady the vessel as she nosed past the forced rent in the fabric of space and into the warp. Matteus leant forward in his chair, feeling the intensity of the merciless pressure winds buffeting them. In the face of this unmanageable power and fury, he felt helplessness and futility deaden him to his core. It was a personal struggle against his own inadequacies that he battled with during every warp jump.

The navigator's scratchy voice rattled over the vox: 'The warp has swallowed us whole.'

Eusoph flicked off the vox-link.

Brock, the security officer, watched the crew for telltale signs of warp psychosis. Seeing none, he relaxed a little. The danger period passed and the bridge crew settled back to their respective duties, anticipating another uneventful journey through one of the safest supply routes in Imperial space.

'Into the maelstrom,' Matteus whispered.

The reserve navigator, curled up in his cot in a recess in the bulkhead and lost in a deep slumber, twitched and whimpered.

THE LIFT SCREECHED slowly down on grime encrusted runnels and settled heavily on the deck. Drant heaved the rusty lattice door open and activated his chair. As he whined down the dank corridor, inquisitive rats poked sleek black muzzles from out of their holes to see what the intrusion was. He ducked his head rhythmically to pass under hissing overhead pipes and wrinkled his nose as the heavy odour of promethium fuel battered his nostrils. For centuries the *Sable Bess* had been a tanker until she was downgraded to a dry freight vessel. She was now consigned to an easy routine, supplying non-essentials manufactured on Vrantis III to the

Imperial Guard garrison on Jared's World, deep inside Imperium controlled space.

The name *Sable Bess* was derived from the black fuel she once towed from supply depot to war-zone, in the more exciting period of her career. But that time was now passed. Her former cargo's powerful smell hung in her holds and corridors, dormitories and gangways like a pungent ghost from the past. The stench was particularly bad near the stern where hold one-forty was situated. Drant glided down the corridor, enjoying the quiet.

He reached the hold door. It towered above him, a rusty orange colour with dark streaks smeared down its length. Under the layer of dirt was painted '140'. He punched in the relevant code on the rune pad set into the door frame. With a grinding roar the huge doors heaved apart and Drant was momentarily stunned by the smell of promethium that wafted over him. But he was more stunned by the scene that confronted him inside compartment one-forty.

The hold opened out immeasurably on either side, the walls receding into darkness. Two portable glow-globes, plugged into the door mechanism lit up an area of floor about fifteen metres distant. Several packing cases had been pushed together to form a makeshift table. Lying on this was a little girl. Her face, white as cotton and turned towards Drant, was fixed with a livid expression of despair; frightened eyes, framed within dark rings of fatigue, were wide open and alive with movement. Her mouth, the edges pulled down in an expression of utter misery, oozed drool. Spittle flicked and her pink tongue lolled grotesquely behind white baby teeth. She hissed as her thin body bucked and arched from the table as if caught in an uncontrollable spasm of agony.

Over her, stooped with intent, was a man. In his bony hand he held a long, liquid-filled syringe that was poised over the struggling girl's neck. At the sound of the opening door he looked up, alarmed. Seeing Drant, he roared with fury and before the medic could react, lunged for him.

* * *

WHEN MATTEUS WAS assured his ship was safely on its way, he handed over the bridge to Eusoph and headed to hold one-forty to see to his stowaways.

As he rounded a corner, whistling lightly through his teeth, the ship lurched, throwing him heavily against the wall. Deafening klaxons sounded and the light globes in the ceiling dimmed, flickered and came back on a deep orange hue. Underneath the noise of the alarms Matteus heard the ship's superstructure groaning like a stricken beast; dread twisted his guts as the noise grew. He reached out a hand to steady himself against the bulkhead and he felt it shiver under his touch.

For a split second his mind flashed back ten years…

…the sickening crunch as the eldar corsairs latched onto his vessel. The ruptured hull imploding inwards. The billowing smoke and crackling flames. The murderous boarding crews, screaming like banshees, seizing his cargo. And his child…

Clutching his numbed arm and regaining his shocked senses, Matteus found a vox-com control on the wall.

'Bridge, this is the captain. What's going on up there?' he said, fighting to hide the panic in his speech.

Eusoph answered, his voice strained but controlled: 'We don't know. You'd better get up here quick.'

In the background Matteus could hear the clamour of the bridge crew, and men shouting urgent orders.

'Did we hit something? Any sign of intruders?'

'No, and there's no damage that we can tell. As yet…'

Matteus winced as the hull around him quivered, sending shallow shockwaves down the length of the corridor. The light above his head shattered in a shower of bright sparks. He cowered as slivers of glass rained down, pattering onto his head and shoulders.

'Tell that to the *Bess*! On my way. And for the love of all that is holy, turn off these alarms.'

Still holding his arm, Matteus pounded back up the passageway as the ship strained and protested around him.

* * *

DRANT'S VISION WAS filled by the quivering needle just a few centimetres from his eye and a rabidly angry face looming behind it. The man's knee was on Drant's chest and his elevation over the chair-bound medic gave him an advantage; but Drant had once been a corporal in the Imperial Guard and, although disabled, he was stronger than most able-bodied men. With one meaty hand he clutched the man's throat, and with the other his thin wrist; but still the point edged closer. Drant struggled, heart beating fast; all he could see was the wicked-looking needle, one drop of clear liquid hanging like a tear from its tip.

Then the ship reeled, and the lock was broken. Losing his balance, the man pitched over Drant's chair and in doing so sent him rolling back against the bulkhead. All the lights went out, plunging the hold into darkness. For a second the light fizzled back into life and Drant had a snapshot of the man picking himself up; and someone else, slight of build and with raven black hair covering her face, leaning over the comatose child who now lay crumpled on the ground.

Blackness returned. He could hear movement, and urgent whispers that echoed confusingly around the enormous hold. Then it went quiet.

Drant tried to control his ragged breathing. He'd seen plenty of combat in his Imperial Guard days, so fear was not new to him, but being consigned to a wheelchair had been an agonizing test of faith and character. He had adapted, with the help of the Emperor. But now his lack of mobility frustrated him; he was fully aware that this disadvantage could be the death of him. He switched off his chair motors, knowing that their use would alert his enemy to his position. He began to roll towards where he thought the door was by turning the wheels manually. Seconds passed. Straining his ears and eyes for his aggressor, he trundled on with agonising slowness. He could see a faint light outlining the door frame. Evidently some of the glow-globes in the corridor had not gone out.

Nearly there…ten more metres…

There was a sudden rush of movement and something heavy collided with his chair, tipping Drant over onto his side. He grunted as all the air was knocked from his lungs. The man brought all his weight to bear and Drant was rendered completely immobile. Hot breath rasped into his ear and a voice, scratchy and cold said, 'This is not your business, cripple.'

Drant, terrified and helpless, felt something cold and sharp against his cheek; it slid smoothly under the skin. He pictured the man's white skinny thumb over the syringe plunger, about to press...

A buzzing sound filled the room and the lights burst back on, burning bright and harsh. Shouts invaded his petrified mind even as all he could think about was the needle in his flesh. There was a guttural roar of violent rage above and the weight of the man on top of him was suddenly gone. From the corner of his eye Drant saw him sprawl onto the ground, robes flying around him and limbs flailing. He smashed into a packing case and fell limp. His neck rested at an ugly, crooked angle; Drant knew he was dead. Towering over the corpse stood a mountain of uniformed muscle, it was Gunnar Larson, the captain's mate, and huddled against the table was the raven-haired woman, cradling the child in her arms. As Gunnar approached her, she snarled, mouth twisting into an ugly grimace.

Drant clawed at the needle that was still embedded in him, pulling it loose. He felt relief beyond measure when he saw that it was still full of liquid. Strong hands gathered him up and set his chair upright. He looked up into the concerned features of Brock, the security officer.

'Drant, can you tell us what in the Emperor's name is going on?'

MATTEUS GAZED MORTIFIED at the ravaged mess behind the stained glass window. The navigator hung half out of his harness, face a tormented mask of agony. Reddy-brown rents ran down his cheeks and, where his warp-eye should have been, was just a raw crimson pit weeping pus and blood.

'What... what did this?' Matteus stammered.

'He did it to himself,' Eusoph said. Matteus looked at him dumbly. Eusoph pointed to the navigator.

'Look at his arm.'

Matteus saw that one scrawny limb rested by his side. He had somehow managed to free it from the restraints. His fingers were curled into claws and stained with dark cerise fluid. The pipes and cables that made up the navigator's delicate connection with the ship had been ripped from his head, leaving deep welts in his ashen skin.

'One minute all systems were functioning and the navigator was guiding us,' Eusoph continued. 'Then he screamed something over the vox. A warning I think, but incoherent. Then he tore himself apart. He used his restraining buckle to pierce his eyes.' Eusoph swallowed. 'There was nothing we could do but watch.'

Matteus tore his gaze from the dead navigator. 'What's our current status?'

'*Bess* is stable but we're adrift within the warp,' Eusoph said. He looked at the dead man. 'Some sort of exposure to the outside elements may have caused this but we should be safe, the navigator's chamber is completely sealed off.'

Matteus calmed a little. Around them, bridge officers barked orders and conflag-servitors were dousing dozens of small fires that had broken out. Smoke filtered away through ceiling vents, and a semblance of order was being restored.

'Organise damage teams to inspect every rivet and bolt on this ship, and I want all tech-priests testing warding beacons and protective veins. Get them praying to their blasted Machine God, whatever…' Matteus checked himself. I must keep calm, he said inwardly. 'I want our secondary navigator linked up in half an hour.'

Eusoph looked troubled, 'We can't wake him. He's in some unholy trance. Filthy psykers, I don't understand them. It will take time to rouse him.' He paused, as if assessing whether he should tell his visibly shocked captain any more.

'There's something else.'

'Go on.'

'Someone's opened compartment one-forty, and there's no reason for anyone to do that. It's empty. I've sent Brock and Gunnar down to see.'

As if on cue the vox-com crackled into life.

'Bridge, this is Brock. We've some uninvited guests. One dead man, one unconscious girl, and one woman screaming blue murder.' In the background Matteus could hear a woman's shrill cries of despair. Brock's voice faded from the voice pick-up. 'Gunnar, shut that harpy up, for Terra's sake.' A slap rang out, followed by silence. Brock spoke back into the vox-com. 'I'm taking the woman to the brig and Drant's going to see to the child in the medi-bay. And what the hell happened to the ship? I almost fell over the gantry on the way here.'

'Tell Drant I'll meet him in the medi-bay. Then I'll see you in the brig. Find out what you can from her, and don't stand on ceremony. I'll talk to you then.' Matteus looked down guiltily, 'Is Drant alright?'

'He's had a narrow escape. This maniac was trying to stick him with a needle as long as my arm. But he's fine.'

Matteus breathed a sigh of relief. 'I'll meet you in the brig.'

'Acknowledged. Brock out.'

Eusoph raised an enquiring eyebrow. 'Who or what was in hold one-forty, captain?'

'I'll deal with that,' Matteus replied, trying to sound as neutral as possible. 'Eusoph, you have the bridge. Get us moving again.' He cast a nervous glance around him, as if expecting daemons to appear through the bulkhead, then strode hurriedly off the bridge. Eusoph stared after him, eyebrow still raised.

BROCK LIFTED THE woman's face up by her hair and looked into challenging black eyes. Manacled to the wall of the brig cell, she glared defiantly back at him, her mouth horribly swollen from where Gunnar had slapped her. Brock kept his expression contemptuous, but in truth the woman disturbed him. She was young, but her face had a haggard look that belied her youth, as if she had seen things so terrible they had aged her prematurely. It made him feel uncomfortable. She held him with her eyes and the depth of experience he perceived within them intimidated him further. A thrill of fear shivered up his spine.

She spat back into his face and the spell was broken. Brock
smacked her hard around the face, angry at himself for losing concentration. She recoiled, ugly words pouring from
her lips.

'Who are you?' Brock shouted, wiping the spittle from his
face. 'And what in the Emperor's name were you doing to
the child?'

A few seconds passed, and then she looked up, her face
calm, 'I would never expect you to understand.' Her voice
was soft and seductive, totally at odds with her weathered,
beaten face; her words were tinged with a strange, melodi-
ous accent that Brock could not place. But underneath was
an unmistakable undertone, like steel under satin, hard and
unforgiving. 'All I know is that you will die.'

Chief Brock frowned, momentarily disconcerted, but he
quickly regained composure.

'You can talk or you can remain silent. It matters not.' He
smiled a thin smile. 'We are reviving that poor girl. She will
tell us what we want to know.' He stepped back to see her
reaction and was shocked by its vehemence.

Her eyes widened in panic and all composure fled her
face. She had a slender frame but became possessed of a
strength born of terror; words gabbled from her mouth and
she struggled with her bonds, arms straining and fingers
bent into talons.

'No, don't wake her!' she screeched. 'Keep her dormant.
They will find her, it will find her.' Her last sentence was
screamed at nerve shredding volume: *'You don't know what
she is!'*

Matteus entered the medi-bay, blinking in the unforgiving
glare of the lights. The infirmary was a sterile white; a room
of scrubbed surfaces and gleaming surgical-servitors. In the
corner, incongruous amongst all the delicate machinery,
hulked Gunnar Larson. His uniform was stretched to tearing
point over his muscular frame, and with his giant hands he
petted his huge rat, Leman. Gunnar cooed and warbled as
the rat sniffed suspiciously at the air. Against the opposite
wall was a line of about a dozen examination slabs, all
empty except one.

Drant was examining the girl's eyes for signs of shock whilst chatting quietly. She perched on the edge of the slab kicking her legs back and forth, seemingly quite happy. She was peering at the polished floor with intense interest at her own vague reflection. Lank black hair like that of her mothers was draped in strands, obscuring her face.

Drant looked over when he heard Matteus enter the room. His genial face turned angry and with a final word to the girl that was duly ignored, he wheeled over to him.

'Are you well, my friend?' asked Matteus with concern.

'I was very nearly killed.' Drant narrowed his eyes. 'Gunnar told me, in his fashion, about the navigator. What have you done to us, Matteus?' he said.

The captain blanched and wiped his perspiring brow.

'That has nothing to do with your... incident. Or the stowaways. Coincidence, nothing more.' Matteus laid a hand on Drant's shoulder. 'The man is dead, the woman is in the brig and Eusoph will have us on our way soon. We'll just have to cover this up.' He glanced at the girl and whispered, 'Has she said anything?'

Drant sighed, placated for now. 'Not a word. I gave her a stimm-drug to wake her and she seems healthy enough, considering her treatment.'

Matteus gazed at the child and was reminded of why he'd agreed to help them. There was little likeness between this girl and his daughter, but she was the same age and build as Nadia had been when she was stolen, and she exuded a vulnerability that Matteus responded to immediately. He felt a deep sympathy for the lost child who sat alone, still staring at her reflection and swinging her legs in the air. He approached her, signalling Drant to stay back. He crouched and looked up into her little white face.

'What is your name, child?'

Her electric blue eyes regarded him levelly. When she spoke her voice was light and clear as dawn in spring.

'Are my parents gone?'

'Your father is dead,' he said gently. 'But you mother is in another room helping us.'

She dropped her gaze and bit her bottom lip.

'Child, your name?' She ignored him and turned away, scratching at the pink needle mark on her skinny arm.

'My friend is coming,' she said, suddenly brightening.

'What friend?'

'My friend. The one I feed sometimes.' She tapped the side of her head. 'I grow him in here.'

'I don't understand,' Drant said. 'Who do you grow?'

A tiny frown darkened the little girl's otherwise serene face. 'My friend,' she said.

Seeing that Matteus still did not understand she leaned close, tapping her temple with both index fingers. 'In here,' she insisted.

Matteus, confused and taken aback by the intensity of the child, stood up, obeying an unconscious desire that demanded he be taller than her and thus regain some initiative.

She looked up at him, smiling happily, her legs swinging like incessant pendulums. 'You'll see who soon,' she said airily.

Matteus, at a loss, shook his head, 'Drant, do you have any truth-drugs?'

A ragged scream echoed upwards through the grilled ventilation cover set into the floor, rising in pitch then suddenly cut short. Silence fell for a split second then another cry followed, higher, and infused with so much fear and dread that Matteus felt his knees go weak.

For the first time that day he took immediate and constructive action.

'The brig,' he ordered. 'Gunnar, to me!' and dashed from the infirmary with the giant lumbering in tow.

Drant, shaking as the shrieks echoed around his infirmary, tentatively approached the girl. She was bouncing up and down, giggling and clapping her hands together. 'He's here!' she said gleefully. 'At long last, he's here!'

Drant grabbed her, sat her on his knee and whirred after the captain.

IT HAD TAKEN half an hour to prise open the navigator's chamber. He had been sealed within for decades and had since never left what had eventually become his tomb. Eusoph coughed in the stale air, holding a handkerchief over his mouth.

'Get the vents working. I can hardly breathe in here.' He cast an appraising eye around the chamber. 'No sign of forced entry, and the hull's intact.' He snorted. 'If it weren't we wouldn't be here any more.'

The secondary navigator had been revived from his self-induced trance and was getting ready to link up to the ship. He could sense the dead body even if he could not see it. Eusoph looked on in distaste as he crept blindly but with complete assurance around the small room.

'What do you think caused him to do this?'

For a moment the navigator was silent, probing the ship and the space around it with his sensitive psychic sense.

'Something on board,' he said in a blank monotone. He turned, empty sockets directed at Eusoph's own grey eyes as if he could see him. 'Something nearby, something close. And more are coming. They circle us like vultures.'

'Ensign Jagg!' Eusoph shouted, louder than he needed to. 'Help our new primary navigator into his harness.' He indicated the former incumbent who lolled precariously from his straps. 'And get that abomination out of there before I vomit on the Emperor's holy floor.'

'Sir?' the young ensign said.

'What is it?' Eusoph snapped.

'I think I can hear something.' Jagg sidled up to the huge gothic window that commanded the entire forward facing bulkhead. An impregnable blast door had been lowered over it for protection. Jagg put his ear to the glass.

Eusoph tapped his foot impatiently.

'Ensign...'

Jagg pressed his finger to his lips. 'Listen.'

Eusoph was about to scream blue bloody murder to the man who had dared silence him when the blast door jolted in its runnels and a piercing scraping sound jarred their ears. Jagg stumbled back, terror etched onto his youthful features. They watched as the bottom corner of the door tilted upward, juddered and then dropped back, as if something with unimaginable strength on the other side was trying to force it open.

Eusoph, eyes wide with shock, did his best to rally the startled crew.

'Jagg, get the navigator hooked up at the double. And seal off this chamber from the bridge when you're done. I want that door welded shut, understand? Everybody else get out, now! I want the engines ready to fire as soon as the navigator's in position.' As he walked with unseemly speed from the chamber he asked himself: where is Matteus?

The new navigator primus said nothing, even as the blast door undertook another brutal assault, shaking the ship from prow to stern.

THE BRIG LAY in the squalid bowels of the ship, directly below the kitchens. Some said the worst part of being there was to smell the swill that the cooks produced that overpowered even the all-pervading odour of promethium fuel. This pungent cocktail was whipped sluggishly by slowly rotating fans on the ceiling.

Matteus stepped off the ladder, wincing as his boots struck the metal gantry with a clang. The brig corridor was dim, lit only sparsely by orange glow-globes set low in the bulkhead. The noise of the engines would normally be more profound here than anywhere else on the ship, bar the engine rooms. The narrow walkway was usually filled with the powerful throb of the warp-drive and the faint cries of the engineers and crews as they toiled with the giant machines. But now it was quiet, except for the mellifluous murmur of ventilation pipes.

Gunnar followed, along with two security ratings who wielded power mauls. Matteus was hefting a heavy piece of pipe; Gunnar needed nothing more than his mallet-sized fists. Matteus motioned for silence as he crept down the corridor. The door to the brig cell hung at an angle, the top hinge torn from the frame. It was buckled outwards, as if something with tremendous power had smashed it open from the inside.

'That door's made from solid titanium,' the security rating whispered.

'Put your mauls on full power,' Matteus said softly, and was heartened as the buzz from the weapons increased behind him.

'Gunnar go first,' a voice as deep as a chasm intoned behind him. Matteus was startled, not by the volume but by the fact that the gigantic man had actually spoken, something he rarely ever did.

'Thank you, Gunnar,' Matteus said, patting him on the arm, 'but I should go first.'

After reaching the door, he hugged the wall and preyed silently, while the other three looked expectantly at him. He turned to them and mouthed, 'One, two, three', and burst into the room.

He stopped short, his mind taking several seconds to register what he saw; he put a hand to his mouth to stem the flow of bile that rose up his throat, bitter and sharp. The others barged in around him, brandishing weapons. Their war-cries died on their lips.

The entire opposite side of the cell was stained crimson. Red streaks spattered the brown-hued steel in garish rainbow patterns, which dripped down to pool in viscose puddles at the base of the wall. Two bodies lay on the ground, one on top of the other, as if locked in a lover's embrace. They seemed fused together, loose flaps of skin and torn flesh overlapped to such an extent that it was impossible to judge whose body they belonged to. Matteus could tell the one on the bottom was Brock only because he could see his ornate security officer's epaulette, almost obscured by a mass of human offal.

The warm air, heavy with a nauseating tang of copper, caught in Matteus's throat. His mind reeled as the violence of the scene hit him like a kick in the stomach. He heard one of the ratings moan as he vomited in enormous, raking heaves. He dropped his club which rolled across the floor and came to rest next to the gently steaming corpses.

Matteus's horror deepened when he noticed the manacles on the wall. Dangling grotesquely like meat joints in a butcher's window were the woman's arms. Gunnar was pounding his fists on the cell wall, his simple mind unable to cope with what he saw.

When Matteus heard the lift door rasp open at the other end of the corridor he found his senses again. He slapped Gunnar hard and indicated for them all to be quiet. They edged back against the wall, grim faced and trying to ignore the terrible vista of death that lay before them. The security rating who had been sick wiped his mouth with a shaking hand. Matteus caught his eye and nodded encouragingly. The rating nodded back. They turned their eyes on the door and waited, with weapons at the ready.

They exhaled in relief as the familiar whine of Drant's chair grew louder towards them. They could hear the little girl's voice over the noise of the motors.

'Don't bring her in here,' Matteus called, but it was too late. They rounded the corner and glided into the cell.

Drant gasped.

'Damn it, get her out of here, will you?' Matteus ordered, but the girl slipped off Drant's knee and padded barefoot into the room.

'Mummy?' she said. The men watched her, not knowing what to do. She turned to Matteus, her blue eyes shining in the gloom. 'Is that my mummy?' she asked.

Matteus looked again at the bloody mess in the middle of the floor, for the first time noticing the coal black hair spread out like a fan.

'Yes,' he said, voice cracking, trying desperately to think of something comforting to say; but the scene of devastation around them negated all words of succour.

She crouched down next to her mother, the bottom of her white dress becoming saturated with blood. Glancing up and cocking her head, she sniffed the air. She looked perplexed, as if inwardly struggling to take in what had happened.

'He's been here.' She fixed her gaze on Matteus. 'Mummy must have made him angry.'

Being under her scrutiny unnerved him. There was something old within her eyes, something old and wise. 'It's best not to make him angry,' she continued.

Matteus swallowed, attempting a smile.

'Best not to make who angry, child?'

'My friend.'

'What is your friend like?'

She looked appraisingly at Gunnar who stood at the edges of the room shaking his head as if trying to clear it of heretical thoughts.

'Bigger than him,' she said. 'Much bigger. He looks after me. But sometimes he can be very messy.' She gestured to the scattered flesh parts and liquid pools around her. 'I can make him come back, if you like.'

'No!' Matteus said, too loudly.

She frowned. 'But I want him here,' she said petulantly. Bowing her head she began to soundlessly mouth words. Instantly the atmosphere in the room became heavy and time seemed to slow down; the temperature plummeted as the girl became the epicentre of a psychic storm, her long black hair standing on end, electrified in whipping blue bursts of energy. It looked like her elfin face was wreathed in headless, writhing snakes. The air around her thickened and shimmered; to Matteus her outline became hazy. The only point of clarity in the unearthly vision that had once been a petite and seemingly innocent child, was a look of hatred centred in her once sky-blue eyes which were now deepest black and vacant of humanity. Leman the rat squealed and leapt from Gunnar's top pocket and dashed out into the corridor. Gunnar bellowed, lunging for the child.

Quick as lightning she spun round to face him. A fleeting look of fear and confusion swept over her face but it was gone as soon as it had appeared. She spat an ugly command and the giant was lifted clean off his feet and hurled bodily out of the door as if he were rag doll tossed aside by a bored child. He smashed into the corridor wall, rupturing pipes. Hot vaporous steam erupted with an explosive hiss. For a few seconds Gunnar sat there, stunned, then he leapt to his feet and pounded off after his beloved rat, weeping in distress.

The other men stood aghast as the child spun to face them with an expression of malevolent fury. The security ratings sprang towards her, power mauls swinging in deadly arcs. She uttered something and they were catapulted into the ceiling, skulls impacting with wet thuds. She held them there, then let them drop to the deck like unstrung puppets.

She turned her gaze to Matteus and Drant, her tiny mouth chanting words of arcane power. Matteus felt them invade his mind and take over his senses...

The chase was over. Rain fell about them, soaking the walls of the blind alley; and she shivered as it ran down her neck. Her parents clutched her to them as the gang advanced. The tallest stepped forward, boots splashing in shiny black puddles. She looked down, frightened, catching her reflection in the water at her feet. She struggled to master her emotions, but did not know how. Something inside her, powerful and possessive, began to surface.

The man pulled back his hood. His face was hard, but his mouth hinted at amusement as he watched the family shiver. Rendered in blue on his high brow was the Imperial spread-eagle.

'Elusive, aren't you?' he said. 'But no one slips through my grasp. The Inquisition will not be mocked by you, Chaos filth.'

'Do as you will,' her father said. 'We serve the true powers of the warp. Soon you will weep before her gaze.'

The inquisitor barked a laugh. 'Then I sentence you to return to her.'

His band of hunters drew forth weapons from their robes.

'Fire at will.'

She felt her mind flex like a muscle, and the air around her became stiff with cold fingers of energy. In her head she formed a shape with claws and a soulless heart. She screamed, clutching her temples as the vision became solid.

She continued to look down at her reflection as the cries of the inquisitor mingled with the sounds of renting flesh and splitting bone.

The vision ended and Matteus found himself on the other side of the closed door with Drant breathing heavily beside him.

'Cultists,' he whispered, almost to himself. 'And the girl...' He looked with uncomprehending eyes at Drant. 'They used her to channel the fiend that is now on my ship.'

'At your invitation, Matteus,' Drant said sullenly.

Matteus heaved on the cell door, but it was wedged shut, held there by the child's incredible psychic strength.

'Where's Gunnar when you need him?' He activated a vox-com: 'Bridge, what's our status?'

Eusoph's voice crackled over the speaker, his usually commanding tones steeped in barely controlled panic.

'We're under attack; they're trying to get through the blast doors.' In the background Matteus could hear fearful cries mingling with the sound of tearing metal. 'There's something already on board. Reports of an intruder are flooding in from all over the *Bess*. I can't get hold of engineering. I sent a squad down to see and they haven't come back. We can hear screams in the vent shafts…'

'Calm down, Eusoph. How's the navigator doing?'

'It's too late for that. Didn't you hear me? They're already on board!'

Matteus slumped against the bulkhead; feeling like someone was filling in a grave over his head. He could hear Eusoph's irregular breathing magnified over the speaker, and behind that, shrieks of terror. Someone was shouting: 'Back to your posts, or I'll drop you where you stand!' Chaos was reigning supreme on his craft. Matteus knew it was time.

'Eusoph, I'm authorising a ship-wide abandonment. All crew to the escape pod, at the double. Tell them to stop for nothing. Don't wait for me. As soon as all personnel are accounted for and I've got the ship out of the warp, abandon her. Just get the navigator hooked in to the ship's systems before you go. Do you understand?'

'I understand. Eusoph out.' Mercifully, the sounds of turmoil on the bridge clicked off.

Matteus knelt down next to Drant. 'That means you too: bail as soon as we drop out of warp.'

'We'll go nowhere without our captain. Besides, you must be held accountable for this, old friend.'

'Get to the pod, you old fool.' In the cell the little girl wallowed in blood. She dangled her fingers in it, giggling, and began to daub patterns on the wall; stylised runes in the shape of ever wakeful eyes. They glowed like beacons. The feeding frenzy in the warp increased in violence. Deep in the ship, something responded.

THE SHIPBOARD VOX-com had been left on an open channel. As Matteus shinned up ladders and sprinted down gangways on his way to the bridge, he heard the shrieks and dying prayers of his crew from the vox-pickups dotted around the vessel. It was obvious that many were not going to make it to the escape pod. He charged across gantries, legs pounding on the steel floors, tormented by the cries of the murdered as they echoed around him. His boots were spattered with blood and several times he slipped in the wetness.

He reached the bridge with the ship quaking under the escalating attack from the warp-creatures as they scratched and lacerated the hull. He stared, awestruck, as part of the blast-shield was peeled away with a tortured screech. He turned his eyes away from the dizzying whorl of distorted stars outside and dashed into the navigator's chamber.

The navigator lay curled on the deck, twitching and jerking spasmodically. Cables sprouted from plugs in his head attaching him to the ship.

Matteus shook him roughly, 'Awake, blast your eye! Get us out of the warp! Drop us out, now!'

The navigator whispered, voice barely audible above the din of the attack, 'So much malevolence t'ward us, strain's too much...'

'No! Get us out, for Emperor's sake, don't condemn us!'

'Trying...' the navigator murmured. A grating sound filled the room as the blast door was at last torn from its housing; a victorious gibbering filtered through from outside. Warp light streamed in, Matteus shielded his eyes and cried out in fear. The navigator screamed as his frail body succumbed to a final violent spasm; the warp-light died and silence descended.

'It is done,' he said, his face tranquil.

Matteus collapsed onto the deck, relief flooding through him.

'We are free,' the navigator whispered through raking gasps.

Before Matteus could thank him, a vision from his worst nightmare lumbered into the chamber, bringing with it a cloying stench of death. Walking upright and fully four metres tall, it stooped under the door; a black shadow of catastrophe. Its grossly swollen head turned left and right, as thick drool streamed from slavering, fanged jaws. Long arms, ending with lethal white talons, lashed out with deadly speed and impaled the navigator through his belly. He let out a weak bleat of pain, and fell silent.

Matteus acted instinctively, dashing through the monster's muscular legs and diving over his command chair on the bridge. He scrabbled underneath and found the shotgun he kept there for emergencies. Training the gun on the door with shaking hands he fumbled for the safety catch; but the creature was on him, foot-long claws raking his arm and sending the shotgun skittering out of reach.

Matteus had a second to register the enormous beast that towered over him; jaws wide in a silent scream of malignant rage; hot, rank breath blasting his face. A part of his mind screamed when he noticed an ear attached to a length of flesh dangling from a gore stained incisor. Matteus shut his eyes and waited for death.

'WE GO.'

'We wait.'

Eusoph looked at Drant incredulously, 'He's dead. Nearly everyone's dead. I'm in command. We go.' He reached over to the launch icon.

Drant grabbed his wrist and pulled Eusoph's face close to his own.

'We wait for our captain,' he said through clenched teeth. 'I insist.'

Something in the old man's eyes told Eusoph it was dangerous to argue. He backed off, chastened.

Ensign Jagg sat in the hatch to the escape pod from where he could see the fifty metre corridor leading back into the *Bess*.

'All quiet at the mo, Drant.'

'Let's hope it stays that way, lad.'

Drant fingered the handle of the autopistol he kept hidden under the armrest of his chair. 'Let it come,' he thought.

HE THOUGHT OF Nadia. Soon, perhaps, he would join her in whatever afterlife the Emperor had prepared for them.

The staccato rattle of an autogun broke his reverie. He looked up to see the creature career away, puce fluids bursting out of its carapace skin. Gunnar burst through the bridge doorway, howling with rage. He emptied the magazine then wielded the gun like a club, laying into the stumbling creature, bludgeoning its swollen head and roaring like a man possessed. It fell over, crashing into a gantry rail, blood oozing from a dozen wounds.

Gunnar turned to Matteus and pointed to a pulsating bulge in his breast pocket.

'Found Leman in kitchen.' He patted the now-buckled autogun. 'Found this also.'

'Thank the Emperor! Let's go.'

Behind them, even as they made their dash for freedom, the creature stirred. It knew this ship and where they were heading. It pounded after them with a hunter's instinct to cut them off.

'Two more corners and we're there,' Matteus cried euphorically. Gunnar grabbed him suddenly by the collar and clamped a gigantic hand over his mouth.

'Leman frightened. He smells it.' He pointed to the corner up ahead and whispered, 'There.'

A vast misshapen shadow was cast on the wall up ahead; the creature had beaten them! Matteus crouched onto the floor, broken at last.

Gunnar tapped him on the shoulder. A grin slowly crawled over his face, the cognitive process for this action taking some time. He pointed up to the ceiling. Matteus followed his finger and managed a smile.

JAGG LET OUT a cry. 'Something's there, at the end of the corridor!'

It came at them in a stooped charge, a solid mass of glistening muscle and scything claws, wide shoulders taking up the entire width of the passageway. Drant scrabbled for his pistol, levelled it in shaking hands and fired a wild volley of shots that ricocheted off the walls, puncturing coolant pipes. Scorching steam gushed out, burning the creature which jumped back, suddenly cautious.

Drant stared at the awful apparition that crouched just metres away, now wreathed in hissing vapours.

'It has come,' he breathed. 'Emperor preserve us, it has come.'

'We go, now!' Eusoph yelled, reaching for the launch icon.

Then a body fell down in front of them from the ventilation shaft in the ceiling of the corridor. It was quickly followed by another larger one. They tumbled inside.

'Launch!' Matteus screamed.

Eusoph hit the icon, and as the creature reached the doors they slammed shut with a resounding clang. A gaping mouth, spraying juices, lashed violently against the glass. The men cowered back, crying out in shock. Gunnar pressed his face to the window, howling in delight,

'Gunnar won! Gunnar won!'

Launch thrusters ignited with a roar, pushing the pod out into the void. The fiend, cheated of its prey, stood framed in the doorway for a second, and then retreated back inside the *Bess*.

'Now they are together, child and beast,' Matteus said, exhausted. 'Which is the bigger fiend, I wonder?'

He glanced around, eyes bright with grief. The shuttle was built to take the full crew complement of one hundred and forty-five men. A tally revealed twelve left, including him. No one spoke. No one could think of what to say.

Matteus stared out of the window as the *Sable Bess* faded from view. A blinding flash and she disappeared entirely, swallowed into the fathomless netherworld of the warp, and taking with it the girl and her Chaos spawn.

ON THE EDGE of a giant radiation cloud that was drifting across the Imperial freight route connecting Vrantis III to Jared's World, a hunter lay in ambush. From hooked nose to elegantly tapered fins, the eldar raiding vessel was a study of harsh, lethal beauty.

'Death can come from anywhere. She waits, then takes you into her embrace.'

And so spoke her captain, Khorach Wyche, who sat poised in her command chair, the very embodiment of a deadly predator, waiting patiently to strike.

'We have a contact,' her pilot informed, relish fairly dripping from his voice.

'Details?'

'Single vessel, probably a freighter, low readings, minimum power. A fat human maggot for us to burst.'

Khorach smiled the coldest of smiles. Easy pickings, yet she felt a twinge of disappointment. It was too easy. The cruel nature of her soul demanded a challenge, a foe that would wriggle and fight in her death grip. This prey would barely whimper before it fell to her guns and boarding crews.

Her pilot was looking at her expectantly. She made her decision, the only possible one.

'Assemble my raiders, I board with them today.'

'As you wish,' her pilot said. 'I have a designation on the ship. It's the *Sable Bess*.'

Khorach waved her hand dismissively. 'Unimportant. I just hope she puts up a struggle.' She licked her thin lips and looked hungrily at the lumbering vessel as it hove across the vision portal.

'Good hunting, lady, and good luck,' her pilot called.

'I won't need luck for this. I anticipate no problems.'

With that she turned and strode out of the bridge.

LEVIATHAN

An Ultramarines story

Graham McNeill

THE FORGE ECHOED to the sound of iron on steel. Sweltering heat rippled the air and Uriel sweated as he worked the narrow, flat-headed hammer along a length of orange-red metal, rounding off the edges to prevent them from folding when it came time to draw out the blade of his new sword.

He worked the hammer up and down the blade, keeping the temperature of the steel as constant as possible. Working it too hot could cause it to burn, resulting in impurities within the metal rising to the surface of the blade and making the weapon brittle. Conversely, working the metal too cold would 'work-harden' the steel, resulting in fine cracks that would greatly weaken the blade.

Satisfied the metal was ready for drawing, Uriel placed it at the correct angle on the anvil and began hammering one edge. He flattened and straightened the resulting twist in the metal, turning the blade over and repeating the process.

His muscles ached from the long day and hot steam burned in his lungs with every breath. The stars glittered through the open roof and a warm breeze sighed in from across the mountains, carrying the scent of evergreen

highland pines. He had not slept in six days, his time on
Macragge as full as he could ever remember it being. The
majority of this time had been spent reorganising the
Fourth Company after the Pavonis expedition and induct-
ing its newest members from the reserve companies, but
he had made sure to set aside time for this work in the
Artificers' forge chambers.

Uriel had until morning to finish the blade. The Fourth
Company had been called to action once more, this time in
the far-away system of Tarsis Ultra, and he was determined
to finish the weapon before departing.

Upon his return from Pavonis he had immediately cast
the metal icon taken from the Nightbringer's tomb into the
deepest vault below the Fortress of Hera. Once removed
from the C'tan's tomb, the metal had become utterly inert,
dead to every form of auspex Techmarine Harkus had at his
disposal. It was resistant to every weapon, furnace heat or
any other form of attack and resembled nothing so much as
a simple piece of carved silver. With the disappearance of its
diabolical master, it had become just a simple trophy of war.
But such an artefact was too dangerous to be allowed to
remain unguarded and sealed away forever in the depths of
the Fortress of Hera, it was as secure as anything could be.

With the Nightbringer's icon secured, Uriel had then
taken the broken blade of Captain Idaeus's sword and
placed it in the Chapter's most sacred reliquary.

He thought back to his former captain and though he still
mourned his friend and mentor's passing, he had now
grown into his role as captain of the Fourth Company.

Idaeus had taught him well and shown him the value of
thinking beyond the strictures of the Codex Astartes, the
holy tome penned by the primarch of the Ultramarines himself, Roboute Guilliman. Uriel would never consider
abandoning the teachings of the codex, but it was clear to
him now that there had to be some way of following the
spirit of the codex, if not the letter.

Pasanius, his oldest and most trusted friend, had accepted
Uriel's leadership without question, having been his only
comrade through their training and already well-used to the

less conventional command style of Captain Idaeus. With the practical mindset of a sergeant, Pasanius had understood the need to adapt to a continually changing battlefield. Learchus, Uriel's other veteran sergeant, had made no secret of his disapproval for such methods and, while he followed his new captain in the manner the Codex Astartes prescribed, he had never accepted the need to deviate from the sacred teachings of their primarch.

So ingrained was the concept of following the words of the codex without question that Uriel still wondered at his breaches of its teachings. Had he made the right decisions on Pavonis? Would there have been more lives saved if he had not taken his own initiative? No, he decided. The world of Pavonis would have burned in the fires of Inquisitor Barzano's Exterminatus if Uriel had not intervened, and he could not bring himself to believe that such an act of humanity was wrong.

But where would such small steps, on what many Ultramarines would consider the path to heresy, lead? Had those Space Marines who had turned from the light of the Emperor and followed the Great Betrayer into war so many millennia ago taken these same steps, still believing themselves acting for the best? How many had fallen without even realising it?

Surely there had to be some middle ground. And if there was, he resolved that he would find it. He owed the memory of Idaeus that much at least.

Shaking himself from such weighty thoughts, Uriel lifted the glowing blade, checking that the sword was the correct length and that it was accurately balanced. He nodded to himself and selected a smaller hammer from a table bearing all manner of tongs, fullers, punches, hammers, files and grindstones.

He began the relatively simple, but time-consuming, task of hammering the edges of the blade. Moisture dripped from his brow, hissing on the heated metal of the blade, and Uriel thought it appropriate that a measure of his own sweat be part of its forging. He worked the hammer backwards along the length of the blade, periodically turning the metal to keep it straight.

The Artificers had metriculators for measuring the exact line of a blade, but Uriel preferred the honest feel of a blade worked by hand and eye.

Finally, he lifted the sword from the anvil and held it before him, checking for any bends or twists in the metal. Finding none, he turned to the roaring forge coals and thrust the blade deep within.

Uriel left the sword to heat and wiped his brow, walking back to the entrance of the forge and lifting a clay jug of mountain water from a battered workbench. He raised the jug to his lips and drank deeply. The water was a day old and had warmed in the forge's heat, but was gloriously refreshing nonetheless. Uriel drained the jug in one long draught and set it back on the workbench. He stared up into the star-filled sky, shutting out the ring of hammers and ritual chants of the Artificers in other parts of the forge.

Working in the forge, with the heat of toil burning in his muscles and the scent of the wilds of Macragge in his nostrils, he was as close to content as he had been following his confrontation with the Nightbringer. Uriel closed his eyes, trying to shut out the image of the deathly apparition of the monstrous alien. He still woke from sleep with the taste of blood in his mouth, visions of death filling his senses and the lingering filth of its diabolical thoughts staining his dreams.

Each time he lay down on the simple bed in his cell, the scent of scorched flesh and burning blood would fill his nostrils. When he closed his eyes he saw severed limbs, spilled entrails and dismembered corpses. But though each body was mutilated with lunatic passion, their bloody eyes stared at him with hateful recognition.

You did this to us, they seemed to say. You and all your kind butchered us and left us to rot on a thousand times a thousand battlefields. Hundreds, then thousands surrounded him, and his superhuman strength was no defence against them. Eagerly they closed in, clawing and tearing at his flesh until his body ran with blood. Only as they reached with grave-dirt-encrusted fingernails for his eyes did he wake, hurled into consciousness with a cry of anguish still-born on his lips.

He shivered and tried to push all memory of the ancient star-god from his mind as he returned to the forge coals and lifted the sword from the fires.

The blade glowed a fierce red-orange and Uriel knew it was ready. He plunged it into a trough of water and oil, steam hissing angrily from the cooling metal.

He pulled the sword from the water and smiled as he turned his gaze to a velvet wrapped object on his workbench. As the sword blade cooled, he unwrapped the bundle, revealing the golden sword hilt that had once held the blade of Captain Idaeus's power sword. As he began the tempering process, he nodded to himself as he felt his former captain's silent approval. The hilt had remained in the Chapter's reliquary until Marneus Calgar, lord of the Ultramarines, had presented it to him as a mark of respect for his success on Pavonis. Uriel no longer needed the sword of his former captain to symbolise his authority over the Fourth Company, but Calgar had understood that Uriel well deserved to carry such a precious relic of the Ultramarines.

By morning he would have the weapon finished, its blade polished and sharp. Then he would take it to the chapel of the venerable Chaplain Cassius and have it anointed with clear water he had collected from the pool at the base of Hera's Falls, at the end of the Valley of Laponis. The Chaplain would sanctify the blade and entreat the spirits of war and battle to impart a measure of their wrath within the weapon.

Uriel could feel the sword's weight in his hand and it felt good, it felt natural.

IT WAS IMPOSSIBLE to tell what manner of aliens had constructed the original starship at the heart of the space hulk. Blue-frosted glaciers and aeons of space-borne detritus had agglomerated across its surface to the extent that it was now buried beneath thousands of metres of ice and metal, grafted in sedimentary layers upon its surface. What *was* obvious was that at some point in its recent history it had been taken over by orks, customised and added to with whatever junk and debris that the green-skinned savages could lay their hands on.

Rusted iron girders formed a tangled lattice across the ice and steel, crude, airtight iron boxes bolted to the ice and rock in a jumble of metal. The hulk was perhaps seven kilometres in length, spinning pieces of debris rippling from the ungainly structures like entrails from a torn belly. In a way, the orkish engineering was a marvel of unwitting skill, luck and blind lunacy, though no member of the Adeptus Mechanicus would ever admit to such a thing.

Its age was impossible to divinate with any degree of certainty. Perhaps it had plied the depths of space for tens of thousands of years before the orks had discovered it – or it had discovered them. Quite how such barbaric and warlike savages had the wherewithal to even get into space, let alone commandeer something so inherently dangerous, was a mystery that continued to baffle the priests of the Machine God. That the orks had ever managed to get their monstrously deformed contraptions space-worthy defied their every theorem.

Regardless of such apparent impossibility, once the orks deemed the hulk ready, it would be crammed full of warriors, with a vast power field bubble trapping the necessary oxygen and then hurled through space on a random course through the stars.

The hulk would ply the depths of space for an indeterminate time, sometimes dropping into the fluid medium of warp space as the ebb and flow of long-forgotten power sources surged and hurled the craft through the galaxy. Where and when such ships would emerge back into realspace – if they ever did – was a mystery to which no one could predict the answer.

If the orks were fortunate, the hulk would emerge in an inhabited system and if they were even luckier, crash on an inhabited planet. The strongest warlord who survived the crash landing would emerge to lead the others in an ork crusade known as a Waaagh!

To say it was a haphazard form of travel was an understatement of colossal proportions.

The arrival of a space hulk in an inhabited system was a portent of great ill-omen and wherever they were encountered, their destruction was given immediate priority. It was a duty that often fell to the Adeptus Astartes, humanity's greatest warriors, who would board the hulk and destroy it from within.

And this space hulk, codified the *Death of Virtue*, was no exception. As it crossed the orbital path of Barbarus Prime, the ninth planet of the Tarsis Ultra system, a ship with crenellated weapon turrets and a cathedral-like command section emerged from the corona of the system's star and moved gracefully into a shadowing position. Beside her, the three smaller vessels of Arx Praetora squadron gathered in her shadow, ready to defend her against any attack.

Scarred with the fires of war, the Ultramarines' strike cruiser, *Vae Victus*, stood ready to send her warriors into battle once more.

LORD ADMIRAL LAZLO Tiberius, captain of the *Vae Victus*, looked up from the pict-slate on his command pulpit and asked, 'Philotas, do you have a firing solution locked in on the close-in surveyors yet?'

'Yes, sir,' answered Philotas. 'Shall I order battle stations?'

'Aye, battle stations,' confirmed Tiberius, descending from the pulpit and striding to the stone-rimmed command plotter where Captain Uriel Ventris and his Master of Surveyors awaited him. The admiral rubbed a hand over his scarred and hairless skull, staring at the new tactical plot that now displayed the exact position, course and speed of the intruder.

'Opinions?' demanded Tiberius.

'Well, it's drifting now,' said Philotas. 'That much we can tell from its speed. It's not travelling under its own power and it's a big one, that's for sure. It's no wonder the Tarsis Ultra system defence ships couldn't handle it. As to its course, it appears to be heading roughly towards the planet Chordelis. On its present heading it should pass out of the system without incident.'

'But we can't take that chance. We must treat it as a hostile contact until proven otherwise,' added Uriel.

'Agreed,' said Tiberius. 'How did it arrive in-system? A jump, or did it just drift in?'

'It just drifted in,' said Philotas. 'It appeared on the outer rim surveyors about five months ago, coming from below the galactic plane, but they are unmanned and the hulk did not pass close enough for a pict-capture. However, it passed close enough to listening post Trajen for the adepts there to get a more precise fix on its position.'

'Damn,' hissed Tiberius. 'Can they estimate where it came from?'

'The senior magos believes it came from the regions of space we know to be controlled by an ork warlord known as the Arch Fiend of Octarius,' replied Philotas.

'What do you think, lord admiral?' asked Uriel. 'Is this the vanguard of an ork invasion?'

'No, I do not believe so,' said Tiberius.

'Why not?'

'Well, we would be seeing a lot more hulks if this was an invasion, Uriel. Orks don't come singly; they come en masse, in a green tide that smashes through anything in its way. You remember the reports we received following the invasion of Armageddon?'

Uriel and Philotas both nodded as the venerable admiral continued.

'Segmentum command at Bakka has issued several warnings of increased incidences of ork migrations from the realm of the Arch Fiend, but the strategos feel they are too fragmentary and disparate to be an invasion, and I agree.'

'Then if not an invasion, what is causing this migration?' asked Uriel.

'I do not know, but then you can never tell with the damned greenskins. Sector command seems to think that the orks are fleeing from something, as unlikely as that sounds.'

'But you think there are orks on board?'

'Aye,' said Tiberus pointing at a fluctuating set of numerals at the side of the display, 'but I do not think they will be alive. The mass readings look about right, but the mean internal temperature is probably too low and there does not appear to be enough interior oxygen voids for anything to survive – even orks. I think we are just looking at something that has split from an even larger ship, but we need to know for sure.'

'Are the auguries picking up any anomalous readings?' Uriel asked Philotas.

'None, but I wouldn't necessarily expect any just yet.'

Tiberius nodded. 'Continue monitoring anyway, I want to be ready for anything unexpected.'

'Yes, sir.'

'Range to target?'

'Nine thousand kilometres, lord admiral.'

A green icon winked into life on the display before Tiberius, indicating that the Thunderhawks in the prow flight-bays were now prepped and ready for launch. The damage to the launch bays caused by an eldar ship en route to Pavonis had been repaired in the shipyards orbiting Calth and the *Vae Victus* was once again operating at full readiness. He pressed the flashing icon, acknowledging the information.

'Uriel, I want you and your men ready to launch within the hour.'

'We will be, lord admiral.'

'Plant those demolition charges quickly and get your men out of there, Uriel,' ordered Tiberius. 'You are not on the hunt for archaeotech here. I just want this thing destroyed.'

'Understood, lord admiral. From the sound of things, I don't expect to find anything troublesome over there, but if we do we'll be ready for it,' assured Uriel.

MASSIVE STONE ARCHES supported the groined stone ceiling of the launch bay and the air reeked of fuel and incense. Three Thunderhawks sat idling on the ready line, their engines growling as the crews built up power before take off. Techmarines circled them, anointing their armoured sides with sacred unguents and removing the arming pins from the missiles slung under the wings in time with the Words of Ordnance.

The armoured deck rang with booted steps as the Ultramarines prepared to take the light of the Emperor into the dark places once more. Techmarines accompanied by engineering servitors chanted mantras of ire to the gunships and cast the runes of war to rouse the battle spirits of each craft.

The crew ramps were lowered, and tracked lifter-servitors loaded cylindrical ammunition crates, supply boxes and the demolition charges that would blow the hulk to pieces into the hold. The pilots and Techmarines walked around the exterior of the gunship, ensuring every access panel was properly sealed. Uriel watched the scene of controlled efficiency before him with pride. Once more his company was going into battle and he relished the thought. It had been too long since Pavonis, and both he and his men were eager to prove themselves once more.

He gripped the hilt of his new power sword. The weapon was yet to be blooded and, despite his belief that the hulk they were to board was lifeless, he hoped that there might be enemies as yet undiscovered aboard that might satisfy his blade. Uriel felt the onset of his lust for battle kindle in his belly and was surprised at its nascent ferocity. He suppressed it for now. Too often had it surged to fiery life at the thought of battle since his encounter with the Nightbringer, images of war and death filling his mind with the desire to shed blood.

The armoured blast door to the launch bay rumbled open and two squads of Space Marines led by sergeants Pasanius and Learchus entered, their bolters held at parade rest.

Uriel marched quickly to where his men had begun performing final checks on their equipment and running through their devotional prayers.

'Officer on deck!' bawled Pasanius and the Space Marines snapped to attention.

'As you were,' said Uriel, raising his hand. The armoured warriors returned to their pre-battle drills as he shook hands with Pasanius and Learchus. Even now, almost a year after the Pavonis expedition, Uriel found it hard to adjust to the idea of Pasanius having a bionic replacement for the limb he had lost fighting the Nightbringer thousands of metres below the planet's surface. The arm shone like silver, its surface smooth and brilliantly reflective. Truly the artificers of Pavonis had excelled themselves.

'Everything is in order?' he asked needlessly. He already knew his sergeants would have everything prepared and trusted them implicitly, but as any commander worthy of the name would say: you could never be too prepared before going into battle.

'Of course,' affirmed Pasanius.

'Do we make for Tarsis Ultra after destroying this hulk?' asked Learchus, unable to mask the anticipation in his voice.

'Possibly,' replied Uriel. 'Admiral de Corte has despatched system defence ships to join us should our charges prove insufficient to destroy it. We will return to the docks around Chordelis to re-arm, but I dare say we will journey to Tarsis Ultra before long.'

Learchus smiled. 'I have heard great things of Tarsis Ultra. The tale of the Warrior's Debt was always my favourite at Agiselus, it will be good to see a planet's populace upholding the ideals of the primarch so far from Ultramar.'

'Ten thousand years is a long time, Learchus,' said Pasanius. 'I doubt many will even remember who Roboute Guilliman was, let alone follow his teachings.'

'What? The worlds of Ultramar prosper under his teachings. Why then should a world choose to abandon such notions of courage and honour? It makes no sense.'

Uriel smiled, hearing the inflexibility of Learchus's argument in every syllable. Learchus could see no benefit in turning from the teachings of the primarch and simply assumed that everyone else shared his view. Any other possibility was unthinkable.

Pasanius pointed to where a Techmarine was giving the thumbs up to the pilot in the cockpit of the Thunderhawk.

'Looks like our chariot is prepared, captain.'

'Gather the men, we depart in five minutes.'

'Aye, captain,' saluted his sergeants.

URIEL'S BOLTGUN NESTLED in the rack beside him, its dull sheen gleaming with sacred oils in the red-lit crew compartment. He had honoured the battle spirit within the weapon before boarding the gunship and his armour was a fresh, brilliant blue, its surfaces smooth and untarnished. The Chapter's artificers on Macragge had repaired its fabric after the damage it had suffered on Pavonis, though the scar where the C'tan's infernal metal had scorched the backplate had resisted their every effort to remove it.

A Space Marine always honoured the battle gear that protected him and the weapons that were the instruments of the Emperor's will. To do any less would be to arouse the wrath of the war spirits that empowered such holy artefacts and no warrior would dare run such a risk.

Uriel gripped the hilt of his power sword and offered a prayer to Roboute Guilliman that he would prove worthy of his Chapter. He had not failed in his duty before this and vowed that he would not do so now.

For this present duty was entrusted to him by no less a person than the primarch himself.

The defence of the Tarsis Ultra system was a sacred task to the Ultramarines, the result of an ancient oath sworn by Roboute Guilliman during the days of the Great Crusade. It had been a time of heroes, when the Emperor's own progeny, the primarchs, had stood shoulder to shoulder and carved His realm from the flesh of the galaxy, wresting His worlds back from the domination of vile aliens and heretics.

Tarsis III had been one such world, liberated from the lies of heretic secessionists by Roboute Guilliman at the head of the Ultramarines Legion. The battles fought to reclaim this world of the Emperor were the stuff of fireside legend on Macragge, taught at every one of the many training barracks throughout Ultramar, as was the courage and discipline shown by the inhabitants in rising to fight alongside the Ultramarines. It was said that a lowly trooper of Tarsis III had saved the life of Guilliman in the last battle and such was the primarch's gratitude that, at its end, he had dropped to one knee and sworn to a mighty oath of brotherhood with the soldier, declaring that should Tarsis III ever be threatened, the Ultramarines would return to fight by their side.

The victory was commemorated in a legendary work that adorned the walls of a giant room in the heart of the

Imperial governor's palace. Named the Tarsis Fresco, it was said to be a gargantuan mosaic that covered the walls and ceiling of the palace's inner sanctum. Tales spoke of a work of unsurpassed majesty and Uriel greatly looked forward to seeing this spectacular mosaic.

Instead of the wastelands many of his brother primarchs left in the wake of their victories, Guilliman left those who could help rebuild the world in the image of his homeworld. The grateful populace eagerly took up the challenges laid before them by the primarch and renamed their world Tarsis Ultra, that they might always remember their liberators.

Once more entrusted with the honour of the Chapter, Uriel knew that his victory on Pavonis had earned him this sacred duty and, though the oath sworn by the primarch was almost ten thousand years past, it was no less binding. He would see that the ancient debt was fulfilled.

This he swore by the spirit of the weapon he now held. He could sense the intensity around him and knew that his men felt the same. He felt the courage of his seasoned veterans, those he had fought beside in the Mereneas Core, on Black Bone Road, on Ichar IV, Thracia and Pavonis. In counterpoint to the calm courage of the veterans, he saw the eagerness of those warriors newly elevated to the Fourth Company. Though they had fought in many battles already, this would be their first engagement as full battle-brothers and the desire not to let their brethren down was palpable.

He felt the motion of the Thunderhawk change as the craft pitched upwards towards the location the auguries had pinpointed as the most favourable location for the gunship to enter the hulk. Uriel watched as the vast shape of the *Vae Victus* yawed from sight through the thick vision blocks, and the screaming of the engines changed in pitch, the pilot making his final approach on manoeuvring thrusters alone. He caught a brief glimpse of the other two Thunderhawks, similarly laden with Ultramarines, making their way to their own designated entry points.

Slowly, the vision port was filled with the undulating flank of the space hulk, frosted metal caked with the residue of its voyage through space and cratered with asteroid impacts. A shiver rippled up Uriel's spine as he wondered where this vessel had been, where it had come from and what calamitous fate had seen it consigned to the icy graveyard of space. The thought of entering the craft filled him with a cold dread, and though he told himself it was simply the unclean nature of the vessel, he wasn't sure he believed himself. During his service in the Deathwatch, the Chamber Militant of the Ordo Xenos, he had cleansed many such abominable places, part of a kill-team whose sole aim was to eradicate alien creatures. He had felt the same sense of trepidation as he felt now and no matter how many times he had boarded one of these hateful vessels, the same primal loathing remained.

Something had once made its home on this ghost ship and Uriel knew full well that none of the things that might do so would be friendly.

He saw a yawning chasm torn in the side of the gargantuan vessel, the twisted metal ringing it looking for all the world like fangs in some alien predator's gaping jaws. The thought was not a comforting one. The view through the block slid from sight as the pilot gently rolled the gunship, matching his speed of rotation to that of the hulk, and turned the ship to face the fanged maw they would fly into. Uriel watched as what little light filtered through the vision block was snuffed out as they flew inside the structure of the ancient leviathan.

The ready light above Uriel's head changed from a baleful red to a gently flashing amber and he knew they were almost in place.

The pilot's voice cracked over the vox. 'Depressurising in ten seconds. All crew go to internal air supply.'

Uriel disconnected his backpack from the gunship's own air tanks and sealed the valve, whispering the prayer of thanks to his armour's spirit as an icon flashed up on his visor, indicating that its integrity was intact. He checked that the air level in his armour's tanks was full and watched as his warriors followed suit.

The thin, engraved purity scrolls affixed to the gunship's venting systems fluttered as the pilot gradually depressurised the crew compartment, readying it for opening into the hard vacuum of the hulk's interior.

Uriel released the harness restraints and slammed a magazine into his bolter as he rose to his feet. The motion of the Thunderhawk shifted again, the engines rumbling and the deck vibrating with the tonal shift. The ready light flickered from amber to green.

Then, with a thump and groan of landing gear, they were down and the frontal boarding ramp dropped, slamming into a pile of twisted wreckage. Uriel nodded to Pasanius and together the two Ultramarines swiftly descended the ramp, weapons at the ready. Surprisingly, Uriel felt the weight of his armour and realised that there was gravity within the space hulk. It could not have been generated naturally, which told him that even if there were no inhabitants on board, then at least some remainder of their technology was still functional. The rest of the gunship's passengers debarked and formed a protective cordon around their leaders as Uriel surveyed the interior of the space hulk. Bright beams of light speared from the frontal section of the gunship, illuminating their landing zone.

The chamber was a vast, echoing cavern of twisted, glittering girders bolted and welded to what must have been the flank of another starship in a random fashion, forming a groaning latticework roof some hundred metres above them. Stalactites of ice drooped from the ceiling and jagged pillars of glistening blue rose to meet them. Steam feathered from the Space Marines' backpacks as they spread out through the frosted chamber, ice crystals crunching underfoot as they moved off into the hulk.

A multitude of beams from the Ultramarines' armour lights criss-crossed through the spectral twilight as Uriel stabbed his hand in the direction of a yawning slash torn through the wall two hundred metres before them.

'All squads check in,' ordered Uriel.

The vox bead in his helmet clicked and hissed with white noise. Crackling voices stuttered through his helmet.

'Squad Brigantus in place and moving inside.'

'Squad Learch... in pla... and... movi... in...'

'Sq…d… arin in p…ce.'

'S…a… terion…'

Uriel cursed as the last transmission faded from his headset, blocked either by the sheer mass of the hulk or some failing of their vox units. Techmarine Harkus had warned him that they tended to fare badly in the depths of hulks. Well, Uriel had personally briefed each of his squad leaders and there was nothing more he could do. He was now beginning to understand something Marneus Calgar had said to him before departing on the long journey towards Segmentum Tempestus and Tarsis Ultra: that there was a world of difference between leadership and command.

He approached the opening in the wall, his shoulder-mounted illuminator revealing a wide, ribbed corridor of glistening, pustule-like growths that stretched off into the darkness. Thin scraps of mist clung to the floor and soft, puffs of gas soughed from sphincter-like orifices in the pustules. Water dripped in a fine rain around the opening from melting ice above, and condensing air gusted around it. Uriel stepped through the opening, feeling his boot connect with something hard and metallic.

Lying on the floor, partially covered in the clinging moisture was a flattened sheet of iron, hammered into a crude representation of a horned skull. The jaw was sawn with elongated fangs, and despite the crudity of the work, it was recognisable as a totemistic ork head.

Pasanius knelt beside the ork head, keeping the hissing nozzle of his enormous flamer pointed down the corridor.

'So it looks like there are greenskins on this vessel after all,' he said.

'Aye, so it would seem,' agreed Uriel. 'But where are they?'

Both Space Marines looked up as the click of something moving from ahead sounded from the oddly shaped walls, throwing the echoes around them. Uriel pressed himself against the undulating wall, raising his bolter as Pasanius motioned the warriors of his squad forward. The Ultramarines moved in two-man fire teams down the corridor in disciplined groups as the noise came again.

Uriel followed his men, his footsteps sucking from the gelatinous, spongy floor. A soft, chittering sound rippled through the walls, the puffs of gas from the pustules feeling like the breath of some disgusting sea beast. If that were the case, then truly they were in the belly of that beast.

The corridor rounded a bend, the wet, organic walls of the corridor abruptly changing to the armoured bulkheads and the rigid mesh of an internal floor so common on Imperial vessels. The walls were scorched black, pocked with fist-sized craters and Uriel knew immediately that they were weapon impacts; too large for most small arms fire and too shallow for heavy weapons.

Human ones at least.

He'd fought orks often enough to know that their weapons were easily capable of these kinds of impacts and opened a channel on the vox.

'Brother Flavian, front and centre, we need your auspex.'

Seconds later a Space Marine with his bolter slung and carrying a hand-held device with a gently glowing plate joined him. A soft chime sounded regularly from the device as the spirit caged within the machine swept the architecture before them with an array of surveyors.

'Brother-captain,' said Flavian, keeping his eyes trained on the device.

'How far to the first waypoint?' asked Uriel.

Flavian consulted the auspex, scrolling through the display and said, 'Two hundred metres, brother-captain. Along this corridor and right.'

'Very well. Let's go, and stay alert.'

HARKUS NODDED, INDICATING that the first charge was set and Uriel led his squad onwards, following the chiming auspex of Brother Flavian. The corridors echoed to the heavy, armoured footfalls of the Ultramarines, throwing their steps back at them in ringing metallic waves. Uriel saw a riot of interiors butted against one another in a chaotic jumble of accidental architecture. Girders stamped with faded Imperial eagles abutted rusted metal structures that were plainly of ork construction, which in turn were welded to portions of ships that Uriel did not recognise at all. Vessels too numerous and strange to guess at had unwittingly supplied the material required to construct this space-borne leviathan; yet another reason to see it utterly destroyed.

Uriel stepped across a frost-limned stanchion, feeling his steps lighten the further he travelled down this particular section of corridor. He raised his fist and halted the advance.

Ahead, the corridor widened into a high ceilinged chamber of blue ice and swirling mist. Glittering shards of ice tumbled lazily through the air, catching the light from his armour's illuminator. Sparkling like miniature suns, Uriel realised that the crystals were floating in a zero-gravity environment. Whatever arcane devices or alien archaeotech had kept gravity functioning in other portions of the hulk was plainly not at work here.

'There is an area of weightlessness ahead,' he voxed to the rest of his squad. 'Engage boot magnets and switch to autosenses; there is a great deal of airborne debris.'

He stepped onwards, feeling the powerful grip his boots now had on the mesh of the deck beneath him. As he entered the chamber, he felt a lurch in his stomach as he suddenly became weightless. There had been no gradual change in environment, simply a switching from one state to another. Ice brushed against him and a spinning bar of metal rang against his thigh armour. His grip on the deck did not feel as secure as he would have liked, the thick ice on the floor preventing the magnetised soles of his boots from gaining a better purchase.

'Be on your guard, the ice is distorting my auto-senses. Pasanius, clear us a path through this mist.'

'Aye, captain,' said Pasanius, hefting his bulky flamer unit as easily as another Space Marine might carry a boltgun. The veteran sergeant unleashed a whooshing tongue of flame into the mist, a hiss of ice flashing to steam and liquid droplets exploded away from the fires.

But rather than simply dissipating, the liquid prome-thium rolled in the air, miniature infernos spinning through the chamber as the fire revelled in the sensation of weightlessness. Removed from the tyranny of gravity, the flames slid like liquid through the air, rippling in strangely lifelike ways. Adhering to icy pieces of tumbling refuse, the splintered fire lit the chamber with the glow of a million dancing fireflies.

Uriel shook his head, entranced by the myriad patterns of liquid fire twisting before him and said, 'We should expect to find many more places like this.'

He pushed on through the icy mist, his senses stretched out before him for any foe that might be lurking in the swirling fog ahead. He saw hummocks of ice on the ground and knelt beside one. Its skin a deathly pale, the ork lay immobile, its limbs welded to the deck by the cold. Uriel saw that the other hummocks were also dead bodies.

'This place is a tomb,' he whispered to himself.

The huge body before him was frozen utterly solid, its wide fanged mouth twisted in a last roar of aggression. Its torso was ripped open in a dozen places and glistening entrails, frozen as they spilled from its belly, coiled around its meaty fists.

'It froze to death while trying to push its guts back inside,' said Pasanius.

Uriel nodded. 'And I just bet it would have survived had the cold not killed it. Obviously the chamber froze before the gravity failed.'

Apothecary Selenus knelt by the body, extending a forceps probe from his wrist-mounted narthecium. The dextrous callipers gripped something wedged in the ork's belly, cracking free a long, chitin-sheathed claw. Its surface was black and reflective, its edge lethally sharp.

'What is it?'

'A claw, and not an orkish one,' said the Apothecary. 'It obviously belongs to whatever killed this brute.'

'You mean something killed an ork with its bare hands?' said Pasanius.

'It would certainly appear so,' nodded Selenus.

Uriel stood and pushed the dead orks from his mind. They had a mission to perform and as diverting as this mystery was, it was delaying them from completing it.

'Leave it,' he ordered. 'We are behind schedule already.'

He waved his men forward and they carried on, passing more stiff, frozen corpses of orks. Eventually the icy mist cleared and Uriel stepped from the glacial sepulchre onto a dripping gantry high above a cavernous drop into darkness. Chains jangled from an unseen ceiling and melting water poured in runnels from innumerable passageways all around them. The weight of his armour settled on his frame and he realised that they had once again entered a gravity pocket.

Brother Flavian joined Uriel and pointed his auspex down the length of the gantry.

'It's this way to the next waypoint,' he said.

Uriel acknowledged him with a nod of his head as he scanned the blurred darkness above him. Shadows and mist coiled high above and rippled with motion.

There was something else on this ship besides the orks.

He just hoped they could complete their mission before they found out what.

URIEL PANNED HIS shoulder-mounted illuminator around the columned chamber, noting the reading of his heartbeat in the lower left corner of his visor display. Higher than normal, he saw, though he wasn't surprised. This place was damned, cursed, and reeked of death. He looked up at the groaning structure above him. Hundreds of bowing columns supported a sagging roof of ice, the soft jingle of dangling chains and dripping moisture masking the sound of his breathing.

For another four hours, the Ultramarines had crept through the baroque interiors of the hulk, ghosting from waypoint to waypoint, planting explosive charges and following the soft, regular chiming of Brother Flavian's auspex. Patchy communications had been re-established with the other squads throughout the hulk, but each sergeant's reports were fragmentary. It appeared, though, that the mission was going well and the remainder of his squads were progressing unopposed.

A circle of light from the Ultramarines' armour lights surrounded the kneeling Techmarine Harkus, who set the last of the demolition charges Uriel's squads were to place. Silently, Uriel willed him to hurry up.

The longer they stayed here, the more his sense of trepidation grew and the greater the threat of encountering something hostile. The lord admiral believed the hulk to be abandoned and, aboard the *Vae Victus*, Uriel had agreed, but now, standing in the twisted, desolate interior, he wasn't quite so sure. The groaning darkness of the hulk was an unsettling place, and Uriel had the constant sensation of being watched.

The hulk creaked, though it was impossible to pinpoint from where the noises came.

'By Guilliman, I'll be glad to see the back of this place,' mused Pasanius, flexing his silver fingers on the grip of his flamer, the blue flame hissing at the weapon's nozzle.

'Aye,' agreed Uriel, glancing upwards as he thought he caught a glimpse of furtive movement. 'It is unnatural.'

Pasanius nodded grimly in agreement. 'It reminds me too much of the darkness below the mountains on Pavonis.'

'In what way?'

'I fear we may meet something as monstrous as the Bringer of Darkness, because this place is a tomb as well. People died on this ship and there are evil echoes here.'

'Evil echoes? That doesn't sound like you, my friend.'

'Aye,' said Pasanius with a shrug. 'Well, I don't like places like this, they bring out the superstitious in me.'

Uriel said nothing, but agreed with his old friend's belief. He had seen enough horrors in his time serving in the Deathwatch to know that places of ill-omen could indeed resonate with ancient evils. The battle with the Nightbringer only reinforced that belief and was another reason to be done with this place.

There were creatures known to dwell on hulks like this and he did not relish meeting any of them.

He watched as Harkus flipped open the glass lens covering a brass dial on the face of the demolition charge and turned the delicate arms of the timer mechanism. A red light winked into life beside the timer and the Techmarine intoned the words of arming.

'Holy Father of Machines, I ask thee to invest this blessed machine with a fragment of your divine wrath and beg your forgiveness for its destruction. *Destructus et abominatus, Omnis mortis justicus.*'

Harkus made the sign of the machine and nodded to Uriel.

'The demolition charges are now set, brother-captain. Within the hour, this hulk will be nothing more than wreckage.'

'That thought fills me with nothing but relief, Brother Harkus. Now let us be on our way.'

Harkus concealed the demolition charge beneath a handful of ice shards and thin sheets of metal as the vox-bead in Uriel's helmet clicked and Brother Covius, his northern perimeter sentry reported.

'Brother-Captain, I have movement before me. I can hear the sounds of many enemies approaching,' said Covius.

'What kind of enemies?' hissed Uriel.

'I do not yet know, brother-captain, I can see nothing beyond the edge of the chamber, but from the noise I believe there are a great many. And they are heading this way.'

'Brother Covius, remain in place until you can give me more information, then get back and join the rest of us,' ordered Uriel.

'Understood.'

Uriel circled his hand above his head and the Ultramarines closed the circle around him. Even as they did so, Uriel could hear the sound of battle erupt in the distance. Gunfire and the crump of an explosion echoed from the chamber walls. He opened a channel to Covius as the vox crackled with reports from the other squads scattered throughout the space hulk.

'Contact!' bellowed Sergeant Learchus over the vox-net.

'Enemies!' shouted Sergeant Brigantus.

Uriel was about to demand confirmation on who exactly was attacking when the answer came in a shout from Brother Covius.

'Brother-Captain, they're coming!'

'Who, Covius? I need better information than that!' yelled Uriel.

But before Covius could reply, the signal was suddenly cut off as a fiery explosion blossomed at the far edge of the chamber and half a dozen stalactites crashed down from the ceiling.

Then through the flames came a wave of screaming foes, their bestial faces twisted in alien hate and their powerful bodies rippling with bulging muscle.

Orks. Hundreds of them.

THE ULTRAMARINES WERE ready for them. Bolters levelled, they unleashed a deadly volley of mass-reactive shells into the mass of charging orks. A dozen fell to the first volley and a dozen more to the next.

The charge faltered in the face of such devastating firepower and Uriel could see an expression that might have been surprise cross the thick features of the closest ork as a bolt detonated within its ribcage and exploded its alien heart.

Pasanius's flamer roared, hurling a liquid sheet of promethium into the mass of aliens. Orks bellowed as the fires consumed them, igniting others as they flailed in their death throes.

Bolter fire shredded the closest orks, but there were simply too many to kill before they reached the Ultramarines line. Uriel slung his bolter and drew his power sword as a massive, iron-jawed ork charged him, swinging a gigantic cleaver with a howling chainsaw blade. Thick sheets of metal were strapped over its shoulders and chest and Uriel leapt to meet the ork, lunging for its unprotected midriff. His sword plunged effortlessly through its flesh, sliding clear with a burning hiss.

The beast roared and bellowed something incomprehensible before swinging its cleaver at his head. Uriel almost failed to dodge, such was his surprise at the beast still being alive. He knew orks could withstand terrible damage, but he had practically cut this one in two!

He leapt to one side as the motorised cleaver hacked a wide gouge in the deck, shrieking in a flare of sparks as it passed through the metal. Uriel turned and swung wide and low, severing the ork's arms below the elbow.

All tactics were gone now; as he spun on his heel and beheaded the brute with one stroke. Another ork barrelled into him, slamming its hard-boned elbow against his head.

He fell, twisting out of the way of an axe blade as it swung towards his neck. He dodged as the axe descended again, kicking out and rolling to his feet as the ork struggled to free the axe from the ground. He stabbed his enemy through the head and kicked it from the blade as he tried to gauge the ebb and flow of the battle.

Scores of the orks were dead, cut down in the initial volleys of bolter fire or hacked down by his warriors. The orks fought with a dreadful ferocity, but Uriel could see that there was a desperation to their fighting. He watched Pasanius smash an ork to the ground with his flamer, hammering his boot down on its neck with a sharp crack. Another reared up behind him, chopping downwards with a huge, broad-bladed chainsword.

Uriel shouted a warning, but the veteran sergeant was already aware of the danger, spinning around and catching the blow on his bionic arm. Sparks flew as the rusted teeth bit into the metal of his arm and even the massive form of Pasanius was driven to his knees by its force.

Uriel leapt forwards, slamming feet-first into the ork's face. Yellow fangs snapped under his boot heels and the creature fell back, blood spraying from its mouth. Uriel rolled as he landed and readied his sword as he sprang to his feet. He drove the weapon through the ork's neck, almost severing its head completely.

In the midst of the furious combat, Uriel saw a hulking ork with a massive, piston-driven claw powering his way through the Ultramarines. Blue-armoured bodies were hurled through the air by the ork, black smoke belching from its rusted weapon and a bellowing roar of fury echoing from the walls.

Armoured in rusted plates of metal that would have taken four strong men to lift, the ork was a powerhouse of primal brutality. Thick, corded muscles bulged on its upper limbs and great slabs of meat layered its chest. A black, horned helm crowned a monstrous, scarred face and burning red eyes. Viscous spittle sprayed from between yellowed tusks, each the length of Uriel's forearm. Bigger than all the others, Uriel knew it must be the war-leader of this particular band of orks and pushed his way through the melee towards it.

The creature turned to face him as he swung his sword for its head, bringing the wheezing claw around to block the blow. Orange sparks flew as the two weapons met and with a speed surprising for such a gigantic beast, it lashed out with its sledgehammer fist. Uriel ducked and threw his sword up as the reverse stroke of the giant claw came at him. An iron-shod boot hammered his armour and even through the ceramite plates, he could feel the strength behind the blow.

He rolled to his feet and spun inside a clumsy thrust of the power claw. He lunged and thrust his sword into the ork's chest. The blade hissed as it penetrated the sheets of iron and the stench of charred alien flesh assailed him.

Uriel grunted as he forced the blade deeper into the ork's body. Its powerfully muscled arms gripped him in a crushing bear hug and pulled him from his feet. Too close to use its power claw without decapitating itself, the ork had settled for merely crushing him to death. He felt the creaking of his armour as it fought against the pressure of the ork's muscles.

The ork's face was a hand's breadth in front of his own, its spittle coating his helmet in slimy mucus as it uttered something in its barbaric, guttural tongue. It chest heaved and its shoulders shook as Uriel twisted the sword in the wound. Blood so dark it was almost black spurted, but Uriel realised the beast was laughing at him.

Even as his armour began to buckle, Uriel felt his fury build at this alien's mockery and released his grip on his sword, leaving it buried in its flesh. The ork's coal-red eyes glared at him and he gripped the meaty flesh of its shoulders, bracing his feet against the tops of its thighs.

With all his might, he lowered his head and slammed his helmet into the centre of the ork's face. He felt its nose break, smashed to splinters by the force of Uriel's head-butt. The iron grip on his body lessened for a second and he hammered his helmet against the ork's face again, feeling more bones of its skull break as it twisted its head in a vain attempt to avoid his blows.

Its grip continued to loosen and Uriel ripped his sword free from the beast's chest in a dark arc of blood. The ork roared as he dropped to the deck, reaching to tear him in two. With a roar of hatred, Uriel hacked the descending claw from the ork's body in one upward sweep. Sparking cables and spurting fluids bathed him as the claw dropped to the deck with an almighty clang.

Uriel did not give the wounded beast time to recover, stepping close and hacking at its flesh like a butcher. Each blow sheared slabs of alien flesh from his foe and even after the brutish monster fell dead at his feet, he chopped in a killing frenzy until the ork was little more than sizzling chunks of scorched meat.

Breathless and immersed in the fury of battle, he turned and thrust with his blade as he caught sight of another giant figure in his peripheral vision. He diverted the stroke at the last minute when he saw that it was Pasanius, skewering a charging ork as it came up behind the veteran sergeant.

Orks swirled around them, and both he and Pasanius hacked all about themselves with great disembowelling strokes of their swords. The chamber rang to the sounds of battle, but within moments, it became clear that the orks did not have fighting on whatever passed for their minds any more.

The few survivors of the charge swept past the stunned Ultramarines, departing the chamber from the opposite side as fast as they had entered it.

BLOOD RAN RED FROM the ork's back where it had been laid open to the bone by Uriel's power sword. Apothecary Selenus knelt beside the mutilated body of the dead ork leader and looked up at Uriel.

'What exactly am I looking for?' he asked.

'Look at the wounds this creature has suffered and tell me what you see,' said Uriel.

Pasanius nodded towards the hulking corpse. 'What are you looking for?'

'I want to know if these orks were attacked by the same things that killed the ones we found earlier in the frozen tomb. I want to know why we beat them so easily and why they didn't stay to fight. Have you ever known orks to run from a battle?'

'No,' said Pasanius, 'but you killed their leader. Orks don't do well seeing the strongest amongst them defeated.'

'I know, but there was more to it than that.'

'Maybe,' shrugged Pasanius as Selenus gave a grunt of recognition. Both Uriel and Pasanius squatted beside the Apothecary, watching as he pulled apart two slabs of skin and muscle from the ork's chest.

'Look here,' began Selenus. 'Brother-Captain, this is where your power blade cut the xenos. As you can see, the edges of the wound are smooth and cauterised from the heat of your weapon.'

The Apothecary then rolled the ork onto its side and pointed to a wound running from its left shoulder to the base of its ribs on the right hand side of its torso.

'So what are we looking at here, Selenus?' asked Pasanius.

'The blow that caused this wound cut through the creature's armour plating on its shoulders and sheared through the thickly ossified bone of its ribs with something incredibly sharp.'

'Another power weapon?' suggested Pasanius.

Selenus shook his head. 'No, the edges of this wound have not sealed or been seared as the wounds on its front have been. This was done by something so sharp it was able to cut through iron and ork flesh with almost no effort at all.'

'Greenskins fight each other almost as much as they fight us,' pointed out Pasanius. 'Maybe another ork did it or it's an old wound?'

'No,' said Selenus. 'The wound is too clean. An ork weapon would have torn the flesh around the wound much more thoroughly than this.'

'Do you know of any weapons that could have inflicted such a wound?' asked Uriel, already fearing he knew the answer and what the orks had fled from.

'Not many,' admitted Selenus, 'but here on a space hulk, there is one thing I know could have inflicted it.'

'Genestealers,' spat Pasanius.

'We need to get out of here,' said Uriel, 'and quickly.'

Selenus nodded as the soft, regular chiming of Brother Flavian's auspex suddenly sounded with greater urgency.

Uriel and Pasanius looked up as the walls seethed and hissed and chittered with sudden movement all around them. Shadows darted across the ceiling, the clatter of claws scraping on metal echoing from the glistening walls.

'Too late,' whispered Uriel, 'they're coming.'

THE WALLS CHURNED with movement, the screeching hiss of aliens seeming to come from everywhere at once. As one, the Ultramarines assumed a defensive formation and began falling back to the entrance of the chamber, bolters pointed outwards at the walls.

Uriel edged closer to Brother Flavian, all the time keeping his eyes trained on the hissing darkness around them. He gripped Flavian's wrist and raised the auspex, watching the sweep of the spirit across the pict-slate as it pierced the gloom with its all-seeing eye.

Distance and direction vectors glowed, and at the edge of the auspex, a blur of movement rippled, expanding and contracting slowly.

The soft chime sounded again, and again, and again. The gap between each chime shrinking each time.

'They're all around us,' whispered Flavian, and Uriel could detect a hint of nervousness in the young Space Marine. Flavian was one of the many new recruits he had inducted into the Fourth Company to replenish their numbers after the Pavonis campaign and, though he was brave, he was less experienced than the majority of the company. Uriel hoped this would not prove to be both his first and last campaign.

Slowly, step by step, the Ultramarines edged back the way they had come.

Then, without warning, their unseen enemy attacked.

Brother Travion was the first to die, four clawed arms reaching from the darkness of the wall and dragging him backwards, ripping through his armoured breastplate in a welter of blood.

Pasanius turned and bathed the wall with liquid fire, lighting up the darkness with a brilliant orange glow.

Firelight glittered from alien eyes and bared fangs as the creatures attacked.

Directed by a single, monstrous imperative, the genestealers boiled from the walls, ceilings and ducts. They were everywhere.

'Fall back! Get back to the entrance!' shouted Uriel.

Bolters chattered and Pasanius's flamer roared as the Ultramarines ran for the exit of the giant chamber. Uriel fired his bolter from the hip, cutting down more of the alien horrors with each salvo.

As more and more of the chamber caught light and pools of promethium burned, Uriel saw the creatures attacking them in all their horrifying glory.

Hunched over, with a grotesque, beetle-like carapace, the genestealers were monstrous, six-limbed creatures, sprinting forward on powerful hind legs. Their upper limbs ended in vicious, tearing claws, and Uriel could see how easily these would rip through ork armour.

Space Marine armour too, were they to get close enough.

But it was the faces of the creatures that horrified Uriel the most.

Bestial and filled with hundreds of lethally sharp teeth, the genestealer's maw was spread wide in a hissing screech, its eyes utterly black and filled with alien malevolence.

Black and impenetrable, they could express nothing beyond the desire to kill.

Uriel shot down three of the creatures as they raced towards him, inhumanly fast. Another three hurdled the corpses, coming at him with clawed arms outstretched. He ducked the first creature, grunting in pain as the claws of the second tore across his shoulder guard and cut through it like paper. Blood welled briefly in the cut, before the

Larraman cells in his enhanced bloodstream sealed the wound.

He swept his sword out, hacking the legs from the third and rolled upright, raising his weapon before him as the first creature came at him again. It leapt, impaling itself on the crackling blue point of the weapon, purple ichor bursting from its jaws as the blade pierced its heart.

Uriel dragged the sword from the beast as the second genestealer leapt upon him from behind, tearing at the eagle on his breastplate with frenzied claws. Preternaturally sharp, they tore through the eagle and scored a deep groove in the ceramite plate. Uriel dived forwards, tucking his head and landing on his back, allowing his heavy weight to crush the beast below him.

It refused to die, kicking spastically with its legs and biting the back of his helmet.

He hammered his elbow downwards into its face, cracking open its skull and spilling its brains across the icy deck.

Alien screams and gunfire filled the chamber. Pasanius's flamer lit up the darkness, drawing shrieks of agony from burning genestealers. Uriel pushed himself to his feet and staggered in the direction of the bunched Ultramarines. Pasanius had cleared a path through the genestealers with his flamer and the blazing exit was now clear of enemies.

Uriel rejoined his warriors, the pain from his lacerated shoulder flaring bright and hot. Three of his men were down and perhaps double that were injured, but none of those wounded were ready to give up the fight. Together they helped carry the bodies of the dead. No Ultramarine would allow one of his fallen battle-brothers to remain in this cursed place.

Uriel was pleased to see that Flavian was not amongst the dead.

Despite the horrendous losses the tide of genestealers had suffered, they were unwilling, or unable, to retreat. Time and time again, they threw themselves at the Ultramarines' ring of firepower and time and time again they were hurled back, but each time reaching a little closer to the Space Marines.

Pasanius backed from the chamber, hosing the aliens with fire and Uriel could see that the flaming spout drooped a little shorter than before. Pasanius saw this too and shared a look with Uriel.

'We can't go on like this!' shouted Uriel. 'We'll be out of ammunition soon.'

Pasanius nodded curtly. 'I've less than a quarter load left in the canister. I doubt it will see us back to the gunship.'

The Ultramarines fell back from the chamber's entrance, firing through at the genestealers that gathered beyond. Already, Uriel could hear the clatter of claws and talons through the walls as the voracious alien predators sought to encircle them. Could the genestealers know their ultimate destination? Would they be able to cut them off before they reached the Thunderhawk? They might be aliens, but that did not mean they were without cunning.

'Back to the gunship, double time!' commanded Uriel. 'We don't have time to waste, those charges will be detonating soon!'

As the last of his squad fell back through the chamber's exit, Uriel turned and followed his warriors, praying that they would be able to fight their way clear in time.

URIEL MOVED TO the head of their advance, keeping the pace fast, but always watching for alien attacks. Flavian's auspex kept them on course, and despite their haste, the pace was nowhere near as fast as he would have liked. Every corner had to be checked by two-man teams, covering the transverse approaches for any sign of a trap.

Chambers and corridors that had seemed simply alien as the Ultramarines had penetrated the space hulk now assumed monstrous dimensions, with every shadow and weirdly angled fixture potentially concealing a deadly killer.

Uriel opened a channel to his other squad leaders and said, 'Ventris to all squads. We are under attack from unknown numbers of genestealers and are falling back to our gunship. Secure your perimeters and make best speed for your own extraction points.'

One by one, his sergeants acknowledged his report.

A crackling voice that Uriel recognised as belonging to Learchus said, 'Brother-Captain, our auspex reads that we are less than three kilometres from your current position. We can come to your assistance.'

'No,' ordered Uriel, 'continue on towards your evacuation point.'

'But captain, proper procedure dictates that all squad members should be–'

'Damn it, Learchus, I don't have time for this now. These charges are set to blow soon and I want you off this hulk before that happens. Ventris out.'

Uriel snapped off the vox-link before Learchus could argue further, knowing that he would obey Uriel's order, though he wouldn't like it.

Pasanius took the lead of their continuing retreat through the hulk, periodically filling the corridors before them with flaming death as they made their way back to the gunship in good order. Every junction and every bend in their route had to be scouted quickly but thoroughly, lest there be alien killers lurking in wait.

The walls echoed with the sounds of pursuit. Every open duct or ragged pipe became a potential avenue of attack. Most proved empty, but many others did not, shrieking genestealers bursting through as a tide of chitin-armoured monsters attacked in concert from either side.

Uriel could sense a fearsome cunning in the timing and co ordination of the attacks. In any military operation, the greatest enemy was confusion and the greatest leaders were those who could effectively co ordinate their forces. The gen-estealers attacked with perfect synchronicity, forcing the Ultramarines to fall back at a much slower pace and Uriel knew that they were running out of time. He checked the chronometer in his visor.

The demolition charges would detonate in less than twenty minutes.

'Come on, we have to move faster!' he ordered.

Something heavy dropped from the ceiling, smashing into his back and driving him to the mesh decking.

He lost his grip on his sword, the blade skittering away from him and its energised edge deactivating. Clawed fingers gripped his shoulder guards and pulled. Uriel felt his back creak under the pressure as his spinal column bent backwards. He felt muscles tear and his strengthened bone begin to crack. He twisted his head and, in the flickering shadows cast by the flames of battle, could see the genestealer's talons rise, ready to plunge through his helmet and into his brain.

Uriel twisted desperately, bucking and thrashing in an attempt to dislodge the creature, but its grip was too strong.

He roared with a last show of defiance as a blur of blue armour entered his vision.

Pasanius said, 'Steal this,' and thundered his gleaming bionic fist through the genestealer's skull, smashing it to bloody splinters. He followed up with a vicious kick, spinning the twitching corpse from Uriel's body.

Uriel lurched to his feet, wincing at the strain in his back and torn muscles. He gathered up his sword and rejoined his men with a nod of grateful thanks to his oldest friend as they continued their retreat to the Thunderhawk.

Another tense quarter of an hour passed and as Uriel felt the weight of his armour lessening, he knew they were approaching the ice chamber with no gravity.

He plunged into the chamber, the magnetic soles of his boots keeping him anchored to the deck as gravity was withdrawn. They had travelled perhaps ten metres through the corpse filled cavern when Uriel noticed that something was different. It took him a few seconds to realise what it was.

The mist had thinned and where once the chamber had been filled with spinning crystals of ice, now it was filled with wobbling droplets of water. Uriel checked the temperature reading on his visor and saw that the temperature had leapt by thirty degrees and was still rising. Instead of a fog of chill mist, a rippling curtain of water droplets filled the chamber.

The ork corpses lay revealed without their frosty coating, their exposed viscera stinking in the warming chamber. Now able to see the far edges of the chamber, Uriel could see the glistening, mucus-wreathed walls were honeycombed with rippling egg sacs. Translucent membranes strained as creatures that had spent unknown centuries in hibernation struggled to break free of the organic stasis chambers that had kept them alive.

Long claws sliced through drooling cocoons whose amniotic fluids spilled from the tears like thick, floating ropes. Hissing monsters with long, bone-ridged heads pushed themselves free from their chitinous slumber. Uriel recognised them with a snarl of revulsion.

Tyranids.

Alien predators from beyond the galaxy, bent on devouring all before them with an insatiable appetite for bio-mass. Uriel had fought this abominable alien race before on Ichar IV and knew how deadly they could be. The Ultramarines' arrival on the space hulk must have triggered the aliens' revivification and Uriel knew they did not have long to escape this place.

Hundreds of rupturing egg sacs lined the ribbed walls of the chamber and though no more than a handful had thus far broken clear, it would only be a matter of time until there were more.

'Run!' shouted Uriel as he heard a growing rush of claws on steel and a boiling tide of genestealers poured into the cavern from behind them.

But here the Ultramarines had the advantage, as their magnetic boots held them to the deck, while the alien creatures had no such ability. Violent hisses of frustration and rage filled the chamber as the genestealers suddenly became aware of this handicap.

Despite the zero-gravity, the momentum of the genestealers carried them through the air towards the Ultramarines. Pasanius turned and unleashed a stream of burning promethium, the weightless streams of fire filling the air with molten liquid. Aliens howled as they were powerless to evade the floating flames and caught light.

The cavern walls gleamed in the sudden burst of light, and Uriel saw a host of scythe-taloned monsters hauling themselves from their lairs to either side. Many were drifting into the air as they tore free of the mucus-like streamers holding them down. Others, quicker to realise the nature of the environment, clamped their claws onto the deck, razor-sharp chitin gouging into the metal floor and holding them fast.

The curtain of drifting water droplets parted and Uriel could see a trio of tall, armoured warrior organisms stalking cautiously through the chamber to block their escape route. Upper limbs sheathed in reflective black chitin twitched above their heads and grasping, taloned hands clenched and unclenched in time with their breathing. Slathered with glistening birth-fluids, the tall aliens bellowed as the Ultramarines approached.

Bolters fired, cutting down pursuing genestealers in droves as they thrashed impotently in the air, frenziedly clawing at their escaping prey. Uriel charged towards the warrior aliens guarding the exit and drew his sword, shouting, 'Courage and honour!'

He swung low at the closest organism, hacking his sword through its ankles and drawing a bestial howl of pain from its throat. Its clawed hooves remained clamped to the deck while its body drifted into the air, spurts of coloured ichor pumping from the stumps of its legs.

The second and third beasts came at him from both sides and he swayed aside as a set of black claws slashed past his head from the left. But the attack was no more than a feint and as he turned to face the creature on his right, its claws closed on his waist with an iron grip and wrenched him from his feet. Uriel raised his sword in time to block a downward sweep of its claws, but he could not prevent himself from being hurled into the air.

The first beast struck him again, its claws punching into his armour, but sliding clear as he was pushed higher. Uriel spun in the weightless chamber, desperately trying to orient himself as he saw the warrior aliens bound into the air after him.

A glutinous stream of ichor coated his helmet as he passed through a floating pool of blood and Uriel quickly wiped it clear as the tyranid creatures closed on him.

He tried to halt his spin as he suddenly realised the import of the blood he had just floated through. Desperately he spun in the air, sweeping his sword out in a wide arc as the tyranid creature whose legs he had cut off at the ankles closed on him from above.

More ichor sprayed over him as his crackling sword chopped through its thorax. The two halves spun off towards the chamber walls.

A swirling layer of water rippled above him and Uriel realised he had floated all the way to the chamber's roof. He twisted his head, seeing the two warrior beasts rising towards him with their claws outstretched and fangs bared. He rolled, bringing his knees up to his waist as his feet impacted on the roof, sending droplets of icy water spraying in all directions.

As Uriel's feet touched the roof he pushed out with all his strength, powering down towards the two tyranids, his sword extended before him. The tip of the glowing blade sliced through the hard carapace of the closest beast's skull and it screeched in pain, wrenching its head to the side and tearing free of Uriel's sword. Its mantis-like claws scythed the air, but Uriel twisted aside and beheaded it with a broad sweep of the power sword.

But his wild stroke had left him spinning and dangerously exposed. He grunted in pain as the last beast's claws stabbed through the back of his thigh armour and pulled him around. He swung his sword in a downward arc, but a massive, clawed fist seized his wrist and twisted. Uriel felt his armour give way and the bones in his wrist crack, losing his grip on his sword, which continued on its downward trajectory and buried itself in the deck.

Uriel rammed his knee into the tyranid's chest, but its chitinous exo-skeleton was like iron. Its jaws snapped against his chest, scoring slimy grooves in the ceramite. Wrapped together in a desperate fight to the death, the two foes spun back down to the chamber's floor. Uriel slammed his armoured elbow into the monster's face, tearing its lower jaw free in a wash of sticky blood.

Still the beast tried to bite him and Uriel pistoned his fist through the ruin of its jaw, pushing through the gory ruin of its neck. Alien flesh closed around his fist as he ripped through hide, cartilage and sinew to grip its ridged spinal column. Alien digestive fluids poured down his arm, hissing as they ate away the top layers of his armour.

Uriel closed his fist on the tyranid's spine and with a roar of hatred wrenched it around, feeling the hard bone bend then snap under the power of his grip.

A froth of bloody matter sprayed his chest as the beast died and its claws released him. Uriel kicked away its corpse and spun his body in the air as he saw the ground rushing to meet him. He rolled his feet around and slammed onto the deck, engaging the magnetic clamps on his boots once more and sweeping up his sword.

The genestealers still spun and twisted through the air and more and more tyranid warrior organisms were pushing their way clear of their cocoons. Most of his warriors were already at the chamber's exit and Uriel hurried to join them as the alien pursuers attempted in vain to follow them.

Eventually they emerged into the organic, pustule-encrusted corridor that led towards the gigantic ice cavern they had landed in, and Uriel had never been so glad to see such a desolate place in his life.

It was then he noticed the decreasing counter in the corner of his visor.

0:06… 0:05… 0:04… 0:03… 0:02… 0:01…

'No…' whispered Uriel.

0:00

As the Ultramarines neared their escape, the devices planted throughout the hulk by the Techmarines finally detonated. Each boxy device was fitted with six kilos of a high explosive compound developed specifically for the destruction of space hulks.

The demolition charges had a wide blast area, and the destructive power unleashed within that area was an order of magnitude greater than almost any other explosive of similar size.

The timer mechanisms had all been calibrated from a single master unit aboard the *Vae Victus* and thus every single bomb detonated within a nanosecond of each other.

As each bomb exploded it instantly vaporised an area one hundred metres in diameter with a huge, reverberating thunderclap. The sounds of the massive explosions spread throughout the hulk, and positioned throughout the ship at key structural points, the effects were devastating.

Agglomerated structures tore free from the hulk's side as their supports were blasted clear, ripping gantries and beams with them. All across the *Death of Virtue*, the structural integrity of the hulk collapsed at an exponential rate as the explosive echoes died.

The explosion from each demolition charge roared into a seething ball of plasma energy, burning with the heat of a star. Those charges closer to the centre of the hulk, where the internal gravity field was strongest, dropped through the deck, turning the core of the hulk molten as they fell.

Slowly at first, but at a hugely accelerating rate, the hulk began to break apart.

URIEL FELT THE deck shift under his feet and heard the shriek of tearing metal as the corridor began wrenching free from the main body of the hulk. The ceiling split and vile fluids poured from the ruptured pustules on the wall, drenching the Ultramarines in noxious slime.

The screech of metal on metal squealed deafeningly and Uriel was thrown to the floor as the deck rolled sickeningly, ripping from its crudely bolted moorings. The door they had first come through appeared to lurch upwards as the decking dropped away and Uriel saw that they had seconds before it was ripped from the side of the hulk.

'Come on!' bellowed Pasanius, hauling fallen Space Marines upright. 'On your feet and get moving. That Thunderhawk isn't going to wait forever! Come on!'

The Space Marines quickly vaulted through the doorway, each warrior turning as he went through to reach back and help the battle-brother behind him.

Uriel backed towards the door, casting furtive glances over his shoulder as he kept watch for anything that might attack them from behind. His nerves were stretched taut.

It was impossible to tell whether anything was approaching over the screech of tearing metal and the distant groaning of the dying hulk.

A hand slapped on his shoulder guard and he turned to see Pasanius reaching down towards him with his gleaming and unblemished silver hand. Uriel slung his bolter and reached for the smooth metal of his sergeant's arm as the deck screeched and dropped from beneath him.

He stumbled as the mesh decking canted to one side, ice and debris spilling down spreading cracks in the metal. Uriel pushed himself upright and looked up to see how far he had fallen. Some three metres separated him from the doorway and escape.

Metal scraped on metal as the deck gradually slid down the inner surface of the hulk, sparks flaring in the darkness as it tore free of the wall.

'Captain!' shouted Pasanius. 'Come on, jump!'

Uriel launched himself upwards, gripping Pasanius's hand and scrambling for purchase as the deck finally broke from the wall and tumbled down into darkness. His fingers slid down the metal of his sergeant's arm and he reached up with his other hand as Pasanius reached down with his free arm and hauled him through the door. The cracked bones in Uriel's wrist flared in pain.

He rolled upright, grateful beyond words to hear the whine of the Thunderhawk's engines spooling up.

'Time to get going, Uriel,' shouted Pasanius over the din.

Uriel nodded as Pasanius turned and jogged through the cavern towards the gunship.

The deck rumbled and heaved, shuddering as though in the grip of a powerful earthquake. Ice cracked, raining fine white crystals into the chamber and stalactites separated from the roof with the crack of gunshots, dropping gracefully to the floor to explode into lethally sharp splinters.

Ultramarines were already boarding the gunship as a yawning chasm split the floor of the ice chamber and gouting jets of steam spewed through the cavern. The buckling floor ahead of Uriel heaved upwards and he was pitched to the ground. He skidded across the deck, fingers scraping a

furrow in the icy floor as he fought to arrest his slide. A sta-
lactite hit the floor nearby, showering him with fragments.
Hot steam blinded him as he felt the deck tip downwards.
He rolled aside, seeing the flare of distant infernos far below
him. Roiling clouds of smoke and venting gasses geysered
towards him.

With the last reserves of his strength, Uriel hauled himself
upwards, desperately clawing his way up the ice-slick floor.
Hand over hand he climbed, rolling clear as the deck section
plunged downwards into oblivion. The cavern bucked in the
hulk's death throes, falling ice and billowing clouds of
steam obscuring everything in a grey haze.

Uriel staggered in the direction of the roaring engines of
the gunship as he saw shadowy figures racing alongside him,
also heading towards the beacon of noise.

At first he thought they were fellow Space Marines.

Then one leapt at him, scything claws reaching for his
throat.

The genestealer's bestial screech was drowned in the
howling gale of the jetwash from the gunship that
emerged from the smoke. Uriel raised his arm to ward off
the blow, feeling the monster's claws tear through his
armour and gash his upper arm. Its mid-section arms
closed around his waist, and the two foes fell to the deck
in a tangle of limbs.

The genestealer's jaws fastened on his helm.

The Thunderhawk's landing gear was up, but Uriel saw the
forward ramp was still lowered. The heavy bolters mounted
on either side of the gunship's frontal section roared, the
noise deafening as heavy calibre shells ripped up the chamber. Genestealers, ice and steel disintegrated under the
devastating fusillade as the pilot swung the nose of the gunship left and right.

The creature's hot breath fogged Uriel's visor, thick ropes
of saliva spattering him as its jaws snapped shut. Uriel
twisted his head and the teeth slid clear, scraping parallel
furrows down the side of his helmet.

He rolled atop the thrashing genestealer and gripped its
shoulders, using his formidable strength and weight to hold

it pinned. Its legs kicked and its upper arms slashed at his armour, ripping one of the shoulder guards clear and raking his flesh.

Uriel fought to hold the creature at bay, but it was like trying to wrestle a snake and it squirmed free of his grip, twisting him around and slamming him back into the deck.

The Thunderhawk swayed in the air behind him. The pilot fought to hold the craft level in the chaos of the collapsing hulk, its frontal illuminator beams stabbing erratically through the smoke. The gunship's bolter shells sawed the air, a curtain of explosive bullets ripping through the chamber at thigh level.

The genestealer's claws raked his sides again, and with a last roar of desperation, Uriel locked his hands around the alien's neck and pushed its head upwards.

His muscles screamed in protest as he fought to hold the creature steady.

The roaring of the guns grew in volume as the gunship swung around again.

He felt his muscles giving. But then the genestealer's head exploded as bolter shells ripped it from its body. Blood and brains spilled over Uriel's armour and he threw the creature's corpse aside in disgust.

Uriel flipped over onto his front, careful to make sure the heavy bolters were not firing in his direction before pushing himself to his feet and scrambling towards the lowered crew ramp. He leapt into the gunship, digging his fingers into the mesh of the decking. Hands gripped his armour and pulled him inside and he rolled onto his back as he saw Pasanius hammer the door closing mechanism.

'Go! Go! Go!' he yelled at the intercom.

The craft rolled wildly, spilling Ultramarines to the floor as the pilot violently swung the gunship around on its axis and hit the main engines.

Uriel slid backwards, the powerful acceleration hurling the Thunderhawk forwards. He gripped onto a stanchion, the deck rolling and bucking madly as the pilot flew them from the disintegrating hulk. Something hard smashed into the gunship and Uriel heard a tortured scream of metal as it swayed drunkenly to one side. Fire burst from a shattered conduit and sparks filled the compartment.

Steam vented and emergency lights flashed.

But then they were clear and the gunship roared away from the hulk, its flight finally becoming level.

Uriel pulled himself upright with a groan and slumped into the captain's chair.

He rested his head against the vision block and stared at the destruction of the hulk. Tongues of flame consumed the massive vessel from within, its structure collapsing as the demolition charges did their work. He saw streaks of light powering away from the hulk and recognised them as the other two Thunderhawks. He wondered how the warriors aboard them had fared and if the people of Chordelis and the Tarsis Ultra system knew how dearly their survival had been bought.

He turned away, satisfied that the ungodly vessel had been destroyed and that they had accomplished their mission.

Not exactly how they had planned, but accomplished nonetheless.

THE MOOD ABOARD the *Vae Victus* was sombre as Uriel stood at the tactical plotter with Lord Admiral Tiberius and two frail, green-robed Astropaths. Both carried simple ebony staffs and both were blind, their eye sockets sealed with black, plasflex hemispheres that just failed to conceal the puckered scar tissue at their edges. The massive viewing bay at the end of the command bridge's nave was still filled with the image of the dying hulk, but none of the strike cruiser's bridge staff paid it any mind.

They had greater concerns now.

'Are you sure?' asked Uriel.

'As sure as we can be, my lord,' answered the oldest of the pair, though it was difficult to judge the age of a psyker accurately. 'Just below the galactic plane, at the edge of perception, a wall of white noise in the ether encroaches. A smothering blanket of psychic interference lurks below us. But it is moving, and it is moving this way.'

Uriel locked eyes with Tiberius and felt a cold dread settle in his soul as he realised the import of the Astropath's words.

'The Shadow in the Warp,' said Tiberius tonelessly.

Uriel nodded slowly.

And that could mean only one thing.

'The tyranids are coming.'

ABOUT THE AUTHORS

Dan Abnett lives and works in Kent. He is well known for his comics work and his considerable output for the Black Library includes *Lone Wolves*, *Darkblade*, the best-selling Gaunt's Ghosts novels and the Inquisitor Eisenhorn trilogy.

David Charters is married with five children and divides his time between London and Devon. In his spare time he sits as a magistrate at Bow Street magistrates' court, and is of course fascinated by the work of the Inquisition…

Matthew Farrer has been writing since his teens, and was first printed in *Inferno!* He has published a number of short stories and was shortlisted for an Aurealis Award in 2001.

Jonathan Green works as a full-time teacher in West London. By night he relates tales of Torben Badenov's Kislevite mercenaries and the adventures of the Underhive bounty hunter Nathan Creed for *Inferno!* magazine.

Graham McNeill. Hailing from Scotland, Graham is a Black Library regular who works full-time for Games Workshop. As well as three novels, he has written a host of short stories for *Inferno!*

Sandy Mitchell is a pseudonym of Alex Stewart, who has been working as a freelance writer who produces science fiction and fantasy in both personae, as well as television scripts, magazine articles, comics and gaming material.

Matt Ralphs. Being the assistant editor at the Black Library has in no way aided Matt's chances of being published; he has to work as hard as anyone else to get his words into print, which he finds rather upsetting.

Si Spurrier has become a frequent contributor to *2000AD* and the Black Library whilst attempting to reconcile the zany partying lifestyle of a neurotic writer with the sombre, lonely existence of a student. This is harder than it sounds.

More Warhammer 40,000 from the Black Library

ANTHOLOGIES

**In the far future of the 41st millennium, the human race must battle for survival amongst the stars.
Three great collections of tales from the dark future of Warhammer 40,000.**

STATUS: DEADZONE

Tales from the savage hive-world of Necromunda

Featuring stories by Jonathan Green, Alex Hammond, Gordon Rennie, Tully Summers and others.

DARK IMPERIUM

Featuring stories by Barrington J Bayley, Andy Chambers, Ben Counter, William King, Gav Thorpe and others.

DEATHWING

Featuring stories by Dan Abnett, Storm Constantine, William King, Graham McNeill, Gav Thorpe, Ian Watson and others.

WORDS OF BLOOD

Featuring stories by Dan Abnett, Andy Chambers, Ben Counter, Graham McNeill, Gav Thorpe and others.

More Warhammer 40,000 from the Black Library

THE SPACE WOLF NOVELS
by William King

FROM THE DEATH-WORLD *of Fenris come the Space Wolves, the
most savage of the Emperor's Space Marines. Follow the
adventures of Ragnar, from his recruitment and training as he
matures into a ferocious and deadly fighter, scourge of the
enemies of humanity.*

SPACE WOLF

ON THE PLANET Fenris, young Ragnar is chosen to be inducted
into the noble yet savage Space Wolves chapter. But with his
ancient primal instincts unleashed by the implanting of the
sacred canis helix, Ragnar must learn to control the beast
within and fight for the greater good of the wolf pack.

RAGNAR'S CLAW

AS YOUNG BLOOD CLAWS, Ragnar and his companions go on
their first off-world mission – from the jungle hell of Galt to
the pulluted hive-cities of hive world Venam, they must travel
across the galaxy to face the very heart of evil.

GREY HUNTER

WHEN ONE OF their Chapter's most holy artefacts is siezed by
the forces of Chaos, Space Wolf Ragnar and his comrades are
plunged into a desperate battle to retrieve it before a most
terrible and ancient foe is set free.

More Warhammer 40,000 from the Black Library

THE EISENHORN TRILOGY
by Dan Abnett

IN THE 41ST MILLENNIUM, *the Inquisition hunts the shadows for humanity's most terrible foes – rogue psykers, xenos and daemons. Few Inquisitors can match the notoriety of Gregor Eisenhorn, whose struggle against the forces of evil stretches across the centuries.*

XENOS

THE ELIMINATION OF the dangerous recidivist Murdon Eyclone is just the beginning of a new case for Gregor Eisenhorn. A trail of clues leads the Inquisitor and his retinue to the very edge of human-controlled space in the hunt for a lethal alien artefact – the dread Necroteuch.

MALLEUS

A GREAT IMPERIAL triumph to celebrate the success of the Ophidian Campaign ends in disaster when thirty-three rogue psykers escape and wreak havoc. Eisenhorn's hunt for the sinister power behind this atrocity becomes a desperate race against time as he himself is declared hereticus by the Ordo Malleus.

HERETICUS

WHEN A BATTLE with an ancient foe turns deadly, Inquisitor Eisenhorn is forced to take terrible measures to save the lives of himself and his companions. But how much can any man deal with Chaos before turning into the very thing he is sworn to destroy?